THE BETRAYAL GAME

THE

BETRAYAL GAME

DAVID L. ROBBINS

BANTAM BOOKS

THE BETRAYAL GAME
A Bantam Book / February 2008

PUBLISHED BY
Bantam Dell
A Division of Random House, Inc.
New York, New York

Book design by Robert Bull

Bantam Books is a registered trademark of Random House, Inc., and the colophon is a trademark of Random House, Inc.

Library of Congress Cataloging-in-Publication Data
David L. Robbins.
The betrayal game / David L. Robbins.
p.   cm.
ISBN 978-0-553-80442-3 (hardcover)
1. Castro, Fidel, 1926– —Assassination attempts—Fiction.
2. United States—Relations—Cuba—Fiction.
3. Cuba—Relations—United States—Fiction. I. Title.
PS3568.O22289 B48 2008
813/.54 22—nwcu—n-us
2007038003

Printed in the United States of America
Published simultaneously in Canada

www.bantamdell.com

10 9 8 7 6 5 4 3 2 1
BVG

For Mark Lazenby, and all
our conversations.

For Zach Steele, and Wordsmiths.

For Susann Cokal, and everything
you have to teach.

AUTHOR'S NOTE

According to the Cuban security service, there have been at least 638 attempts on the life of Fidel Castro. Most took place under the first four of the ten American presidents Castro has outstood in office, beginning with Eisenhower. These assassination efforts were either direct operations of the CIA or delegated by them to proxies. In addition, there have been hundreds of volumes written by political historians and assassination theorists speculating that some portion of the apparatus put in place by the CIA and the Mafia to kill Castro turned around on John Kennedy and murdered him for his perceived betrayal of the Bay of Pigs landing.

This novel is grounded in the months leading up to the doomed rebel invasion of Cuba that began on April 17, 1961. During this period, CIA-trained covert hit squads were landed on the island, poisoned cigars were sent Fidel's way, bombs, bullets, aerosols, bacteria, and LSD were aimed at him; a panoply of plans were put in place by CIA to make him lose his voice, his beard, his sanity, or his life, with a degree of inventive perniciousness that would have made Borgia, Machiavelli, and 007 proud. Castro was targeted not only by the CIA, but by the American Mafia, the Cuban underground, other Caribbean and South American leaders, as well as many of his former closest associates. Fidel survived them all, sometimes inexplicably.

The great fun of writing this novel was describing some of those unexplained mysteries, and positing an answer: Dr. Mikhal Lammeck.

The majority of what *The Betrayal Game* portrays is thinly fictionalized fact. Annotations appear at the rear of the novel to amplify, for the interested reader, many of the details of the several assassination attempts and actual events described on these pages.

The Annotations are divided into two sections. The first, you may read along with as you make your way through the book. These should add to your enjoyment of and amazement at the real history that forms the spine of this story. The second Annotation section, I ask you to leave unread until you have finished *The Betrayal Game*. My reason is simple: there's a surprise that I don't want ruined. So be patient, and let the story play out at its best for you.

A few people have helped along the way with this novel and deserve a quick word of appreciation. My editor, Kate Miciak, and my William Morris agent, Tracy Fisher, have been longstanding in my corner. Dan McMurtrie kept me company on my research travels. Dr. Jim Redington again served as my medical expert. Dr. Stu Goldman and Elma Brantingham provided much of the language translations. David Whitford was my shooting guru. My friends and colleagues in the James River Writers serve as inspiration for their dedication and talents in their own crafts.

David L. Robbins
Richmond, Virginia

Our allies think we're a little demented on Cuba.

—President John F. Kennedy

*I'm not worried about assassination. I will not live
one day longer than the day I'm going to die.*

—Fidel Castro

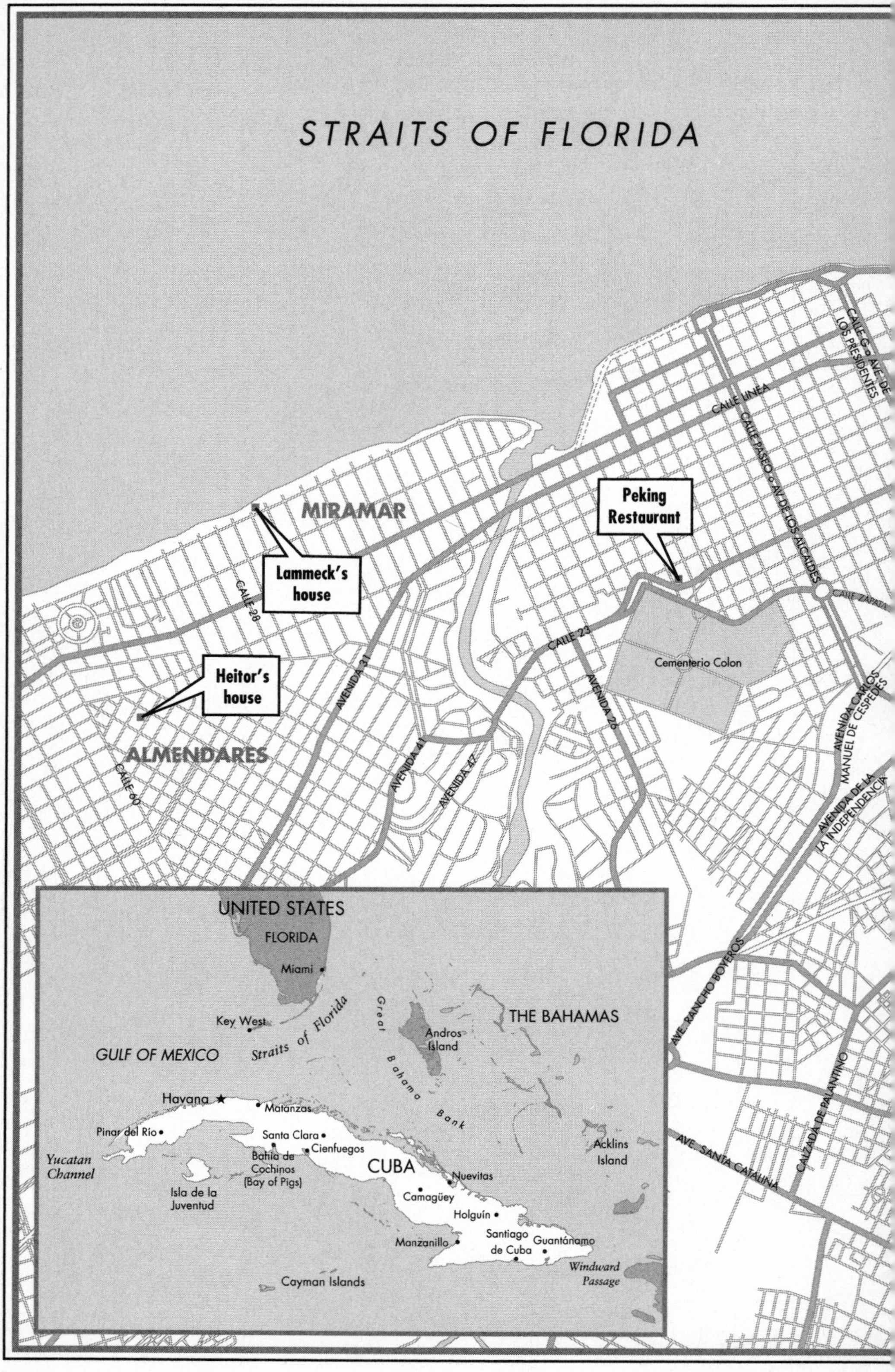

STRAITS OF FLORIDA
MIRAMAR
Lammeck's house
Peking Restaurant
Heitor's house
ALMENDARES
CALLE 28
CALLE 60
AVENIDA 31
AVENIDA 41
AVENIDA 47
CALLE 23
AVENIDA 26
CALLE LINEA
CALLE PASEO • AV. DE LOS ALCALDES
CALLE G • AVE. DE LOS PRESIDENTES
CALLE ZAPATA
Cementerio Colon
AVENIDA CARLOS MANUEL DE CESPEDES
AVENIDA DE LA INDEPENDENCIA
AVE. RANCHO BOYEROS
AVE. SANTA CATALINA
CALZADA DE PALANTINO
UNITED STATES
FLORIDA
Miami
Key West
Straits of Florida
GULF OF MEXICO
Great Bahama Bank
THE BAHAMAS
Andros Island
Havana
Matanzas
Pinar del Río
Santa Clara
Cienfuegos
Bahía de Cochinos (Bay of Pigs)
Yucatan Channel
CUBA
Nuevitas
Isla de la Juventud
Camagüey
Holguín
Acklins Island
Manzanillo
Santiago de Cuba
Guantánamo
Windward Passage
Cayman Islands

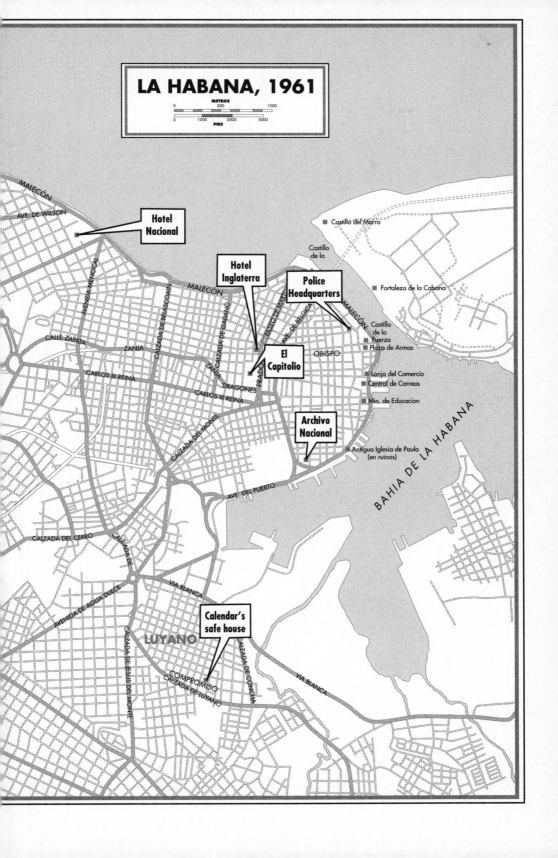

LA HABANA, 1961

METROS

PIES

Hotel
Nacional

Hotel
Inglaterra

Police
Headquarters

El
Capitolio

Archivo
Nacional

Calendar's
safe house

MALECÓN

AVE. DE WILSON

AVENIDA MENOCAL

CALLE ZAPATA

ZANIA

CARLOS III REINA

CALZADA DE BELASCOAIN

CALZADA DE GALIANO

MALECÓN

PASEO DE MARTI

AVE. DE BELGICA

PRADO

ZANIA

DRAGONES

CARLOS III REINA

CALZADA DEL MONTE

OBISPO

Castillo del Morro

Castillo
de la

Fortaleza de la Cabaña

MALECÓN

Castillo
de la
Fuerza

Plaza de Armas

Lonja del Comercio

Central de Correos

Min. de Educacion

Antigua Iglesia de Paula
(en ruinas)

BAHIA DE LA HABANA

AVE. DEL PUERTO

CALZADA DEL CERRO

CALZADA DE

VIA BLANCA

AVENIDA DE AGUA DULCE

LUYANO

COMPROMISO

CALZADA DE LUYANO

CALZADA DE JESUS DEL MONTE

CALZADA DE CONCHA

VIA BLANCA

THE GAME

CHAPTER ONE

★ ★ ★

March 7, 1961
Bahia de Cabañas
Cuba

THE OLDER BROTHER MOVED first. More competitive, faster, he grabbed his swim fins, mask, and spear from the backseat. He dashed down the slope. The younger one hooted after him, not caring so much to win a race to the water. He knew his luck ran better; he would catch the most fish, as always.

"Rodrigo!" his brother called to him up the hill. He walked carefully, barefoot over the limestones and scraggy shells. "Slowpoke!" Manuelito made a show of putting on his mask and fins at the water's edge. He held up the spear, then splashed ahead. Rodrigo watched his brother kick, chopping froth behind his fins, to be first into the bay.

Rodrigo sat unconcerned in the sand. He wet the fins to slide them on better and spit into his mask. He stepped into the water, pleased at the flatness of the surface today. The sun shone from straight above, the visibility underwater would be ideal.

Rodrigo walked until the water rose to his knees. He kneeled forward and let his buoyancy take over, then propelled himself with a kick of the fins. He gazed down and ahead; the shelf of sand fell off quickly to deeper water, to the small coral reef only fifty meters from shore that was off-limits.

Schools of yellowtail and blue creole wrasses swam to meet him with curiosity. When Rodrigo offered nothing of interest, they dispersed. He paddled along the surface watching the sand bottom slope away. When the depth reached eight meters, the outskirts of the reef began to appear, small brain coral heads and elkhorn coral, sea whips and sea fans. Rodrigo and Lito did not know this reef so well as the ones of Bahia Honda fifteen kilometers west. Those were closer to their home and not the private preserve of Fidel Castro. But the boys had speared wonderful Nassau grouper in this place twice before, and had not been caught or bothered by anyone. They decided to come again today, a perfect day.

Staying on the surface, Rodrigo kicked until the reef beneath him grew denser. The tops of the coral lay ten meters below him, the sand bottom three meters more. He swam a wide circle, looking for Lito. For minutes he did not see his brother; Lito was the stronger swimmer and could stay down fantastically long. But Rodrigo had eyes for movement, a knowledge for fish his brother could not match. While Lito thrashed about on the bottom, lunging into holes, chasing, and stabbing, Rodrigo cruised, quiet and belonging on the reef, until his spear betrayed his intent.

He saw bubbles dribble out of the coral. Lito was in a crevice, chasing something. His brother emerged empty-handed, cheeks puffed with the last of his lungs. He did not speak when he surfaced beside Rodrigo but only gulped air, then propelled himself again to the bottom. Upside down, Lito looked up to Rodrigo and held his hands apart, to imply a medium-sized grouper.

Rodrigo drew a deep breath and dove. He kicked easily, wasting no motion or air. He settled on the sand beneath a jagged brow of the coral. Here in the blue depth the greens and aquas muddied to gray, orange faded toward bilious brown, and when a spear caught a fish in the heart, the brilliance of blood was never more than rust.

Rodrigo waited, releasing no bubbles. He held himself on the bottom with a hand gentle on the reef, to break nothing. He listened to the grinding rustle of sand on the other side of the coral wall where his brother worked to corner his grouper. Rodrigo stayed patient, knowing Lito might spook something out of the reef his way.

He exhaled a slow stream of bubbles to ease his lungs. Smaller denizens of the reef came to investigate—some grunts too little to take, a spider crab peeked at him then retreated. Rodrigo peered into the shadows at the bottom of the coral to be certain no morays lived there.

A burst of Lito's bubbles boiled out of the coral. A metallic thud sounded. Lito had loosed his spear but the noise was metal striking rock. Lito had missed. Rodrigo caught a flutter to his left; a grouper sped into the open trailing frightened puffs of feces. He watched his brother rise out of a crack in the reef, loose spear dangling at the end of its tether. Lito reeled the lance in and kicked to the surface for a quick breath. Rodrigo loaded his spear in his own hand, pulling the long shaft back, stretching the rubber belt anchored around his wrist.

That moment, a large blackfin snapper ambled around the corner of the coral head not two meters from Rodrigo's fins. The fish had seen Lito, had watched the grouper escape, and decided to follow suit while the predator was away. Rodrigo rolled to his side, swinging the spear into play before the snapper could react. He let go the long shaft, the sling launched the spear forward; the tip pierced the snapper just behind the gills. The fish went crazy. Blood inked the water in the ragged circle the snapper danced, tugging the lanyard at Rodrigo's wrist. He hauled the fish in, grabbed the still shivering lance, and showed it to Lito who was nearing the surface. His brother shook a fist down at him. Rodrigo had struck first.

Lito took a breath and headed back down. Rodrigo kicked to the surface, to take the snapper to shore to put it in the cooler in the car. A small barracuda arrived to watch, keeping its distance, intrigued by the blood.

The snapper weighed on Rodrigo's arm. It flicked its fins, desperate to get off the barbed tip of the spear. Rodrigo felt every spasm of the dying fish through the shaft. He lifted his head above water to take a breath and look to shore.

A man stood in the sand on the edge of the water.

The man saw him and waved both arms. He was big, stout in a green *guayabera* and khakis. He wore something around his neck, sunglasses. No, binoculars.

Rodrigo lifted his mask to see better. He snorted to clear his ears, then heard what the man was yelling at him.

"Get out of the water!"

Rodrigo licked his lips, salty. Under the surface, the snapper struggled.

"Fidel!" the man shouted, pointing at the road.

Rodrigo raised a hand, to say he had heard and understood. He pulled the mask back over his eyes. The snapper wriggled, refusing to die. Rodrigo took a deep breath and dove to fetch his brother. There would be trouble if they were caught fishing in Fidel's private cove. Of all the *mala suerte*.

He spotted Lito on the bottom, on the trail of the grouper. Rodrigo could not catch up to his brother quickly if he dragged this snapper along. He couldn't wait for Lito to surface; his brother could stay down minutes—too long, with Fidel on the way. Without regret, he pushed down the barb and slid the fish off the lance. The snapper fooled itself that it was free and kicked once. That exhausted it; the fish rolled over dead.

Rodrigo surfaced, to move faster and put himself above his brother. Below, Lito crept hand over hand along the reef, not as sensitive as Rodrigo to the life of the coral, thinking only of the grouper. Unseen to Lito, his grouper scampered out the other side of the coral, staying low across the sand flat.

Rodrigo kicked hard. If they were found here, there was no telling what Fidel would do to them. Fidel was a man of the people, a revolutionary, but he liked his sport and this was his reef, everyone knew that. The brothers might be taken out of school and put in jail, they might have to serve in the militia. They could lose their father's car. Rodrigo had no more time to count his fears; his brother was swimming over the top of the reef, suspecting now where the grouper had fled. Rodrigo, fighting to control his breathing after the fast swim over the surface, took a breath and dove.

Lito was in the sand flat now, on his knees staring after the grouper, deciding whether to give chase again. Rodrigo saw him shrug and look up. Lito had still not seen him.

Rodrigo figured his brother was about to rise. Instead Lito turned his mask downward again, at the sand. Just a few meters to his right, a perfect conch shell lay in the open, the pink of its belly so bright the water could steal little of its hue. Lito flattened on the bottom and flipped his fins to glide to the shell. Rodrigo hovered behind and ten meters above, worried. This wasn't the time, with Castro bearing down on them, for his brother to be collecting shells.

Lito set his hand on the conch. Rodrigo, without a full breath in his lungs, considered surfacing to see if they were already caught. Before turning for the surface, Rodrigo admired the shell his brother had found; it was large, filling Lito's hand lifting it.

An explosion ripped out of the sand. Rodrigo erupted away in a torrent of foam and mad water. He was catapulted past the surface of the bay into the air, his mask torn away, the fins gone. He landed on his back still holding the spear, but he let that go and it trailed away on its tether. He brought his hands to his head, to quell the pounding in his ears, behind his eyes, from the pressure of the blast. He could not shake off the black dots in his vision. What had happened? What had Lito touched? Rodrigo opened his mouth wide and, with pain, drew in all the breath he could hold to dive for his brother.

Without his mask, the water was a confusion. Whipped-up sand clouded what little he could discern. Rodrigo panicked. He kicked for the surface, gasping. He looked at the water he treaded in and saw the brown stain. He screamed, "Lito! Lito!"

A stinking mist hovered on the surface. Rodrigo kicked to lift himself higher, to see and shout through the haze. Dead fish bobbed to the surface. He thought to yell for help, and spun around to face the shore. The man who'd called to him was gone.

Rodrigo turned back to the open bay, fighting tears. The water began to settle from its terrible roiling. The shock that struck first in his chest swelled into his arms and legs with the pricks of needles.

Through stuffed ears, he heard a splash. His eyes flashed across the surface. In the haze, twenty meters off, a hand rose, then dropped.

Rodrigo swam in alarm and hope for his older brother. Approaching, he saw that Lito did not have his mask either. Lito was barely able to keep himself above water, probably would not have were he not such a strong swimmer. Rodrigo stroked closer, calling out how scared he was.

Lito answered only by again raising one arm out of the water. Then Rodrigo realized how much darker was the water around them both.

"Grab on, Lito! I'll take you back to shore!"

Rodrigo reached out. Lito clapped his raised arm around his brother's neck. He waited for the slap of Lito's left arm across his shoulders, to complete the clasp before towing him back to the beach. But the touch of his brother's second arm did not come.

Rodrigo screamed when he saw the protruding bones. Splashing water kept them white, washing off blood that pulsed out of the shredded muscles around the joint, the meat of his brother as pink as the conch shell.

Rodrigo looped an arm beneath his brother's one intact shoulder. Crying, he rolled Lito to his back and kicked for land. He could not look back, and did not know what he would do to save Lito when they reached shore.

Before he could take more than a few strokes, with his brother's moans in his ringing ears, three jeeps roared onto the beach. The vehicles stopped behind their father's car. A dozen bearded men got out, some in swimsuits. Paddling hard, fighting not to fail in his strength, Rodrigo shouted for help.

One man, the tallest, heard and began without hesitation to run down the slope. Others tried to stop him, the cove stank with the smoke of the explosion. The tall one broke free and dashed, barefoot and bare-chested, over the sharp ground. Rodrigo recognized him and felt a surge of relief, also dread. Fidel dove into the bay.

CHAPTER TWO

★ ★ ★

March 10
aboard a Helio Courier L-28 STOL
10 km northeast of El Volcán
Cuba

TWO THOUSAND FEET BELOW, the earth lay blacker than the midnight sky. Vast swaths of tilled land and uncut forest unfurled, uncannily dark, with no homes or lit barns to strike a single sparkle. The few narrow roads were vacant at this hour. In the northern distance, Havana glistened. From this height, even the faint gleams of Matanzas a hundred kilometers to the east were visible.

The pilot, an exile code-named Pronto, circled a finger at the windshield, aiming ahead and down. Calendar looked closely where the man pointed. In the next minute, it was Pronto who saw the lights.

The darkened plane banked left. Pronto cut back the rpm's, aligning the nose of the Helio with the flashes from the ground. Three red dots appeared on the left, three green on the right. The

Unidad team below marked the landing strip. The demarcated space was maybe no longer than a football field.

An anxious hand touched Calendar's shoulder. He twisted in his seat to the four men in the rear seats. Each of them wore black, head to toe, with greasepainted faces. All had satchels in their laps stuffed with clothes, money, false papers, and Dragunov SVD 7.62-mm sniper rifles. On their hips rode Heckler & Koch pistols. The four were Cubans, CIA-trained assassins.

The one tapping on Calendar's shoulder made a gesture with his hands to express how small the landing zone looked. The man seemed unsure. Calendar hid his annoyance that a Cuban trained to blow off Castro's head would be scared over a plane landing.

Calendar pressed an open palm at him to assure that everything was okay. There wasn't time to explain that the STOL in the plane's name meant Short Takeoff and Landing. Calendar again masked his irritation that this guy didn't know the Helio was designed for this sort of operation: come in low, slow, and short; leave these four guys behind, then get out.

The Cuban sat back, uneasy. He shouted something to one of the other shadows. All of them were lit only by the plane's dials. Pronto lined up on the red and green flashes, the landing zone edging closer. He brought the plane in at thirty knots, quickly shedding altitude. Calendar watched the silhouettes of treetops rise against the charcoal sky. Pronto made small, almost hectic adjustments with the yoke. Calendar had not flown with this pilot before and had to rely on faith that he was good enough to set the STOL down without landing lights, in pitch black with no idea what sort of surface he was landing on. A bead of sweat dribbled under Calendar's eye.

The wings waggled as Pronto adjusted to a cross breeze. Calendar stared where the ground was supposed to be and could not tell what lay ahead. The Helio slowed, almost drifting downward,

slowly, maddeningly, leaving plenty of time for Calendar to con-
jure trees and power lines out of the night. The red and green flashlights remained the only illumination as the plane sank, sank, then
bounced hard.

The hands of the assassin behind him went to both of
Calendar's shoulders, clutching in fright. Calendar swept the
man's grip away, angrily disengaging himself from the touch of
fear. *Get off me!* he thought. Pronto straightened the taxiing Helio
and depowered the prop. They'd landed on a road, a narrow asphalt stripe cut through a dense forest. Calendar wiped his lips,
gazing out the windows at the walls of tree trunks on either side.

"Holy shit," he muttered, forgetting for the moment he was
wearing a microphone. Ten feet left or right.

Pronto laid on the brakes and used just enough prop to turn the
Helio around, to face the direction from which they'd flown in.
With damp hands Calendar undid his seat belt. He yanked off his
headphones and pulled the door handle. Jumping out on the road,
the spinning prop wash rippled his jacket.

"Go, go, go!" he shouted at the darkened snipers in the back-
seats, pistoning his arm. He reached in to grab duffel bags to toss
them on the asphalt. He did not touch the Cubans, letting them
fumble out of the plane on their own. Shapes appeared out of the
darkness, *Unidad* men. Calendar had nothing to say to them,
though they were his assets. As soon as the last assassin was out,
Calendar gave them all a thumbs-up, then climbed back into the
plane. Animatedly he pointed up the road, for Pronto to hit the gas
and get back in the air.

The pilot took his foot from the brake, goosed the throttle, and
the Helio began to taxi. Again the colored flashlights came on
ahead, marking the road. Pronto spiked the rpm's. In seconds the
Helio's wheels came off the road. Calendar did not buckle his seat
belt. Instead, he pivoted to look back. The red and green lights

went out. Instantly, they were replaced by other flashes, orange ones.

Gunfire.

"Shit!" Calendar yelled into the cockpit, drowned by the prop and engine. Urgently he twirled his index finger, signaling Pronto to come around over the landing zone.

Pronto circled above the scene, banking Calendar's window to the chaos below. Calendar kept his eyes on the ground, catching pops of gold and orange flecking the dark. He followed the ambush by the flashes of gunplay. Troops had the landing zone surrounded, their guns sparked in a broad circle. From the amount of rounds fired, the ambush looked to be in squad strength, forty or fifty soldiers. The *Unidad* team and the assassins defended from the center, trapped on the open road, dashing to escape into the trees but running right at soldiers.

The ambush was over before the Helio could make a third loop. The road and the trees lapsed back to darkness.

Suddenly, Pronto yanked the plane out of its circling bank. Calendar, without his seat belt, pitched sideways, slamming his head against the window. Before he could curse, a series of flashes blinked on the ground like firecrackers. Castro's troops had turned their rifles to the sky, at the sound of the unseen plane. It would take a lucky potshot, but with enough of them shooting...

Sparks struck on the engine cowling; a bullet had zinged off it. Pronto pulled on the yoke and worked the throttle for all the climb he could get. Calendar tugged his gaze off the ground to face into the blank sky. In his earphones, Pronto muttered, *"Hijo de puta."*

The entire operation had been rounded up. All the training, resources, plans, lives squandered.

"Goddam underground," Calendar growled into his mike. "Riddled with informants."

Pronto nodded.

"All the best people left for Miami," the pilot answered. "There's nothing but *pendejos* left in Cuba. That's why we're coming back."

The Helio leveled off at six thousand feet. Calendar buckled his seat belt. Pronto angled west, away from distant Havana. Calendar sat back and shut his eyes. Images of the four men he'd left dead on the road waited for him, and visions of Fidel's firing wall, after questioning, for those who were captured alive.

He opened his eyes to stare into the blur of the prop. The images departed.

Calendar looked across the huge island sliding by below, soon to give way to the dark coast and Florida Straits. In an hour, he'd land in Key West. He'd pour himself a drink or three in his room.

He balled a fist, slamming it into the roof of the plane, once, twice, a third time. With every punch, he shouted, "Damn it! Damn it!"

"Hey!" Pronto shouted into the earphones. "Easy, man. You're gonna dent the plane. *Jesús.*"

Calendar lowered the fist, knuckles throbbing from the pounding. He stared at glowing Havana off to his right.

"How hard can it be to kill this guy?"

He rammed his fist one more time into the ceiling.

CHAPTER THREE

★ ★ ★

March 13
First Avenue
Miramar
Havana

TOWERS OF SMOKE CORKSCREWED out of the blaze. The fire, raging on tons of spilled oil, burned out of control in the first minutes after the initial explosion. By the time fire crews responded, the outcome was decided: nothing could save the refinery. Arcs of water soaked the steaming superstructure, but could not keep it from buckling. The high-leaping flames turned aside the darkness with a flaring, frightening light.

Dr. Mikhal Lammeck drank a morning beer, popped peanuts in his mouth, and watched. His Spanish was good enough to follow the television news commentary: last night, sometime after midnight, underground wreckers, backed by the rebel mercenaries and America, had sabotaged a Texaco refinery in Santiago de Cuba. The refinery had been chosen by the underground for destruction because, two years ago, it was one of the first U.S. assets in Cuba nationalized by the revolution.

The news show switched to film of the refinery taken only an hour earlier. The skeletal remains were scorched. Firemen continued to douse it with water.

Behind Lammeck's sofa, a warm Caribbean breeze filtered in the window. The sheer curtains hoisted, causing a cotton caress to rise and fall along his neck. A salted scent from the Florida Straits trailed on the wind. Lammeck smiled at the mayhem on the TV. The announcer stated that Castro would speak that afternoon in Havana's Parque Central. Fidel would address the sabotage and rising tensions in the country. A gathering of twenty thousand was expected. Arrive early, the announcer advised.

Lammeck stood. He shut off the television, closed the wooden doors of the RCA cabinet to hide the screen. Leaving the den, he went to the front hall. He lifted his briefcase and stepped outside into the early sun. The 9:00 A.M. taxi he'd arranged to pick him up idled at the curb.

He rode to Cespedes Avenue, to the National Archives. Lammeck instructed the driver to go the long way, on the coast road, the Malecón. He enjoyed the view of the ocean, the varying moods of the blue water against the seawall. Along the way were monuments, parks where kids tossed baseballs, and the crumbling facades of marvelous Spanish architecture. The highway curved south at Morro Castle, at the mouth of Havana Bay, past the spot where the U.S. warship *Maine* blew up at the end of the last century, igniting the Spanish-American War. The taxi drove by leviathan warehouses that, until Fidel seized them, had belonged mostly to American corporations. The biggest was the pier for American Fruit, the company that for sixty years was the largest landowner in Cuba. The name of the firm remained painted on the immense metal roof. The ships that docked at these quays now had the hammer and sickle emblazoned on their smokestacks.

Lammeck gave the driver a hefty tip and told him to come to the house tomorrow morning, again at nine. Inside the archive, he walked to the carrel he'd staked out as his own, in a sunny corner of the second floor. The old librarians saved it for him each morning. He sat with books untouched from the previous day's work. Some of the reports were in English, left behind by American administrators and accountants. Lammeck's Spanish skills were enough to decipher the rest.

Out of his briefcase he took a notebook brimming with notes. He flipped to the place he'd left off, and resumed his research into the long history of the plundering of Cuba.

Lammeck did not arrive early to the Parque Central. The crowd was a sprawling throng by the time he reached Prado Boulevard. Traffic was blocked on the approaching streets. Lammeck did not edge forward for a spot to see or hear better. Instead, he nudged his way to the outdoor bistro of the Inglaterra Hotel, across the street from the park.

He waited to catch the busy eye of Gustavo, the waiter he'd been grooming with large gratuities. Gustavo waved a hand in recognition. Lammeck pointed at the packed portico and shrugged. Gustavo stuck out his bottom lip and nodded over the packed heads. He lifted one finger, to signal *Give me a moment*.

Quickly, the waiter emerged from a thicket of *guayaberas* and cigarettes to guide Lammeck to an elevated table set for him on the small bandstand. The hotel's five-piece band would not be playing during Fidel's speech. A cold beer waited on the table. Lammeck slipped Gustavo five pesos.

Across Prado Boulevard, in the heart of the *parque,* stood a statue of José Martí, the greatest hero of Cuba's liberation from Spain. Martí was Fidel's role model: both men were prolific political writers, supporters of equality for all races, uncompromising in their desire for independence. The two were children of Spaniards who'd come to Cuba at Spain's invitation to whiten the island's population. Both were filled with that fierce Spanish brand of personal honor. In 1895, still a young man, Martí was shot dead out of the saddle of a pale horse. The hero's bronze face looked across Fidel's crowd. Lammeck wondered if the similarities would continue, and martyrdom awaited Fidel, too.

Gustavo brought Lammeck a *cubano* sandwich, a grilled and pressed concoction of ham, roast pork, cheese, and pickle on Cuban bread. Sipping beer, he counted the platforms hastily erected around the park for the television cameras. Castro, like his American opposite Kennedy, knew the value of this new medium. The two men made better use of television than any other world leaders.

Lammeck finished his sandwich and beer. He had a good view of the stand a hundred yards off where Castro would speak. The television announcer's estimate of twenty thousand in attendance seemed conservative, the park and streets teemed with a festival air. Vendors worked the crowd selling tobacco, lottery tickets, nuts, and sweet rolls off trays strapped around their necks. Gustavo brought Lammeck a fresh beer. Then, with no introduction, Fidel ascended the platform.

Like a jet engine, the crowd sent up a deafening roar. Fidel waited before a bouquet of microphones, nodding, clasping his hands behind his back, an austere and martial air about him. Ten other men stood on the stage. Half wore beards and khaki uniforms like Fidel. The others, civil servants of the revolutionary government wore *guayaberas*. Lammeck recognized only one on the stage beside Fidel, the most famous of the *barbudos,* Che Guevara.

At last, Castro raised his hands. The crowd quieted on cue, practiced. A red light glowed on top of one of the TV cameras. Castro stepped to the microphones.

"Students, workers, and citizens all." In person, his voice emerged in a lower timbre than on the TV newscasts Lammeck watched in the States. Fidel spoke in rapid-fire bursts, without notes or cue cards. Lammeck was pleased to understand so much of Castro's speedy Spanish.

Even from a distance, he saw how Castro's lips inside his beard curled outward when he spoke, like the bell of a trumpet. Fidel leaped on his sentences, knifing his hands to punctuate. He rose to his toes, fell to his heels, and rocked as if the words coming out of his mouth had a recoil. A sea of heads nodded in unison. The crowd interrupted him a dozen times with applause. Fidel did nothing to quiet them in these moments of approval. He let them express themselves, their fervor for him. Lammeck noted the makeup of the crowd: blacks, whites, men and women, young and old, men in business suits, factory workers, students, brown girls with babies on their hips, all side-by-side to hear and be heard in the park.

Fidel was a remarkable orator. Lammeck had seen only short squibs of his speeches. On American newscasts, Castro was always fiery, but with nothing of the power and charisma he displayed in front of his people. Lammeck was impressed, too, with the man's mind; it must have been extraordinary, to speak so confidently, eloquently, and at such excruciating length.

Lammeck raised his hand to catch Gustavo's attention for another beer. He mimicked forking a bite off a plate, their signal for an order of flan.

Castro, after relating at length the virtues of the revolution, turned his attention to Kennedy and America. Lammeck, who'd begun to slouch in his chair, perked up.

"President Kennedy always finds an occasion to make his insidious statement that he loves the people—but not the revolutionary government—of Cuba. Well, then, let Mr. Kennedy realize that the government is the people."

The crowd shouted "Fidel, Fidel!" Castro, with his impeccable timing, paused, then kept the momentum building.

"Let Kennedy realize that he cannot separate us from the people, as we cannot separate him from the monopolies and the millionaires."

More applause.

"The people and the revolutionary government in Cuba today are the same thing, just as the millionaires, usurers, and the government in the United States today are a single thing."

The crowd chanted "Castro, yes! Yanquis, no!" Fidel waited, pursing his lips and nodding while above him the bronze Martí gazed over his shoulder. Castro let the crowd settle, then drove home his point with a finger jabbing the sky.

"This is not a government by a rich caste, not a government of thieves, not a government of exploiters, not a government of petty politicians, not a government of high ranking officers. This is a government of the people, by the people, and for the people. This is the revolution of the humble, by the humble, and for the humble!"

The enormous gathering went wild. Castro stood wrapped in the rumble of his citizens. Lammeck raised the last of his beer in admiration.

He got a quick sense that Fidel might have seen him lift his glass, for across the thousands of cheering voices the bearded caudillo nodded solemnly straight at Lammeck.

Once Fidel began another stanza of the speech, Lammeck tucked pesos under his emptied dessert plate. He stood slowly, in case Castro really had seen him.

He stepped down off the bandstand, to make his way through the crowd to an open street, to hail a taxi for home and an afternoon nap. He'd had one more beer than he should and this made him sleepy; he'd leave for tomorrow his research at the archives. Before he could walk away from the Inglaterra, Fidel launched into a sermon about the CIA, the Pentagon, and the impending invasion of the island by Cuban exiles backed by America.

Surprised, Lammeck stopped to listen. He said aloud to no one, "How the hell does he know?"

"Everyone knows," answered a voice in English beside him. Lammeck shot the man a look. He was heavyset, about Lammeck's age, but not familiar, though he looked back with a smile as if they were old friends.

"Walk with me, Professor Lammeck?"

The man held out an ushering hand. Lammeck hesitated.

"Do I know you, *señor*?"

"No. I apologize if I have startled you. I am Police Captain Johan."

"Have I done something wrong?"

"No, Professor. Absolutely not."

Again, the man gestured with his open hand for them to walk. Unsure, Lammeck accepted and strode ahead on Prado, along the rim of the tightly packed crowd. Castro continued his breathless screed against the CIA and the U.S., preparing and alerting his country for the impending assault.

Johan walked beside Lammeck without speaking, until they reached the outer edges of the crowd. Castro's voice still boomed in the distance behind them.

"How do you know who I am, Captain Johan?"

The policeman smiled. He was of Lammeck's generation and seemed of similar temperament, thoughtful before speaking.

"You are quite well known, Professor. Your work precedes you, even in Cuba. I've looked forward to meeting you for some time."

Lammeck was quietly pleased to be recognized. But how could this Johan know Lammeck was coming to Havana?

Before he could ask, the policeman pointed across the boulevard.

"Ahh, there. Do you know this building?"

"The national capitol."

"The former national capitol. It is currently vacant. May I teach you something, Professor Lammeck? About Cuba?"

"I suppose."

"Well..." Johan grinned. "Obviously, the capitol is an exact replica of the American Capitol. Do you see? Every detail is there on a smaller scale—the dome, the pillared wings, high white steps. In 1929, it was built for us by the United States to house the Cuban Senate. More important, *El Capitolio* was designed to remind every Cuban that we were an American possession. A little copy of your Capitol, given to us as little Americans."

Johan said this without rancor; in fact, he smiled as if he'd made a jest.

"After the revolution, Fidel called it a symbol of Cuba's suppression. The place was abandoned. But as can you see"—the police captain swept a hand across the wide grounds, filled with children and adults playing baseball or eating lunches on the tall marble steps—"*El Capitolio* still serves the people."

They rounded the corner of the capitol lawn. Ahead stood the Partagas cigar factory.

"You spend too much time in the library, Professor. I should like to show you some of the real Havana. We are not a people who can be captured so well on the page."

Lammeck narrowed his eyes. "I'm not sure I like the fact that you've been following me."

Johan waved this off. "I will explain and you will forgive me. But not right now. I have to return to the park and Fidel. I have responsibilities there. I cannot be gone for long."

"And when do I get this explanation? Or will I just turn and find you there again?"

Johan inclined his head. "I shall leave you here for a taxi, Professor. You should not have a long wait." Johan gestured at the cigar building. "I would like to bring you a gift of a box of Partagas number twos. They are my favorite. Che prefers the Montecristo and Fidel the Cohiba Lancero, but my taste runs to the milder Partagas."

"And you figure I'll like what you like?"

"Yes," Johan said, with a touch to Lammeck's forearm. "I have reason to hope we have much in common, you and I. Tomorrow night, seven o'clock, I will come to your home. Then we will talk."

"About how everybody's sure there's an invasion coming?"

"And many more surprises. Tomorrow night, then."

The policeman walked off. Lammeck opened his mouth, not certain if he could object.

Johan called over his shoulder, "Don't worry, Professor, I know your address."

CHAPTER FOUR

★ ★ ★

March 13
Miami Beach Convention Center
Miami Beach

WITH TEN THOUSAND OTHERS, Bud Calendar shot to his feet. The whole building shook with the crowd's cry when Floyd Patterson's back hit the canvas. Calendar shouted with them, "Ohhhh!" but without worry. He knew the champ would get back up. Patterson had been knocked down more than any heavyweight champion in boxing history, but, as Patterson had said, he also "got up the most."

The Swedish challenger Johansson bounced on his toes waiting for the champ to resurrect. The referee's count reached four; black Patterson took his time to get the wobble out of his legs before he stood. The big Swede looked to be in the worst shape of his three bouts with Patterson. Even so, he'd drawn first blood and ten thousand gasps.

Calendar glanced away from the mat, where Patterson had risen to one knee at a seven count. Celebrities caught Calendar's eye— Sinatra, Jackie Gleason, Joan Crawford, and Sammy Davis Jr. All ringside.

Inside the ropes, Patterson bounced to his feet, pounding his gloves together. *Lucky punch,* the gesture said, but it wasn't and Calendar could tell that Patterson knew it. The champ had leaped in, careless and too aggressive. He'd lowered his guard to loose a roundhouse right; the Swede stayed cool and popped him with his own right hand, the one he called "Thor's Hammer." Calendar reached into his pocket to finger the boxer's mouthpiece he always carried. *Getting old,* he thought. Old habits. Even so, he figured he could have stayed on his feet longer in this first round than the champ did.

Patterson wasn't upright long before Johansson planted him again with another stiff right to the chin. Calendar bolted out of his seat with the crowd, this time genuinely concerned. The Swede had already beaten the champ two years ago, then last year Patterson pounded him, becoming the first heavyweight to lose the belt and win it back. Tonight was the rubber match. Right now, on his back for the second time in just the first round, the champ hadn't lifted his head yet, with the ref over him sweeping fingers past his face.

Calendar shouted with everyone in the arena, "Get up! Get up!" Patterson shook his head; under the hot kliegs, sweat beads haloed off his brow. The ref shoved an open hand—"Five!"—in front of the champ's nose. Calendar flicked his eyes to Johansson. The big Swede wasn't bouncing this time. The boxer stood flat-footed, glaring down at his black opponent. Johansson was compelling Patterson to stay down, adding the weight of his will to bind Patterson to the mat. Johansson knew the champ's heart better than anyone in the world. *This is what it's about,* Calendar thought. *This right here.*

Patterson slid his gloves under him. He sat up, and even with the ref's count at eight, took a moment to push his mouthpiece back over his teeth. The look he gave the Swede made Johansson start bobbing again, dancing away as if Patterson weren't sitting on the mat but standing and charging already. By ten, the champ's legs were under him and firm. The ref swiped Patterson's gloves on his shirt to clean them, then diced both hands through the air to say: *Fight, boys!*

The spectators stomped and screamed. Calendar shouted to the unknown man beside him, "Like a fucking Lazarus, this guy!" The man nodded, then cupped his hands to holler his own support for the champ.

The rest of the opening round continued with the two boxers parrying, no advantage taken. Patterson had weathered the best Johansson had for him. With seconds left, the Swede came in, fierce and unprotected, trying to finish Patterson off. Johansson knew, Calendar knew, it was now or never. In response, Patterson clipped him with a big left hook. Johansson crumpled. The building exploded. The bell sounded in the din, saving the Swede.

The crowd was slow to take their seats between rounds, they were so charged with the event. Calendar eased a hand into his other pocket to touch a little glass bottle. With what was inside it, there was no one CIA Agent Bud Calendar could not put down. And they would stay down.

★   ★   ★

Fontainebleau Hotel

Calendar lifted his chin to the moon and closed his eyes. In each hand he held one of his shoes. He'd rolled his pants legs above the calves. Between his toes, sand shifted under a withdrawing wave.

"This is what I'm talking about," he said to the warm water at his feet and the Miami night. "Way too much time in the cold."

A balmy breeze caressed his cheeks, seawater foamed at his ankles. He recalled a massage from a long-ago woman in Berlin that felt this good. Or was it Moscow? Prague? He couldn't remember; it was somewhere cold.

He opened his eyes and looked around. Up and down the beach, evening strollers walked the sand, or, like him, stood barefoot in the shallows.

"After I get Castro," he muttered, setting his resolve one more time, "I'm done. I'm moving down here. Screw the cold."

Calendar listened to the sounds of the curling and withdrawing at his feet.

"Just lemme take care of Castro."

Calendar kicked through the shallows to the sand, then to the boardwalk steps leading into the courtyard of the Fontainebleau. He used his socks to dry his feet, then rubbed his soles before cramming them back into the hard shoes. He thought how many countries they'd stood him upon; his stalwarts, these two knobby white feet, never failed him. Never got bloody like his hands. He slid on the socks and promised his feet he'd never wear shoes again, not down here in Miami, only sandals.

Before heading inside, he took another full, salty breath of the Atlantic. Calendar felt every one of his fifty-four years. His twenty years in intelligence work. He was tired and he wasn't finished. *But this is what it's about,* he thought. *Like Floyd Patterson. Get up off the mat and slug another round, 'til you're done.*

The Fontainebleau's lobby décor reflected Miami Beach's deco style, with all the pastels of a coral reef, blues, pinks, greens, yellows. Moving through it, Calendar imagined himself a fish on such a reef. What kind of fish would he be? Not some scared little denizen but a shark, a feeder. He liked the comparison. Feeders and bleeders, that's all there was in the world. He indulged in a vision of frenzy, bloodied water. This freshened his sense of his own girth, and the power the United States had deposited in him. Calendar straightened his posture and widened his stride.

In the elevator, Sinatra crooned "The Best Is Yet to Come." The elevator rose creakily. Calendar used these moments with Frank to dump the last of his fatigue. These men waiting for him, they were sharks, too. They could sense if you weren't swimming right. Calendar crammed his hands in his pockets; sifting through loose change and his room key, he fingered the poison pill bottle, then shifted his touch to the plastic mouthpiece he always carried in case of a fistfight.

The elevator doors parted. The hallway carpet glowed watermelon red. Standing on it were two oversized men in sunglasses. This was a habit Calendar disdained, wearing shades indoors. It made a man conspicuous.

"You Calendar?" one of the guards asked.

Walking forward, Calendar answered, "You the Bobbsey Twins?"

He did not pause for the pair's scrutiny but ambled down the hall toward another shaded goon standing outside a room.

"You Calendar?"

"I get asked that a lot."

"Lemme see some ID."

Calendar reached into the pocket with the mouthpiece. He withdrew his hand holding up the middle finger.

"Here you go. Don't it look like me?"

The sentinel pulled down his sunglasses to tuck them in his jacket. His small eyes did not blink.

"You a funny guy?"

Calendar smiled. "I dunno. Is your Uncle Sam a funny guy?

'Cause that's who I am. Now let me inside or I turn around and walk. And you can explain to your bosses how you and I quarreled and I left with my feelings hurt."

The man's quandary was interrupted by the door opening. The knob was in the hand of a tall, bald, round-faced man. He didn't look Miami, and he didn't look New York, in sports coat and slacks. He was California, lightly tanned and smugly grinning.

"Mr. Calendar? Come in."

Before entering, Calendar faced the guardian.

"What did you think? Was I funny? Yes, no? Well"—he patted the guard's shoulder—"you can tell me later."

The man answered by sliding his sunglasses on, aiming them blankly into Calendar's face.

Inside the closed door, Calendar shook hands.

"We meet at last," the tall man said. "Bob Maheu."

"Bud Calendar. Everybody here?"

"Right on time. You need any briefing before we start?"

"Do you?"

Maheu's grin flatlined. Calendar guessed the man's shirt and silk tie cost what his own suit was worth.

"Not at all. Mr. Calendar?"

"Yeah."

"I appreciate the tough talk like what I heard through the door. I do. But...it might not go over so well with these gentlemen. If you catch my drift."

Calendar donned an understanding demeanor. "Certainly, Bob. And that explains why they get along so well with you." He showed his teeth in his own smile. "Shall we?"

Maheu nodded, eyes narrowing, calculating the CIA man. *Not what you expected,* Calendar thought, *am I?* Maheu knew to bite his tongue. The man had connections, but Calendar didn't care about Maheu's power, or that of anyone else in the next room.

Whatever they had, it didn't stack up to the U.S. That's who Bud Calendar represented.

Calendar followed Maheu through the chintz fabrics of a large sitting room. The man walked elegantly, a seamless flow of long arms and legs. The view out the windows faced the Atlantic, moonbeams broken on its dark surface to the horizon. Calendar didn't covet power—he had plenty of his own—but he did admire the view.

Maheu opened the door to a meeting room. A long oval table held the center between eight padded leather chairs. Again, the décor was tropical, a vibrant kiwi carpet beneath white and lime striped wallpaper. Lamplight cast a green hue over the three men, who did not stand upon Calendar's entry.

Maheu tapped the back of a seat at the open end of the table. Calendar ignored the suggestion and sat where he chose, in what was probably Maheu's spot, to the left of a hawk-nosed little thug with big, veined hands at the head of the table. The balding man wore a plain white shirt opened enough to show a hairless and sunken chest. He had hunter's eyes, quick and narrow, a deeply lined mouth.

Next to him, across from Calendar, sat a pudgy man in a dark suit and black tie. Perched on his flat face were black rimmed glasses, beneath a receding hairline. A hangdog look made him appear droopy and sad. Beside him was the muscle, with Brylcreemed white-gray hair in a black Ban-Lon shirt. The older gents smiled and nodded when Calendar sat. The big guy scowled. The first two were bosses. This third one reeked of soldier.

All three had their fingers knitted on the tabletop. Calendar made a show of doing the same, lacing his fingers and dropping them on the polished wood.

Maheu slid into his leather seat as if buttering it. He did the introductions, indicating first the large man.

"Bud Calendar, I'd like you to meet Johnny Roselli." Calendar reached across the table, receiving a meaty mitt decked with two fat gold rings. "How you doin'?" Roselli muttered. Calendar nodded and answered breezily, "Good. You?" He pretended to be impressed with Roselli's handshake. "Hey, you work out? Wow." Roselli sneered, patient.

Maheu cleared his throat, to move Calendar past Roselli.

"This is Joe the Courier."

Calendar shook hands with the man in the suit. The hand was flaccid, gentle after Roselli's paw.

"Thanks for coming, Joe," Calendar said. "Maybe we can get you into a pair of shorts, huh? Hey, it's Miami. Loosen up a little."

Joe the Courier sniffed, a jolt of amusement. "I'll see if I got some in my car." He cut his eyes to the hawk-nosed man, to communicate that they had a joker at the table with them.

"Hey, so you live around here?" Calendar said. "I'm thinking of getting a place in Miami myself. Maybe you can help me out, show me the good neighborhoods."

"Yeah, maybe." Joe the Courier stared at Calendar, confounded.

"So, you really a courier?"

"Yeah."

Calendar nodded approvingly, as if this were a wonderful profession.

Maheu interrupted. "Mr. Calendar?" He aimed his manicured nails across the table. "And this is Sam Gold."

This one ran the show, Calendar decided, shaking hands with the man beside him. The eyes, the casual dress, the seat at the head of the table. Sam Gold said, "How'd you do on the fight?"

"I don't gamble."

"No? Too bad. If you change your mind, I can get you set up."

"I'm sure. How'd you do?"

Sam Gold chuckled. Roselli, too. "Good," Gold said. "Fucking good. That moolie Patterson. You can't keep him on the mat. You'd hafta shoot him, for Chrissakes."

Joe the Courier pushed up his glasses and interrupted Sam's clucking over his winnings. "Before we get going, I'd like to know the connection here. Who knows who?"

Big Roselli answered: "I'll go first. I met Bob Maheu out in Vegas two years ago. We hung out, broke some bread, he seemed okay. Then it turns out he's Howard Hughes's righthand guy. Then, when I was in LA once, I gave him a call. We hooked up, did some lunches and got to be pals. One time I was at his house for one of them clambakes he throws."

Maheu cut in, "I used to live in Maine and we did this all the time. Buckets of lobsters and steamers, plenty of liquor."

"Sounds great," said Sam Gold, still expansive.

Maheu kept going. "Anyway, I heard Johnny was in town so we invited him. At the party he met one of my pals, Sheff Edwards. Sheff checked Johnny out and was impressed with his résumé and"—Maheu indicated Sam Gold and Joe the Courier— "connections."

"Edwards is CIA," Roselli said. "We talked a little about this and that. Next thing I know, I get a call from Bob saying Edwards wants me to put together a sit-down."

Maheu motioned to Sam Gold and Joe the Courier. "Johnny brought you gentlemen to the table. And the CIA has graciously sent us Mr. Calendar to handle their side of things. I'm just the broker in the middle."

Maheu smiled in his unctuous way. Joe the Courier and Sam sat satisfied, adding nothing, letting others talk. Roselli beamed to be in the room with this much firepower, obviously thinking well of himself.

"It's an odd alliance, certainly," Maheu said, "but one that I think can do something great."

The mood around the table was complacent, everybody happy to consider great deeds and their boxing winnings. The fruity interior made the meeting bright, seem like fun. And who ran this meeting? Fashion-plate Maheu, Howard Hughes's go-fer?

No, Calendar thought. America ran the meeting. Why? Because Uncle Sam had more money than Hughes. And he'd killed a few millions more than Sam and Joe.

Calendar slipped his mouthpiece out of his pants pocket into his hand.

"So," he piped up, "Joe the Courier. Sam Gold. I like those names. I got to get me one of those nicknames like you guys."

The two winced at Calendar, Joe from behind his big glasses. He said, "What?"

"Yeah." Calendar smacked his own forehead. "I just came up with one! Tell me what you think. Bud the Vacuum. Huh? Got a ring?"

Roselli pressed his forearms into the table. "What are you doin'?"

Calendar swiveled his attention to Roselli. He matched the man's posture, leaning in. He kept the mouthpiece tucked in his fist.

"Ask me why," he said to Roselli.

The soldier blinked once, slowly. "Why?"

Calendar put a hand under his own chin. "Because I'm up to here in dirtbags."

At the end of the table, Maheu shot to his feet. "Calendar! I told you to curb your goddam mouth."

"Bob," Calendar calmly said, not prying his eyes off Roselli, "sit down and shut up."

Calendar reached into his jacket pocket. Roselli stiffened on instinct when Calendar's hand disappeared into his coat. He said, "I hope you know what you're doin', big fella."

Calendar withdrew the hand slowly. Sam Gold motioned for Maheu to take his seat. On the table, Calendar unfolded a page out of yesterday's Sunday *Miami Herald.*

"Let's see what we got here. Uh huh, here we go."

He spun the newspaper around to face Joe the Courier and Sam Gold.

"See anybody you recognize there, boys?"

Beneath a banner reading "America's Most Powerful Mafiosi," seven black-and-white photos had been laid out to mock a lineup. Below each picture ran their names: *Joe Bonanno, Frank Costello, Carlo Gambino, Meyer Lansky, Charles "Lucky" Luciano;* then Joe the Courier's round face and black rims in profile leaving a Tampa courtroom above the caption *Santo Trafficante Jr.* Bringing up the rear, Sam Gold had been caught in a jaunty straw hat and fat smile. The name under his picture read *Sam Giancana.*

Calendar waited while Giancana and Trafficante took in the spread. Roselli leaned across, curious. Calendar glared at Maheu. Then he tapped the table with the flat of his palm.

"I'm the United States government, boys. Who you think you're dealing with? Do you even know what the CIA does? Who we are? Sam Gold, Joe the Courier. Gimme a break."

Calendar paused. No one spoke; Roselli's threatening manner had vanished.

"So, should I get up and walk away now and handle this situation on my own? Or are you gonna stop lying to me like a bunch of two-bit hoods?"

Maheu tried to speak, but Calendar broke him off with a glance.

"Because I hate being bullshited by people I'm trying to do business with."

He crooked an elbow on the table and pointed at Trafficante, who sat stonily peering through his black rims.

"Santo Trafficante Junior," Calendar announced. "Born in America, one of the few men to actually succeed his father as a Mafia don. Head of the Tampa family. You lived in Havana from '46 'til Castro chucked you out in '59. One of the first mobsters to get into the hotels and casinos in Cuba in a big way. That was back in the heyday, huh? How much you losing every month, with no business in Cuba, Santo? A million?"

"Two."

Calendar turned on Giancana.

"Sam 'Momo' Giancana. You run Chicago. Used to be muscle for Capone. Chauffeur for Paulie Ricca. Moved up pretty fast through murder and rackets. You like to hang out with the stars. You're a good pal of the Kennedys. And you and JFK are both fucking Marilyn Monroe."

Roselli leaped out of his chair. Calendar rose fast; on his way up, he popped the mouthpiece past his lips and clamped down. The broad table separated them enough to make both men consider how to get at the other, long enough for Giancana to bellow, *"Basta!"*

Roselli froze at the command. Calendar licked the outside of the mouthpiece, then spit it into his hand.

"Sit down, Johnny." Trafficante had his hand on Roselli's thick wrist. "We're all friends here. Aren't we, Mr. Calendar?"

"Sure. I'm even dating Johnny's sister."

Another tug on Roselli's wrist was needed to get him back into the leather chair.

Roselli asked through thinned lips, "Calendar, have you asked yourself lately whether you're right in the fucking head?"

At the head of the table, Giancana smiled sagely.

"It's okay, Johnny. Mr. Calendar here does in fact know what he's doing. He's just letting us all know who's the boss in this affair. I respect that. I think Santo does, too."

Trafficante nodded. Roselli still glared, wary. At the far end of the table, Maheu looked disgusted.

Giancana continued: "In our business, Mr. Calendar, we learn to take a shot. And we're good at giving one back. Live by the sword, die by the sword. Remember that. Now, for the record, your friend Mr. Roselli there is my representative in Las Vegas and Hollywood. And, of course, Mr. Maheu, a former FBI agent, works closely with the richest man in the world. So, Mr. Calendar. You know our credentials. We don't know yours. Do you mind?"

Calendar breathed through his nose, quieting his pulse. He took his seat, pocketing the mouthpiece.

"Sure."

Calendar looked around the room. He wasn't cleared to say anything he was about to. But what the hell, he thought. Everybody at this table lived in a world of money and murder. All of them were surely discreet. Or they'd be dead.

"Ten years ago, it dawned on the CIA that there was no way we were ever going to roll back Communism. The countries that were Red were gonna stay Red unless we went to war with them. Fair enough, they weren't gonna change us either. So, we decided the better way to fight the Commies was containment. That means there isn't going to be a global war, because no one wins that one. The real battleground is small engagements in Third World countries that are still in play between the Reds and us."

"Cuba," said Giancana.

"And Viet Nam, and Congo, and Panama and the other half of the planet that's got their palms out waiting for one of the big boys to fill 'em up. We play hard, both teams do, but we play in secret. That way the odds of a mushroom cloud are less."

Trafficante asked, "So where've you been playing, Mr. Calendar?"

"A few places. Maybe you heard of them. Iran. In '53 we put Pahlevi back on the throne. And we did Guatemala the next year. CIA engineered a coup to get rid of Arbenz after we figured out he was taking money and arms from the Soviets. We faked an invasion, dropped some smoke bombs on the capitol, and Arbenz got cold feet and lit out for Mexico."

Trafficante seemed unimpressed. "Who gives a crap about Guatemala?"

Calendar answered, "The Commies. That's why we give a crap. Lately, we've had our eye on Congo. You've probably heard that Lumumba's gone missing. What you won't hear on the news is that he's been chopped up with a hacksaw and dropped in sulfuric acid. I'm sorry to say we weren't directly responsible for that one."

Giancana nodded approval. "Even so, nice."

Calendar brightened. "Okay, Santo. Even you'll like this one. You heard of Sukarno?"

"Indonesia."

"Bingo. We did a blue movie, with him as the star."

At the far end of the table, Maheu jerked. "You were behind that?"

"Yes, Bob, I was."

Calendar continued addressing himself to the two mob bosses. "Back in '58, Sukarno was starting to get cozy with the Russians. Uncle Sam was concerned, as you can imagine. So, we did some checking, and found out that Sukarno is quite the poon hound. Isn't that right, Bob?"

Maheu grimaced at Calendar's vulgarity. "President Sukarno has an ample sexual appetite, yes."

"CIA found out that Sukarno had been shacking up at the Kremlin with a KGB agent. She'd been posing as a stewardess on his flights to Moscow. The classic honey trap. So, we hired Bob here to set up a little porno movie for us out in Hollywood. He got a hot little blonde hooker who looked just like the KGB gal from behind, and some Hispanic guy in a bald cap to play Sukarno. And you're gonna love who Bob got to produce this little number. Bob, tell everybody."

Maheu did not like the role of second banana Calendar had set out for him. But he cleared his throat, and said, "Bing Crosby."

"Get the fuck outta here!" Giancana rocked back in his seat. Roselli waved both hands in the air. Trafficante rubbed his big forehead.

"I call *that* living by the sword," Calendar said, knocking Giancana in the shoulder like a comrade, "huh, Sam?" Giancana accepted the gesture with a merry wink.

"Anyway," Calendar mopped up, "all we had to do was circulate some stills from the film around Indonesia. Sukarno had to stop seeing the gal. And the Soviets aren't such great pals of his as they once were."

Again, Giancana said, "Nice." All three gangsters looked at Maheu, the proper California gent with his silk tie, niceties, and his high horse.

Trafficante glanced at his watch.

"Mr. Calendar. All due respect, but we're not here tonight to make any dirty movies. If you catch my meaning. Sukarno's a sick fuck. Arbenz got scared." The mobster rubbed fingers down his long, sad jowls. "We got a different situation. Castro don't scare."

"And that," said Calendar, "is why, if we can't turn him, we're going to kill him."

In intel circles, this word was never spoken. They called it *Executive Action, the magic bullet, the button.* There were any number of euphemisms to smother the ethical dilemma of murder. Calendar savored saying to these unflinching men exactly what they were going to do.

Across from him, Trafficante finally stopped fingering his face in concern. He laid his hands flat on the table.

"And how do you figure this should take place, Mr. Calendar?"

"First of all," Calendar asked the dapper man at the end of the table, "Bob? Do you want to hear this? Or is Howard Hughes not paying you enough to be an accomplice?"

"Proceed, Mr. Calendar. Mr. Hughes won't cry when Castro is removed, but he's not involved in this operation."

"Then what's your reason?"

"I'm a patriot, Mr. Calendar," Maheu answered with a blank face. "Same as you."

"You sure it's got nothing to do with the fact that your boss makes about a billion bucks a year supplying the U.S. government with weaponry? Maybe Howard's a bit of a kiss ass. Maybe he's more involved than you think. And maybe you're a good employee, as well as a patriot."

"Maybe, Mr. Calendar."

"Okay, then. We're all on the same page. Here's some ground rules first. This is a cutout operation. That means it's a one-time shot. The CIA and the mob are not gonna start holding hands after this. Understand? One deal, then it's back to cops and robbers."

Nods all around. Calendar pressed on.

"Tell you the truth, we've been trying to hit Castro on our own for six months now. We tried giving him poison cigars last year while he was in New York at the U.N. Couldn't get close enough to make the delivery. We've been providing the Cuban underground with every weapon they ask for to clip Fidel. Plastic bombs, sniper rifles, you name it, and every time they come up craps."

Giancana asked, "What's wrong with the underground?"

"Too many snitches. Castro's police have infiltrated just about every cell on the island."

Roselli pitched in, "Fucking Cubans can't keep a secret anyway."

Calendar thought Roselli was right, but didn't say as much. He kept on describing the CIA's tough luck in getting to Fidel. "We thought about putting thallium salts in his boots to make his beard fall out. We made plans to get him high on an aerosol LSD before one of his radio talks. We tried more poison cigars. Considered jabbing him with a shellfish poison needle like Gary Powers, that U-2 pilot who got shot down, was supposed to stick himself with. Just last week we got real close. We wired a mine under a conch shell where Fidel goes spear fishing. Some kids were poaching on his private reef. One boy got his arm blown off right in front of me. Two goddam minutes before Fidel showed up."

Giancana nodded sympathetically. "Murder on television looks real easy, don't it? Not so easy to do in real life."

"Then a couple of days ago, we had a sniper team get picked up the minute they landed."

"Too bad," agreed the mobsters.

"Anyway, I'm done with the underground. I may as well publish what I'm doing in the newspapers as deal with those blabbermouths. That's why I'm here, gentlemen. I need names, people I can trust in Havana. I'm sick of dealing with nothing but patriots. I want your guys, greedy and scared to death of you. I'll be honest, this *omertà* thing you people have got, it's a CIA man's wet dream."

Trafficante, ever the businessman, asked, "Alright, Mr. Calendar. You've figured out you need our help. And from the sound of things, you're right. How does this go down?"

"The CIA's first choice is a gangland-style hit. You guys find someone in Havana to do it with a lot of noise, a submachine gun in a public square, a drive-by, something out of that TV show *The Untouchables,* you know? We want it to look like the Mafia did it. Revenge murder for Castro closing down the casinos."

Roselli nodded, enjoying the image of Fidel splayed out and bleeding, the doing of it. Trafficante remained staid. Giancana stroked his chin.

Calendar said, "The government's willing to pay a pretty penny for this operation. You pull it off, you name your price."

Trafficante replied, "We'll do it for free." As the Florida crime boss with mob jurisdiction over Cuba, this was his call. "Lansky's already got a million-dollar price on Castro. We're covered."

Giancana shook his head. "Nah."

Trafficante asked, "What's the matter, Momo?"

"You'll never get anyone to pull the trigger," Giancana said. "It's in the middle of Cuba, for Chrissakes. What kind of *stunad* you gonna find for that idea? Gun down Castro and do what? Fucking shoot yourself next, is what. Nah. It's gotta be quiet."

Calendar began to respond but Giancana cut him off.

"Frankly, we don't need the CIA or anybody if we want to gun Castro down. We'd have done it already. If we're gonna hit the son of a bitch and get away with it, we gotta work together. We got connections inside Havana. You got all those secret weapons. No other way to make it work, if you want us involved."

Trafficante immediately agreed with the logic. Roselli shrugged, clever enough to have no opinion but clearly saddened not to re-live one more time the old Chicago days of blasting away from the running board of a speeding coupe.

Calendar let this percolate for a moment. He'd anticipated the mobsters' reaction. Then he nodded.

"If that's what'll get the job done, okay. Pills, it is. Bob?"

"Yes, Mr. Calendar?"

"You're liaison. If the CIA wants additional contact with these gentlemen again, we'll go through you. If anyone says anything about this meeting or any event that comes out of it, they'll not only be called a liar, they will engender the ill will and full attention of their government. Not good, trust me."

All these men, including the absent Howard Hughes, made their livings ducking and weaving Uncle Sam. All knew better than to poke him in the eye.

"The concept, gentlemen, is plausible deniability. By that I mean that neither the CIA nor any branch of the U.S. government can be put in a position where we're linked to the assassination of a foreign leader. This will be a civilian operation. Understood?"

Giancana fingered a thick gold ring on his left hand. "What you're saying is, if this goes bad, you don't know nothing."

"Nothing. And nobody."

Trafficante tapped fingertips below his chin. Giancana spun the gold ring, and Roselli drummed fingers on the table. Maheu shook his head in a barely perceptible display of loathing.

Calendar reached into his pocket. Between finger and thumb, he held up for the men at the table the small amber glass vial.

"These are the pills."

Roselli reached for them. Calendar held the bottle away.

"Botulinum. Sprinkle one of these babies on food or in a cold drink. Nothing warm. In six hours, paralysis starts at the feet and crawls up the body until it hits the organs. They shut down, the lungs quit next. Castro'll be dead twenty-four to forty-eight hours later."

Calendar set the bottle on the table. Giancana picked it up. The Mafioso peered closely into the glass, as if trying to see a life trapped inside like a genie. "These'll do the trick, huh?"

"No antidote."

Giancana passed the bottle to Trafficante, who also gazed into the little shaded glass at the six white capsules. Roselli was next. Maheu did not desire a closer look.

"Okay," said Calendar. "Now that Uncle Sam's anted up, I'll need something from you. A name."

Trafficante exchanged glances with Giancana. The two nodded.

"When?" Giancana asked.

"I'll let Bob know. It'll be inside the next couple weeks."

"Okay," said Trafficante. "I got a guy in mind. You say the word, Mr. Calendar, I'll bring him here for a sit-down."

"That'll work."

Giancana spoke. "One last thing."

"Yeah?"

"Plausible deniability."

"That's right."

"So, who's the patsy?"

Calendar stood to end the meeting.

"I got my eye on one. As we speak."

CHAPTER FIVE

March 14
First Avenue
Miramar
Havana

A STRONG EVENING BREEZE blew across the Florida Straits. Mikhal Lammeck stood in the backyard of his rented house, hearing the wind in a royal palm left leaning after some old hurricane. He looked over the waves and whitecaps to the northern horizon. Ninety miles that direction, under the same purpling sky, lay America.

The actual distance, Lammeck thought, was not so great. It was nothing, crossable in an hour by plane, three hours by powerboat. Ninety miles was a poor measurement of what separated Cuba from the U.S. today.

He checked his watch: 6:00 P.M. He left the rear yard and entered the house, passing through the kitchen. Pouring himself a tumbler of rum, he went to the front porch, out of the wind, facing the road, to wait.

He sat on the step. His house was the only one on the block that had an inhabitant. The others had been abandoned over the last two years, furniture left inside, cars still in the driveways. The homes were beginning to show the effects of tropical weather and neglect. Their owners and families took what valuables they could carry to travel that ninety miles north. Most settled in Miami. All gnashed their teeth over Castro.

Lammeck sipped the dark rum, letting the taste swirl on his tongue. He'd been in Havana a week; rum and sunsets had become his early evening ritual. Then he would call a taxi and head back into old Havana to eat, have another few drinks, and listen. But not tonight. Lammeck set the glass of rum on the porch and let the warm Caribbean evening fall.

Johan arrived on time, at seven. A powder blue and white '56 Ford Fairlane pulled up. Lammeck did not rise or lift a hand in greeting. This meeting was not something he'd asked for. The man coming up the sidewalk was not someone he knew better than a five-minute conversation could tell him.

"Professor."

Lammeck inclined his head. "Captain. Right on time."

"It is my profession to be exact, Professor. As it is yours."

"What have you brought me, Captain?"

Johan showed a cigar box. "The Partagas, as promised." He set the box on the porch beside Lammeck, then handed over a bottle. "And *añejo* rum."

Lammeck admired the bottle, then gave it back to Johan. "I'll fetch you a glass, Captain. Open that and have a seat."

When Lammeck returned from the kitchen with the tumbler, Johan had already poured Lammeck's glass full. A new, snipped Partagas cheroot waited beside it.

Lammeck sat on the step and tilted the glass at Captain Johan beside him. The policeman returned the salute. Lammeck took a swallow.

"This is good."

"Thank you. It is the *siete* rum. I assume you have been drinking the *quince*."

"I have."

"That is for tourists and export, Professor. In Cuba, we know to drink only the seven-year rum, especially with cigars. The *siete* has gained all its flavor, and lost nothing. The fifteen-year is too old."

Lammeck tipped the glass again Johan's way. "It is possible to be too old. I worry about that every day."

Johan shook his head. "No need, Professor. You are a fine-looking man." Smiling, the policeman patted his own stomach. "We are of a kind, in that department. Here, let me light your cigar."

Johan produced a Zippo and set the flame to both cigars. Lammeck breathed in the good Cuban tobacco, then sipped the *siete*. Johan was right, the dark flavor of the younger rum married the tobacco's tang better than the *quince*. The two tastes filled each other's gaps.

Johan savored his own smoke and glass. "This is a fine home, on a wonderful street. You are fortunate."

Lammeck shrugged. "I made the arrangements in December, before the U.S. broke relations in January. The Cuban government owns this house. Someone decided to let me keep the contract."

Johan smiled. *"Por nada."*

"You?"

"I am particularly fond of historians, Professor. I am in charge of approving American entry visas since the break. I thought it might be a good thing to let you come, despite our countries' disagreements."

A tingle crept up Lammeck's spine. He rolled the glass of rum in his hand and chose his next words carefully.

"How long have you been following me?"

"Let us say I've simply been waiting for a good opportunity for us to meet. I wished to give you a chance to get settled, before I introduced myself."

Lammeck eyed his guest. "Why don't you do so now?"

The man set his own rum on the stoop and rose. Slightly shorter than Lammeck and not as stout, he had the same firm rotundity; he was strength and excess in tandem, a powerful blend like the cigars and rum. The posture Johan struck was meant to be comic and self-deprecatory but Lammeck made no mistake: this was no regular policeman.

"I am Captain Pablo de Santana Johan Guerrero. I have the honor of serving on Commandante Castro's security force." Johan clicked his boot heels and bowed. The move was Germanic, a lampoon. Johan was trying to take the sting out of who he was.

"You're with the secret police."

Johan shook his head. "Really, I am more a policeman of secrets. That is why I have an interest in you, Professor. May I?"

"Please. Sit."

Johan returned to the porch.

"And exactly why have you been following me? You could have just met me at the airport. Or dropped by the house."

"You are an expert in assassinations, Professor. It is known you have had high-level affiliations with your government in the past. And you are an American during this unfortunate time of conflict between our countries. It was considered wise to keep an eye on you for a little while, to be certain you have no agenda here in Cuba other than research, rum, and cigars."

"I have none, I assure you."

"That is excellent to hear. Do you know, Professor, I have read your book? Years ago. *The Assassins Gallery*. It remains the definitive work on history's assassinations."

"I'm flattered."

Johan studied the tip of his cigar, then said, "This is my assignment, you see. Protecting Fidel from the very people you describe so brilliantly in your book. People that you continue to study, I understand. Assassins."

"I do."

"I am, as you say in English, a fan."

"What did you do before the revolution, Captain?"

"I have always been a policeman."

"You married? Family?"

"No. I'm afraid my work has been my home. It has been full at times, empty at others. I know you have not married either."

"Another similarity between us."

Johan allowed a delicate pause, for the wives and children they did not have. Then he raised his rum in toast to Lammeck and the lives they did. The two men drank.

"I assumed you wished to come to Cuba to continue your research. That is why I decided to allow you. You know something, or you suspect something is going to happen. You are like a raven. You are a harbinger."

Lammeck drew on the Partagas. "You're a clever man, Captain."

Johan grinned behind the rim of his glass.

"Like you, Professor, I have lived more than my half century. And we have both, I believe, lived it well. One learns along the way, yes?"

"Yes."

Johan finished his rum. He set the emptied glass on the table with a flourish. "Have you never been to Cuba before this trip?"

"No."

"Why not? We are, as Kennedy is so fond of reminding you and your countrymen, only ninety miles south of Florida."

"I'm from New England, Captain. Warm weather reminds us of how unhappy we are. We avoid it."

Johan laughed. He got to his feet.

"Come, Professor. Take a walk with me by the ocean. I will tell you things about Cuba you do not know. And you will teach me something about assassinations."

Johan put Lammeck in his Ford Fairlane, but did not drive far. He headed east toward old Havana, then parked on the wide seafront road, the Malecón.

"My favorite walk in all of Cuba," Johan said, climbing out of the car. "In all the world."

Lammeck, too, marveled at the Malecón every time he strolled it. The waters of the Florida Straits, when driven by the north wind as they were this evening, beat against the seawall with waves rolling in ten feet high. Plumes of spray leaped into the air, then cascaded across the road, soaking traffic and pedestrians. Lammeck had always stayed on the opposite side of the wide boulevard, out of reach of the flying water. Johan stood beside the seawall, waiting for Lammeck to join him.

"Come, Professor. Let us gamble."

Lammeck moved up on the wet sidewalk. Johan pointed ahead. A mile and a half farther east, heaving up to the edge of the water, was the old city. Standing on the wet concrete, he glanced across the street where the walkway was dry and mostly empty. Dozens of *Habaneros* strode the ocean-side with Johan and Lammeck, testing their luck on the fickle Malecón.

"It is a tradition," Johan told him. "It is Havana."

Traffic flowed past, Fords, Chevrolets, and Buicks from the 1940s and '50s. Many glistened and swished windshield wipers from a dousing they'd taken farther up the road. Lammeck imagined being waterlogged and sitting through dinner. But Johan smiled like a boy. Lammeck stepped beside him.

"I appreciate that you are trying to trust me, Professor."

"It's not so easy to do. You've got a few advantages on me. I don't know a thing about you. And you've been following me."

"Let me rectify that. Ask me questions."

"How high up are you in the government?"

Johan raised his thick palms. Lammeck noted they were similar to his. He knew what had made his own hands that way, decades of weapons and martial arts training, all for research into the tools and skills of history's assassins. He wondered at Captain Johan, at his careful refinement, and what it concealed.

"I am not so important," Johan answered. "I am the number three official in the protection service around Fidel. I have enough authority to approve an American historian's entry visa and his application for a rental house. And to, as you say, follow him to one of Fidel's speeches and a restaurant. Beyond that, I deal with paperwork. Others handle Fidel's physical security. I am like you, Professor. Somewhat of a theoretician. I handle information. I search for... tendencies."

"Fidel must be difficult to protect."

"He is a man of his people, definitely. Not a week goes past when Fidel is not eating in a restaurant, swimming in the sea, playing baseball with youths, visiting a hospital. He sleeps in different places all week long, at odd times. Remember, Fidel is only thirty-five. He has energy. So, yes," Johan chuckled, "Fidel is difficult."

"Where are you from?"

"I was born in Las Tunas, a small city in the heart of Cuba. My family were landowners. They farmed sugar cane."

"Sounds a lot like Castro's background."

"Yes. Both of our parents came from Spain in the '20s."

"Were you with Fidel during the revolution?"

"I was not with him in the mountains, but I joined the resistance to Batista here in Havana."

Lammeck eyed the man. Johan smiled at teenagers they passed lounging on the seawall, he dipped his head to older couples taking the air before dinner. Johan did not seem suspicious and hawkeyed. This secret policeman was gracious, measured.

"Does that mean you're a Communist?"

Johan cast Lammeck a sideways glance. This was the first hint Lammeck got from the man's face that he was not completely open. Then the look was gone, replaced by a wily grin.

"As I said, I suspect I'm very much like you, Professor. Simply a man trying to understand what history determines is just, and what it does not."

In the next instant, Johan grabbed Lammeck's elbow and yanked him into a sprint. A column of water shot overhead and spilled behind them, bathing a passing car and the sidewalk where they'd strolled seconds ago.

Huffing but pleased, Lammeck said, "Your instincts are pretty good."

"Thank you. And you are agile for a portly professor."

The two walked on. Several streetlights were broken, making the street patchily lit. Teenage boys beat salsa rhythms on congas and bongos, struck chords on yellowed guitars. Others sang, often in adept melodies. Their girls snapped fingers, joined in the singing, or reclined on the seawall with heads in their boys' laps. Sometimes, in the places where the lights were out, the girls kissed their boys or danced for them, hiking skirts above brown thighs, swishing their hems to the beat.

Lammeck and Johan walked blocks without speaking. Johan let Lammeck take in this damp side of the street, the authentic Havana. Lammeck watched the others on the promenade, the cars, and the wild sea. He kept his ears peeled for the sound of a wave whacking the seawall, to see if he could be the one to warn

Johan against a cold soaking. He had one false alarm and ran up the sidewalk alone. Johan stayed behind, dry and laughing.

"Tell me, Professor," the policeman said when he caught up, "about your instincts. I expect they are better than mine in many areas beyond the Malecón."

"Such as?"

"Assassinations. You have come to Cuba. You've rented a house with no time limit on when you intend to go home. You are the world's leading expert on the subject. Your instincts tell you something is going to happen in Cuba. What? And just as important, why?"

Lammeck was reluctant to get into a political discussion with Johan, a government official, or anyone in Cuba. Since arriving in Havana, he'd been mindful that he was an American; anti-U.S. sentiment ran high on the island. Lammeck made no reply to Johan's question.

"Please, Professor. I would be very grateful for your insights. I will not lie to you. I can be a useful friend here in Cuba."

Lammeck looked down at the dripping sidewalk. He could walk on without Johan, out of range of the waves whacking the wall behind him. But the policeman claimed to be a theoretician. Lammeck had theories to spare.

Lammeck eyed the water. He spotted a tall roller coming in, coursing at the Malecón. This one would blast water thirty feet high.

"Okay."

The policeman put a hand in the small of Lammeck's back and pushed. The wave pounded against the seawall; the pair galloped out of the shower just before it landed. At a safe distance, both turned to look back. Mist drifted over them.

Johan pointed at the place in Lammeck's back where he'd put his hand.

"You grow more interesting by the moment, Professor."

"Do I?"

"You have a knife under your jacket. In the waistband of your trousers."

"Is it illegal?"

"No, certainly not. But, without wishing offense, it is odd to think of you, a scholar, as a man who goes about armed. Do you have enemies, Professor?"

"None that I know of."

"Of course," the police captain agreed. "Weapons are for the enemies we do not know of. May I see it?"

Lammeck reached under his coat for the four-inch dagger. He slid it from the leather sheath tucked inside his belt.

"The handle's black bone. The blade is Cordovan steel."

Johan nodded. "Marvelous. It appears quite old."

"Sixteenth-century Spain."

Johan turned the dirk over in his hands, testing the balance. He seemed no stranger to weaponry.

"Is it special? Has it done something of note?"

Lammeck smiled, enjoying the question, the opportunity to show his knowledge.

He tapped the knife in Johan's hands. "It was involved in what Spaniards still call the most spectacular assassination in their history, the killing of Guiterrez de Castro."

"Ah," breathed Johan, recognizing the event. "The *mater alevosamente*."

"You know this?"

"*Sí*. It was in your book, of course. But every Spaniard knows this murder, even those of us born in Cuba. We have even given it a name: 'To kill with treachery.' Guiterrez de Castro was the governor of Burgos district. He was opposed to church influence in state matters. One day in 1869, while praying in the cathedral, he was stabbed to death by priests. By priests! And this is one of the knives they used to murder him. *Dios.*"

Johan offered the dagger back to Lammeck, plattered on two hands. The knife was a prized item of Lammeck's Assassins' Collection he was building and curating at Brown University. He took the blade from Johan and slid it into the sheath at his back. He'd chosen to bring this particular dagger with him to Cuba in a sort of irony; this knife had killed a man named Castro.

"I will not ask why you carry this, Professor. I will respect your secrets, as I have a few myself. I will, of course, expect this marvelous blade to stay in its sheath while you are in Cuba."

Lammeck was relieved not to have to lie. He would have concocted something flimsy, and not have told Johan that every day for the last sixteen years, since meeting an assassin named Judith—the most dangerous human he'd ever encountered—he never left home without a weapon on him somewhere.

For the Providence collection, he'd even managed to secure Judith's twelfth-century knife, a dirk from the Assassin cult of ancient Persia. That knife, which had fought the Templars during the Crusades and murdered more than a few in the twentieth century, was the most precious of the thousand artifacts in his collection.

He said, "I'll do my best."

Johan nodded, accepting this.

Their walk had taken them to the end of the Malecón. Here, at the ruins of Punta Castle, the road turned south to run along the entrance to Havana Bay. Across the broad channel loomed Morro Castle, a sprawling, intact stone redoubt built by Spain to protect this valuable Caribbean harbor. Lammeck was still learning his Cuban history, but he knew a great deal about Spain. For centuries, untold tons of gold, spice, animals, tobacco, rum, and sugar left Cuba for Madrid through Havana Bay. What came back were more Spaniards and African slaves.

From the seaward tip of Morro Castle, a lighthouse swung a shaft of white light over their heads. Lammeck watched the beam circle. When he finally brought his gaze down to Johan, the policeman said, "Professor, I see you are reluctant to speak with me about why you've come to Cuba. I know you are here because you strongly suspect, as I do, that something may soon befall my country. You also believe that Fidel is ripe for assassination. I agree with you. And I have a job to do. So, to encourage you to trust me further, I will speak first."

Lammeck leaned against the stone wall. The Morro lighthouse flashed overhead.

Johan said, "Four days ago, there was an attempt on Fidel's life. A seashell was wired to explode underwater near a reef where he is known to spearfish. The charge was set off by two local boys only minutes before Fidel arrived. One boy was badly hurt. His arm was torn off at the shoulder. Fidel himself drove the child to a hospital."

Lammeck shook his head, mortified and at the same time thrilled to hear this bit of intelligence.

"We do not presume the Cuban underground has such capabilities, or the imagination," the policeman said. "It was CIA."

"And there have been other attempts?"

"Oh, dear." Johan laughed, an odd response. "Your CIA is very keen on disposing of Castro. I know of several assassination plots. In New York last year, someone tried to slip him a box of poisoned cigars. We have learned of American schemes to make Fidel lose his hair or his sanity. In the last three months alone, bombs have been defused in Santa Clara and Havana, all at places where Fidel was to appear. In February we intercepted a squad of four exiles dropped off at a remote airfield. They were black operations, trained and equipped in Florida, then flown in by the CIA, to kill Castro."

"You know these things how?"

Johan did not lose his breezy manner. "We have friends, Professor. Contrary to what you hear in America, the vast number of Cuban people love the revolution. They are the first tier of defense around Fidel."

"Informants."

"A nasty word. But, yes, of course."

"And when you don't have friends?"

"We interrogate. Make no mistake."

Lammeck paused with images of Johan's interrogations. He reminded himself to be careful with this agreeable policeman.

"I tell you these things in confidence, Professor. If they appear in your research, I expect you will make no mention of where you received the information. It would be an inconvenience for us both."

"Certainly. You'll learn that about me, Captain. I can keep a secret."

The policeman nodded. It seemed to Lammeck that Johan believed this about himself, as well.

"In addition to the CIA," Johan said, "we're on constant guard against the underground, the exile groups, and your American Mafia. All of these want Fidel dead."

"It must make for a busy day."

"Indeed."

"And you want me to tell you why."

"I have my own theories. Nothing beyond the obvious, I'm afraid."

Lammeck straightened from against the seawall. A lit-up cargo ship entered the channel between the two guardian castles. The registry on the bow read Bulgaria. Johan followed Lammeck, waiting for his reply.

"Tell me the obvious," Lammeck said.

"The underground and exile groups are counterrevolutionary.

They oppose Fidel's changes, the agrarian reform laws, the suspension of elections."

Lammeck was quick to respond. "Fidel's looking more and more like a Communist, Johan. Don't be surprised if people who're accustomed to freedom wind up opposing a Communist revolution."

"Yes." Johan smiled blandly. "As I said, the obvious."

"And the Mafia. That's just about money."

"Clearly. But the CIA. Your country. Why such fervor to kill Fidel? Why not rely on diplomacy? Does your country try to murder every world leader it disagrees with? Of course not. The U.N. would disintegrate if that were the case. Why, then, is Fidel so dangerous to America that you cannot leave him alive? That you cannot deal with him at all?"

Lammeck eyed Johan. The man had been forthcoming about the attempts on Fidel's life; he'd traded good value for Lammeck's advice, and perhaps would continue to be a source of information on the exact subject of Lammeck's research. Where else could Lammeck get information like what Johan could provide? Exploding seashells and black operation hit squads would not be in the papers or the archives.

Johan might be, as he mentioned, a useful friend here in Cuba.

Across Cespedes Avenue, an outdoor bistro fragranced the evening air with odors of simmering meat, black beans, and coffee. Christmas lights were strung between palm trees above red and white checked tablecloths.

"Buy me dinner," Lammeck said to the policeman, "and I'll tell you."

Lammeck avoided talking about his theories until the food came. He and Johan ordered Cristal beers, to be followed by the Cuban

national dish, black beans, rice, and roast chicken. The evening remained fine, a tropical cool that in New England would have been
a perfect midsummer's night. Lammeck steered the conversation
to Johan himself, to learn more about the captain. The policeman
volleyed questions back at Lammeck, to do the same.

"Your English is exceptional, Captain. Where'd you learn it?"

"In the American schools in Havana. For the sixty years your
country occupied Cuba, we were taught to love everything Ameri-
can. Your language, your cinema. Baseball. There was no bigger
thrill than to go to the casino at the Nacional Hotel and see
George Raft greeting guests, or Johnny Weissmuller and Mickey
Mantle seated at the blackjack games. I used to wait tables there.
My English got me the largest tips. Once Marlon Brando and
Casey Stengel each gave me a hundred dollars on the same night.
And your Spanish? Where did you learn it?"

"A few years back, I decided I was interested in Cuba. I pick up
languages pretty well. I learned Russian in the fifties so I could
read *Pravda* and *Izvestia*. I had a fascination with Stalin for a
while. That was one murderous son of a gun."

"A few years back. In other words, when the *Fidelistas* won."

"Yep."

"You knew then that Castro might be assassinated?"

"I knew that I was looking at a classic candidate for it, yes."

"Classic, you say. Very interesting. Tell me why."

Lammeck paused. He wasn't finished finding out about Johan,
this seemingly reasonable and educated man, and secret policeman. Lammeck decided to prod. If Johan was going to be a source
for him, he needed to know how the information would be
colored, what lenses Johan wore when viewing the revolution, and
how far Lammeck could trust the man.

"First, what about the oppressions, Johan? How do you stomach them?"

Johan tilted his head and considered Lammeck. He worked his lips before answering.

"The 'oppressions,' as you call them, are made necessary by the mercenaries and rebels. A revolution—and you know this well, Professor—cannot be made on niceties."

"Free speech suspended. Political opponents sent to prison or the *paredón*. Elections eliminated. Manipulating the courts. Secret police like you. Informants. You're right, Captain—these are definitely not niceties."

"Elections are not something a hungry people cry out for. There are other human rights besides free speech. There is food and shelter. There is work. And the firing wall, the prisons, the intelligence gatherers like myself, these stay busy only so long as the wreckers do."

"Beautifully put, Captain." Lammeck grinned. "If they had elections in Cuba, you could run for office."

"I would not do so, Professor. Like you, I prefer the background. I am a civil servant. Fidel is the reformer."

"And that," said Lammeck, "makes him a sure bet for assassination."

Johan uttered, "Ahh," now that Lammeck had arrived at the point of their meeting. The food showed up in that moment. Johan lifted his hands in anticipation of the meal set before him. Lammeck couldn't help liking this dodgy man.

The captain smiled. "This is why you may have your elections, Professor. You are not so hungry as a Cuban."

Lammeck sliced a bit of the roast chicken. He forked it in, followed by black beans and a swig of beer. Johan was already a quarter through his plate. Lammeck felt a bit let down by how the food distracted Johan's attention from him. He raised a finger to renew his point. Momentarily, the gesture recalled Castro's own style. Johan looked up from his food.

"Reformers seize power for their own purposes. That means they have to kick somebody else out of power. And they're not just working to change the name on the door. Reformers and revolutionaries transform the entire system of governance. Wealth and authority shift hands dramatically. That makes for very big, very dedicated enemies. People who've got everything to lose. In turn the powers that be use everything to keep themselves in power. That, of course, includes assassination. Off the top of my head, in the twentieth century alone, I can think of Zapata and Pancho Villa. Mohandas Gandhi. Just last month, Patrice Lumumba."

Still chewing, Johan added, "There were several attempts on Hitler's life, who from a purely historical perspective can be considered a reformer."

Lammeck continued, "In 1918, Lenin was shot. Then Trotsky..."

"Mercader," Johan jumped in, referring to the man who'd taken an ice axe to Trotsky's head. "Did you know his mother lives in Cuba? I've met her. Cantankerous old woman. We keep her at a distance from Fidel. Not a good family."

Lammeck laughed with Johan, who had to use his napkin to keep some of the food in his mouth.

He said, "In his own way, Franklin Roosevelt was a reformer."

Johan patted his lips with his napkin. He eyed Lammeck with curiosity.

"And was Roosevelt assassinated?"

Lammeck grinned. He dusted off an old and spectacular secret, admired it once in his memory, then put it away.

"There were attempts on FDR's life. But no."

"Now, Professor," Johan demanded, finished with his meal, "tell me. You've come to Havana because you are convinced something is going to happen. I should like to know what that is."

"I'm working on a new book."

"Yes, good."

"You know the nature of my work, the central question I examine. What makes history—individuals or events?"

"Of course."

"I've come to Cuba because I think the answer's going to be played out here."

"Here. Really?"

"I've come to watch what might be the last of the Cuban revolution."

Johan's eyebrows arched. "The last of the revolution. You mean this seriously?"

"I believe it may end. Soon."

"And the assassination of Fidel?"

"Inevitable."

Johan pushed away his emptied plate. He slid his beer in front of him, then sat back, fingers knitted over his shirt buttons.

"Alright," Lammeck began. "Two years ago, when Fidel took over, the whole world sat up and noticed. After all, it was America he kicked out of Cuba. Christ, Johan, *no one* boots America out. So I got curious as to how and why. I started researching our relationship with the island. Mostly I've been looking into the economics, examining bank records, corporate reports, government white papers, United Nations studies, newspapers. I'm finding some pretty damning stuff."

"I can imagine."

"It might actually be worse than you think. Since the end of the Spanish-American War, the U.S. absolutely dominated Cuba's economy. We forced the whole island into dependence on sugar, a single commodity. Nothing else you had to offer, like tobacco, nickel, coffee, none of it was allowed to compete for open farmland. Sixty percent of tillable Cuban soil was owned by American corporations."

Johan pursed his lips in a silent whistle. "I did not know it was to that extent."

"Because Cuba couldn't diversify, and because you had only one principal sugar customer, us, you were never able to fully enter into international markets with any other product, or pursue other large buyers. Cuba couldn't even produce its own needs. Do you realize that more than fifty percent of what the Cuban people consumed they imported from the U.S.?"

"I remember eating American ice cream as a child. I wondered even then, where was Cuban ice cream?"

"We even made you buy our candy and flowers. You couldn't go on a date without us dipping into your pocket."

Johan nodded, recollecting.

"If Cuba traded with any foreign markets we disapproved of, we stuck tariffs on the transactions to cripple them. Whole sectors of the Cuban economy went bust: leather goods, textiles, dairy. This focus on sugar created large-scale land ownership at the expense of the middle class. The whole economic structure in Cuba got out of whack, weighted toward the extremes. Wealth for a few, poverty and farm labor for the rest. And it was done on purpose, Johan. On bloody purpose."

"How better to rule a people?" Johan asked. "Why allow them to prosper? Best to keep them dependant, corrupt, and servants."

"And ignorant. The illiteracy rate in Cuba was forty percent."

There was more Lammeck could have told, that the American Mafia operated ninety percent of the casinos in Cuba, how at one point there was not a single major hotel in Havana that did not have underworld owners. All of this with the knowing wink of the American government. By 1959, the poorest forty percent of Cubans earned only six and a half percent of the island's income. The United States owned ninety percent of Cuba's telephone and electric utilities. Then, in Eisenhower's last term, Fidel showed America the door.

"All that," Johan said deliberately, "is the stage Fidel stepped onto."

Lammeck got the sense that Johan was weighing him, to see what kind of American he was at his core. Did Lammeck lament these things, or approve? Or was he what he claimed to be, simply an academic keen on history's trail?

"And that," he said, setting down the glass, "is why Fidel has to die."

Johan narrowed his eyes.

"Be careful how you phrase these things with me, Professor."

"You asked me to tell you specifically, Johan. That's what I'm doing."

Coolly, the policeman said, "Proceed." Then, mercurial, Johan smiled again. "I apologize. It is a professional instinct of mine to view such statements with...distaste."

"I understand. And you understand, Captain, I'm just an observer."

"Please," Johan said, "continue."

"The real problem is that these conditions, poverty, illiteracy, trade imbalances, colonial histories, racial tensions, all of them exist right now throughout the Caribbean, as well as Central and South America. If a Communist revolution can happen in Cuba, it can happen in any of those places."

"Yes, I know this. But why can't the United States *negotiate* with Fidel? Why not engage with him, win him over? Buy him off? Anything but murder."

"Here's the key." Lammeck leaned his elbows onto the table for emphasis. Johan remained motionless.

"Your young Fidel Castro conducted the first and the only Communist revolution in the last thirty years that was not supported by either China or Russia. It was *indigenous*, Johan.

Completely homegrown. Not one Soviet tank, not one peso from Mao. That scares Washington. Because it proves that someone very dangerous might've been right."

"Who?"

"Karl Marx."

"I see."

"Right now, Khrushchev's doing backflips over Fidel, the new poster boy for world Communism. And like I said, there's nothing to stop this revolution from inciting others in the Western Hemisphere."

"The American hemisphere."

"Some like to call it that, yes."

Johan bobbed his head up and down, calculating, seeing all the connections.

"The invasion," Lammeck said.

"Yes. Of course."

"You said you'd tell me how you know."

"Professor, it is an open secret. There is so much rumor in Miami, so much in the American press, that our biggest problem is sifting through it all for truth. But now I see how obvious it is. All this recent activity to kill Fidel. It is a signal that the rebel landing will be soon. The invasion is inevitable. The two surely go hand in hand."

Johan stabbed a finger at Lammeck. "You are an American. Do *you* feel it is necessary to kill Fidel, to save America?"

Lammeck measured his answer, and the man he would give it to. Lammeck was an historian. He did not delve into what ought to happen, only what had and what might. But, as an American, he believed the menace of Communism was real. Revolution *could* spread. Fidel, the reformer, could be the match to the tinder. Karl Marx predicted this, that Communism would be the "engine of history." Marx actually predicted Fidel. The CIA was right to remove Castro. Lammeck knew this because it was his own conclusion.

"Frankly, Captain, I can discuss both sides of the ethics of assassination. History hasn't made up her mind, yet."

"I will let you go without answering. I see it makes you uncomfortable. Let us agree that we both wish it were not so. We will talk about it another time, perhaps when events have helped clarify your thinking."

The waiter came to clear the plates. Johan fixed his eyes on Lammeck, a wince of approval furrowing his brow.

"You see all this in an historical context, Professor. The many elements and currents, across centuries in both directions. Though I find everything you've said very disturbing, all the more so because it is believable. Tell me one last thing."

"If I can."

"Why Cuba? There are many revolutions going on in the world right now. Many places are teetering between Communism and democracy. In Africa, Asia, Central America. What made you center your research on my country?"

"The central question, Johan. What creates history? Men or events."

"You believe Fidel is the answer?"

"I think Castro might be that rare individual who's truly indispensable to history. For four hundred and fifty years, this place needed a revolt. Martí got close, but he couldn't make one. Cuba waited a long time for Fidel. Not Che, Raúl, or Cienfuegos, none of them, could have pulled this off. Only him. If Fidel's assassinated, I'll have the best chance of my career to watch what history will do afterward. Continue in a straight line? Or veer off?"

"Please tell me you are not hoping for this to happen."

"I'm not, Captain. I'm waiting."

"But doesn't the United States understand? Che and Raúl, those two are next in line. They are both far more militant than Fidel."

"Fidel's the personality. He's the one with history's kiss on his cheek."

"So, Professor." Johan rubbed his hand over his chin. "What is your guess? What will happen to history's kiss if—or as you expect, *when*—Fidel is assassinated?"

"The revolution ends."

"And with it, the danger to America."

"You've got to figure that's what they're thinking up in Washington. If he's left alive, even if the invasion succeeds, I'm betting he'll be back. If not in Cuba, then in Haiti, Nicaragua, Africa, somewhere else that needs a revolution."

"So one man can indeed change history, yes?"

"We'll see. The CIA believes it. That's why they're after him. And I suspect it. That's why I'm here."

Johan ordered two *cafés con leche* and cognacs. He pulled from his coat pocket a pair of Partagas cigars. Lammeck took one and accepted the flame from Johan's Zippo.

The policeman sat back with his glowing stogie. "Who knows who may make history?" He looked troubled, but blew a satisfied cloud of smoke above the table. "Perhaps it will be two lonely old men. You and I, eh?"

CHAPTER SIX

★ ★ ★

March 20
First Avenue
Miramar
Havana

LAMMECK DROPPED HIS BRIEFCASE on a table beside the front door. He peeled off his shoes and socks and headed for the kitchen. Along the way, he shed his jacket, tossed it over the sofa, and untucked his white shirt.

After pouring himself a glass of water, he grabbed a slab of sliced pork from the refrigerator. Popping it in his mouth, he walked to the rear porch, carrying the meat in his teeth like a dog. Lammeck's eyes were exhausted, he'd been cooped inside the archives for seven hours without lunch or fresh air. He wanted to sit on his porch, close his eyes, let the late afternoon breeze blow over him. This was one of the compensations of age, he thought, to know what you want and go directly at it. He bit a chunk out of the pork and chewed, leaving the rest of it hanging from his lips.

Lammeck was aware that he looked unsavory. He considered this another reward of age and living alone.

He pushed open the back door. On his wicker lounger lay a newspaper. On top of it rested an unopened bottle of dark rum. The *siete*. Lammeck put down his water glass, removed the paper and bottle from the seat, and collapsed into the chair, tired to his bones.

The paper was the *New York Times,* three days old. It had been folded to page three, where an article declared that an invasion of Cuba was imminent in the next few weeks.

Johan.

Before reading the article, Lammeck wolfed down the rest of the pork. Dumping the water into the yard, he peeled the label from the rum cap, unscrewed it, and poured a glass. He gulped the liquor, relishing the sizzle at the back of his throat. He was out of cigars but did not want one, only a relaxing shot of rum in his blood and his feet up in the Caribbean breeze.

The ocean ran mild. The Malecón would not be flooded this evening. Lammeck decided to stay in tonight, forage in the fridge, go to bed early. His head was full. He committed himself to reading nothing for the rest of the night after he looked over the paper Johan had slipped onto his back porch. He intended to sit here until hunger drove him from the chair, then return for the sunset and most of this bottle. Lammeck made up his mind to pass out drunk on the porch.

The slender *Times* article was neither a revelation nor a scoop. It was speculation, based on some rumor, some fact. Fifteen hundred Cuban exiles were known to be training in Guatemala and at secret sites around south Florida and Louisiana. The Kennedy administration was ramping up its anti-Communist rhetoric. Kennedy called meeting after meeting with his military staff, CIA, and political advisers over the "Cuba problem." Fidel himself warned daily against an invasion from the American-backed exiles, whom he called *gusanos*—worms. Lammeck had heard this at two more speeches over the past week. Fidel's ability to lecture at immense length, without notes, beggared description. Lammeck would never have believed a man could go on for so long, keep crowds of thousands thundering over his words for hours. Fidel Castro was remarkable. Every day that Lammeck read about him, or saw him, spoke with Johan about him, he became even more convinced that Fidel was indeed the anomaly that Lammeck believed him to be, the one in a million who, alone, could change history—and as such, was absolutely marked for death.

In the last week, Lammeck had switched his research at the archives from the economics of the island to recent Cuban history. He focused on sources not available to him in American libraries or press: the Communist newspaper *Granma,* and eyewitness tales from the *barbudos,* the bearded ones who'd been guerrillas in the mountains with Fidel. In every instance the accounts spoke of Castro's extraordinary magnetism, his unbending persuasiveness. No other man, Lammeck thought, no one in his right mind would have sailed from Mexico with eighty-two others, not a one of them with military experience, to conquer a nation. After a disastrous landing, Castro's cadre was quickly whittled down by Batista's troops and bad luck to a dozen men. He endured two years in the mountains, hunted by the government, short of food and supplies, through swamps and jungle, recruiting an army of illiterates and cane cutters. And won a nation. What other revolutionary of the twentieth century had taken such risks? Lenin had waited out the beginnings of the Russian Revolution in the safety of Zurich. Stalin held up banks and trains, then spent time in Siberian jails, serving only as a military administrator during the Russian Civil War. Mao controlled vast armies against the Kuomintang and the Japanese, but never suffered privations or danger. Yugoslavia's

Tito led troops from a safe headquarters and enjoyed American and British protection. Ho Chi Minh was imprisoned and did not lead soldiers against the French. Khrushchev had not fought in World War II, he'd been only a commissar. Hitler screamed in beer halls while confederates brawled and slit throats for him. Castro had slept with a rifle barrel tucked under his chin in case he was caught in the night.

Every day the people of Cuba saw Fidel in his fatigues. He reminded them of the struggle, that he was a true *guerrillero*. Judging from the endless rallies, the people loved him.

Lammeck didn't make it out of the chair. He watched the sky darken above the straits. He felt the breeze scour away the closed-in sensation of his day spent in the dusty stacks of the archives.

He made it through a quarter of Johan's rum and half the *New York Times* before he got his wish and fell asleep, barefoot.

Lammeck's hand flashed to the small of his back. He jerked erect on the wicker chair, planting his feet, ready to jump. His eyes cut into the darkness for the rustle of someone unannounced on his porch.

"Whoa, whoa." A silhouette spoke, hands up in surrender. "Easy, Professor."

Lammeck's head pulsed from the sudden waking and the remnants of rum in his system. He kept fingertips on the hilt of the knife, sliding it partway out of the sheath.

"Who are you?"

The man kept his palms up. He took a step forward, still little more than a black figure. "I'm with the government. Your government. The United States."

Lammeck blinked and snorted once, to shake off the last of his sleepiness.

"What are you doing on my back porch?"

"I knocked, pal. Nobody answered."

With his vision clearing, Lammeck could make out enough to see that the slowly approaching intruder was broad shouldered, with a flattop crew cut. He was dressed like a Cuban in *guayabera* and loose pants. Lammeck didn't pull his hand from the dagger.

The stranger took another stride. He lowered one hand to point at Lammeck's arm, still angled behind his back.

"You can take your hand off the pig sticker, Professor. My name's Bud Calendar. I'm with the CIA."

"Does CIA recommend you walk up on people in the dark on their own property? There are rules, Mr. Calendar, even for your sort." Lammeck continued to grip the blade.

The agent pushed open the screen door to the back of the house. He stepped inside and found a lamp to flick on. He returned to the porch washed in sallow light. Lammeck saw better now what a brute his government had sent him. He'd be more than a handful in a fight.

"Rules?" Calendar eased into the other wicker seat. "No. There's not."

Calendar jerked a thumb over his shoulder at the interior of the house. "You want a cup of coffee or something?"

"I'm fine." Lammeck noticed the open rum bottle and the empty glass on the table beside him. He felt a bolt of embarrassment at what he must look like, some sorry aging alcoholic conked out in a chair.

"Good. How about making me one, then?"

Lammeck released a long breath. He let go of the knife and rose from the chair. Calendar stayed on the porch when he went into the kitchen. They spoke through the screen door while Lammeck filled the percolator with water and ground beans.

"What branch of CIA are you with?"

"Special Operations Division. Out of Quarters Eye."

Lammeck pursed his lips, setting the coffeepot on a burner. He wondered at all the sudden attention he'd gotten in the past week. The Cuban secret police sent him an emissary. Now the CIA had sent one.

He went to the screen door while the water boiled. He caught Calendar finishing a swig of rum from the bottle.

"I can get you a glass."

"Nah." The big agent waved off the suggestion. "Coffee's good. Black."

Calendar set the bottle aside without screwing on the cap. Lammeck eyed the man a moment longer, comparing him to Johan. Both were sizeable and exuded real power. But Johan seemed to possess a respect for boundaries this one did not.

Lammeck poured two cups, accepting that he could use some coffee. On the porch, he handed down the hot mug and sat opposite the CIA man. He watched Calendar sip and nod at the quality of the coffee. The night breeze had stiffened a little. Lammeck took a sip from his own cup in the yellow light of the one lamp inside.

"You mind?" Calendar indicated the *siete*. He tipped a splash into his cup, then offered the same to Lammeck, who held forth his mug. The rum agreed with the coffee. Sitting, drinking, Bud Calendar seemed no less threatening than he did the first inky moment Lammeck saw him in shadow. He had the brow and skewed nose of a pugilist, his hands were thick and indelicate on the coffee mug.

"Why're you here, Mr. Calendar? Have I done something to attract the CIA's attention?"

"Oh, yeah."

"I'm in Cuba on a research visa. I can show you the stamp in my passport."

"That ain't it."

Lammeck changed his mind about the rum in his coffee. The smell under his nostrils incited the liquor already in his head. He set the mug aside.

"Fifteen years ago you wrote a book about assassination. Pretty damn good book, I hear."

"You haven't read it?"

"Apologies. I've been busy. A world to save and all that. You speak four languages. You're skilled with weaponry from a dozen different centuries. Martial arts, in four separate disciplines. All this so you can understand assassins better. An admirable work ethic, Professor. Back in the big war you were a weapons trainer for Jedburgh teams in Scotland. Came home to the States, cushy teaching job at Brown. Kept up your studies, started a museum at your college. And for some reason that's not in your dossier, you started carrying a weapon everywhere you go. Even here in Cuba, sitting on your back porch for a little nip in the evening."

Lammeck did not move in the chair. He narrowed his eyes.

"I have a dossier?"

"A fat one."

"You're having me followed."

"It's not just me, Professor. You've been followed for the last sixteen years since Roosevelt. Look, I don't know what secrets you lug around in your head. I don't need to know. Whatever they are, the government keeps pretty close tabs on you. And yes, on occasion that includes following you."

"Are you going to require an explanation about the knife, Agent Calendar? Because as you can guess from my fat dossier, I'm not going to give you one."

"Not at all." Calendar reached into a pocket to dig out a little plastic horseshoe. A boxer's mouthpiece. So, he *was* a fighter. Calendar held the thing up for display, then tucked it away. "A man with no enemies hasn't done shit in his life."

"So you say. Should I be curious what else you know about me, or can we just assume that it's enough for me to be annoyed, and enough to make you come see me in the middle of the night?"

Calendar sipped his coffee. "Works for me."

"If you don't mind my getting to the point, what are you doing here?"

"You know."

"I do?"

"It's why you're in Havana. Why Johan's made buddies with you."

Lammeck did know. But the answer was clouded in its own magnitude, and he'd been slow to admit it in the minutes Bud Calendar had been on his porch.

"You're trying to kill Castro."

"I'm going to kill Castro," the CIA agent answered.

Lammeck sat back in his wicker chair, fully awake and sober now. Calendar was a government assassin—for Lammeck's own government! Lammeck had a thousand questions to ask. He knew he'd get answers to none.

The agent said, "When we saw you were coming to Havana for research, we got interested. Made sure you got your research visa. Then the plan sort of fell together."

"Agent Calendar, I'm an historian. That's all I am. Why come here to tell me about a CIA plan to kill Fidel? Unless you want me to put it in the book I'm writing, which I very much doubt."

Calendar raised a finger. "And which you're very much not gonna do."

"Then why are you telling me?"

"Because you're gonna help me."

Lammeck did not see this shocker coming. After a moment, Calendar reached for the rum bottle. He offered it first to

Lammeck, a testimony to the look frozen on Lammeck's face. Lammeck shook the offer off, then watched the agent pour himself another shot.

"Tell me, Mr. Calendar. Why do you use the name 'Bud'?"

"What do you call the guy on the street? The guy you don't know? That's me. I'm Bud. I'm everybody and nobody."

"You're probably a very dangerous man."

"I need to be."

"So this might not be well advised on my part, but are you out of your mind?"

Calendar smiled at this. "Doesn't change anything if I'm nuts. Frankly, with some of the things I've done, I'm betting it helped. In any case, Castro's going down. And you're gonna be part of it."

"No. I'm not."

The agent sat back, crossing his big legs at the knees. "Out of respect, Professor, I'll let you go first. You tell me why you're not, then I'll tell you why you are."

"I'm not a killer."

"You don't have to be. I've got a different job for you."

"Johan. You know he's been following me."

"I know everything about Johan. Him striking up a gab with you is actually a bonus. We can use him for information. Don't worry about Johan."

"You want me to be a conspirator *and* a rat?"

"Yep."

"No. I won't do it."

Calendar unfolded his hands out of his lap. "That's it? That's your argument?"

Lammeck did not like his predicament, but this agent didn't need to take such pains to condescend to him, treat him like a child or a pawn.

"Alright. Make your point, Calendar."

The agent caught the shift in Lammeck. He sat straight on the wicker, the strawlike weave creaking under his weight.

"The United States government has put the highest possible priority on this operation—"

Lammeck interrupted: "There's an invasion coming, and killing Castro goes hand in hand with it."

At this, Lammeck reached to the floor for the *Times* article Johan had left for him. In the lamplight, Calendar took it and read the narrow headline.

The agent set his elbows on his knees. "Whatever happened to secrets? We invaded goddam France with half a million men and no one knew a thing." He lifted his head. "Yeah, there's an invasion of Cuban exiles coming and, yeah, Castro needs to be dead when it hits the shore. Did Johan give you this?"

"Yes. The Cubans know, Calendar. You're screwed."

"Not if Castro's dead. They can be waiting right there on the beach when the exiles land and it won't matter a damn."

"You're counting on chaos, a popular uprising."

"Exactly."

"Forget it. You're not going to get it. These people are too supportive of the revolution, and of Castro personally. Have you seen the guy speak in public? He's like Babe Ruth, Buddy Holly, and Patton rolled into one. You kill him, you'll turn him into a martyr."

"Too late to change the plan, Professor. The decision's been made. And you of all people should have figured out the reasons why."

Lammeck had guessed at this inevitability, had described it to Johan.

He asked, "How soon?"

"Don't know, it's still being debated in Washington. But you can bet it's around the corner. The exile brigade's getting ready..."

"In Guatemala." Lammeck tapped the newspaper in Calendar's hand.

The agent licked his lips in displeasure. He set the paper aside.

"Okay, Professor, I get the point. I don't know when and I don't know where. And I don't really give a shit. My orders are just to take Castro down. Let's assume the invasion will follow fast enough."

A silent moment passed between them.

"One last thing," Lammeck said. "Why can't you do it yourself? You're the spy. I'm just an academic."

"A little thing called 'plausible deniability.' The United States can't touch this operation, not officially. The political fallout of an American agent caught in a hit on Castro would be...well, real fucking bad. This whole Cuba project is illegal. In one way or another, invading Cuba and assassinating Castro violates the Neutrality Act, the Firearms Act, the Munitions Act, the regulations of the IRS, FAA, Immigration and Customs, and I'm sure the enabling charter of the CIA. Plus the laws of about six states and several nations."

"Calendar, in case you didn't notice, I'm an American citizen, too."

"Yeah, but like you said, you're an egghead. So you're perfect. An international specialist on assassinations, come down to Cuba to keep tabs, be close to the action. Maybe you got carried away when some underground types approached you about knocking off Fidel. A once-in-a-lifetime opportunity to not just watch history but make it. You couldn't resist. You're freelancing, with no official connection to the U.S. government. Very believable."

"Very risky."

Calendar took up his coffee mug to pour himself more of the rum. He eyed the half-full bottle and chose to leave it. He set his cup on the table and waited.

"I'll pass on the offer," Lammeck said. "Attractive as it is."

The agent filled his lungs with the Caribbean evening. He looked out, past the edge of Lammeck's rented yard to the moon-raked ocean. "You finished?"

"For now."

"Alright," the agent said, "let me give you some answers. First, I can't personally do it. Like I said, it would be a debacle of biblical proportions if I got nabbed. Second, if something happened to me, the whole operation would stop and there'd be no way to nail Castro before the invasion lands. I'm the last CIA agent in Cuba."

"And what if I get, as you say, nabbed? That sounds like some kind of breakfast food, Calendar, *nabbed*. It's not. It's a dawn in front of a firing squad."

"First of all, you won't get nabbed. Second, if for some reason you do get picked up, you're still an American citizen. We've got some juice left, even here in Commie Cuba. Kennedy raises a back-channel stink that you're this famous academic who's simply researching a real important and timely book on Cuban politics. You might've strayed too close to the flames, but hey, that's why you're a good historian. Anyone who claims you were involved in an assassination plot is a liar and covering his own butt. You were framed. Plausible deniability. Behind the scenes, worse comes to worst, we extract you. We're not going to let an American citizen end up in one of Castro's jail cells. And especially not you, with what you carry around in your head. But, lookit, Professor, you're not gonna be swinging an axe at Fidel or anything. I just need you as a courier, between me and the names and addresses I give you."

"Courier of what?"

"Information and instructions. And these."

Calendar dug into a pants pocket. He tossed to Lammeck a small glass vial. Lammeck caught it and looked inside at six white capsules.

"Botulinum," the agent said. He described the symptoms, the creeping paralysis. Death between twenty-four and forty-eight hours. Untraceable. Irreversible.

Lammeck lobbed the poison back.

"No."

Calendar caught the amber bottle but didn't stow it again in his pants. He set it on the table beside the *siete*.

"Professor, do you agree that Castro has to go?"

"From the standpoint of the United States and the CIA, I can see your logic. But that's in the abstract. It's different when I'm asked to take a direct hand in murder."

"So you're afraid, then."

"In addition to my ethical qualms, yes. Who in his right mind wouldn't be?"

"Me."

"Of course," Lammeck observed. "But there's that issue again of whether or not you're out of yours."

The flesh beside the agent's eyes crinkled. He breathed deeply once more, seeming to regret what he was going to do.

"Well, if no is your answer, let me tell you what that's gonna look like from your end of the stick. First of all, the IRS will be your new best friend. You don't need a description of that particular hell, I assume. Next, the government contracts at your university in Providence won't be renewed. You'll be fingered for some suspicious reason that won't stand up but, hey, it won't matter. You can forget foreign travel. Visas are going to be impossible for you, so get used to sea-to-shining-fucking-sea for your research and vacations. And that's just for beginners. We'll come after your job, your money, and your reputation."

"You wouldn't do that."

Calendar turned his head to the side, appealing in a disgruntled mutter to some phantom jury. "I tell the guy I'm gonna kill Castro, but he doesn't believe I'd wreck his life." The agent looked back at Lammeck. "Yes, Professor, that's exactly what I'd do."

Lammeck felt the crosshairs of America intersecting between his eyes. What had he done to get himself targeted like this? How to escape? All he wanted was to study and write, to leave a legacy in the worlds of ideas and history. But his own government had been marking him for sixteen years, and now they'd sent this ape to Cuba to threaten his livelihood and good name. Lammeck's heart sank. Escape? This was America they were talking about.

"And if I cooperate?"

The corners of Calendar's mouth relaxed. "You'll be permitted to write the book you're researching right now, with two large changes. First, you'll have complete access to every record of the Cuban invasion, soup to nuts, plus everything you want to know about the assassination plans, the ones that've failed and the one that will work. The second change is the book you write will have to stay secret in CIA archives for fifteen years. That does you no good right now, but you'll have the opportunity to write the definitive insider's history of one of the twentieth century's greatest adventures. How America stopped Communism in the Western Hemisphere. You want to make a name, Professor, that'll give it to you in perpetuity. You'll definitely make professor emeritus at your college. Plus all the doors a secretly grateful nation will open for you."

Lammeck sat staring at Calendar, weighing. The big agent was right; he'd be given the chance to write a secret history, a seminal analysis of invasion and assassination, with unparalleled access to government source material. A colossal and important undertaking.

But murder? Lammeck had spent his career studying assassins. Could he become one? How would that affect his posture as a professional historian? Could he take part in such a killing, then maintain the proper—indispensable—academic distance? And what about the larger question, the only one that really mattered: the moral issue. Is killing murder when done by a state? This was the endless query, the subject of volumes and centuries of debate by the greatest historians and philosophers.

To inject himself directly into that debate? To be in simultaneous roles—political theorist and assassin? Who could question his authority, or insights? Even if he had to wait fifteen years for the secret history to come out; even if he was dead when it did. Who could top Dr. Mikhal Lammeck? Emeritus.

He rattled his head to chase these thoughts off. He was not faced with a metaphysical scale to decide what he ought to do, measure the aftermaths in his own life, good and bad, or parse a complex ethical question. He was not staring at a choice, at all. Seated in front of him, waiting for an answer, was a burly and lethal CIA agent with enough power vested in him by the strongest nation on earth to do everything he claimed he would. Kill Castro. Lavishly punish or reward Lammeck.

I'll be just their courier, he thought. *Names and addresses. If not me, Calendar will just find someone else. And Castro will still die.*

Lammeck knew this was temporizing. He recognized himself for what he was, a coward and a pawn, exactly why Calendar and America had picked him.

"What names?"

Calendar rose from the wicker chair. Without a word, not of thanks or assurance, he set a white envelope on the table beside the vial of pills. With less sound than when he'd arrived, he strode off the porch into darkness.

CHAPTER SEVEN

★ ★ ★

March 23
Obispo Street
Havana

FOR TWO DAYS, LAMMECK could not go back to the archives to study, not with capsules of poison in his pocket.

Instead, he roamed the streets of Havana. He wanted to see as much as he could of the life of the city before the change fell. The pills would be a major cause of that change. He kept the little amber bottle with him all the time, hidden like the knife in its black sheath beneath his *guayabera*.

Lammeck walked everywhere now, taking a taxi home at night only when he was too tired to traipse the long, wet Malecón. He hadn't seen or heard from Captain Johan in two days; this was one of the reasons he stayed away from his rented house where the policeman might find him. Johan had said Lammeck would not be followed anymore, but since his encounter with Bud Calendar,

Lammeck was wary of all who walked behind him. It was unnerving to think of how much of what he'd done in the past years, and weeks, how much of his life had been secretly observed.

Lammeck had been in Havana almost three weeks, and now that he'd pulled his nose out of books, he'd begun to more fully realize the size and complexity of the city. It was much larger than New Orleans, and a hundred years older than the United States itself. Havana was dense, laid out in warrens and skewed angles like a European town, growing organically with the flow of centuries and prosperity. Streets uncoiled in every direction. Lammeck looked above the throngs and traffic, block after distant block built by Spain, then by the U.S. Sixteenth-century churches stood alongside seventeenth-century carriage houses, stone keeps, and twentieth-century banks and offices built with American money. On the narrow streets, Fords and Chevrolets jostled alongside boxy Czech Skodas, Tatras, and Russian-made Zaporozhets. Many avenues were blocked from traffic by two-hundred-year-old Spanish cannons buried barrel-down into the cobbles as barricades. Inside doorways, Lammeck caught glimpses of marble stairs, stained glass, black terrazzo, bronze inlays, terra-cotta, wrought iron, wood paneling, the remnants of grand Caribbean riches.

Lammeck entered Obispo Street. The cobbled road narrowed, grew crowded with pedestrians. Several storefronts were shuttered, their businesses closed, the operators gone to Miami and the sanctuary of America. But the rest of the cobbled lane rippled with vitality. Vendors had set up *vidrieras*—kiosks for cigarettes, candy, and cigars—in open windows and alleyways. Above every shop door, bright canvas awnings argued their colors and claims. Old women hawked rolled paper cones packed with *cucuruchos*, roasted peanuts, to calls of *"Mani, mani, rico mani!"* Everywhere was music and the aromas of white pork and tobacco. On every corner were games of chance, men wearing triangular hats made of printed numbers selling lottery tickets, four numbers for a peso. Vendors waved chits for lucky ball and bingo, or ran dice and card games. Others sold slips of paper for the *bolita,* the unofficial street lottery. Olive-clad police strolled absently through the crowd, not looking for infringements, knowing their presence was probably enough and that enforcement was discretionary. In echoing courtyards, alleys, and plazas, teenagers swung broomsticks at tossed tennis balls and bottle caps. Reminders of the revolution's short history lingered on many walls in graffiti damning Batista or praising Fidel, in posters of Che pasted over old commercial signboards for American beers, sodas, and airlines. Above the commerce and bustle of the streets, on the balconies of the upper floors, hung the ubiquitous shirts, dresses, and diapers of Castro's people, now liberated to dry their laundry or play baseball anywhere in the city.

Lammeck strolled through the bustle. He wanted to stop to buy a pastry, or be a spectator of a game of bottle-cap ball in an alley. But he pressed onward to his rendezvous. The pill bottle in his pocket, rolling over in his fingers, was like the button to a bomb, with the power to sweep it all away, backward in history as if the revolution had not happened. Lammeck wondered if the thousands of assassins he'd studied had felt this way, robbed of choice by a history they could not fight.

He arrived at his destination, a corner saloon under a pink neon marquee, El Floridita. This was all Calendar's note had specified, to be here at 5:00 P.M. today. Lammeck stepped inside. The room was cozy in dark paneling. A lustrous mahogany bar ran its entire length; wooden stools stood along it tucked up to a brass foot rail. All the bartenders wore white shirts and black bow ties. Behind the counter, a hundred different bottles and pyramids of stacked glasses gave a crystalline fragileness to the place, a counterbalance to the aged hardwoods and tobacco smoke hazing the air.

This was Hemingway's bar. Pictures of the writer hung in a cluster on one wall: Hemingway with a leviathan fish strung up by the tail, laughing with a shotgun over his shoulder, shaking hands with a young and admiring Fidel. Lammeck understood why Hemingway would gravitate to El Floridita; the intimate room seemed as much a cloister as a bar. Here Papa Hemingway could drink his mojitos without being accosted. The place was spare, like Hemingway's writing. But the writer, too, had retreated to America. Somehow the revolution had not been good to Hemingway; that photographed handshake with Fidel had not borne out, or he would still be here.

The place was not crowded. Lammeck took a seat at the bar near the wall bearing the writer's photographs. Beside him, a plaque inlaid in the bar's surface explained that he was seated next to Hemingway's favored spot. Lammeck ordered a mojito.

Halfway through the minty drink, twenty minutes past the appointed time, Lammeck had not been approached. He bore no instructions from Calendar what to do other than sit and be conspicuous. He felt self-conscious on the stool; in his imagination, the poison in his pocket continued to single him out among the Cubans and few European tourists in the bar. He grew uncomfortable on the stool, glancing around, obviously waiting for someone. Lammeck nursed a growing agitation over Calendar's selection of him for this gambit out of an Ian Fleming novel, playing James Bond, cool over a drink in a famous Havana saloon waiting for his cloak-and-dagger contact.

He bought a Partagas from the bartender, who gave him a light. Lammeck puffed, knowing he looked nervous. He smoked until the hour struck six, burning through the cigar with fidgeting fast inhales. The stool next to him was filled and vacated several times by men who did not speak or even look his way.

When the cigar was down to the label, Lammeck set the stub in an ashtray. Blaming Calendar for this waste of his time, he chewed on his anger and figured that if this was how tightly the CIA ran its operations, it was no wonder Castro was still alive. Fidel could, in fact, expect a long life under such would-be assassins.

Lammeck stood. He was hungry and too annoyed to stay in Hemingway's bar any longer. A man with a shaved head blocked his path.

"Professor Lammeck?"

The man stood close. He was several inches taller than Lammeck, with a gaunt, white Spanish face, thin frame, and long arms. He wore gray slacks and a blue business shirt rolled at the cuffs.

"Yes."

"My name is Felix."

Lammeck nodded. "Felix?"

"*¿Sí?*"

"Was I early or were you late?"

"We have been watching, *señor*. To see if you would wait. And to see if anyone else was following you. *Bueno*. We may go now."

The bald man's voice was soft, almost feminine. His physique was that of a whip. Lammeck clamped his lips against more complaint.

He followed not out the front door but through the bar. More stealth, Lammeck thought, more spy novel folderol. He wanted to turn gangly Felix by the shoulder, slap the poison pills in his hand, and go get himself dinner.

Felix pushed open the rear door to the bar. He held it aside for Lammeck to walk through. Lammeck stepped into the alley, but his path was blocked by a long, emerald, fin-tailed Cadillac. The car stood empty, idling. Dusk had fallen.

The Cadillac disappeared behind a rupture of light and pain. Lammeck was struck hard on the back of the head. He struggled to stay conscious. He was hit again. The pain swelled. Spangles of false light drifted through his vision. The last, fading things he was aware of were his knees striking the cobblestones of the alley, and a hand under his *guayabera* reaching to the waistband at his back, taking his knife.

The pain woke Lammeck. His head hammered. Opening his eyes to utter darkness, he drew a sharp, alarmed breath at the instant flood of his situation. He'd been blindfolded. He lay on his side on a moving, jittering surface. He heard tires on a road, smelled exhaust. He was in the trunk of a car! Feet and hands bound!

Uncontrolled, Lammeck began to pant, puffing his cheeks with the panic of enclosure, the terror of being tied. His instincts demanded him to shriek, kick his heels at the walls of the trunk. Who'd done this? Who was Felix? Did Calendar know this was happening? Something had gone terribly, terribly wrong.

Lammeck could kick his legs against the trunk wall. Felix—was he even the driver?—would stop the car and open the trunk. The blindfold would be taken off, Lammeck would see and breathe open air. He'd explain! Explain what? That this was a mistake, he was caught up in something far past his intentions? He was just a scholar, an academic, not James Bond? He was only supposed to deliver the pills. He'd hand them over. That's all he had of value; he knew nothing else they could want, whoever they were.

Wait...was Johan behind this? Was Felix his henchman? Did the secret police get wind of the CIA plot and kidnap Lammeck away from it, to wring the details out of him? He had no details, only the pills. But they alone were enough to get him executed! All he knew about Bud Calendar was a name, a description. Not enough.

Or what if his being snatched out of the bar had nothing to do with Calendar, Johan, or Castro? There remained plenty of poverty in Cuba; what if Felix was simply a criminal, part of a plot to hold Lammeck for ransom from the U.S.?

Lammeck forced himself to breathe through his nostrils, slowing the panic. Listening to the sounds of the road rubbing against the spinning tires, he struggled to calm himself, to think straight.

The car was moving slowly, in fits and starts. There must be stop signs, people, they were still in old Havana. Lammeck didn't know how long he'd been unconscious; judging by the hangover and how he'd been tied up, he'd been knocked out cold.

Voices, were there voices? No, that was a radio.

Again, he considered shouting, kicking. Maybe someone on the street would hear, make the car stop, save him. No, he reasoned. He had no idea who'd grabbed him or what they were capable of. More likely than salvation was another clout on the head, or worse. Lammeck decided to keep still and focus. When the trunk was opened, wherever it was he was being taken, he'd need his wits.

"Sons of bitches," he whispered, not knowing who the curse was aimed at.

Against his earlier judgment, Lammeck thumped the wall of the trunk with his bound heels as hard as he could, to let them know he was awake and not going to be pleasant when they opened the lid.

"I'm an American citizen!" he shouted.

But he was an American in a country where diplomatic relations no longer existed. There would be no U.S. embassy to expect help from. The revolution here was still young, these were dangerous times. An American might easily go missing, especially one traveling by himself, one who'd rashly agreed to take part in the murder of the nation's leader. But how could they know? Who had betrayed him? Calendar? Johan?

Lammeck lay for a black and indeterminate time—he guessed a half hour—until the car stopped. His joints ached, and his bladder nagged for his attention. He kept his eyes closed behind the blindfold. Fear and anger combined to confuse him. Claustrophobia crept in. He wanted fresh air, light, and an explanation for why he'd been stuffed in this trunk. With the car no longer moving, Lammeck's temper began to assert itself.

The engine was cut. All four car doors of the Cadillac opened and shut. Boots scraped on pavement, men getting out of the car.

A key was inserted into the trunk lock. The lid was lifted.

Voices traded in Spanish above Lammeck. Someone ordered one of the others to lift him out.

Hands touched him. Without thinking, Lammeck lashed out. His bound heels struck dead center in a torso. He felt someone hurled backward, heard the gong of a head banging the bottom of the trunk lid.

He reeled in his legs to kick out again, waiting for his next captor to reach in for him. "Come on," Lammeck growled, "*chingarros.*"

He heard laughter. Someone moaned and cursed, "*Ay, coño.*"

"*Viejo,*" a voice told Lammeck, "it will not be a difficult thing to take you on another ride. If you prefer this."

Lammeck recognized the voice. "Get this blindfold off me, Felix."

"Soon. For now it must stay. May we put you on your feet?"

Lammeck's sudden temper gave way to pragmatism. He'd taken one good shot; time to get out of the trunk and get the blindfold off. He lowered his legs. "I've got to piss."

More laughter when this was translated. The mild voice beside the car said, "You kick like a mule, old man. Perhaps you piss like one."

Lammeck's ankles were gripped. The rope binding them was sliced away. More hands dug under his armpits, hoisting him to a standing position. Blinded and stiff, wrists still tied behind his back, Lammeck's balance eluded him. He was caught when he stumbled.

"Untie my hands," Lammeck demanded.

"Not yet. Diego!"

More laughter. Footsteps shuffled closer.

"*Ay yi yi,*" unhappy Diego muttered, fumbling with Lammeck's zipper.

Lammeck closed his eyes behind the blindfold while clumsy fingers dug into his pants, through his underwear for his penis. When he was clear, he let go his stream. Lammeck heard his urine splash and puddle. He imagined the Cubans standing around watching. Pride made him push hard and piss for a long time in a lengthy jet. When he was done, Lammeck bounced on his heels, knocking off the last drops. Again the men laughed. Lammeck was put back inside his pants, his zipper pulled up.

"I am going to assume," the gentle voice said, "that you have enough lumps on your head, *viejo*. We can give you more. Or you can walk quietly with us so we can have a talk."

Lammeck nodded. He was led forward. He imagined awful things ahead in his blindness: these men could walk him off a ledge or into a lake with his hands tied behind his back; they could stand him at a *paredón*, he was already blindfolded. Lammeck's fears joggled in his gut. He resolved to keep them hidden as best he could.

By the footsteps and the different voices around him, Lammeck determined there were four men. He was prodded down a set of stairs, out of the open air into an enclosure fusty with the smells of concrete dust and mildew. A basement. The hands under his arms tugged him to a stop. A chair was dragged across a bare floor. Lammeck was pushed to sit. He was relieved to find the chair beneath his rump, not a prank and another humiliation.

Another rope was added to his bonds, this one tying him to the chair. Felix issued instructions. Others left the room. A door closed. Lammeck heard only one man move and breathe.

The one remaining man stepped close. He stood in front of the chair. Lammeck heard him scratch stubble on his chin.

Fingers touched Lammeck's brow, digging under the blindfold to push it down around his neck. He blinked to focus. The first things he saw were Felix's dangling hands; broad and veined, they made his white arms resemble axe handles.

"Hold still." Felix probed the crown of Lammeck's head, poked the twin bumps there. Lammeck sucked through his teeth at the pain.

"No need for stitches. You have a hard head, *viejo*."

The basement was broad and bare, unfinished with exposed framing and hanging wiring. Light came from one bare bulb. The only other piece of furniture was another metal chair. Felix carried it over to set in front of Lammeck. He sat and leaned forward. Muscle shifted in the Cuban's forearms.

"I wonder," Felix said, "how hard that head still is."

He eyed Lammeck. He appeared to hope that this threat might suffice. Lammeck gazed back.

"Who are you?" Lammeck asked. "Police? Or maybe just a criminal."

"*Viejo*, this is not going to be like one of your American movies where you ask me questions and I am impressed with your courage or outsmarted, so I give you answers instead. This is Cuba. I will ask *you* questions, and I will beat you until you give *me* answers."

The bald man said this softly, malevolently.

"I don't know anything," Lammeck told him. "Beating me won't change that."

"Ah, but it will verify it."

Felix stood. He scraped the chair back a few paces.

"Professor Lammeck, let's begin."

"You know my name."

"I know a few things. You are a teacher and a writer of some notoriety in America. Why are you in Cuba, Professor? Why would a teacher of assassinations come to an island where a revolution has just been won? A revolution, of course, that is very unpopular in your country. Are you working for someone, Professor? Perhaps you are doing more than writing about an assassination? And please, do not say you are here on vacation. I won't believe you."

Lammeck licked his lips. He leaned his head back to look into Felix's face.

"Vacation."

Felix bent to bring his face level with Lammeck's.

"I don't believe you."

Before Lammeck could cringe, Felix whipped his hand furiously across Lammeck's cheek. The force of the strike rocked Lammeck's chair onto two legs, almost toppling him sideways to the floor. Felix caught Lammeck by the collar before he could tip over.

The right side of Lammeck's face sizzled. His senses flurried, blown loose like trash.

Felix kneaded the back of the right hand with his left. He said something, but to Lammeck the sound was fuzzy, as though swallowed by the roar of Klaxons. Lammeck probed his tongue between cheek and molars, sensing swelling but no loose teeth. He spat once. The wet dab on the floor was threaded with blood.

"I admit," Lammeck muttered, "it's not much of a vacation."

Felix fetched his chair and sat in front of Lammeck.

"Why does Captain Johan come by your house to visit, Professor?"

The question shook Lammeck. He didn't know who Felix worked for, but he expected to be asked about other topics. Johan was a secret policeman. Perhaps, then, Felix was not. Or was he a rival of Johan's? Was Johan himself involved in something illicit?

"Felix?"

"*¿Sí?*"

"Don't hit me again. *¿Comprende?*"

The bald man grinned. "I shall try to restrain myself, Professor. But that will require cooperation on your part. Now, why has Captain Johan befriended you?"

Lammeck blinked. The pulsing in his right cheek grew worse by the heartbeat.

"We play checkers."

"And what do you talk about over checkers, you and our police captain? The assassination of Fidel? Come, Professor. Fidel is your sole interest for being in Cuba. And that is Johan's concern, as well. This is not an accident that the two of you have become comrades. What does Johan know? What has he told you?"

"That the *siete* rum is better than the *quince.* Doesn't make sense, but he's right."

"Anything else?"

"Cuban women. And cigars."

Felix nodded at this.

"Of course. You are an American. Your opinion of us would be demeaning. *Bueno.* I will allow you a touch of bravado. But I suggest you get it out of your system quickly. Let me try a different question. Who is Bud Calendar?"

Again, Lammeck was taken aback by Felix's inquiry. Didn't he know? It was Calendar who'd sent Lammeck to El Floridita in the first place! How could Felix have intercepted him without knowing something about Calendar? Who was Felix? Who was behind him? Lammeck fought to keep any reaction from his face. He was certain of only one thing: that he could not answer. He didn't know what Felix was capable of beyond kidnapping and a few wicked blows to the head. But Lammeck was dead sure of Calendar's power, and the CIA agent's willingness to use it. And Johan? He was Fidel's protector; it was not a job you got without being ruthless, even with his affinity for historians.

"I don't know the man."

Again tall Felix massaged the knuckles on the back of his jackhammer hand. "Why are you protecting these two men, Professor? If I accept what you say, you do not speak with Johan about the killing of Fidel, though I know you do. And you do not know Calendar, when I am convinced you do."

"Someone's lying to you, Felix."

"Yes. That is certain. And the liar is you."

Felix stood again from his chair. This time he raised his right hand slow and high, backhanded again, to use the studs of his knuckles. Lammeck stared straight up, marveling, even as the blow swept in, at the degree of his fear of Calendar and the CIA, to take this punishment instead of telling everything he knew of them. He turned his cheek, to let the wallop land on his right ear.

The pain was not worse than the first shot, but this time Felix didn't stop the chair from tumbling over. Lammeck landed on the concrete, banging his left shoulder and cracking his head.

He lay on his side, listening to himself groan. He tried to open his eyes but failed. He wanted badly to rub them but with his hands tied could not. When he could see again, he looked into the dirty tips of Felix's shoes.

The tall man kneeled beside Lammeck's head.

"I did not think I would be impressed with you, old man. But you have a mean streak."

Felix dug a hand under Lammeck's cheek, lifting his head off the bare concrete. He pulled the scarf up across Lammeck's eyes, returning him to blindness and the smell of dust.

"You will be driven back to your house, Professor. You will be watched closely here in Cuba. I hope you have enough sense to make your visit short. And when you do go back to your powerful, comfortable homeland, drink your own rum, screw your own women, but take some of our excellent cigars with you."

Felix patted Lammeck's shoulder. Lammeck heard the man's shoes grind in the grit of the bare floor, walking away. Felix called for the others to come back into the room.

Lammeck was sliced free of the chair; his hands were left bound. Arms hoisted him off the floor to return him to his feet. Hands under his elbows kept him from stumbling while making his way up the steps out of the basement. Someone used a kerchief to stanch blood off his forehead where he'd struck the concrete. Under the blindfold, Lammeck's right cheek took up a murderous, bloated throb.

On the arms of Felix's henchmen, Lammeck entered open air again. Quickly, he was folded into the car, this time not into the trunk but the backseat. He sat on his bound hands. Men pressed in on either side of him.

Lammeck's blindfold was lowered. He looked at the four men with him in the car. Felix sat in the front passenger seat. The three others were not remarkable in any way. Two were white Spanish like Felix, the third was mulatto.

"I suppose you don't mind if I get a good look at you all," he said.

Felix pivoted to reply, "And who will you tell?" Felix challenged. "Johan? Will he believe you said nothing to us about your conversations? Calendar? You think I was harsh in my interrogation? Be my guest with Castro's secret police. Or your CIA. No. I have no concern that you will make any trouble for me."

Lammeck asked, "Which one's Diego?"

Beside him, the mulatto nodded. The man whispered, *"Siento."* Sorry.

Lammeck nodded back. He glanced outside the car to get an image of where he was. The street was dark, the brick houses nondescript. Hedges rimmed the yards, trees shadowed the few working streetlamps. A lone motorcycle puttered past, but no pedestrians were on the evening sidewalks.

Felix said, "Turn around."

Lammeck faced the rear window. His arms were gripped and raised. The rope tying his hands was snipped. Instantly, blood flowed back painfully into his wrists. They itched. Lammeck massaged the flesh, turning back to Felix. The man held Lammeck's four-inch dirk.

Felix pointed the blade at Lammeck's battered face.

"I like this knife, Professor. I think I will keep it."

Lammeck rubbed his wrists, working his fingers to animate them.

Felix waved the knife once, a bully's threatening gesture.

Lammeck, sure of his hands now, acted with long-practiced instinct and speed. With one eye swollen shut, he moved by feel and pressure. Swiftly opening his left palm, he slammed it against Felix's big forearm, pushing the knife to the right. He wrapped his fingers around Felix's wrist, pressing his thumb hard into the back of the man's hand to bend it inward, a quick aikido disarming grip. In the same instant, Lammeck's open right hand smashed against Felix's exposed knuckles, shoving the hand in farther, painfully, forcing the tendons to open the fingers around the knife handle. Flexing his right hand wide between index finger and thumb, Lammeck swept the haft out of Felix's suddenly weakened grasp. In less than a second, Lammeck held the blade. In the next moment, before Felix or any of the men could react, he released Felix's arm, then reached his left hand behind the bald head, pulling forward, pinning the Cuban against the front seat. Lammeck laid the sharp point of the knife into the flesh below Felix's shocked left eye.

"Concerned *now*?"

Above the knifepoint the man's eyelid fluttered wildly. Lammeck pressed the knife; a drop of blood bubbled beneath its point.

"Everyone out of the car," he said evenly.

No one moved. Lammeck waited.

Felix repeated the command in Spanish. The two were left alone.

"Felix."

"*Sí*, Professor."

Lammeck let a little of the man's blood slide onto the silver blade.

"I'll be taking my knife with me. It's a museum piece. And it's drawn better blood than yours. The sheath, please."

Lammeck watched the nervous eyeball above the knife shift up to meet his gaze, then down again to the red-dribbled blade.

"*Sí*."

Felix fumbled on the seat beside him without looking away from the steel. He produced the leather case for the ancient priests' knife.

"Toss it on the seat next to me."

The man obeyed, with his head clamped between Lammeck's palm and the dirk at his eye.

"And understand, I'll have this knife on me at all times. Including the next time I see you. Yes?"

In his soft voice, Felix answered, "Yes. Of course, Professor."

"Now, it's my turn to ask a question. Who do you work for?"

Under his hands, Lammeck felt Felix's head shiver, to tell him, *No.*

Lammeck pressed in the tip. A thicker trickle of blood sluiced down the blade.

"Let's try again. Who are you working for?"

Felix's eyeball cut left and right, his jaw worked, but these were the only parts of his head he could move in the vise of Lammeck's grip.

"Easy, Professor. Let him go."

The voice came from outside the open car door. Lammeck didn't look.

Calendar.

"Felix," Lammeck asked, "is this your boss?"

The bald man leered, as if he'd been spared in the nick of time and there was nothing Lammeck could do.

"*Sí.*"

Lammeck flicked the knife away from Felix's socket, but kept his left hand tight behind the bald head. Swiftly, he raised the knife backhanded, exposing the hard metal knob at the bottom of the handle in the meat of his fist. He slammed his fist on top of the bald head, once, then harder, twice, his other hand braced behind Felix's neck.

Lammeck let him go. He watched Felix sag back against the Cadillac's dash. Before he faded too far, Lammeck unleashed one more good shot, this time a fist hardened around the knife's handle, aimed dead into the bleeding eye socket, for what would become a splendid shiner.

"I believe you," Lammeck told Felix. He put the knife in his free hand and shook the sting out of his knuckles. He collected the black sheath.

The three men on the sidewalk hauled Felix out of the front seat, off the floor mat. Lammeck pulled the bandanna from his neck. He threw it into the street at their feet.

Watching the others lug Felix away, he slid the dagger into its case. Lammeck, his ear still buzzing, let out a slow breath.

With his anger subsiding, his hands began to shake.

"Climb in the front," Calendar said, leaning in. "I'll drive."

The agent tossed a duffel bag into the backseat, then drove away.

Lammeck glared. He padded fingertips over his burning cheek.

Calendar shot him a glance. "You thinking about having a go at me, Professor?"

"I'm not ruling it out."

"Well, rule it out. And get back to thinking things through, before you do something else stupid."

The Cadillac knifed through a tight neighborhood of working-class homes, brick, with front stoops. People took their strolls before dinner, a Cuban custom. Calendar swung the big car at a fast clip down narrow streets. He knew the area.

"Where are we?" Lammeck asked.

"Luyano. South of the *centro*. That was my safe house."

"You were there? You let Felix beat me up in your basement?"

"I was upstairs, Professor. Cool down. I didn't know he was gonna go that far. Hey, I told the guy just to knock you around a little, scare you. Felix went overboard. I got nothing to do with that."

"Plausible deniability?"

"You can say that."

"Did you have him put me in the trunk, too?"

"I had to know, Professor."

"If I could keep a secret?"

"Exactly. You got no idea how much is riding on this operation. Far as I knew, you were just some chubby egghead from Rhode Island come down here to play on the edge. Now I got a real idea what you're made of. You can take a licking and keep on ticking. I saw that for myself. Now we can move ahead."

Calendar brought his finger around to wag in Lammeck's face. "And listen to me. It's square between you and Felix, understand? You evened the score, so I got no more beef with the guy. If you do, keep it to yourself."

Calendar wended the Cadillac out of the warren of streets onto a wider avenue along Havana harbor. The car sped past the behemoth sugar and fruit warehouses where four Soviet-marked cargo ships were moored. Great cranes swung pallets from the ships' holds onto the quay, lit by floodlights.

"Russian arms," Calendar said, indicating the freighters. "Artillery, trucks, tank parts. More good reasons to take Castro out."

Calendar was trying to deflect the conversation back to their mission. But Lammeck was not finished; he figured he'd paid for some answers.

"Who's Felix?"

"Need-to-know basis, Professor."

"Calendar?"

"Yep."

"I'm pretty pissed off. Now's a good time to show me you trust me."

Calendar eyed Lammeck again.

He nodded. "Those guys were all Cuban Mob."

"The CIA's working with the Mafia?"

"They're bookies. I got their names from a couple of Miami syndicate big shots. They're paying off some debt to Lansky. He handed them over to the guys I'm working with."

"I don't believe this."

Calendar shrugged. "The Mob hates Castro as much as anybody, believe you me. They're losing millions a week since they got kicked out. So we throw Lansky and his pals some bread, and tell 'em we'll turn our backs for a while after we get everything shipshape again down here. At the moment we're all on the same side, Professor. The enemy of my enemy is my friend. Sun Tzu said that."

Lammeck was tempted to lay out for Calendar what he knew about Sun Tzu, which would fill a two-hour lecture. Or he could tell the agent what he'd learned about the damage the Mafia had done to Cuba's economy. Plus what American Fruit, Domino Sugar, and nine U.S. presidents had done. But Calendar couldn't be made to care. Cuba wasn't his concern. Only America was. Probably not even that, Lammeck considered. What Calendar cared about was the game, the assassination. It began to dawn on Lammeck that, for the time being, he'd be better off if he did the same.

"What about the underground?"

"We're still doing business with them. But the infiltration rate's too high. These gangsters, on the other hand. You don't just join up with them because you nailed an anti-Castro poster to a pole somewhere. They got a code. They know each other. They keep their mouths shut, and they police their own. Best thing is, they're greedy. I can work with greed. We're pulling out all the stops, Professor. Anyone, fucking anyone. Mob. Cubans. You."

Lammeck dug into his pocket for the pill bottle.

"And these?"

"You're catching on." Calendar took the amber bottle. He opened it. "Want one?"

"No."

The agent popped a white capsule in his mouth. "Sugar pills." He capped the bottle and lobbed it back into Lammeck's hands.

"Why?"

"You can figure this one out."

"To make sure I wasn't going to flush them."

"Botulinum's expensive to refine, Professor. Besides, the real pills aren't prescription, you know. If the wrong people got hold of one, it'd be a definite link back to CIA. Not good for business. But you kept 'em in your pocket, where they belonged. That took *co-jones*."

The Cadillac zoomed onto the Malecón. The boulevard glistened with spray. Couples walked along the seawall, daring their luck before dinner. Lammeck asked no more questions until the car turned onto First Avenue in Miramar. Calendar parked in front of Lammeck's rented house. He shut off the headlights and cut the ignition. Above the dark house, the first stars of the Caribbean night glittered over the Florida Straits.

Calendar grabbed the duffel from the backseat and hoisted it onto the bench between them.

Lammeck looked at the bag.

The agent slapped a hand on the canvas. "Don't open this 'til I tell you. Hide it."

Calendar pulled from his pocket another small amber bottle. Inside were six more identical white capsules. He handed them over.

"These are live action, Professor. Listen close. One of these is for you. Keep it on you every minute of the day, next to your bed at night. If this operation goes sour, if you get caught, take it. Shut your mouth until the poison shuts it for you. This operation is bigger than you and me, by far. Tell me you get this."

"Let me just be clear, Calendar. If I walk away, you take my job and ruin my reputation. But if I help you, and I get caught, I have to kill myself. Is that right? Because walking away from this just started looking a lot better to me."

Calendar opened his hands to show they were empty of more lies at the moment.

"Okay. I couldn't exactly tell you this early on, but if you do walk away, I gotta kill you."

Lammeck's heart plummeted, but he wasn't stunned to hear this. He understood secrets, and he was aware that he already carried too many of Calendar's. The assassination plot, pills, the invasion, the Mob.

"Is this how the CIA recruits? Death threats?"

"Let me lay it out for you. We're at war with Communism. Every chance we get, this is how that war's fought, in secret. It's a hell of a lot better than a nuclear fireball. Right now Cuba's a battleground. Consider yourself a soldier. This is a soldier's deal. Win or die trying."

"Does that include poison cigars and blowing the arm off some innocent kid who got in the way?"

"Johan tell you that?"

Lammeck was silent.

"The answer is yes," Calendar said. "It includes that. And a lot more, if necessary."

The big man lifted the bag off the seat. He laid it in Lammeck's lap.

"Hang on to those pills until I tell you who to deliver them to. It might take a week or two. And put something on that cheek, Professor. That's gonna swell if you don't."

Lammeck got out of the Cadillac, lifting the duffel behind him. Without another word, Calendar pulled from the curb. Lammeck hefted the bag and walked to his front door.

Inside, he clicked on one light, then dragged the duffel onto a couch. He didn't hesitate to untie the string at the end of the duffel and spread open the bag.

Lammeck stood back, as if the bag belonged to Pandora. He paused, staring at the open mouth, then cinched the drawstring tight without looking inside.

In the kitchen, he poured rum over some cubes from the freezer, and returned to the den. On the sofa were the duffel, the pill bottle, and a white envelope. Lammeck stood, sipping the *siete*, looking over these bits of Calendar that were lodged in his life now like shrapnel. He held the cooling glass to the bruises on his face.

CHAPTER EIGHT

★ ★ ★

March 29
National Archives
Havana

"PROFESSOR?"

Lammeck gazed up from the chaos of books on his desk. One of the old librarians, Miró, approached.

"*¿Sí?*"

"Your dinner is here."

Lammeck answered in Spanish. "I don't think I ordered any food."

"I do not know, *señor*. But a man has brought it for you. Should I send him up?"

"Do you know this man?"

"No. And he gave me no name."

"I'm too busy to eat. Thank him and send him off."

Miró hesitated. Lammeck asked, "With respect, is there something else?"

"Professor, I see the work you are doing. I think it will be good for my country, your work. I see also you are careless with your health at times. You should eat. For the sake of the work."

"I agree." Captain Johan rounded a wall of shelves, bearing a brown paper sack. Grease splotched the bag's sides.

"Thank you," Lammeck said to Miró. The librarian inclined his head to Johan on his way out.

The captain set the bag on a table near Lammeck. Without a word, he spread open the sack and laid out paper plates, napkins, and plastic forks. Three cardboard containers were opened; the aromas of meat, rice, and beans curled under Lammeck's nose like a beckoning finger. From Johan's jacket pocket came a silver hip flask.

"You have been working too hard, my friend. The old man is right. What good does it do to ruin a promising book and yourself in the process? Come along. *Coma.*"

Lammeck rose from his carrel, realized he was standing for the first time in hours. Johan handed him the flask while spooning out portions of white rice, black beans, and seasoned pork. Lammeck allowed himself a strong pull of the *siete* he knew would be inside the flask.

Johan sat in front of his own heaping plate. He accepted the flask for a swallow, then tucked into the meal. Lammeck's hunger was slower to arouse.

"I have not seen you in almost two weeks," the policeman remarked. "Did you get the *New York Times* article I left on your porch?"

That was the night Lammeck first met Bud Calendar. "Yes, thank you."

"You have been very busy. How is your book coming?"

Lammeck's head was a repository of facts mined from the dusty archives, priceless nuggets for his research. But more distracting were the events of the past eleven days. Lammeck fixed his gaze on Johan before answering, trying to gauge what the man might know, if he might see some vestige of swelling on Lammeck's cheek, if he had any sense of the secrets Lammeck carried, the conspiracy he'd entered into. He tamped out of his face and voice any hint that, ever since accepting the botulinum from Calendar, he'd been waiting for Johan to arrive at his house to arrest him. "It's consuming me," he answered.

"I see it on you, my friend. Your eyes are bloodshot. Besides, you've labored long and hard in your life to get such a magnificent waistline. Why let it all wither away? Cuba is not a place for such self-sacrifice."

Lammeck forked a portion of pork and rice. Johan watched him, beaming.

"It pleases me to see you, Professor. I have missed our chats. And while I respect your discipline, I must insist we see each other more regularly."

"I'm sorry. It's just lately, I've been putting a lot of pressure on myself."

"Why lately?"

Lammeck chose his words carefully. "I just have a sense something might be happening soon. I wanted to get in as much research as I could before that."

Johan raised his fork to buy a moment while he chewed. When he'd swallowed, he chased the meat with a swig of rum.

"Professor," the policeman said, smacking his lips happily, "your instincts are correct. I have news."

Lammeck set down his plastic fork; his appetite for information was greater than for the meal.

"I could not mention this before. I did not have all the facts, and it is quite a major development. But we have completed our interrogations, and now I can tell you in better detail. On March 18, in

Miramar not far from your house, we intercepted a very important meeting of anti-revolutionary leaders. We detained several of the coordinators of the underground's military wing. These traitors were discussing a plan to place a *petaca*—a plastic explosive— under a platform where Fidel was scheduled to review a parade next week. One of the conspirators, Humberto Sorí Marín, was a minister in Fidel's cabinet. He was also the chief of *Unidad*'s underground military wing."

Another disaffected government official. Instantly, Brutus came to Lammeck's mind, with Fidel in the role of Caesar. When Caesar saw that Brutus, his friend and protégé, was with the assassins in the Senate, he covered his face with his robe and submitted to the knives. Lammeck doubted that Fidel Castro, when he found out about this Sorí Marín, was so heartbroken as Caesar.

"This was to be a putsch of huge proportions, Professor. A number of highly placed officials were ready to take part. The undersecretary of finance, the deputy commandant of the San Antonio de los Baños air base, the president of the Cuban Sugar Institute, several navy flag officers, and, in a personal shock to me, the chief of the secret police."

Johan raised the silver flask in toast to himself. "I have been promoted. I am now the number two official in my department."

Lammeck's jaw hung open at the scale of the planned coup. He forgot to congratulate Johan and could only say, "You're kidding."

"I could never concoct a joke this sordid. I am not kidding."

The policeman seemed amused, even impressed with the plot as he described it. "Once Fidel was eliminated, rebel officers were to seize the air base. At the same time, several naval ships would undergo mutinies. The plan was to exert control over the air and sea around Havana. Next, the University of Havana was to be taken over by dissident students. The police in the city would be led into revolt by my former superior, wretched man. Across Cuba, the underground would immediately seize or destroy all communications and public utilities. Without Fidel, the revolution was expected to fall into bedlam. The rebels would seize power. Then Che, Raúl, and any others of importance who opposed them would be shot. I flatter myself into thinking I would have been among those put against the *paredón*."

An alarm rang in Lammeck's gut. Were Felix or any of the others in his crew part of this plot? Had one of them betrayed Lammeck? Had Johan brought him a final meal and a flask before taking him away? Lammeck looked down at his food, to hide his eyes while he calmed himself. He dropped a hand beneath the table, to finger through his pant leg the poison capsule in his pocket. No. Felix wasn't in the underground; he was Calendar's asset, the same as Lammeck.

He reached for the flask from Johan.

"Without question, Captain, you would've been among the first to be shot."

"Thank you."

"The scope of the conspiracy. It sounds huge. Is the underground that big?"

"Many in the privileged classes continue their resistance. But the people, the men and women on the street and in the fields, they love the revolution. There will be no bedlam, Professor."

Lammeck drank. Johan smiled with satisfaction.

"How much of this is public knowledge?" Lammeck asked.

"The arrests will be announced soon. The full extent of the plot is being held in confidence for a time. But, as always in Cuba, little is kept quiet. We do what we can. You understand, Professor."

Lammeck nodded. "Not a word."

"After we have a clearer picture, I will feel free to allow you more curiosity."

"What'll happen next?"

"More arrests. A handful of show executions to loosen tongues."

Lammeck couldn't keep his distaste from his face. In his research, he'd tallied over five hundred firing squad executions in the first four months of the revolution alone. So much blood spilled, he thought, how could this be liberation?

Johan noted Lammeck's discomfiture.

"How can you quibble over this, Professor? Your nation's official policy is to assassinate Cuba's leader. We both know your CIA has been involved in the same sort of murderous schemes in other nations. Yet when Cuba defends its own government against saboteurs, you wrinkle your nose. This is monumental hypocrisy." Johan pointed at the cooling plate of food in front of Lammeck. "Eat. You are not thinking clearly."

Even reproving, Johan stayed good-natured. Lammeck forked another bite. But Johan had put his finger squarely on the debate which had obsessed Lammeck all his life: How can a state advocate political murder?

"There is more," Johan said, interrupting Lammeck's thoughts. "Today. A momentous event. Perhaps even more dangerous than the Sorí Marín plot."

Lammeck wrestled down one more wave of worry that Johan was going to spring Felix on him.

"What happened?"

"This morning, your president suspended the last of the United States' sugar quota with Cuba. That is the end, Professor. Sugar was the final link between our two countries. Now there is neither diplomatic relations nor trade. You and I are officially enemies."

"And I'll bet the Soviet Union stepped in and agreed to buy all the sugar Fidel can sell them."

"Before Kennedy's ink was dry on the suspension."

"Johan."

"Yes, Professor, I know. This is a prelude to war. I came to advise you this may be a good time for you to go home."

"I can't."

"There are very few Americans in Cuba right now, my friend. My office keeps track of them all. Each is being advised to leave. Anti-American sentiment is only going to get worse. You and I both suspect this invasion is coming soon. When it does, I will have my hands full protecting Fidel. I do not want the added burden of worrying about you."

Lammeck thought about the duffel bag hidden in his kitchen cabinet. There was more that Calendar was going to ask of him. The CIA agent had made it clear: Lammeck was a dead man if he left Cuba. Now Johan was saying he might get strung up by a mob if he stayed.

He shook his head; to Johan it looked like a *No,* but Lammeck was ruing what he'd gotten caught up in. Again, he sensed that momentum that could only be the current of history, sweeping him along. He made himself remember what it felt like, should he be left alive to write about it.

CHAPTER NINE

★ ★ ★

April 1
Havana harbor

THE DOCK WAS WELL lit. Huge cranes unloaded crates, pallets, whole vehicles, and set them on the quay where fifty men swarmed over them with forklifts, wrenches, and hammers. The shouts back and forth around the maze of wooden slats, from beneath bulging nets being lowered to the concrete, were in a Babel of languages, English, Spanish, Czech, Portuguese, Malay. In all the activity and electric glare, Calendar backed into one of the few deep shadows he could find.

The hull of the moored ship towered four stories above the dock. Lines tying the freighter to hawsers were as thick as a man's leg, the anchor was the size of a truck. Calendar, for all his travels, had no love of the ocean. His interests had always been land based.

This cargo ship carried Malaysian registry, but her name on the prow was in English. That afternoon, *Eastern Princess* had stopped in Freeport, Bahamas, to pick up one last round of cargo and two passengers.

Calendar waited twenty minutes, watching from behind a shed wall down the quay. He wished for a cup of coffee. The late hours of spy work were the worst part of the job. That, and being kept waiting. If your job was to kill people for politics, you needed to be better than your targets. Stronger, smarter, have a taste for sacrifice, be at least as dedicated to your ideals, and punctual.

Finally he stepped out of the cloaking shadow. He issued a low, tweeting whistle.

A young woman stood alone under a dock light, looking up and down the quay. She wore a knee-length black leather coat, wrong for the weather. At Calendar's whistle, she walked his way. He receded back into the dark.

He watched her move toward him. She was maybe five foot six, brown curly hair cut above the shoulder. Nothing special, except her eyes. They were blue, intense, under heavy brows. She stopped at the edge of the shadows. Calendar spoke in Russian.

"*Skolko tebe let?*" How old are you?

She cocked her head.

"*Deviatnadtsat.*" Nineteen.

"*Skolko Aliku let?*" How old is Alek?

"*Dvadtsat odin.*" Twenty-one.

Calendar muttered in English, "I don't fucking believe this."

The girl crossed her arms against her leather coat. A large handbag hung off her shoulder. She shifted her weight to one leg. Her English came hesitantly. She drilled Calendar in the gloom with a blue, petulant stare. "Is problem?"

"Yeah, this is problem. I wasn't told I was gonna be getting Spanky and Darla."

"Who? We are not these people."

"They're kids. I wasn't told I was gonna be getting kids."

Switching to Russian, she retorted, "And I was not told I was getting an asshole." She returned to English to finish. "There. Problem, too."

Calendar ran a hand over his crew cut. He checked his watch, but the radioactive dial had lost its glow. He jutted his wrist into the light. 1:46 A.M.

"Where've you been? You're a half hour late."

"Trachalas s Alikom." Fucking Alek.

Calendar made a fist and bit his lip. "Where is he, honey?"

"Customs. Bringing luggage. He come now."

"What does he know?"

"Ya nye ponimayu." I don't understand.

"What does he know about you?"

"I will be loyal wife. He got mystery job. I support, he trusts. Is all."

"What's the cover story?"

"No cover story. Marry when we return Minsk. Is real story."

Calendar turned away, leaning a shoulder against the shed wall. None of this was good news. He was being asked to run an incredibly sensitive operation, with global implications, and to pull it off he'd been sent two engaged pimply-faced kids.

"Calendar?"

He answered without turning. *"Tchto?"* What?

"Alek comes. Go forward or no. Say now."

Calendar balled his fist in the blackness, then released it with an exasperated breath.

"Yeah, Rina." He turned to her. "We go forward. Christ."

She seemed not to know if this was a curse or a wish for luck, but she replied, "And Christ to you, Mr. Calendar."

Calendar mumbled a curse at the idiocy of those who pulled the strings. Stepping into the light, he walked the direction of the gangplank, where a skinny young man slumped under the weight of two fat suitcases. Rina stayed behind. As Calendar approached, Alek put the bags down. He extended a sweaty palm. Calendar recalled what the girl said they'd been doing while he waited. He shook the hand reluctantly. It was pale and narrow, artistic in a way. A good shooter's hand.

"Welcome to Cuba. I'm Bud Calendar. Let me grab one of these bags."

Alek looked around with tired gray eyes. "Long trip. It's warm here." His voice was soft, reedy thin.

"It ain't Minsk. Come on. I got a car."

The two hefted the luggage. Alek was almost a head shorter than Calendar, at least seventy pounds lighter. On all sides, dock workers unloaded the freighter, transferring her cargo into the sprawling warehouse.

Alek asked, "You met Rina?"

"You're getting married, she said."

"Yeah. Look, did you tell her anything?"

"Why would I do that? I don't want to get to know her, she's your problem. Make sure she doesn't turn into mine and everything'll go like butter. But she seems like a good egg for a Russkie."

The boy nodded, lugging his suitcase, too weary to take offense. Or maybe he had enough discipline to shut his mouth. Calendar didn't care which. The bag he carried was unexpectedly heavy. Shambling beside him, Alek complained about Rina's packing, like any normal young man on holiday with his fiancée. It was eighty degrees in Cuba, Calendar thought, how many clothes did she need?

With the girl still fifty yards up the quay, Calendar said, "I got what you asked for. Winchester 70. Collapsible stock. Weaver scope."

"Chambered for a .308?"

"Just like you said."

Ahead, Rina waved. Even from a distance, Calendar saw how her eyes changed when she looked at Alek. She really was nineteen, and she really did love this skinny kid. Calendar set down his bag. Alek followed suit. Rina saw them talking and kept her distance.

"Alright," Calendar said, "before we start, you're clear on everything?"

"Sure."

"Look, I mean everything. What you do if the op goes right, what you do if it goes wrong. I'm not gonna be around to nursemaid you."

"Where you going to be?"

"Close enough. I got another guy. A civilian. Some brainiac Ivy League teacher. But he's a weapons expert, and he knows his shit. He's reliable. He's your contact." Calendar handed over an envelope. "Here's what you need to know for now. The rest'll play out when the time's right. If everything goes smooth, you won't see very much of me after I drop you off at the hotel. Now, like I said, are you clear?"

"I don't want to work with anybody else."

"I'm not giving you that option. Now, tell me you're five by five."

"Yeah. Five by five."

Ahead, Rina tapped her foot under a light pole, impatient. She, too, began to look worn like Alek from their long journey.

"As for her, see that she doesn't get in the way," Calendar said.

"What do you mean 'in the way'?"

Calendar stabbed a thick finger into Alek's scrawny chest. "I mean in the fucking way. No one slows you down, except me. Got it?"

Alek screwed up his narrow face, glancing down at Calendar's finger in his sternum. He pushed the agent's hand down. As he did so, Calendar caught a glimpse of the assassin he'd been promised.

CHAPTER TEN

April 3
Havana

THE PATIO BISTRO OF the Inglaterra was not busy this
Monday afternoon. Lammeck tipped the five-piece band to stand
by his table and play a few songs. During his month in Cuba, he'd
taken a liking to Afro-Cuban music. The lyrics were often ballads
of unabashed romance, like the tunes of the 1940s and '50s he
loved, and that were already fading out of style. Today's American
tunes were grating, hectic in a sort of hillbilly way, and measured
to be jukebox hits. The words to the songs had lost their imagination and seemed to Lammeck little more than expressions of being
shook up.

After the band bowed and returned to their platform, Gustavo
came with a *cubano* sandwich and a fresh Iron beer. He lingered
beside the table. There were few other customers to pull him away.

"The next time, ask the band to play 'Manteca,' Professor. It is my favorite."

"I'll do that. The restaurant is not busy today, Gustavo."

The waiter looked beyond the restaurant's railing into the city.

"There is a mood," he said, and did not explain.

"I like Cuba," Lammeck offered, not certain why except that the other man seemed troubled.

"Yes. I know." The waiter crossed his hands in front of his apron. "This is a problem, you see—this American affection for Cuba."

"I didn't mean it that way. You know that."

"Yes, Professor. Of course." He pointed to the wait station, where two other servers gathered. The pair smoked and leaned on elbows to listen to a black transistor radio. "We hear more from your American president today."

Lammeck took a bite of his sandwich. He enjoyed Gustavo. The man was political, well-read, and talkative.

"Not good news, I take it."

"It depends on who you are. Good news if you are a demon or a buzzard."

"What did Kennedy say?"

"He has announced America's intention to support a democratic government in Cuba."

Gustavo sucked his teeth.

"Where does your president think this democratic government is going to come from? Does he think Fidel is going to form one? Why doesn't he just come out and say it? An invasion is coming to take back what America believes belongs to it."

The waiter took in the sum of the empty chairs around the patio. Lammeck glanced with him and saw what Gustavo was observing: Havana, always vibrant, today seemed lackluster. Across the street in the park, around Martí's statue, where gaggles of men clotted daily to smoke and argue politics or *beisbol,* few gathered. The streetcars clattered nearly empty; downtown traffic had not snarled into honking knots. The sidewalk beauty pageant that was *Habanera* women had few contestants this afternoon.

"Yes," Lammeck echoed, "a mood."

Gustavo nodded. "I do not like being a messenger, Professor. Please ask your friend not to bring these here anymore." He laid a matchbook on the table beside Lammeck's beer. "I must tell you, I know this man. He is a gambler and a black marketeer. You should avoid him."

"He's not my friend, Gustavo. And I'll make sure he stays away. Thank you."

The waiter walked off.

Lammeck unfolded the match cover brought by Felix. Inside, a message had been scrawled:

Tonight. 9. Tropicana. Tuxedo.

Needles of nerves prickled under his skin. What was this about? Was it the poison capsules, the duffel bag, or some extra angle of murder Calendar wanted Lammeck to work? Some *new* risk the CIA had decided he would take? Perhaps another round of threats? Lammeck despised this spy business, stumbling forward, always into the dark. He was a scholar; knowledge was his mainstay. But this constant edging around blind corners—he figured he'd be dead of an ulcer long before he'd ever need the poison pill in his pocket.

Lammeck pulled a fresh Partagas from his *guayabera.* Though he had not finished his lunch, he bit off the tip, struck one of the matches, and puffed the cigar to life in case anyone was watching, wondering why Gustavo had brought him matches.

★ ★ ★

Marianao

The taxi ride west from Miramar took an hour. The tuxedo he'd bought that afternoon fit well enough; the hug of the cummerbund plus the constriction of the bow tie held him in a sort of cocoon. Lammeck fell asleep in it through the second half of the trip.

He awoke when the driver asked for his fare. Lammeck dug Cuban bills from his wallet and climbed out when a young valet in a red bellhop's livery opened his door. The taxi pulled away, replaced immediately by another in a line of cars. Lammeck had to move out of the driveway to avoid being bumped by headlights.

He stepped onto the curb beneath twin concrete shells that resembled a giant woman's bikini top. The main doorway was set in the center. Beside it, an electric sign blazed in sky-blue letters, TROPICANA. Across the drive, a stylized sculpture of a ballerina posed mid-twirl in the center of a placid fountain, bathed in floodlights.

Lammeck stepped through the Tropicana's entryway, borne along with a crowd in eveningwear and minks. Inside, he was stunned. The nightclub's landscape sprawled in a dream of modernist architecture, carved out of a tropical jungle. Slender arches in high parabolas, geometric facades, towering walls of glass and steel, more concrete shells and chrome trappings surrounded an acre of white linen on tables, silver ice buckets, rose and chrysanthemum bouquets, and a thousand cocktail glasses filled with colorful rum punches. At every table, cigarette haze swirled around patrons in white linen suits, black tuxedos, satin gowns, and diamond sparklers. Waiters cruised between the tables balancing trays of champagne and wine. All this was enclosed by tall mamoncillo trees and royal palms, flowering shrubs, and a limitless black sky punctured by stars bright enough to pierce the vista of white pillar candles and hundreds of klieg lights.

Lammeck stepped into the warren of tables and gliding servers. Onstage, beneath a great crystal arch, an orchestra on a tiered bandstand blared a brassy, percussive tune driven by maracas, bongos, congas, and claves. On the platform below the band, four women with hourglass figures in sheer gold organza crooned. One shook maracas. Their dresses were slit high, exposing calves and thighs cased in glittering fishnets. The girls and the band were spattered with colored lights and the brilliant reflections off the glass and steel span rising behind them. Lammeck continued to stroll closer to the stage and the dancers, amazed and drawn.

He was intercepted by a maitre d'. Politely, the man asked if Lammeck had a reservation. Lammeck did not know, but gave his name. The maitre d' dipped his head, left, then returned to lead him to a table near the dance floor.

A young couple was already seated there. Lammeck hesitated, as though a mistake had been made, then wondered if these two were why he'd been summoned. Both were so young, barely out of their teens; in their formal outfits they looked like a prom night date. Lammeck felt a spark of anger at Calendar that these children should be involved; the CIA was, just like the agent had claimed, pulling out all the stops. Lammeck tipped the maitre d' and put out his hand to the young man.

"Hi. I'm Mikhal Lammeck." He had to lean in to be heard over the music.

The young man had a large hand for his short stature, a firm grasp. He was narrow boned and had a natural pout about his lips.

"Alek Hidell." He indicated the girl beside him in her shiny, sea-green chiffon gown. She was pretty, with arresting blue eyes, lean bare shoulders above the dress. She was very pale. "This is my fiancée, Rina."

Lammeck reached across the table to shake her hand, too. Reaching back, Rina inclined her head and smiled. He took his seat and surveyed the table. Empty glasses stood in front of the couple.

"What are you drinking? I'm buying."

Alex answered for them both. "Vodka gimlet for Rina, straight Stoli for me. Thanks, Mikhal. Can I call you that?" His accent was American.

"Of course."

Lammeck turned in his seat to snag the attention of a waiter. Across the table Rina rose. She was shorter than Alek, wiry like him.

"I go. You must talk. Mikhal, drink? I shall buy."

Rina had an accent. Lammeck had assumed she, too, was American. He couldn't place her tongue at first. European? Slavic? He took a guess.

"*Rom so lidom, pozhaluista.*" I'd like a rum on the rocks, please.

Rina put fingertips to her breast, pleased. "You are Russian speaker?"

"*Da.*"

She widened her eyes prettily and left them.

Alone with Alek, he wasn't certain how to proceed. If Calendar had brought them together, why? What was this kid doing in Havana with his fiancée? A Russian girl, at that. Where did Lammeck fit in? What was the next step in this clandestine dance? Small talk, scribbled notes? Go straight at the matter and ask if Alek was in town to kill Castro? Lammeck was stymied and could do nothing but look at the boy.

Alek didn't seem comfortable in his tux and fiddled with bits of it, the bow tie and cuff links. He didn't know how to begin either.

"Vacation? You and Rina?" Lammeck asked.

Alek nodded. "Yep."

"Where are you from?"

"Born in Louisiana. Lived all over."

"There aren't many Americans left on this island. Most are gone or have been warned to leave by the Cuban government."

"You're here."

"I'm doing research for a book. They're tolerating me." Lammeck pointed to the empty seat where Rina had been. "Congratulations, by the way. She's very pretty. Russian, right?"

"We met in Minsk. At a party. Love at first sight."

Lammeck liked this notion and warmed to the boy. "What were you doing in Minsk? Exchange student?"

Alek hesitated, blinking his way through some calculation. "I'm a defector."

Surprised, Lammeck paused before asking, "To the Soviet Union?"

Alek did not shy from this. "Yeah."

Lammeck sat back, eyeing the skinny boy, the historian in him curious to know more. "Son, aren't you supposed to have a cover story? Something else besides being an American defector?"

Alek raised his hands. "Calendar didn't say I needed one."

Just like that, Calendar and the CIA were spilled onto the table between them. Lammeck knew the ugly sway that the agent held over his own cooperation. What threat did he hold over Alek? What role did a young American turncoat have in the killing of Fidel?

The boy seemed vulnerable, unsure, and so young. Lammeck felt a rush of sympathy, almost protectiveness. He knew how confused the world was. Morality, loyalties, love—the war with Communism was clouding all of it, everywhere in the world, like ink staining water. What sense could a boy of twenty-one make of it?

Across the Tropicana's crowded floor, weaving her way through music and packed, candlelit tables, Rina came carrying three high-ball glasses.

"Tell me quick—what does she know?" Lammeck asked.

"That I'm a spy."

Lammeck snorted at this second shocker in a row.

"What?"

"It's okay, she likes it. I trust her."

"What the—?"

Lammeck cut himself off as the girl arrived at the table with the drinks.

Alek kissed her cheek and welcomed her back to the table in fluent Russian. Lammeck recovered enough to join the couple when they lifted their glasses in toast to one another. With his glass held in the air beside theirs, Lammeck asked Alek, *"Esti khoti kakie nie budi idei po povodu togo, tchto mne nuzhno delati?"* Have you got any idea what I'm supposed to do?

The boy smiled, disarmingly lost. He replied in English, "Not a clue. But I reckon we'll find out."

Rina danced the rumba very well. Lammeck counted silently 1-2, 1-2-3 to keep the pace. The bandleader at the head of the orchestra reminded him of Desi Arnaz on the *I Love Lucy* television show; the man stroked a conga held under his arm while he sang.

Between dances, Lammeck spoke to Rina in Russian. He asked where she and Alek had met. At a party in Minsk. How long ago? Two weeks. Love at first sight, she said, blushing, repeating Alek's words. Lammeck accepted this could actually be so. He suspected it might be true at least for the boy. Rina was attractive, bubbly, athletic, expressing an eager intellect. Lammeck didn't know what Alek's part would be in Calendar's design, but the boy seemed to relish playing some secret role, saying he was a "spy." Obviously Rina encouraged that. After all, hadn't she agreed to marry him after two weeks?

She told Lammeck that Alek had suggested Cuba to celebrate their engagement. Somewhere warm and far from Minsk. She had an uncle in the government. He'd pulled strings for them and paid for their tickets.

She asked about Lammeck. He told her he was a political science professor, in Havana for research into Cuban history. No wife, no children. "Just my work." She smiled and patted his lapel in sympathy.

Alek watched from the table. He did not come to cut in, but applauded from afar when Lammeck spun the girl; he laughed with Rina at Lammeck's awkward *cha cha*. After four dances, Lammeck was tuckered. They returned to the table. A fresh round of drinks awaited. The band struck up a slow bolero. Lammeck was glad not to have to dance again; he'd sweat up his tux, while the girl was still fresh.

"Thanks for the drink." Lammeck took up his icy rum.

Alek answered, "It wasn't me. The waiter told me they came from that guy over there."

Lammeck glanced across the nightclub to the bar. From a stool, a gray-haired man dipped his head when Lammeck caught his eye.

"Excuse me." He rose with the rum.

"Mikhal." Rina stopped him.

"Yes?"

"May I tell you a truth?"

She did not use the common Russian word for truth, *pravda*. Instead, she said *istina,* implying something spiritual, a gospel truth.

"Yes."

"You are good man. I am sorry."

"For what?"

"You have no wife. No heirs." She lapped her arm around Alek's slight shoulders. In English, she told Lammeck, "It is no way."

Lammeck nodded, saddened for a moment. He looked at the two, wishing he could do something to preserve them, certain at the same time that he would prove powerless to do so in the face of the forces and events that lay ahead.

He wended his way through the well-heeled patrons of the Tropicana. Like the rest of the nightclub, the bar appeared to have been etched out of the jungle. Mature acacia trees and ferns surrounded the long curved bartop. Space-age chrome stools and high-design chairs of blond woods blended the bar into the modern motif of the rest of the nightclub.

Lammeck approached the fellow who'd nodded to him. The man watched him come, calmly shooting the cuffs of his tuxedo. Lammeck neared. The neighboring stool opened, as if prearranged. Lammeck took the seat.

To his left, a woman in a chinchilla stole laughed loudly with a mustachioed man. On his right, the gray-haired man extended an open pack of cigarettes. Lammeck waved away the offer.

"Don't smoke?"

"Cigars. And only here in Cuba."

"Ah, the best in the world. Why not? They will not be available soon in America."

"How did you know I was American?"

"I watched you rumba, *señor*. What else could you be?"

The man chuckled alone. He waved his cigarette about as he spoke, animated and Latin.

"How do you like the *Bajo las Estrellas* here at the Tropicana? Dancing under the stars?"

"It's beautiful. Never seen anything like it. Thank you for the drink."

"The *añejo* rum, yes? The *siete,* not the *quince.*"

"Do I know you, *amigo*?" Lammeck said bluntly.

"No. A lucky guess." The man circled a manicured finger. "Please turn around and face forward, Professor Lammeck," he warned. "We do not want more than our small share of attention. *¿Sí?*"

Lammeck obeyed, looked into the great mirror behind the bar. He wondered if he'd ever get accustomed to people knowing his name before he met them, shadows showing up on his porch, fragments of secrets scattered like unmatched puzzle pieces, always the cloak of plausible deniability. He kept his hands around his rum glass to keep from betraying his nerves.

"Drink with me for a few minutes, *señor.* Your two young friends will wait."

Lammeck looked over his shoulder. Alek and Rina were on the dance floor. Alek was as poor a dancer as Lammeck.

"Alright. For a few minutes."

Without turning, the stranger spoke: "Speak without facing me. Talk only loud enough for me to hear you over the music. Do not show too much interest in anything we say."

The man pushed away his own empty glass. He raised his ample chin to the bartender to bring another.

"My name is Heitor Ferrer."

"You seem to know who I am, so I'll skip my introduction."

Lammeck sipped his *siete,* doing as he was told. He and Heitor both looked at the futuristic mobiles hanging above the bar.

"Did you know that every great entertainer of the day has played the Tropicana?" Heitor asked. "Nat 'King' Cole, Sinatra, Josephine Baker, Xavier Cugat, Paul Robeson, Liberace. Carmen Miranda sang here two days before she died."

"Very impressive."

"Yes. Fidel shut the Tropicana down, along with all the nightclubs and casinos, for the first year of the revolution. Then he allowed them to reopen. He realized that too much money is brought to the island by tourists seeking games of chance. But Fidel does not like gambling. It does not fit the Communist view of the world. Everyone is an owner of everything. So if I gamble away my money, I also gamble away my neighbor's money. It is not the only absurdity of Marxism, but it is sweet in a naïve, humanist sort of way. Very much like Fidel himself."

"You know Castro?"

"Ah, yes. Indeed. I am a retired tobacco engineer and executive. It was a very important job, as you can imagine. I have known Fidel and Che since 1958, back in the Escambray mountains when we were ducking Batista's soldiers. We used to break the cane stalks to suck the sugar water inside. It's amazing I have managed to grow so fat again, the weight I lost running through those woods."

Lammeck kept himself from reacting. This man knew Castro, had even been a guerrilla with him. And he recognized Lammeck. What else did he know? Calendar, Alek, the pills? Lammeck fought off the urge to glance around, to see if guards were moving in. He steadied his gaze on the artwork overhead.

"You are in no danger from me, Professor. I am going to help you and your young man kill Fidel."

Lammeck whispered, "Don't you think we should've met in private? We're in the middle of a nightclub."

Heitor maintained an upbeat tone. "Calm yourself. What if we are discovered in private, hmm? Then we have no alibi. Here, we can always claim we met serendipitously, you and I. We sat next to each other in a bar, what is sinister in that? Relax. Drink your rum. Listen a bit. Then we will part. We will have the secret meeting you desire later."

Lammeck wrapped his hand again around his sweating highball

glass. Heitor stubbed out his cigarette. He spoke while grabbing up the Zippo to light another.

"After the debacle with Sorí Marín, *Unidad* had to move quickly. Many of our top people were rounded up. So far, they've managed to keep their mouths shut in Fidel's prisons, but for how long? If it were me in a cell in *La Cabaña*, I would be singing like Caruso. The parade where Sorí Marín was to blow up Fidel by a *petaca* is coming soon. We have switched strategies, Professor. Fidel is not going to be blown apart on his reviewing stand. He is going to be shot."

Lammeck revolved on the stool enough to look back at Alek. Rina had her head on the boy's shoulder.

Lammeck turned back, to gaze at Heitor's reflection in the mirror.

"Yes. By your young man, Professor. He is a trained Marine sharpshooter."

Lammeck hoisted his rum and gulped it in two swallows. The bartender delivered another rum seconds after Lammeck set down the rattling bare ice.

"And my part in this?"

"Needless to say, *Unidad* is running out of time. And resources. We have only this one last chance. We assume the invasion is coming soon. The CIA has told us to eliminate Castro beforehand. So, we cannot afford another failure and the arrests that follow. You, Professor Lammeck, are going to help us ascertain whether to let our young assassin proceed."

"How am I supposed to do that?"

"You do yourself a disservice. We know all about you. The world's leading scholar in assassinations. Who better than you to tell us if young Alek Hidell has the makings, eh?"

The man was discussing the murder of an old comrade, his country's leader. Lammeck imagined this conversation with John

Wilkes Booth, Cesare Borgia, Charlotte Corday, Josef Gabčik, Jan Kubiš. He wondered if all the calculated plotters and killers of history were this cool before the deed?

"What else do you know about him?"

"Nothing except his assignment, and whatever you will tell me tomorrow. I am the only one in *Unidad* who knows his name, and I wish I did not. I suggest you limit your knowledge of young Alek, as well. It cannot serve you, Professor. It is not safe for any of us to become too familiar. Learn only what you must. No more. Trust me in this."

Lammeck understood the purpose of Heitor's admonition. What if he, or Heitor, any of them, were arrested and questioned? A man cannot blurt what he does not know. Lammeck felt the small mound of the poison capsule in his pocket. A corpse can't betray anyone either.

"Tomorrow," Heitor said, "I will pick you up in the morning at your house, then young Alek at his hotel. I will drive you both into the country. I understand you have the rifle the boy requested?"

The duffel bag. Calendar had already given him the murder weapon.

"Apparently, yes."

"Good. You will spend a day observing the boy, training him as necessary. Then you will tell us whether you believe, in your skilled opinion, that Alek Hidell is an assassin. If so, *Unidad* will take over from there."

Lammeck fingered the cold glass. He pushed it away, his appetite for the *siete* slackened. He wanted to tell Heitor right now that Alek was not a killer. That the boy was barely in his twenties, he had a young fiancée, he was a defector, he was confused, and this was a rotten thing to do, taking advantage of him this way. Heitor might not know these things, but Lammeck did. And he knew instantly how Calendar, if he was here, would answer: It's war, Professor. Alek Hidell is a Marine. That makes him old enough to die for his country. So he's old enough to kill for it. You just tell us if the kid can shoot straight.

Lammeck responded to the Calendar in his head: Why would a defector, a man who'd rejected his country, kill for it? What vise grip did Calendar have on young Alek Hidell?

"Your enthusiasm for this work is not what I'd hoped it would be, Professor. I apologize for your involvement, but there is little alternative for us."

"Somewhere there's bound to be a Cuban weapons expert who can do this. Why's it got to be me?"

"Because you have been specifically named by your government for this part. I cannot change that. As you may guess, we in the underground are not in a good negotiating position with your CIA."

Calendar, Lammeck thought. *He put me here. Why?*

"But I don't get it. *Unidad* doesn't really need me or the CIA at all. Just go ahead and kill Castro."

"Understand, Professor Lammeck, we cannot do this without the cooperation of the United States. Yet, paradoxically, we cannot do this *with* the cooperation of the United States. So there must be someone interposed. Someone in the middle. A private individual with no official connection to either Cuban or American politics. You have no pivotal role or interest in Castro's revolution or its reversal. And that, *mi amigo,* makes you pivotal. You see how this goes? Paradoxes within paradoxes."

"Plausible deniability."

"An excellent phrase. I have not heard it before. In Cuba we have a different name for this concept: *La prueba de la luz del día.*"

"The test of the daylight."

"That is a bit literal but yes. Something that cannot stand being brought into the open. But the Spanish is so typically poetic and lax. Your American term is much better. Very exact. 'Plausible de-niability.' It is quite technical."

Lammeck didn't reply. Heitor might have believed the thin rea-son for Lammeck's involvement, but he couldn't shake the sense that there was more beneath the surface, out of the daylight, than what Heitor explained. CIA was playing chess with Lammeck's life, and this was one of their moves. Lammeck had no counter but to play along, push his own life into position, and see where it led.

Heitor scooped up the Zippo and waggled fingers to the bar-tender at the drinks on the counter, to lay them on his tab.

"We are all counting on the invasion, Professor. I am going to assume that soon after Castro is dead, the exiles will arrive on a beach somewhere on the island. Not far behind them will be the Marines and the U.S. Navy. Please tell your CIA that many of us are willing to die to free Cuba. But the firing squad holds little ap-peal. We are not eager to be martyrs, only heroes."

Behind them, at the opposite end of the open-air nightclub, the dance floor elevated into a stage. Waiters wove through the crowd snatching up the last china from the four-course dinner. Heitor, Lammeck, and all the patrons at the bar rotated on their stools to watch. The lights dimmed. The little flames of candles danced on every table, so did the pinholes of stars over the treetops. The Tropicana jungle garden sat motionless, flickering. A spotlight jut-ted from a tower down to the stage. The master of ceremonies walked into the beam and announced the evening's cabaret, *Pachanga en Tropicana.*

The orchestra struck up. Two dozen dancers swept onstage, kick-ing and shimmying in time to the fast merengue beat. All the men wore tight, Latin-lover costumes, and slicked hair. The women swayed in risqué outfits of spangles, sheer stockings, and false eye-lashes.

"You see the way they move?" Heitor leaned over to Lammeck.

"The grace, the sensuality? In Cuba this is called *sandunga*. There is no English equivalent for this word."

"Or those dances."

Heitor nodded and said only, "Cuba," as if that were explanation enough. He rose from the bar. "I will see you at eight tomorrow morning, Professor. I apologize for the little games we find it necessary to play. But that is why Fidel must die. *¿Comprende?*"

Heitor filtered away into the crowd. Lammeck kept his seat. The bartender noticed him.

"A vodka gimlet and a Stoli." Lammeck jerked a thumb after Heitor. "On his bill."

He left the bar with the drinks. Alek and Rina sat enjoying the show curled close to each other. They were dapper in their eveningwear, flushed from liquor and dancing. Alek, the Marine-trained sniper, a defector to the Soviet Union, recruited by the CIA to come kill Castro. Rina, his Soviet girl who chose her man after less than two weeks, who loved him and knew he was a spy. Lammeck set the drinks in front of them. They both thanked him in Russian. Lammeck wanted to tell Alek to drink, get so drunk you can't wake up tomorrow when Heitor comes for you. Don't get involved, Alek. Go back to Minsk. Leave history alone. She is never, ever kind.

"Alek. Walk me out. I'm leaving."

The boy and Rina stood. She came around the table.

"Good night, Mikhal. We will see you again, I hope." To his surprise, she stood on tiptoe and kissed his cheek.

"Good night, Rina."

Lammeck led the way out of the music and lushness of the nightclub. Walking between the concrete shells that framed the main entrance, he gestured for the doorman to hail him a taxi.

"Tomorrow at eight in the morning. That man I met at the bar will come get you. Be ready."

Alek was confounded. "Tomorrow morning? That's too soon. I'm not—"

"No, it's not happening tomorrow. Don't worry, he'll explain when he picks you up. But it *will* be soon. Alek, look."

"Yeah?"

Outside the cabaret, away from the noise and lights, the hundreds of others in tuxedos, beyond the red cheeks and loving eyes of Rina, Alek appeared even more a boy, almost a child, in a grown-up and dangerous world.

"Son, you're pretty mixed up right now, that's obvious. You've got a wonderful girl in there who's crazy about you. You've got plenty of time to figure things out, the rest of your life. It can be a long and happy one. Think about this, think hard. And if you don't want to do it, don't get in that car tomorrow."

A taxi rolled to a stop in front of them. The doorman opened the rear door for Lammeck.

He eyed Alek one more time before climbing into the taxi. As the cab drove off, he loosened his bow tie, closing his eyes. The boy would be there tomorrow. Calendar and the CIA didn't make that kind of mistake. Their hooks were into this kid deep. Like they were in Lammeck.

CHAPTER ELEVEN

April 4
Miramar

LAMMECK AWOKE TWO HOURS before Heitor was expected. In his boxers, he carried his coffee mug to the porch to watch the sun rise. He wished he'd known Havana before the revolution, when well-to-do Americans like him had used the island as a playground. What a place, he thought, gazing across the turquoise water, listening to the sawing of insects in the trees and grass, feeling the sun on his bare thighs. In Rhode Island he'd be freezing, looking outside at slush or mud, thinking about being elsewhere. He realized that, from now on, that other place would be Cuba. The island had grown on him, the coffee, cigars, people, climate, food, music, intrigue. No wonder Spain took it, America took it from them, Castro seized it, and America wanted it back so desperately. Perhaps, if Lammeck survived and the revolution did not, he might find a way to buy this house.

Lammeck went into the kitchen. He tugged the duffel out of the cabinet and lifted it to the Formica-top table. Undoing the draw-string, he poured the contents out.

A zippered canvas rifle sack slid out. Lammeck partially undid the zipper and peeked in at a customized Winchester Model 70 bolt action, with a skeleton wire collapsing stock and a custom five-shot magazine. *Good choice,* he thought; the Win 70 was a reliable weapon popular with U.S. Army snipers in Korea. A folding bipod for prone shooting was secured to the barrel. He ran a finger over the bolt. Oil filmed his fingertip. The gun was clean. The serial number, as expected, had been filed off the receiver ring behind the barrel. He closed the sack. Behind it came a smaller case containing a Weaver 10K telescopic sight. Another good selection, with parallax control built in. A stubby range telescope and tripod emerged next. Two boxes of .308 rounds. The last things in the duffel were five paper bull's-eye targets. From beneath his kitchen sink Lammeck pulled out a ten-ounce plastic bottle of Clorox. He poured the bleach down the drain and put the empty bottle into the duffel, along with a dispenser of masking tape.

Lammeck repacked the bag and secured the drawstring. He showered, then cooked himself a big breakfast. When Heitor pulled up in a cherry red 1953 Ford Sunliner convertible, Alek was already in the car. Lammeck put the duffel in the trunk; a Styrofoam cooler was packed there. He yanked a thumb at the boy to tell him to get in the backseat.

Heitor beamed as Lammeck climbed in. The crimson and chrome car was as garish as anything on the road. Lammeck shook his head as Heitor pulled from the curb. The man remained committed to doing everything possible in the public eye. Maybe he was right. Johan had said it: the wreckers moved in secret. Heitor Ferrer, as much as any conspirator Lammeck knew of, did not. And while others paced in Fidel's prisons, Heitor rode freely in the sun, his own plot still intact. Lammeck admired the Ford and let go some of his anxiety.

"Where'd you get this beauty?"

Heitor lifted his hands off the wheel, palms to the blue heavens. "A gift. It was left in a driveway with the keys in it. The owner, I assume, is driving something far less spectacular in Miami right now. Che once told me it is too vulgar for a revolutionary to drive. He wants me to garage it. I view this as one more rationale for the revolution to fall. This is not a socialist car."

Lammeck turned to greet Alek. The boy had his head back and his eyes closed. He was paler than Lammeck recalled from last night at the Tropicana. Alek lived in Minsk, where like Providence the weather was mired in the last gasps of winter. He wore blue jeans and a green OD T-shirt, probably Marine issue. The sun painted bright across him on the white upholstery and, again, Lammeck had the thought of how small the boy was. He did not know Alek's story, and Heitor had advised him to learn only what was necessary. But looking at Alek Hidell, how little there was of him, how he soaked up the sun and wind, Lammeck guessed the boy hungered, for something.

Lammeck considered the thousand assassins he carried in his head as his comrades, tutors, and only family. He'd noted long ago that they were a young bunch: Guiteau who shot Garfield, von Stauffenberg whose exploding briefcase barely missed killing Hitler, Gandhi's murderer Godse, Fanya Kaplan who plugged Lenin—they were all in their mid-thirties or forties. But the vast majority of killers were closer to Alek's age. The teenage disciples of Hassan-i-Sabah, the Old Man of Alamut, who invented the term *assassin*. The royal knights who cleaved Thomas à Becket to please Henry II. Jakob Yurovsky, the Soviet soldier who led the firing squad against the Romanovs before dumping their bodies into a Siberian well. The boys Lammeck trained to be saboteurs and executioners behind enemy lines in World War II. Like Alek, all were young, impressionable, and sent by the *viejos*.

Heitor drove them along the Malecón, toward Havana Bay. He followed the waterside road south, tracing the harbor until the docks faded behind and the convertible headed east, into humbler neighborhoods. The streets were not teeming with American and Soviet cars but bicycles, horse-drawn wagons, loose chickens, women carrying mesh grocery baskets, dusty men hauling building supplies across their shoulders, and children punting soccer balls. Here, at the fringes of Havana, the people's skins turned darker, the pace slowed. The small houses seemed clean and in repair. The streets were swept. No one walked barefoot, or stood aside useless. No one begged.

"No poverty," Lammeck said.

"That is Fidel's great aim," Heitor replied. "And no wealth."

They entered a broad freeway and sped up. The road bore them quickly into the countryside until the land opened to savannah and sparsely spread farms. Tractors and mules plowed for the early spring planting. Along the road, school-age youths and workers in overalls by the dozens stood hitchhiking with thumbs out.

They drove southeast. Lammeck turned several times to check on Alek, but the boy appeared asleep. Lammeck looked over the landscape, impressed and surprised at the size of Cuba. Far off to the north, a mountain range serrated the horizon. Fifty miles outside Havana, the fields became immense. The convertible passed towns, factories, convoys of trucks on the highway; all of this fired Lammeck's amazement at Castro's achievement, to have wrested this entire island from a power with the might and determination of America. To have done it with peasants and cane-cutting *macheteros* for his troops. Lammeck watched the land roll by, imagining the depth of sentiment Castro must have tapped into. In the first green blooms on the cropland, the scattered electric lines, factories, villages, horses, tractors, mountains in the distance, he sensed the people of this island rise.

Was this boy in the back the one to undo all that?

Ninety minutes outside Havana, Heitor turned off the highway. The Ford left the gravel road a mile later, whipping whorls of dust. In the back, Alek sat up and looked around. His face registered nothing. Lammeck noted the boy's natural stillness. A sniper's trait.

Minutes later, Heitor stopped beside a copse of cottonwood trees. In every direction Lammeck saw acres of cane brake. Much of the flat earth had been seared black.

Heitor swept a hand over the landscape. "In winter, the cane stumps are fired to burn away the dead leaves. It is not an attractive place, Professor, but you will have full use of this field. The people who farm it have been instructed to ignore what they hear today."

Lammeck climbed out of the Ford, standing on bare soil. Sugar cane stalks, scorched and chopped close to the ground, dotted the vast field. Lammeck bent to inspect one. A yellow, tender shoot emerged out of the cindered stump, the renewal of the cane.

Alek got out behind him and busied himself yawning and stretching. Lammeck took the keys from Heitor and opened the trunk to lift out the duffel bag and cooler. Heitor spoke from the driver's seat: "I will come back for you in three hours. There are water, beer, and sandwiches in the cooler. Train him and the weapon for a five-hundred-meter shot."

Lammeck slammed the trunk. With Alek, he watched the scarlet car streak from the scorched landscape.

"What's with that guy?" the boy asked.

Lammeck pointed at the duffel for Alek to lift it. He took the cooler.

"He doesn't want to know anything about you. Don't take it personally. It's for your own protection."

The two carried their loads under the shade of the cottonwoods. Alek sat on a root, elbows on spread knees. He looked around at the burnt field, displeased, as if this was not much of a way to spend a vacation.

Lammeck busied himself with the duffel. He slid out the canvas rifle bag first, handed it over to Alek. The boy set the case across his lap and did not open it. This told Lammeck he knew what was inside, he'd specified the contents. Lammeck began to attach the range scope to its tripod.

"How 'bout you, Mikhal? You don't seem scared of me."

The fittings of the scope and tripod matched well. Lammeck spread the legs and set the assembly upright. He pocketed the caps from the eyepiece and barrel, then worked to sharpen the focus on another stand of trees at the far side of the field. Looking into the range scope, he said, "I'm not."

He heard the boy unzip the rifle case.

"How come?"

"I have my reasons."

"It does make sense, though, if we're spies and all, not to get too cozy with each other. 'Case something goes wrong."

Again, the botulinum pill in Lammeck's pocket, the blade in the small of his back, prodded him. They were his only protections. Neither was comforting. Lammeck brought his eyes up from the scope.

"Do you know what to do, Alek? If something goes wrong?"

He watched the boy slide the rifle from the canvas sack. Alek fiddled with the Winchester, extending the wire stock, hefting the gun for balance, taking long moments before answering.

"Yeah."

Lammeck made no more inquiry. He emptied the rest of the duffel, laying out the boxes of .308's, the paper targets, and the Clorox bottle and tape. Alek reached for the plastic bottle.

"What's this for?"

"I'll show you later."

Lammeck watched the boy handle the Win 70. Alek attached the Weaver 10K scope using a pocketknife. He was confident with the weapon. Though his arms were thin and not well muscled, he hefted the gun fluidly to his face, took up a sitting shooting position to aim. His cheek nestled the pad on the wire stock, his eye settled unblinking behind the scope. He didn't wave the gun about but picked a spot at a far edge of the field. He was oblivious to Lammeck's observance, blotting out everything but what lay beneath his crosshairs.

Lammeck, too, was mesmerized for these moments. This boy and rifle, attached so naturally, were so insignificant, just slivers really. But what the two of them were intended to do, the impact of a twitch of Alek's slender finger, would be monumental. This was the historic power, perverse and out of all proportion, of the assassin.

The boy pulled back the bolt to chamber a phantom round. He pulled the trigger. The Win 70's hammer clicked.

★ ★ ★

Quarters Eye
CIA Headquarters
Ohio Drive
Washington, D.C.

Calendar checked the tuck of his white shirt, then knocked. He paused before turning the knob. He didn't push the door all the way open, just enough to peek in, as if there might be a fire on the other side.

"Bud, come in."

Calendar entered the office of Richard Bissell, chief of Clandestine Services. He'd never been in Bissell's office before, but this didn't bother him; Calendar's place was in the field. Calendar noted the broad view of the Potomac, Virginia on the far shore.

"Take a seat." Bissell did not stand. On his very clean desk stood a model of the U-2 spy plane, conceived and built under Bissell's guidance. The U-2 had been hailed as the single greatest breakthrough to date in intelligence gathering. Bissell's star at CIA had risen high. Now, it was tethered to Calendar.

Calendar settled in the leather chair at the edge of the desk. He set his forearms on the armrests and laid his heels flat to the floor. This was the same posture as Lincoln in his huge marble memorial, uncomfortable.

"Bud."

"Yes, sir."

"You know, I don't know your real first name."

"Brewster, sir."

"You're ex-military, right?" He didn't wait for a reply. "Normandy. Bulge. Rhine. All the way with Patton's Third, I understand."

"Yes, sir. Those were great days."

Bissell nodded. "I never knew the general well. Met him only a few times while I was working on the Marshall Plan."

Calendar never met Patton either, so had nothing to add. Bissell's war was bureaucratic, Calendar's was muddy. He'd seen Patton from a distance, following him across France into Germany.

"I heard Patton was a racist and an anti-Semite," Bissell said. "Pretty shoddy things for a man of his position."

"I don't know about any of that, sir."

"He was also a firm anti-Communist."

"Yes, sir."

"Bud," Bissell asked with an inscrutable blink, "do you know what the moral about Patton is?"

"No, sir."

"He was anti-Communist. That dwarfs anything else he was."

Bissell stood. He made no invitation or gesture that Calendar should do likewise. He walked to face one of his high windows, fingers latched behind his back, looking out at the glinting river.

"Yesterday the State Department issued a White Paper on Cuba. Schlesinger wrote it. They're preparing public opinion in advance of the invasion. Lots of rhetoric condemning our old friend Batista. Castro started out with promise but has turned his back on the Cuban Revolution for his own ends. You know the song."

"Yes, sir," Bud said to Bissell's back.

"There was one thing, though. . . . I think the phrase was: 'We acknowledge past omissions and errors.' What do you think that was about?"

Calendar knew, and so did Bissell. So why was the chief asking? Schlesinger was making a passing admission of what was common hindsight: that it was the United States' self-serving social and economic policies on the island, plus the fact that the U.S. quashed every bid for independence there for the past six decades, that shoved Cuba to the brink of revolution. To a large extent, America created Castro.

"How dare they," Bissell said. "How dare Kennedy and his whelps admit something like that on the eve of an invasion. Only one thing matters, Bud. One thing. That we are anti-Communist." Bissell turned from the river. "Kennedy held another meeting this morning at the State Department. He brought in a dozen advisers. The President conducted a poll of whether to go ahead with the invasion."

"And?"

Bissell cracked a grin. "They approved it. Word for word. They set a date. April 17."

Monday after next. Calendar shot from his chair; a man couldn't stay seated for news like that.

The two faced each other. Bissell, ramrod stiff, said, "Bud, you and I have worked together quite a few times. I have no recollection of you ever letting me down."

"Nor do I, sir."

"In this particular instance, however, I'm not hearing encouraging reports out of Havana."

Bissell would not say it, no one in Washington would, but he was asking: *Why isn't Fidel dead?*

"I'm coming at it from a couple different angles, sir."

"I don't need to know."

"I've got everything in place. It's just a matter of days."

"Are we sufficiently detached?"

"Deniability is guaranteed, sir."

Bissell brought one hand from behind his back. He aimed a long finger at Calendar, a finger that had brought down kings and governments.

"I assume you need no reminder how important your role is."

"None, sir."

"Kennedy agreed to the invasion in large part because of the Executive Action component. I've assured the President of my personal confidence in you."

Calendar had nothing to say. Bissell shifted the finger from dead center in Calendar's chest to the door behind him.

"Good hunting."

★ ★ ★

10 miles west of Jagüey Grande
Cuba

Lammeck walked in long strides. Beside him, the boy kicked at blackened cane stumps, looking bored.

When Lammeck had counted one hundred steps, he drove two cane stalks into the dirt and taped a paper bull's-eye between them. He marked off another four hundred strides, where he pushed two more posts into the dirt and fixed a second bull's-eye between them. Behind this last target another two hundred yards stood a small forest as backstop. The .308 rounds would still be supersonic when they struck those trees. Lammeck turned back for the cottonwood stand half a kilometer away by the dirt road.

"That's gonna be a long shot, Mikhal."

For the first time, Lammeck noted Alek's slight Southern accent.

"What kind of training did you get in the Marines?"

"Sharpshooter. Mostly out to three hundred yards. Some five. This looks like five."

"It is."

"Why so far?"

Lammeck swept a hand over the wide cane brake. "My guess is you've done mostly range work, open field like this. Some jungle training."

"Yeah."

"Judging by the bipod you had CIA put on the Win 70, you're a prone shooter."

"Right."

"This shot's going to be different. It's urban. Buildings, streets, alleys—all those make canyons of wind. Havana's an oceanfront city. Always a breeze. My guess is you'll be elevated, in a window or on a rooftop. Four, five stories at the most. I don't want you so high you can't get out fast."

"I never did much downhill work."

"Don't worry about it. At five hundred, the extra distance is about one yard. Simple trigonometry. Elevation's not a concern."

"But it's not my best range." The boy said this sulkily.

"The point, Alek"—Lammeck patted the boy's narrow shoulder—"is for you to hit the target and get the hell out of there. There's going to be a lot of people looking for you the second after you pull that trigger."

The two tromped over the ugly field in a rising morning heat. Alek stuffed hands in his pockets, walked with his chin down. He seemed a loner, lost without Rina.

"Alek?"

"Yeah?"

"When did you join the Marines?"

"Five years ago."

"How'd you like it?"

"It was rough sometimes. Got to see some of the world, mostly Japan. I went to language school. Learned my Russian."

"When did you get out?"

"Fifty-nine."

"Was that when you defected?"

Alek shook his head, still kicking at scorched clumps. "I don't think we ought to be talking too much about this stuff."

"I'd like to know."

"Why? We both been told it isn't smart to do that."

Lammeck did not tell the boy he had a poison pill in his pocket that would seal his own lips if he were found out and arrested. He wasn't worried about keeping secrets.

"I'm an historian. To be honest, you might be an historic figure. An assassin. Those are the people I study."

"You're saying you want to study *me*?"

"In a way."

Shyly, Alek chuckled. "That's a first. No one ever wanted to do that before. 'Cept Rina. She wants to know everything."

"You two are crazy about each other. I can see it."

"Yeah."

The boy had deflected the question. Lammeck asked again. "Why, Alek? Why leave the United States?"

"I don't like the way things are there. Racism, unemployment, exploiting the workers."

"But why go to a Communist country?"

"I'm a Marxist."

No you're not, Lammeck thought. This wasn't the 1930s, before Stalin and the purges, the war, when people came from around the world to help build the new socialist paradise. Lammeck had made his career teaching young men. He was certain this one was no ideologue. Those answers about America—racism, exploitation— were stock criticisms. They sounded coached. Alek was just a confused boy. A boy Calendar and the CIA were using to do their bloody work.

"How long have you been in the Soviet Union?"

"A year and a half."

"What's it like?"

"The way you'd figure. Folks are nice, for the most part. But there's too much bureaucracy. Too corrupt. And it's pretty much a police state."

"So why come to Cuba to shoot Fidel? He's a Marxist, too. Don't you like him?"

They were within fifty yards of the cottonwood stand where the rifle, range scope, and cooler waited in the only shade.

"I don't want to talk anymore, Mikhal. No offense. Let's just shoot."

Alek picked up the Winchester and sullenly set about loading the magazine with five .308 rounds. Lammeck stood aside and watched. When the mag was full, Alek slid one more round into the chamber and closed the bolt.

Lammeck took the rifle from him. He opened the bolt, flipped out the live cartridge, and caught it in midair.

"That's not good range safety, son. Always leave the bolt open 'til you're ready to shoot. And clean up your attitude. Right now."

The boy spit once in the dirt between his boots before lifting his gaze.

"Yes, sir."

Lammeck did not hand the Win 70 back. He reached to the Styrofoam cooler and from the lid broke off four small white bits. He handed down two to Alek.

"Stuff your ears."

He plugged his own, then fired the rifle into the earth where the boy's spittle had landed. Dirt and bits of cane sprayed up from the small, sudden crater. Alek jumped.

"What the hell?"

Lammeck worked the bolt rapidly, firing the remaining four rounds into the earth. When he was done, he handed the rifle off to the boy.

"Can't calibrate a clean barrel. Load it again."

Alek obeyed. One more time Lammeck emptied the rifle into the ground, away from Alek this time, enjoying the speed of the Winchester's bolt, getting a feel for the trigger. With only the wire stock, absent the weight of a big piece of walnut, the recoil was magnified.

He handed the rifle to Alek with the barrel warm.

"Alright. Load five rounds. Keep the bolt open. Set up prone."

Alek did as he was told. He lay on his belly in the dirt. Lammeck drank water from the cooler, then set himself behind the range scope. He found the hundred-yard target and sharpened the focus.

"Alright. Let's zero this rifle. Give me one round on center at the first target."

Lammeck pulled his eye from the scope to watch Alek take aim. The boy's small frame worked to his advantage; he splayed behind the rifle and scope with ease. Alek let out a breath, deflating his torso even flatter to the ground. His head was solid on the cheekpiece, both eyes open, his right eye did not flinch behind the scope. When he fired he took the recoil firmly into his shoulder so the rifle would not jump off target. His right hand was quick and practiced off the trigger, to the bolt chambering another round, to the trigger again, in under a second. Through the Styrofoam plugs, Lammeck heard the echoes flee the field.

Lammeck bent to the range scope. A hole pierced the target's outer ring, six inches low and three inches right.

"Make your adjustments, Alek."

The boy unscrewed the caps off the elevation and windage knobs of the Weaver scope. Lammeck made no suggestions, he needed to see the boy's skill. Alek wound the elevation knob counterclockwise twenty-four clicks—one click for each quarter-inch of elevation at one hundred yards. The windage knob he turned clockwise only eight clicks, not the twelve Lammeck expected. Alek was admitting that one of the three inches right of the target was his own error, not the rifle's. *Good,* Lammeck thought, *good.* He has feel.

When the boy was set again behind the Winchester, Lammeck instructed him to fire when ready. Alek took only moments to squeeze off another round. Through the scope, Lammeck watched a neat hole punch into the left edge of the center bull.

"Alright, reload."

Alek pressed two more rounds into the Winchester. The chest of his OD T-shirt was encrusted with clinging black dirt.

Lammeck said, "Slow fire, at will."

He let the boy fire thirty rounds, taking time between shots and reloading to make minor adjustments to the elevation. When he was done, the heart of the target was perforated and the Win 70 was zeroed in. Lammeck watched, saying little, letting Alek get comfortable behind the trigger, with the extra recoil, and with taking instruction. Lammeck didn't know what lay ahead for either of them, but his suspicions of Calendar and the CIA were acute. He wanted to lay the groundwork for Alek to trust him and accept his authority. Lammeck knew he was tied to the boy beyond what he could guess; in the end, Alek's reliance might not matter, or it might save both their lives.

"Reload."

Alek snapped five more cartridges into the magazine. He fixed himself again to the Weaver scope. Lammeck sensed the boy's focus was a tactic to avoid talking.

"Upper right-hand corner. Give me a small grouping. Five rounds. Rapid fire."

The rifle barked in Alek's hands. The next instant he flung back the bolt, ejecting the spent casing. Never pulling his eye from the scope, he fired again. With remarkable pace, he chambered another round, fired. In under ten seconds, Alek emptied the magazine. Lammeck checked the target. All five rounds formed a star in the upper right-hand corner, three inches across. If this had been a torso, they all would've been killing shots.

So this was Alek Hidell's special skill. Speed.

"Reload."

When the magazine was full, Lammeck said, "Again. Lower left. Go."

Lammeck observed the target while Alek drained the magazine. Hole after hole tore into the target exactly where he'd ordered, at an uncanny rate. He muttered under his breath, "Holy smokes."

To the boy, Lammeck said, "Pick up the casings. Then grab a sandwich."

Alek sat up, flicking dirt clods off his shirt. He left the Win 70 and set about gathering the spent brass. Lammeck walked away, to let the boy collect himself in the silence he preferred. He headed to the hundred-yard target.

What did this odd boy know? That he was part of a fantastically broad campaign to assassinate Fidel in advance of a military invasion? That he was just one strand in a web spun by the CIA, the Mafia, *Unidad*? That he was no different than the exploding seashells, black operation hit teams, plastic explosives, poison cigars, toxic pills?

Lammeck reached the tattered target. He detached the paper and kicked over the stakes. The center of the bull's-eye seemed to have exploded out of the sheet. One .308 round could do this to Fidel's chest.

Lammeck strode back to the cottonwoods. Alek had already finished a sandwich and a beer. All the empty shell casings had been gathered into the box.

Without appetite, Lammeck picked up the duffel bag. He rolled it into a rough pillow. This he rested on top of the cooler.

"We'll go for the five-hundred-yard target from a seated position. Get set up."

Wordless, Alek collapsed the bipod at the end of the rifle. He settled himself on his rump in the black dirt behind the cooler, lifting the Winchester's barrel onto the duffel. Lammeck watched him yield to the gun, pull it close, and cradle his eye, cheek, and hands to it. A finger crept to the trigger.

"You've got to adjust for the extra distance."

The boy didn't raise his head. "Already did. Five hundred yards. Fifty-one clicks."

"How about windage?"

"I'll fire a test round."

"You think you'll have the chance to do that when you're aiming at Fidel?"

Alek pulled his eye from the scope. He licked a finger and held it up.

"Don't do that," Lammeck said. "We're looking at the wind a third of a mile away. Over that distance your round's going to lose a third of its speed. For the first two hundred yards, the bullet's got enough velocity to push through the wind. We want to adjust for the second part of the trip. Look through your scope. The shot you'll take will be about this time of day. The temperature should be similar. Look at the ground. You see a heat mirage?"

The boy peered for seconds before responding. "Yeah. I do."

"What's the wind doing at the target? Read the wavers in the heat."

"Figure . . . five to seven knots, right to left."

"So at five hundred yards?"

"Each minute of angle is five inches of correction."

"How much correction for that wind?"

"Call it three minutes to the right. Twelve clicks counterclockwise."

"Do it. Slow fire when ready."

The first round missed the center by one ring, left of center. Carefully, Alek emptied the magazine. He scored no bulls. His best two rounds struck an inch out. The rest landed in the second and third rings. If these were head shots, he'd miss. If his aim was Fidel's torso, they would all be hits, but not kill shots.

While he reloaded the magazine, Lammeck lectured: On the day
of the shot, look for flags, pennants, cigarette smoke, anything
near the target that'll tell you the wind's direction and speed.
Correct for it, and if you guessed wrong, forget the windage knob
and make the adjustment with the crosshairs on the fly. With your
swiftness on the rifle, you'll get off at least one deadly shot.

"But try to do it with one bullet. If the wind is too unpredictable, go for the chest."

Alek launched five more rounds into the target. When he was
done, two were bulls. Alek was right, five hundred yards was a
challenge for him. But with the right conditions, he could do it.
Lammeck had him turn back the twelve clicks that corrected for
today's five-knot breeze. The Winchester 70 was set up now for a
zero-wind, five-hundred-yard shot, as Heitor had instructed.

"Give me the rifle. And take out your earplugs."

Alek handed over the Winchester, then dug the Styrofoam pieces
out of his ears. Lammeck picked the plastic Clorox bottle out of
the dirt. He unscrewed the cap.

"Hand me the tape."

While Alek watched, he secured the empty bleach bottle to the
end of the rifle barrel with several wraps of the tape.

"This is a trick a Spetznaz soldier showed me once. Here. Load
two rounds."

He handed the weapon to Alek. The boy slipped two more
.308's into the magazine. Lammeck pulled out his own earplugs.

"Aim and fire once."

Alek rested the barrel on the rolled-up duffel. He took his position behind the gun and dropped his eye to the scope. He pulled
the trigger.

Instead of the loud, sharp burst of gunfire, the rifle issued only
the *pop* of a balloon. The bottom of the plastic bottle burst open
like a party favor.

Alek lowered the Winchester. He nodded, impressed with the ruptured bottle.

Lammeck explained: "It's better than a suppressor. No loss of trajectory. Quieter. No extra weight to carry around."

The boy pulled it off the end of the barrel and cleared away the tape. "Okay."

"Understand, anyone along the path of the bullet is going to hear a supersonic crack when the slug flies past. But they won't be able to pinpoint the direction. This little trick will get you a single quiet shot at Fidel. After that, if you still need more rounds, you better be quick."

Alek tossed the bottle on the ground. He rubbed a hand down the rifle in his lap.

"I will be."

"One more round," Lammeck told him. "Take up the gun."

The boy blinked, surprised. There was nothing left to calibrate on the Winchester. He hefted the rifle into place, worked the bolt to chamber the last round, and found the target through the scope.

"Alek."

"Yeah."

"I want you to see Fidel Castro under the crosshairs. Imagine his head. His beard, glasses, white skin. He's giving a speech in front of twenty thousand people, waving his hands, his mouth is open. There are men and women on the platform next to him. They'll watch him die. The crowd will see him die. The world will see it on television. You'll see his head explode and his body go down. You'll see it for the rest of your life. History might call you an assassin but in your own heart you'll be a murderer. Forever. This is your last chance to walk away. Right now. I'll handle Calendar and Heitor. I'll tell them you weren't right for the job."

The boy peered through the scope. He blinked.

"Let me stop you, Alek."

"No."

He set a hand to the boy's shoulder that was pressed against the wire stock.

"What's Calendar got on you? Tell me. I can help."

Alek chewed his lip. Lammeck waited.

The boy wheeled his face around from the Winchester.

"Promise me you won't do that, Mikhal. Promise you won't try to stop me."

Lammeck rubbed his beard, searching for more to say. But there was nothing. The momentum was too great to halt. *History,* he thought again, *is not kind.*

Lammeck nodded. The boy dipped his eye to the scope. He fired.

After the last round, Lammeck and Alek cleaned their presence out of the field, then waited in the shade of the cottonwoods. Lammeck ate his sandwich and split a beer with the boy.

Passing the bottle between them, Alek brightened from the brooding quiet that cropped up whenever Lammeck inquired too deeply about him. Lammeck asked instead about Rina. The boy became effusive.

Rina was a pharmacy worker at a hospital in Minsk, where Alek worked in an electronics factory. He met her at a local dance hall only two weeks ago, but he knew they were in love. Her father had been an engineer, but got labeled an enemy of the people after a bridge he designed proved faulty. He died in a gulag. She'd lived in several places in the Soviet Union: Archangel, Murmansk, Moldavia, Leningrad, and finally Minsk, with her uncle.

"He's a bigwig in the lumber industry," Alek said.

"Is she a Komsomol member? I expect if her uncle's a big shot, he's a Party member. He'd want her to be in the youth group."

"Yeah, she is."

"She want you to join up?"

"No, she thinks it's boring." Alek raised a finger off the beer bottle to point at Lammeck. "And we're not gonna talk about me anymore. Your turn, Mikhal."

"Alright. Shoot. Pardon the pun."

"You study killings, huh?"

"Assassinations. Yes."

"Why?"

"Actually, what I study is history. I'm trying to determine if individuals or events are more important when it comes to guiding history. The one place where those two forces collide is assassinations. If you suddenly remove a key person at a vital moment in time, what course do events take downstream? Do they change direction, keep in a straight line, or go a new direction altogether?"

Alek scratched the back of his neck. Lammeck noted how big the boy's ears were, what an exceptionally average-looking young man he was.

"So after I kill Castro, you'll watch and see what happens next. Then you'll know."

"Then I'll have evidence. No political theorist can ever know. The best we can do is guess."

"Seems like a pretty cold way y'all look at killing someone."

"Yes. It does."

"Is that how you got roped into this? So you could get a good, close look at a real assassination? Is that what Calendar's got on you?"

Alek was clever, Lammeck realized, and had a mean streak.

"I suppose you're right. Too many questions."

The boy lay back on his arms behind his head and stared into the leaves of the cottonwood. Lammeck watched the road for Heitor.

The red convertible arrived fifteen minutes later, trailing a comet tail of dust. Lammeck loaded in the packed duffel, Alek the cooler. They took their seats in the car. Heitor lifted his eyebrows, inquiring how the session had gone. Lammeck nodded.

For the two-hour ride back to Havana, no one spoke. Alek mimicked sleeping again in the rear seat. Lammeck watched the countryside fly past and dodged his own critical judgments of himself.

Heitor drove first to Lammeck's house, reaching it at the height of the afternoon's heat. Lammeck removed the duffel from the trunk and took it inside to hide again. Calendar had instructed him to not let it out of his sight. The red convertible pulled from the curb, with Alek watching from the back. Lammeck closed the door. He stashed the duffel.

In the bedroom, he opened a window and fell across the mattress. No breeze stirred, the curtains hung limp. Perfect conditions, he decided, for a five-hundred-yard shot. The room was stifling. The air, and his thoughts, did not let Lammeck rest.

CHAPTER TWELVE

★ ★ ★

April 5
Fontainebleau Hotel
Miami Beach

CALENDAR STROLLED ACROSS THE suite, swapping the penthouse view of the Atlantic for the panorama of Biscayne Bay, only a third of a mile to the west. He stuck a hand in his pocket, fingering his plastic mouthpiece. A dozen private yachts lay at anchor in the bay, all of them with white lights strung between bow, smokestack, and stern as if today was a holiday. Sailboats, waterfront homes, bright pinpoints of wealth described the bounds of the bay.

Momo Giancana busied himself in the kitchen dicing peppers for a vegetable tray. Johnny Roselli munched out of a bag of Lay's potato chips he carried around. Maheu perched on the back of the sofa, quiet and poised. Calendar sipped from the glass of champagne Giancana had handed him when he came into the suite.

Calendar turned from the high windows. The view reminded

him only of what he did not have. It made him competitive with the men who owned those yachts and the women they surely had on them. This, he figured, was not fair. He focused on what he'd managed to collect in his life instead: power.

He waved Roselli over and grabbed a wad of chips from the bag. The salt tasted sharp against the champagne.

"How's it goin' in Havana?" Roselli asked. "I must've missed that article in the paper that said Castro was dead."

Calendar thought about wiping the greasy chip shards from his hand onto Roselli's black camel hair coat, adding to the crumbs already there. But this lug was just a soldier; nothing other than pleasure was gained by aggravating him.

"I'm coming at it from several angles, Johnny. Stay tuned."

Giancana entered the room bearing a pewter platter festooned with asparagus, cauliflower, peppers, celery, and cherry tomatoes. He set it on a coffee table, and swung back for the kitchen, announcing, "I got onion dip."

Roselli crunched on a fistful of chips and grinned. "Don't worry, G-man. I'm tuned."

"Okay," Giancana chirped, coming back with the dip and another bottle of Dom. "Everybody got everything? Bob, you not drinking?"

Maheu shook his head and blinked owlishly.

"Suit yourself." Giancana slipped into an easy chair, dainty and eager against the size of Roselli, the posing of Maheu. The mob boss used a celery stalk to scoop a furrow in his onion dip and filled his champagne flute.

Calendar grinned. He liked Giancana, a personable little gangster. Not like the bulky Roselli who carried a challenge on his shoulder like it was a talking parrot. Or Maheu the ex-FBI stoic. And not Trafficante, always worrying, scrunching his eyes behind his glasses over money, body count, messiness. Giancana cooked, drank, lived, and murdered like the man he was, a short-timer on this planet who took advantage of the days.

"Hey, Calendar."

"Yeah, Momo?"

"You still thinking about retiring down here? Getting a place?"

"Maybe."

"When the time comes, you need anything, my feelings'll be hurt you don't come to me."

Calendar imagined borrowing money or taking favors from Sam Giancana. The devil, he was always taught, must be invited in. The Mob and the CIA both worked within the same constraint.

Roselli tossed the chip bag onto a table and brushed himself off when a knock came at the suite door. He opened it. Behind Santo Trafficante, a thick-lipped, unsmiling man stepped in wearing black frames similar to Trafficante's. Lammeck figured him for a Cuban before Santo made the introductions.

"Everyone, this is Tony Varona. Tony, this is everyone I was telling you about." Trafficante shot his hawk-nosed face at Calendar. "Watch that one," he warned his guest.

Barrel-chested Varona shook no hands. His manner was dour. Without being asked, he expanded on his name: "Former prime minister of Cuba Manuel Antonio de Varona." He inclined his head, closing his eyes for the moment. This was an uncomfortable, royal sort of gesture, expressing *At your service,* and clearly a lie.

From the sofa, Giancana breezily called, "Tony, hey! Good you could come."

Trafficante moved to the glass dining table. Behind him the Fontainebleau's tall windows peered east over the starry ocean. Out there, Calendar thought, take a right, go south a hundred and fifty miles. There's Cuba. Commies and Castro. Revolution. An invasion on the way. Eyes of the world. Maybe the flashpoint for a war. Calendar fetched his briefcase, forgetting the wealthy men floating on Biscayne Bay. He was happier with the views over the Atlantic. The bay was money. The ocean was power.

"Let's get to business," Trafficante carped. "It's late already."

"Bob," Giancana addressed Maheu, "see if Tony wants anything to drink."

Varona passed on all offers of libations, dip, and potato chips. Giancana carried his veggie tray and champagne bottle to the table. The six took seats. Calendar faced the ocean.

Trafficante began. "Tony's the guy I was telling you about, Momo. Prime minister under Prío for two years starting in '48. When Batista kicked Prío out, Tony left for Miami. In '59, after Batista split, he went back to Havana with Prío. He and Prío didn't see eye to eye with Fidel."

Giancana nodded. "I can imagine."

Roselli asked Varona, "And now you're where?"

"I reside again in Miami."

"Uh huh." Roselli pursed his lips. Plainly, he disapproved of Tony Varona, who'd turned tail when plenty of Cubans stayed behind to fight the Communists.

Varona spoke. "I came back to coordinate the counterrevolution in Miami. I am a leader with the *Frente*. And I have my own small action group, *Rescate*."

Trafficante jerked a thumb at Varona. "He met with JFK."

"Yes, I am pleased with the support of the Democrats in their opposition to Castro. Eisenhower was...less generous."

Maheu asked, "Is that why you take money from Lansky?"

"Meyer Lansky has been a business associate for years," Varona said placidly. "Nothing more."

Maheu pressed. "And you're telling us Lansky's million-dollar bounty on Castro has got nothing to do with it. This is all for Cuba, right?" Maheu glared, in his schoolmarm fashion.

Varona's thick lips cracked an insincere smile. "Of course. All for Cuba."

Calendar had no problem with Varona's involvement, even his obvious private agenda. He knew what Varona was getting out of his association with the Mob: gambling concessions worth a fortune after Fidel was dead. In the meantime, Varona got funds for his little *Rescate* from both the CIA and the Mob, plus he had a shot at Lansky's million-dollar bounty on Fidel's head. Varona got to play the big shot while sleeping safe in Florida. Later, in a free Cuba, he'd be able to brag how much he contributed.

Calendar didn't care, because America didn't care. The bottom line: Varona, Lansky, Giancana, Trafficante, Roselli, none of them were Reds. Fidel was. Plain and simple, like Bissell said.

Giancana pointed the stub of a carrot stick at Calendar. "Show-and-tell time, Buddy boy."

Calendar reached down for the briefcase. Laying it flat on the table, he flipped open the twin locks. For a moment, Calendar admired what lay inside. Then he tipped the briefcase and spilled the banded bundles of dollars on the glass.

"Ten thousand," Calendar said. "And a thousand bucks' worth of communications equipment is in the trunk of a Chevy in the parking lot. Everything you asked for."

Calendar, Maheu, and the mobsters gave Varona a few moments of silence with the cash. They watched the Cuban stack the bundles in a little green wall. While Varona toted the bills, Calendar again counted his blessings that in his own life he'd dodged this vice of greed. The three mobsters almost licked their lips looking at the dough; Calendar could tell each was devising ways to separate Varona from it.

Calendar tried to break the reverie around the table with a snap of his fingers. Varona was the last to look his way.

"Tony? Tony? Hey..." Calendar reached across the glass. He swept a hand through Varona's orderly arrangement of the money. Bundles flew to the floor. He stood.

"Listen to me, Tony. You hear this voice? Whenever you hear it, you stop what you're doing and pay attention. I want to see your ears perk up like a dog for dinner. Got me?"

Varona stared at him.

Calendar pressed his point home. "You're not prime minister of anything right now. That's Uncle Sam's money. And as far as you're concerned, I'm Uncle Sam's first fucking cousin."

For a second, Varona let his eyes leak to the floor where the cash lay scattered. Then he yoked his attention on Calendar and stayed there.

"Pay who you got to pay with that. You can get Green Stamps with the rest, I don't give a rat's ass. All I want from you is what I was promised. A name."

He turned his back on the table, to let Varona gather up the money.

★ ★ ★

Onboard Tejana
Florida Straits

The wind in Calendar's face caused his cigarette to burn too fast. He considered moving to the stern to block the breeze but kept his stance at the bow. He liked the view of the water coming, the fretted moonlight like highway stripes on the sea.

He gave up on the smoke, tossing it over the rail. He took a seat on a stack of crab pots strewn about the deck for disguise. The 110-foot *Tejana* ran swiftly, cruising at thirty knots on its German pancake diesels. An old World War II subchaser, she was long and narrow-beamed; the *Unidad* crew often fought seasickness on the short trips between Cuba and Key West. One more reason why Calendar lingered up front, away from the stink of puke.

An hour out of Key West, the far-off glow of Havana tinted the southern horizon silver, obscuring the lower realm of stars. *Tejana*'s crew left the pilot house to mount her half-dozen .30- and .50-caliber machine guns; these had been removed when she entered American waters. Castro had a small navy and *Tejana* had never been accosted. But if the ship was intercepted, she would fight.

The vessel closed on the island after midnight without incident or notice. Five miles off the coast, the seas calmed. The ride smoothed. *Tejana* made for Bahia de Cabañas, an empty bay thirty miles west of Havana.

A hundred yards from land, she stilled her big engines. All running lights were off. She bobbed broadside to the shore. Calendar looked over the moonlit cove, gray palms and brush behind the long white beach. The water was clear enough to see the bottom. A mosquito that landed on Calendar's neck died in his palm.

Onshore, a flashlight blinked three times. Down the starboard rail, a crewman answered with flashes from the boat. In the next minute, Calendar heard the puttering of dinghies headed from the beach.

He moved to the center of *Tejana*'s beam and clambered over the side, down a ladder. Below him, a wooden boat arrived, a wizened fisherman at the tiller. Once aboard, the skiff pushed off from the subchaser's hull. Immediately, other boats motored alongside to accept lowered crates of weapons and matériel intended for the underground.

The fisherman said nothing on the way to the beach. Calendar avoided getting a good look at the old man's face or giving one of his own. The moment the skiff bellied in the sand, Calendar jumped out. He shoved the bow backward so the fisherman could reverse and return to *Tejana* to help with the off-loading. On the beach, two pickup trucks waited, motors off. Calendar strode past them to an idling taxi.

The cab driver did not turn when Calendar climbed into the backseat. The man hit the gas the moment the rear door closed, jostling Calendar before he was fully seated. Calendar looked into the rearview mirror to see that the driver's eyes were on him. He slid to his right, closer to the window, to get out of the reflection.

He said only, "Miramar."

CHAPTER THIRTEEN

★ ★ ★

April 6
First Avenue
Miramar
Havana

LAMMECK JUMPED AT THE touch on his bare foot. He awoke flailing defensively. He saw the big silhouette at the foot of his bed just as his hand gripped the knife under his pillow.

"For God's sake," Lammeck breathed, letting go of the blade. "How do you do that?"

"Get a dog," Calendar told him. "I could never fool a dog."

Lammeck sat up on the mattress. He gazed down at his boxer shorts, bare chest, and round waist. He reached for his pants hung over the back of a chair.

"Don't bother getting dressed," Calendar said. "I'm not staying long. And leave the light off."

Lammeck rubbed his eyes. "What do you want?"

The agent folded his arms and leaned against the wall.

"You met the kid."

"Yeah."

"He can do the job?"

"He's not a natural marksman, Calendar. He's fast, but at the distance you've set for the shot, I don't know."

"Did you work with him?"

"Yeah, but only for a few hours."

"More than enough for you to tell me, yes or no. Can he do it?"

"I think it's a shame, but yes."

"I appreciate your restraint, Professor. But this is the kind of evil we call necessary. He's young. We're old. His ass goes on the line. Ours doesn't. It's called war. You've seen this before."

Calendar took an envelope from his coat. He set it behind him on the dresser top.

"Here's a name. You meet him tonight, at the Nacional's casino. Give him the pills. He's going to hand them off to a connection of his in town, a cook in one of Castro's favorite restaurants. The cook's been told not to do anything until he gets the signal."

Lammeck didn't understand. Why wait?

"If you can poison Castro, go ahead and do it. Why risk Alek?"

The agent uncrossed his arms. He moved about Lammeck's small bedroom, a black and foretelling ghost.

"CIA's preference is to have Castro taken down by a bullet, if we can get it. Makes it look like a gangland hit. Fidel gets popped, we scoot Alek and his gal off the island, then we blame the Mafia."

"And if the kid doesn't pull the job off...?"

"We go to the pills as backup. Simple."

"What happens to Alek?"

"Alek's not your concern."

"He is if you want my help."

Calendar's shadow stopped stalking along the wall.

"You want to argue with me about this, Professor?"

"Yes."

"We ship the kid back to Mother Russia. And we let him stay there. Satisfied?"

Lammeck let more seconds pass with no reply. Calendar resumed talking.

"*Unidad*'s going to take over with Alek. Heitor will contact you for the rifle. When he does, give it to him. Just get the pills to the Nacional tonight. Then keep your head down. The invasion's coming. As soon as Castro's hit, I want you off this island. I'll send you a taxi. He'll take you to a boat outside Havana, after midnight. The *Tejana*. Get the hell on it to Key West. Then, when we're in charge down here again, we'll bring you back."

Calendar stepped toward the door. He tapped a finger on top of the dresser, on the envelope.

"If everything goes the way it's supposed to, you won't see me again."

"And if not?"

Calendar made no sound leaving. Only his voice trailed behind.

"Then not."

The destiny of peoples cannot depend on one man.
Behind me come others more radical than I;
assassinating me would only fortify the Revolution.

—Fidel Castro

A man who wants to make a profession of good in all
regards must come to ruin among so many who are not
good. Hence it is necessary to a prince, if he wants to
maintain himself, to learn to be able not to be good, and
to use this and not use it according to necessity.

—Niccolò Machiavelli
The Prince

Without violence, nothing is ever accomplished in history.

—Karl Marx

THE BETRAYAL

CHAPTER FOURTEEN

★ ★ ★

April 7
Nacional Hotel
Havana

THE LOBBY BUZZED with guests in tuxes, suits, and evening gowns. Lammeck, in white dinner jacket and bow tie, strode the length of the opulent hall. Along the walls, between leather furniture and potted palms, stood easels supporting black-and-white photographs touting the revolution. Che Guevara rakish under his black beret, Fidel in his big glasses, crowds carrying banners in the streets shouting *¡viva!* The well-heeled guests of the Nacional ignored the placards on their way to the casino. Among them, Lammeck heard very little Spanish, mostly German, English, and French.

Inside, a massive crystal chandelier glittered above green-topped games and rapt players. Women in boas and scanty outfits strolled with trays of cigarettes and liquor. Many older gamblers had younger women in tow. At the teller cage, Lammeck secured two hundred pesos in chips, a one-to-one exchange for dollars. He moved through the tables: baccarat, dice, roulette, pai gow poker. A seat opened at an unlimited blackjack game.

He played for a half hour. The cards never turned his way. Finally he slid his chips off the table and tossed a five-peso tip to the dealer despite the poor cards.

Lammeck strolled the smoky casino, looking for an open seat at a lower-stakes table. He recalled the clandestine meeting that started at El Floridita two weeks ago; was he being watched again, or was the contact simply late? Lammeck tried not to appear jittery, but his luck was flat tonight. He was already down a hundred pesos.

He slid into a seat at a ten-peso game. Instantly the cards favored him. Lammeck won several hands in a row. He did not let this make him bold with his luck but continued to obey the rules of chance and tendency. The others at the table began to nod at his play, and everyone started to win.

In twenty minutes, he built back his loss. When the dealer tossed a queen on top of his ace, he heard a giggle behind him. He turned. Rina stood there, applauding his good fortune. The Russian girl wore the same green-chiffon dress she'd worn at the Tropicana four nights before.

In Russian, he asked, "How long have you been there?"

"I saw you sit down. I did not want to disturb you."

"Where's Alek?"

"In the room. He drank too much. I put him to bed and came back to watch the games. I saw you."

"Then you must be my good luck charm. Don't go anywhere."

Rina beamed, blue eyes luminous. "I won't, Mikhal."

Lammeck played with the girl at his shoulder. He went up forty pesos while teaching her the game as the cards came and went. A few times he let her make the call whether he should hit or stand pat. After fifteen minutes he put Rina in the chair with fifty pesos in chips. She held her own. Ten hands later she left the table up thirty. Lammeck let her keep the winnings.

They walked out of the casino, into the lobby. Rina took Lammeck's arm to lead him past the leather chairs and images of the revolution, to the rear courtyard of the Nacional. Over a Saltillo tile floor, they crossed beneath a tall white colonnade into a vast open garden, built on a knoll overlooking the Malecón and the moon-gray ocean.

They took chairs at a wrought iron table on the lawn and ordered drinks: Lammeck's rum, Rina's vodka on ice. For a moment, Lammeck looked at himself seated with the girl, thinking he appeared no different from the rest of the old *libertinos* in Havana with their *chicas*. The thought embarrassed him, and he sat back from her to make it clear, in case he was being watched, that she was not his liaison.

"I'm very glad to see you, Mikhal."

"Likewise. You look very nice in that dress."

"I am sorry you must see me in it every time we meet."

"All women should find one excellent outfit and wear it every day. Maybe you'll start a fashion. Be the new Jackie Kennedy."

"I would have worn something else if I had been with you and Alek yesterday."

Lammeck crossed his arms to hide how this startled him.

"I was jealous," she said, "that I did not get to visit with you. So this is my reward, to see you tonight."

He quelled the urge to question her about what she knew of their shooting day. Was the boy so indiscreet? Didn't he realize the danger? Rina was lovely and she seemed earnest, but the two had known each other for less than a month. Alek swore he trusted her, but did he know he was trusting her with his life? *And* Lammeck's? If Calendar heard this, he might throttle all three of them.

The drinks arrived. Lammeck raised his glass to her.

"To love at first sight."

She smiled widely and drank.

"Tell me how you knew," Lammeck asked. "That he was the one."

"Oh, I didn't at first. We met at a dance. He was most insistent, breaking all the rules, asking me for many dances in a row. I let him, but only because I was trying to make someone else jealous. Afterward, my friends took me to a house where one of their mothers had just returned from America. Alek was there, too. He spoke about America and all the girls liked him. He helped clean up the dishes after we had cake. Alek was the only American in all of Minsk. He had his own apartment. I decided I'd let him be my boyfriend."

"Just like that."

"No, not the way it sounds. Alek was different. An outsider. I've always liked that sort of person. I am a loner, too."

"Will you tell me why?"

Rina paused, a gentle gaze on Lammeck.

"I did not know my father. Alek's died before he was born. I struggled to finish my education. Alek has only gone to what you call in America the ninth grade. I was raised by a stepfather who loved his other children more than me. A mother who loved her husband more than me. Then she died. I have been passed around to relatives like an old heirloom no one wants. Alek joined the Marines very young to find a home for himself. I live now in Minsk with my aunt and uncle. They are happy I will be living with Alek soon. Alek is very sweet. And very clever. He wants me. I will have children with him. We will live a long time happy."

The girl sipped her vodka. Lammeck watched, unable to warn her, to protect her. Nothing was in his hands, not even his own fate.

She glanced down shyly. "I have a confession."

"Yes?"

"I am glad to see you here tonight. I did not expect you. But you have saved me a trip to your house in the morning."

Now Lammeck's heart began to twist. Another step into the labyrinth, he thought, more dark corners, deeper into things he could not control.

"Why would you come to my house? How do you know where I'm staying?"

"Alek told me. He took the address when the taxi dropped you off yesterday."

Lammeck cursed himself. This was the sort of stupid mistake he was bound to commit. He was not a spy. He had not been trained to be careful with that sort of thing.

"Rina, what do you want?"

"Please do not take that tone. I'm afraid for Alek. Who else can I ask for help but you?"

"Alek tells you more than he ought to," Lammeck said, more brusquely than he intended. "That's all I can say."

"Sometimes he brags to me." She appeared on the verge of tears. "I encourage it. Other times I make him tell me. It's not his fault."

"What did he say to you?"

The girl looked quickly over her shoulders to be certain no one was near. She leaned close to whisper. The gestures struck Lammeck as hackneyed, almost a performance. Then he remembered the girl was nineteen. Drama was natural.

"That you and he are spies. That is why he brought me to Cuba. Because he is on a mission. With you."

"He's lying, Rina. He's making that up to impress you."

"I hope that is true, Mikhal. On my mother's grave I do. But..."

Another couple strolled by. Though Lammeck and she were

speaking Russian, Rina broke off, in her flair for secrecy. She and Alek both seemed to relish the attention that came with *avoiding* attention.

Behind the couple came a four-piece band, searching the court-yard for guests to play for and tips. Lammeck handed them several pesos to go away.

Rina continued, "I know the two of you are involved together. If you are not spies, it is still something he is hiding from me. You, too. Tell me this much is so, Mikhal."

Lammeck let out a long breath. Calendar had told him Heitor and *Unidad* were going to take over Alek. Now this girl was drag-ging the dangerous boy back into his path. She and her fiancé might cost him his life. He knew he should get up and walk away.

"What do you want me to do, Rina?"

She said, "Alek told me of a meeting he must go to in the morn-ing. I asked him if you would be there. He said no. Mikhal, I do not understand what is going on. But I will die of fright if I am not certain you are watching over him. I know you will. I know it. Please, go to the meeting with him. Keep him safe. Promise me."

Lammeck guessed the meeting was with Heitor and *Unidad*. If Calendar had wanted him there, Lammeck would've been given the instructions on the agent's nocturnal visit.

"I'll go with him. But I'll stay outside the meeting. I don't want to know anything more about what Alek is doing than I have to. That's all, Rina. I'll go, because you asked. But that's it."

"Is Alek in danger?"

"Not tomorrow, no."

"But he will be?"

"I don't know."

"Mikhal..."

"What time tomorrow?"

"He said they are coming to pick him up at ten in the morning."

"I'll be waiting. When he comes out, I'll get in the car with him."

Lammeck stood, to tell her he was done talking. He still had not met his contact tonight, more than an hour after the scheduled time.

"Go upstairs to him, Rina. Don't tell him we spoke. Can I trust you not to do that?"

"Yes."

"Good night."

"Thank you, Mikhal."

She took his hand from his side, squeezing it. With a sweep of the sea-green dress, shimmering under the moon and gas lamps of the garden, Rina left him. Lammeck signaled for the waiter, to order a cigar and another rum.

When these were in hand, he strolled down the slope of the courtyard, to the lowest reaches of the manicured grounds, to the rim of the cliff above the Malecón. There, to his surprise, a network of trenches and bunkers had been newly dug, facing the open sea. A dozen soldiers manned machine guns inside hardened redoubts. A single fat howitzer stood vigil on a concrete pad surrounded by flowering shrubs. Castro had his guard up.

Lammeck turned to the sound of heels coming his way. A tall dapper man in a black tux strolled up. A cigarette lolled on his lips below a trimmed, pencil moustache.

In Spanish, the man said, "No one knows where, or when. But everyone in Cuba is convinced the exiles are coming."

"It's a shame," Lammeck answered in Spanish. "To ruin the hotel's garden like this."

"It's only for show." The man pulled the cigarette off his lips, daintily using just the fingertips, then swept a hand over the indentations in the Nacional's courtyard. "To remind the people that we have an enemy there." He pointed the cigarette north, at Florida's unseen lights. "Once the invasion is done, it will all be put back to right. One way or another."

Was this his contact? Or just a gentleman taking the night air? "What do you think?" Lammeck inquired. "Is America an enemy?"

The man considered the question, still looking north. "Like all nations, America is self-interested, Professor Lammeck. So long as her interests are the same as mine, she is not my enemy. Nor are you. You have something for me?"

Lammeck put his hand in his pocket, fingered the poison bottle.

"You know my name, *señor*. What is yours?"

"I do not have comfort telling you about myself. Is it necessary?"

"Let's just say I have no comfort talking with someone who knows who I am but not the other way around."

The man put the cigarette back to his lips. He held the smoke in for a long moment before letting it seep from his nostrils.

"Juan Orta Córdova."

Orta. This was the name Calendar's note had said to look for, before Lammeck burned it.

"Where have you been? I waited in the casino for an hour."

"You waited over an hour," Orta corrected. "I am not allowed in the casino, *señor*. Did you not notice? Cubans may not play in the casinos, they may only work in them. It is one of Fidel's many nanny laws. He takes his belief that we are his children quite literally. Also, you were quite taken with your young lady friend. I could not interrupt. She is Soviet, yes?"

"How do you know that?"

"Though you tried, the two of you did not keep your voices down. And the stage whisperings, it was like watching Shakespeare. I do not speak Russian, but I am concerned, Professor. Where is your caution? On an evening when you are to meet me, you draw such notice to yourself. I find it disappointing."

"But you're speaking to me anyway."

"I do not have the luxury of time."

"Are you with the underground?"

Orta grimaced. "Certainly not. I do not burn department stores. I am with the government. I am Office Chief and Director General of the Office of the Prime Minister."

The man dropped his cigarette to the grass. He crushed it underfoot.

"And that, Professor, is all I will tell you about myself or my intentions."

Lammeck didn't like Orta, his imperious manner wedded to an assassin's purpose. And the man's motives worried him: Orta claimed no allegiance to the underground, so he wasn't driven by politics or power.

True to his word, the man clammed up. Lammeck reviewed the legion of assassins he'd studied, searching for the category that oily Orta belonged in. The grand and affected mannerisms, the tailored tux: This man was corrupt to his soul, and his motive was greed, blood money. History recorded only a few examples of this ugly sort. It preferred to commemorate the names of more colorful characters, lovers, patriots, regicides, and the mad.

A little shamed, Lammeck handed over the poison, keeping one pill in his pocket.

★ ★ ★

April 8
First Avenue
Miramar

Barefoot, Lammeck carried his coffee to the back porch, looking north to see how the wind blew across the straits this morning. The wind seemed to determine so much in Havana: the spray on the Malecón, pennants in the revolution parks, the rain, sidewalk cafés, often the mood.

Stepping outside, he avoided a folded newspaper left at his threshold.

Another *New York Times*. Johan.

Lammeck looked down at the paper, considering that he ought to get a different house. This address was becoming too popular with all the spies in Havana.

The breeze blew out of the northeast. A turn in the weather was coming. Good, he thought. A cool, drizzly day would be comforting, a reminder of New England. This afternoon, he would stay in, read, relax under a lap blanket on the porch, and watch the seas whip up. He still had the lion's share of a bottle of *siete* rum.

He bent for the newspaper. Unfolding it, he saw immediately the headline Johan meant for him: "Anti-Castro Units Trained to Fight at Florida Bases." The article made a strong case that the invasion of Cuba was looming. It claimed that the training of the exile brigade had been halted because the rebels were now adequately prepared. The offensive had entered its final phases. The men and machines were moving to their staging ground in Guatemala. Soon they would depart for the journey and the assault on the island.

Lammeck tossed the paper on a wicker chair. He had no curiosity for the rest of the *Times* or what was going on in America right now. Cuba was his focus.

He watched morning clouds gather. The brightness of the tropic light dimmed, cooling with his coffee. Lammeck went inside to eat his accustomed big breakfast. He shaved and dressed in loose khakis and *guayabera*. Tucking his bone-handled knife into the waistband at his back, he left the house and walked by the ocean, to the blustery Malecón, then a mile to the Nacional Hotel.

Along the way, he circled blocks, ducked through alleys, and monitored the cars and pedestrians over his shoulder. Up to now, Lammeck had been less than vigilant in his movements and security.

Today was not a day to be followed.

★ ★ ★

Nacional Hotel

Alek walked out the front door, held open by a doorman. He stopped at the top of the steps, looking down.

The boy said nothing, made no reaction. He came to stand next to Lammeck. Like Rina last night, he was dressed in an outfit Lammeck had already seen, the Marine T-shirt and dungarees he wore when they'd gone shooting. Lammeck thought how impoverished the young couple must be back in Minsk. Yet Alek didn't look so young today. There seemed a mature readiness about him.

Beside them, guests of the hotel queued for taxis entering the long oval drive. The boy spoke quietly. "What're you doing here?"

"Rina."

"When did you talk to her?"

"Last night. At the casino."

"She asked you to come with me?"

"You're the one who told her about the meeting."

The boy curled his lips. "Goddammit."

"Yep."

"I don't know about this. That guy Heitor didn't say anything about you coming along."

"I don't report to Heitor. And I promised Rina."

Alek cursed again. Lammeck wondered what his invectives were aimed at: Rina's prying, Alek's own recklessness, or Lammeck's intrusion? No matter, Lammeck decided. He didn't report to Alek either.

"Why?" the boy asked.

"She thinks it might be dangerous."

"It's just a meeting."

Lammeck smiled. "Good. I'm not looking for danger. I've got other plans for my day. But, Alek, what you and I are involved in, you understand the magnitude?"

The boy nodded, resolute.

"You've got to stop even hinting at it. She's a clever girl." Lammeck sighed. "Enough said. I'll tag along. I'll stay out of your way. Don't worry. It'll be fine."

The two entered a taxi, Lammeck in the backseat. Alek gave the driver an address, Calle 11 in the Mendares neighborhood, near Miramar. When he was sure they were within several blocks of the meeting place, Lammeck tapped the driver on the shoulder to pull over. Alek glowered at him for asserting himself despite his guarantee to stay out of the way. Lammeck paid the driver, climbed out, and motioned Alek to join him. The boy did, and opened his mouth to complain. Lammeck cut him off.

"From now on, you and I are both going to be a lot more careful. Not just with Rina, but every step we take. You're planning to assassinate the leader of this country. There are lots of forces in place to stop you from doing that. So we're going to walk. We're going to see if anyone's following. And we're going to keep walking if we're not sure we're clean."

Lammeck strode away. After a moment, Alek got in step beside him. He kept his eye on the boy, to measure whether he followed orders or chafed. Lammeck was prepared to tell Heitor he'd changed his mind about this thin lad, that Alek Hidell was too much of a loose cannon, too callow and irresponsible to be reliable. With his braggadocio and attentive Soviet fiancée, he was a risk to reveal the conspiracy. Lammeck would tell Calendar to give nasty Orta the word, to go ahead and poison Fidel because the shooting plot was off. But Alek walked with his head up, eyes darting front and back to make sure they walked without scrutiny. Lammeck caught no petulance in the boy, nothing but a marine's march in his gait. With a pang, he looked across his own shoulders, memorized cars driving past, and let events proceed.

On Calle 11, the address which Alek had given the taxi driver, was a large, canary-yellow house. Royal palms swayed overhead, shading a short, suburban street. Lammeck could smell the ocean here, only a half mile north, on today's strong breeze. There was hibiscus in the wind, and jasmine, too.

Alek said, "You look like a dog sniffing like that."

"I've been told dogs are hard to fool. Come on."

They crossed the street to the front gate of the house. Heitor and a woman sat on the patio watching them. Heitor waved. Lammeck returned it, figuring Heitor was keeping up appearances. He could not be pleased to see Lammeck uninvited this morning.

Heitor rose and held open the iron gate. A table on the patio held playing cards and a tea service. The couple were in the middle of a game of rummy. Lammeck walked to the woman, smiled, then turned to Heitor.

"This is my wife, Susanna," the Cuban said. The woman had long legs and gray hair hanging to her waist. She did not look like a conspirator; rummy and tea were not Lammeck's image of killers' pastimes. It seemed so middle-of-the-road, sane. He thought of Richard Lawrence, who in 1835 became the first man to attempt an assassination of an American president when his two pistols misfired against Andrew Jackson on the Capitol rotunda. Lawrence was a madman, believing he was the heir to the crown of England; Jackson was keeping him from his throne. In 1892, Emma Goldman became a New York prostitute to make money so her cohort Alexander Berkman could buy a gun, to shoot industrialist Henry Frick. And the Roman emperor Caligula, who had thousands killed, enjoyed fencing with gladiators whom he had armed only with wooden swords against his sharp steel. Lammeck considered Heitor and his handsome wife, their yellow house and pleasant habits. He smiled privately at the magnificent and diverse cast of characters in history's long play.

Lammeck took her hand. "Madam."

Heitor shot Alek a sharp glance.

"Go inside. Wait in the parlor."

The boy complied and disappeared unaccompanied into the house.

Heitor motioned to an empty chair on the patio. "Would you like some tea?"

"Do you have time?"

Heitor laughed. "Why go to all this trouble, Professor, if at the end of it all, there is no time for a cup of tea?"

"Certainly, then. Please."

While Heitor fetched another cup and saucer from the kitchen, Lammeck complimented Susanna's home. She answered that she and Heitor had been lucky out here, several miles from the city center; the revolutionary housing councils had not yet appropriated the buildings on their street. They still lived alone. But it was only a matter of time. Then, the same way Lammeck had minutes before, she lifted her nose to the rising wind.

"A storm," she said. "Out of the north."

When Heitor returned, Susanna excused herself with a curtsy.

"My wife," Heitor said, "is anonymous. She must stay that way."

"I understand."

Heitor poured Lammeck's tea. "If that is true, what are you doing here?"

Lammeck explained his reason. He assured Heitor he would

stay on the porch until the meeting was completed. "Maybe Susanna would like to play me in rummy."

"With respect, we will leave my wife uninvolved with you, Professor. Drink your tea and speak with me instead. The meeting will wait. I understand you have an interest in the matters of revolution and assassination."

"I do."

"You may ask me a few questions. To be honest, your compensation for so much risk seems quite small. You receive some insights into the upheaval coming to our island. I, on the other hand, get a freed country."

Lammeck asked Heitor how he'd become involved with the counterrevolution.

The man answered that, once the revolution was won, after he and the other *barbudos* came down from the mountains, he'd been a staunch supporter of Fidel's.

"I was in the front ranks when we walked into Havana. We looked fearsome, I tell you, bearded and dirty. Fidel arm in arm with brother Raúl, handsome devil Guevara, Camilo Cienfuegos in his bush hat. The people waved flags from the balconies of every house, from the Malecón to the *barrios* in Montejo."

Heitor explained how both he and Susanna had accepted some difficult truths: that, in the beginning, some *Batistianos* had to be put against the *paredón,* some had to be jailed, others had to be exiled, and many with no affiliation at all, just raw dissatisfaction, would flee to America.

"This was how a revolution worked if you were truly going to start a new way of governing. To think otherwise was to be naïve."

But after the first year, when Fidel announced there would not be elections, when Soviet Foreign Minister Mikoyan came to Parque Central and Fidel embraced him on the stage for the world to witness, and finally, when Castro announced he was ending all private and religious education in the country, Heitor and Susanna secretly broke ranks.

Parodying himself, Heitor concluded, "Why go to all this trouble, if at the end of it . . . ?"

He joined *Unidad*. He had not told his wife the depth of his involvement in the underground. She believed his contribution to the counterrevolution was to make their house on this out-of-the-way block in Mendares available for an occasional *Unidad* meeting.

"We have had some successes recently," he said. "In the past weeks, our *petacas* have blown up several theaters across Cuba. Last week, incendiary bombs destroyed one of Havana's major department stores, La Época."

This was what Orta had referred to, that he did not blow up department stores.

"I can see on your face, Professor, you wonder what good comes from destroying theaters and stores."

"They're civilian targets. Why do you think that endangering civilians and burning their shops is political opposition? It's terrorism."

Heitor sipped his tea, a dainty counterpoint to the violent topic.

"Castro and his revolution intend to make all who oppose him powerless. There is no legitimate channel for resistance. No free press, no public rallies, no opposition parties. With those explosions, the underground accomplished three things. First, we told Castro that we exist and we defy him. Second, we told the United States we are here and we need their help. Third, and most important, we in the resistance got to tell ourselves that we indeed have teeth. That we remain men of power. True, it is just a shadowy, nighttime sort of power, planting *petacas* then cheering the rubble like vandals. We excuse the casualties of innocents as accidents.

We blame Fidel. But just like the revolution, there are hard truths that must be accepted to stage a counterrevolution."

Heitor did not wait for Lammeck's reaction. He stood.

"Now you will pardon me, Professor. I must go inside. Your young man needs to meet the others who will assist him. Please make yourself comfortable. Keep an eye out. We will be an hour."

Without ceremony, Heitor entered his house. Lammeck watched him go. The man cut no imposing figure; his gentle wife with long gray hair did not suspect him as a planter of bombs. Lammeck reminded himself that the vast majority of folks who made history were just ordinary people in extraordinary times. Most did not carry their names with them into the annals; their roles dissolved with them into dust. As Heitor had said, with luck, both he and Susanna would remain anonymous.

In the time Lammeck waited on the patio, the weather socked in. The sun disappeared behind tufted clouds, palm branches swayed noisily above the yellow house.

After thirty minutes alone, he grew bored and stiff sitting. Susanna did not come back outside to keep him company. He played a few hands of solitaire with the cards left on the game table. He might have liked more tea but felt he was not allowed inside the house to ask. Lammeck stood and pushed aside the iron gate. He walked out to the sidewalk, stretching his legs, gazing up to gauge the swirling weather.

He strolled up the block, moving north, toward the smell of the ocean. The meeting would be over soon. Lammeck would guide Alek to Avenida 5 and tuck him into a taxi. Then he'd walk the half mile to Miramar, back to his own porch to watch the clouds and the rising straits. He'd take care that he was not followed, would remind the boy to do the same. After that, he'd hear from Heitor only when to deliver the rifle, then not see him, Alek, or Rina again. He planned to stock up on groceries, cigars, and rum, to do what Calendar suggested, hunker down until Castro was dead by bullet or poison. His research at the archives would be on hold. He'd go home carrying secrets and skeletons locked in his head. He would wait to write them, expose them, as Calendar promised.

Just before turning back at the end of the block, Lammeck caught a curious sight. A fair-skinned woman, middle-aged and in an apron, ran from between two houses. She hauled behind her a little boy running barefoot. The woman came up the street at a dead sprint in Lammeck's direction, the child barely able to keep up. Her hair and apron flew around her, the child complained. She whirled to say something to keep the small one moving. Dashing past Lammeck, she glanced at him.

"*¡Salga!*" she called. Go away!

She and the child ran until they disappeared into a home across the street from Heitor's iron gate.

On the sidewalk, Lammeck froze.

What was happening?

He stared ahead, up the lane between the houses where the woman and child had emerged. Nothing. The neighborhood stayed hushed. A light drizzle began dotting the sidewalk.

Then Lammeck heard them.

Boots.

His spine sizzled. He muttered, "Soldiers." A spike of dread surged into his legs, demanding he get out of there.

He looked back at the yellow house. He remembered his promise to Rina, and he played out in his head what would happen if Alek were arrested and interrogated.

The first soldier came from between the houses, submachine gun carried at his chest. Five more soldiers followed. Lammeck turned, forcing himself not to break into a run. At a brisk pace, he walked the hundred yards to Heitor's house.

Lammeck didn't knock but pushed open the front door. In the foyer, he shouted, "Heitor!" He kept calling, moving cautiously down the hall. He assumed that somewhere in the house the men he'd come to warn carried weapons, so he advanced with care.

Through a swinging door, Susanna rushed into the hall. She held up both hands to intercept Lammeck, to quiet him.

Susanna came at him. "*Señor, señor,* please . . ."

"There's no time." Lammeck waved her away. The troops out- side were closing in and he had seconds to alert the conspirators, then get Alek and himself out. "Where's Heitor? Right now! Where is he?"

At the far end of the hall, a door flung open. Heitor stormed out.

"What is it, Professor?"

"A patrol. They might be on their way here."

Heitor snapped his eyes off Lammeck, to his wife.

She told him, "It could be just a routine patrol."

Heitor shook his head. "And it might not." He touched her wrist. "Go."

"No."

Heitor sighed. To Lammeck, he said, "I'll get the boy. Take your time. Do not run from this house."

He spun on his heels to disappear through the door. Lammeck looked at Susanna. With a sad smile, she said again, "Perhaps it's only a routine patrol." He watched her go out the front door, to take her station on the patio.

At the far end of the hall, the door opened. Alek emerged,

looking unsure. Immediately, Lammeck measured their chances. They could go out the front door, as Heitor instructed. The soldiers would see them leave. If the patrol was simply cruising the neighborhood as Susanna hoped, there might be no problem. But what if the soldiers were coming here? What if Alek and Lammeck were stopped and questioned? Two Americans in Cuba on the eve of an invasion which everyone on the island seemed to know was coming? There was no time for Lammeck to coordinate a story with Alek and Susanna for why they'd been in this house.

And what of the running woman and child? She knew or suspected something; what was her transgression that made her dart and hide?

If the soldiers were in fact headed for this house, then leaving it seconds before they arrived would be no protection. If this was just a normal neighborhood patrol, the best thing to do was stay out of sight, and trust Susanna to turn the armed men away.

Uncertain, but aware he needed to act immediately, Lammeck pivoted in the hall. Wordless, Alek followed.

Lammeck tapped on the door. Heitor opened it.

"We can't leave. It's safer to stay here."

Heitor nodded.

Inside, eight other men boiled in mounting alarm. Heitor shushed them. As Lammeck expected, each of the conspirators, Heitor, too, had reached for pistols.

The room was bare of furniture and decoration save for a long refectory table and a single chair. On the table a large map of central Havana was spread. Red and blue circles and arrows had been drawn across the sheet. Cigarette smoke purled in slow eddies lit by a single small window. All the cigarettes had been snuffed in an ashtray.

One of the unnamed Cubans pressed a revolver into Alek's hand. Lammeck wanted to insist the boy put it down, but kept

his silence; Alek was a Marine, and if a fight was indeed coming, they'd be better off with Alek armed than empty-handed.
Lammeck considered the knife in his waistband; it was nearly useless in this tight spot. He moved as far from the door as he could
get, to stand beside Heitor behind the table.

Heitor said, *"Todo será bien."* It'll be alright. "My wife will
persuade them that everything is normal. She is remarkably con-
vincing. She is a teacher, you know."

"I'm a teacher. And I'm about to shit my pants."

"You are an historian, as well, yes?"

"Yes."

"Well, now you must ask how much of history has been made
by men and women exactly in your condition, eh?"

Heitor put a hand in the middle of Lammeck's back to comfort him. He felt the sheathed knife tucked under Lammeck's
guayabera.

"Professor," Heitor murmured, "we are not so different, I
think."

Lammeck had no time to consider this or to reply. On the opposite side of the door, boots tromped over the tile floor. Susanna's
voice approached in the hall, trying to redirect someone. Lammeck
heard the word *sargento.*

The men in the room, Alek, too, tightened the grips on their
pistols.

One of the men whispered, *"La ventana."* The window.

Heitor nixed this idea with a harsh shake of his finger. He
pointed at his ear, then toward the door. *It's too late,* he gestured.
The soldiers would hear.

A voice beyond the door said, *"Abre esta."* Open this.

Susanna answered, *"Es sólo almacenamiento."* It's only storage.

One conspirator, who seemed to be the youngest, defied Heitor's
order. He slipped behind Lammeck to the window. Quickly, he

unlocked the frame and slid it partly open. The rising panes let out a hushed squeal.

The young man pointed at Heitor, then the window. He whispered, *"Jefe, vete."*

Lammeck scanned the room. To a man—even Alek—they curtly nodded. Each jutted his pistol at the door, to buy Heitor and their cause whatever seconds they could.

Heitor cast an emotional smile at his comrades. Then he turned to Lammeck.

In quiet words, not a whisper, he said, "Professor, please tell America to free our country."

With that, Heitor raised the window, careless of the noise. He stabbed a finger at Alek.

"You first. Go."

Alek tucked the pistol in his belt. He stepped quickly for the window, not conflicted about leaving. He lifted a leg over the sill, then slipped through to the ground outside.

Heitor rolled the map on the table into a scroll and shoved it into Lammeck's hands. "Go."

Heart pounding, Lammeck took the map and moved to the window. He shoved one leg outside. Twisting to squeeze his shoulder under the top panes, he saw Heitor overturn the heavy refectory table. Several men joined him in a skirmish line behind the table, pistols facing the door.

The door busted open. The heel of a boot flew into the room with splinters of wood.

Heitor Ferrer pulled his trigger. The bullet spooked the first soldier who jumped against the hallway wall. In awe, Lammeck hesitated on the sill, frozen until he caught sight of a second soldier in the hall behind Susanna drop to a knee and level his Czech submachine gun.

Lammeck tumbled out of the window. Landing awkwardly, he rolled to his back. Behind him, the panes shattered, showering him with glass and bits of mullion. He let go the map, shielding his face with his arms. Out of the opening came the *pows* of pistols and the vicious unmuffled ripping of automatic fire. Lammeck lay covered in sharp littered slivers, beneath the horrible clamor of screaming men and blasting guns. Then came the shouts, *"¡Me entrego! ¡No tire!"* The firing ceased.

Alek squatted against the wall below the window, glaring at Lammeck.

He hissed, "Get up, get *up!*"

Lammeck grabbed the dropped map and scrabbled off the ground. A shard in the grass sliced into his palm.

Together they ran through the backyard. The cut on Lammeck's hand had gone deep, his pumping arms spattered blood onto his pants and the pockets of his white *guayabera*. No perimeter had been set up in the backyard before the soldiers went into the house. *Where were they?* Lammeck wondered. He reached the tall bordering hedge. Tucking his head behind his arms, Lammeck bulled through the shrubs. Alek dove in right behind him.

They emerged into an alley, Lammeck wheezing and dripping blood. The boy was in much better shape. Lammeck's *guayabera* was torn, pants grass-stained, both blood-spattered.

"Holy cow," the boy panted. "Okay, okay. What do we do now?"

Lammeck didn't know. He was disoriented, badly frightened. He sucked air to slow his breathing. He needed to concentrate but the pinging pulse in his temples, the bellows in his chest, the throb in his right hand, all fought off his senses from returning. Behind him, beyond the hedge, the silence from the yellow house was ominous. What had happened to Heitor, Susanna, the conspirators? Lammeck could do nothing for them except survive and get Alek away.

North. They should go north, toward the ocean. They'd catch separate taxis at Avenida 5. If asked, he'd claim that he'd been assaulted, cut by a thief's knife. He was lucky to be alive and scared—true enough.

Which way was north? The wind.

He lifted his cheeks to feel the breeze, smell the salt. The direction revealed itself in the palms and oaks arching above the alley. Lammeck took a step, and saw the soldier.

The man was at the end of the alley, a block away but walking straight toward Lammeck and Alek. He carried his submachine gun at the ready, though there was no urgency in his stride. He raised his hand to hail them, to signal for them to stop where they were.

Instantly, Lammeck discarded his plan. He knew he and Alek could not wait for the soldier to approach, not with Lammeck disheveled, bleeding, and clutching a map displaying the details of Fidel's upcoming assassination.

But they'd all seen each other. To turn and go the other direction would appear evasive, because it was.

Lammeck did the only thing he could do.

He said to Alek, "Run."

The boy held his ground, a resolute glint in his eyes. He tugged the pistol out of his belt. Lammeck foresaw a disaster if Alek chose to shoot it out.

"Put that away," he commanded.

The boy did as he was told. Lammeck tore off down the alley away from the soldier, Alek behind him. He sprinted with every bit of his speed, which he knew was not much at his age and girth.

The gash in his right palm continued to seep, blood trailed off his elbow. He glanced over his shoulder; the soldier was gaining ground. Lammeck could hear the rattle of his submachine gun bouncing on his chest.

Alek looked back, too, at their pursuer. He shouted at Lammeck: "Split up!"

The boy lowered his narrow shoulders and crashed full bore through the hedge running along the alley, into some backyard to lose himself among the houses. Lammeck, with the soldier still hot on his trail, felt abandoned. Twenty yards ahead the alley dead-ended into an intersection. Lammeck was not going to outrun the dogged soldier. His only hope was to shake him somehow. He decided to hit the intersection, turn left, and seek an opportunity in that direction. Both he and Alek were on their own now.

Rounding the hedge, Lammeck's sandals skidded in the gravel. Entering the turn, he almost smashed headlong into the bumper of a fat, green, fin-tailed Cadillac idling in the narrow way. To stop himself, Lammeck propped his hands on the Caddy's wide hood, impressing a bloody palm print.

He had no time, the soldier was closing fast. Lammeck glanced through the windshield; a man in the front seat glared back at him. Lammeck scuttled down the length of the driver's side, to keep running.

The driver's door opened, blocking his path.

Felix got out.

Lammeck jerked in surprise. *Thank God,* he thought. *Felix can get me the hell out of here!*

On the other side of the Cadillac door, Felix asked, "What are you doing here, old man?" Under his left eye, Felix had the purple ghost of the bruise Lammeck had put there.

Lammeck blurted, "I'll explain later! Get in the car!"

The tall man reached across the door to grab Lammeck's torn *guayabera*.

Lammeck looked at the big hand clenching his sleeve. Felix yelled, *"¡Aqui!"*

The footfalls of the soldier sounded around the corner.

Felix took his eyes off Lammeck, to shout again to the soldier: *"¡Aq—"*

Lammeck drove the joined fingertips of his bloody right hand into Felix's Adam's apple, crunching the voice box. Felix finished his shout with only a quick, bug-eyed croak. With his left elbow Lammeck jammed inside Felix's grip on the *guayabera,* circling the arm with a swift release maneuver; in an instant he had Felix grappled and turned away. In the same moment, Lammeck swept the ancient four-inch blade out of its sheath at his lower back. He raised and lowered the dagger in an expert act of butchery, slashing hard across the top of Felix's right shoulder from the collar bone to the biceps to immobilize that arm. Felix crumpled in sudden pain; Lammeck held him up long enough to hack deep into the left shoulder, slicing the deltoids there to shut down that arm, too.

Felix sank to his knees. Lammeck scrambled around the car door, sheathing the knife. Blood had splattered on the Cadillac's green roof from Lammeck's bleeding hand. Felix's blue *guayabera* sprouted the buds of dark wings below both gashed shoulders.

Furious, Lammeck grabbed Felix under the armpits. He hoisted the man off the ground; both Felix's arms hung limp. He threw Felix onto the front seat, strong enough in his rage to heave him into a crumple on the passenger side of the bench. Lammeck flung himself behind the wheel, shifted into first gear, and popped the Caddy's clutch.

The big car hurtled forward, slamming shut the door. Lammeck hunched behind the steering wheel, barely seeing over the dash in case the soldier came out of the alley behind him with his machine gun lit up. He shoved into second gear, mashing the accelerator. Passing the intersection with the main alley, he ventured to sit up enough to look in the rearview mirror. The soldier stood behind the speeding car but had not brought up his gun in time to loose a burst. The boy had done the right thing, letting the car go without firing in a residential area. Lammeck spun the wheel to turn into the street.

Slowing to avoid attention, he took stock. Blood was smeared everywhere in the car, across the front backrest from Felix's torn shoulders, over the steering column from Lammeck's bleeding hand. The crisp tang of copper made Lammeck curl his nose. He fought the urge to retch. Turning to the window, he took a gulp of fresh air.

He laid his right hand in his lap, pressing the wound into his shirt to stanch it. He noticed Felix, eyeing him. Felix tried to speak, but only coughed out of his bashed throat. The man tried to raise his hands but neither hobbled arm would lift out of his lap.

Lammeck drew the black-handled knife again from its sheath. He reached across the seat to press the tip into the flesh beneath Felix's chin.

Lammeck didn't know the address of Calendar's safe house, the one Felix had kidnapped him to a few weeks ago. Right now he drove in Miramar. Calendar had said the house was in Luyano, south of the *centro,* near Havana Bay. He guessed that by now the soldier he'd eluded was describing to someone the Cadillac that had escaped him with the running *viejo.* There wasn't time for Lammeck to get lost in Havana's streets. A police hunt for this big green Cadillac with blood splashed all over it would begin very soon.

Lammeck shoved the edge of the knife higher under Felix's chin. He felt the scrape of the man's beard along the blade. Felix stretched his neck as if in a noose.

"I'll slit your throat. I'll dump your body in the street. *¿Com-prende?*"

Felix, afraid to nod with the steel at his skin, choked out, "Yes."

"Good." Lammeck heard his own tough talk. He watched a red pearl drip from his hand onto Felix's shirttail. He gave the knife a nudge.

"Take me to Calendar."

Felix, who could not raise his arms and would not move his head, rasped, "Left . . . at the corner."

CHAPTER FIFTEEN

★ ★ ★

Compromiso Street
Luyano
Havana

CALENDAR HAD NO UMBRELLA and he wore no slicker.
Drenched, he stood in the backyard of the safe house, puzzled.

Under a tarp drizzling rainwater was Felix's Cadillac. Calendar
recognized the car's big outline, the distinctive fins. What was it
doing back here? Why was it covered?

He approached, keeping an eye on the windows of the stucco
house to see if anyone noticed his arrival. Something was out of
whack; he kept himself ready to bolt in the opposite direction at
the first sign of trouble.

He reached the car and took one long, careful glance in every direction. Lifting the tarp beside the driver's window, he muffled a
curse.

Streaks of rusty blood were smeared across the seat back, finishing at twin dribbles and dark patches on the passenger side. More

blood had dried on the steering wheel and shifter. Calendar tugged the tarp back to check the rear seat. It was clean. Only the driver and passenger had bled. His gut tightened.

Calendar dropped the tarp. He looked one more time to the rear of the safe house. No one watched him. He mopped water out of his eyebrows. Time to go inside and get rid of the heartburn that busted plans always gave him.

The kitchen door was unlocked. Calendar quietly pushed in. No one greeted him. He grabbed a dish towel off a rack to dry his face, arms, and hands. Then he stepped into the living room.

Felix sat collapsed in a chair in the center of the room, head slumped to his chest. By his color, Calendar could tell he'd lost a lot of blood. Felix looked up. He was not tied to the chair. His arms hung lifeless at his sides. Crimson dribbled down his long forearms below his *guayabera*. Felix's big fingers dripped into red pools shining on the marble floor. Both shoulders had been badly gashed. Felix's wounds looked professionally done.

Calendar wasn't sorry for him.

In front of Felix stood Lammeck. The professor's right arm was also drenched in blood. Four others from Felix's cadre of gamblers stood behind Lammeck.

Weakly, Felix parted his lips to say something. Calendar spoke first.

"Professor."

Lammeck's bearded face seemed blank, as drained as Felix's.

Calendar beckoned him with a curling finger. "In the kitchen."

Felix dropped his head.

Calendar waited for Lammeck to shuffle past him into the little kitchen. He pointed at one of the men.

"Diego, get out back. Clean that car inside and out."

The mulatto started to object because of the rain, then shut his mouth. He stalked past Calendar to grab paper towels and a bucket from a closet. To the three others around bleeding Felix, Calendar held up a flat palm, for them to stand pat and do nothing until he said otherwise.

In the kitchen, Calendar added to his directions for Diego: keep the Cadillac under the tarp until dark, then drive it to Matanzas; strip the license plates and leave the car with the keys in the ignition. Diego accepted this, and with his supplies left out the back door into the downpour.

Calendar walked up to Lammeck, assessing him. The old man's arms and bearded face were scratched, but the right palm seemed his only serious injury.

"You alright?"

"Not by much, but yeah."

"How long you been here?"

"Maybe thirty minutes. I'm not sure."

Calendar poked his chin back toward the living room. "You do that?"

Lammeck nodded.

"I said you wouldn't see me again if things went well. I guess that was too much to hope for. Alright. Let's tend to that paw."

Calendar turned on the tap to warm the water. From a cabinet he took a white dish towel. "Turn around."

He put a hand on the professor's beefy shoulder to turn him. Swiftly, he unsheathed the bone-handled knife he knew Lammeck kept in his waistband. Blood clotted along the razor edge of the dagger. Lammeck made no remark that the agent held his weapon.

Calendar cleaned the knife in the sink, then used it to cut the towel into strips.

He put his hand out, snapping his fingers. The professor winced when his gash was pulled under the running tap water. Calendar scrubbed off the dried blood to look at the wound. He spread apart the flesh; a clean slice. Bandages and a month would heal it.

Calendar shut off the water. He began to wrap the hand with the strips. "What happened?"

Lammeck watched his hand being swathed. The corners of his eyes flinched.

"Heitor Ferrer set up a meeting with Alek. Soldiers raided it."

"Where's Alek?"

"He and I jumped out a window. Heitor gave me the plans." Lammeck sent his gaze to a crumpled scroll on the countertop, then back to his hand. "The soldiers kicked the door in. Everyone started shooting. I fell out the window into the yard and cut my hand."

Lammeck hadn't answered the question. Calendar tugged a cloth strip tighter, felt Lammeck flinch.

"Don't fuck with me, Lammeck. Where's Alek?"

"I don't know."

Calendar knotted the last of the bandage. He stepped back, leaning his rear against the counter. "You don't know?"

"A soldier saw us in the alley. Alek and I ran together for a block, then he jumped through a hedge into somebody else's backyard and disappeared. The soldier followed me. I rounded a corner and there was Felix in his car."

Calendar nodded. He picked Lammeck's knife off the countertop, examined the black handle. The heft of the old dagger was superb, perfectly balanced. He tested the blade's edge. Lammeck kept it honed.

"Calendar?"

"Yeah."

"Felix grabbed me. He yelled and tried to hold me for the soldier. He was the one who informed on the meeting."

"Seems that way. So you cut him up and brought him here."

"I didn't know where else to go."

"You did right, Professor, you did right. Nice job, by the way. Very skilled. Now, tell me something. What were you doing there? Far as I know, you weren't supposed to be at that meeting."

"Rina, Alek's fiancée—"

"I know who she is."

"I bumped into her last night at the Nacional casino, before I delivered the pills. She asked me to go with him. To protect him."

Calendar chewed on this for a moment. "Why would she ask you to do that?"

The professor slid out a kitchen chair and sat. He rested his wrapped hand across his lap.

"I don't think she knew what the meeting was for. But Alek tells her a lot. She was worried."

"I'll have a word with the boy when I get my hands on him."

"I didn't sit in on the meeting. I stayed outside."

"Have you looked at those plans?"

"No. What's going to happen to Heitor and his wife? The others?"

"They're already dead, or they will be. Executed. Questioned first. By the way, that's a good damn reason for you not to have been there. Now, because you're pigheaded, we have a problem. If Heitor's alive, he's in Castro's jail. He knows your name and that you're involved with Alek. The others know your face. And you know me."

"I'm aware of that."

"I'll bet you are. Anyway, we'll see how long they can hold out. I never met Heitor or his crew, but the *Unidad* guys understand the stakes. They'll buy us a few days. That's all we need. Now tell me about Felix. What's he said?"

"Only that he wouldn't talk 'til you got here."

"Good." Calendar patted the flat of Lammeck's long blade against his palm. "Good."

He took the bone handle in his right fist, locking eyes on Lammeck.

Something on his face made the old man stand from his chair, hold out his one good hand.

Lammeck said, "No."

"Don't worry, Professor." Calendar shook his head. "It ain't you."

He left the kitchen, fingers tightening on the dagger. The gamblers in the living room made no move to intercept him. Sensing the professor at his back, Calendar closed the distance, dropped his right shoulder, and drove forward.

He stabbed Felix with such force that the chair toppled backward.

The chair back hit the floor. Calendar landed on top of Felix, using the concussion to shove the knife all the way to the hilt. He twisted the blade, widening the channel for the blood to run out. The effort made him grunt, like winding a large and difficult clock. Felix's open mouth gasped. The man's pupils rolled upward. Calendar cranked the blade one more time and heard only an empty exhale, a dead bellows. He rolled off the body, listening to his own quick breathing now.

No one helped him off the floor. The gamblers stood back, gaping and waxen. When he stood, Calendar glared down at Felix, still in the upended chair. His arms were spread wide, an odd, welcoming sort of posture. Calendar set a foot on Felix's ribs, careful not to step in the blood-soaked cloth of the *guayabera*. He leaned down to yank the black bone handle of Lammeck's knife out of the man's heart.

"Get a rug," he ordered. "Roll him up in it. After sundown,

put him in the trunk of the Cadillac before Diego takes it to Matanzas."

He turned away from the corpse, holding the knife. Lammeck stood there, like Calendar, in bloody clothes. The two looked like slaughterhouse workers.

"Professor, you want to say something?" He heard the snarl in his own voice.

"What could I possibly say to you? What would make a difference?"

"Nothing."

"Then I'll just shut up before you tell me to."

Calendar walked past him into the kitchen. "I'm gonna shower and change clothes. When I'm done, I've got a car a few blocks from here. I'll drive you back to Miramar."

He dumped the knife into the sink. Let the professor wash it.

CHAPTER SIXTEEN

★ ★ ★

Luyano

ON THE DRIVE TO Miramar, Lammeck searched the agent for some mark of the killing. He saw none, no speck of blood under the man's nails, not a telling word or glance. The deed had been erased from Calendar, while Lammeck still wore ripped clothes sprayed with Felix's blood and his own; the murder weapon was in Lammeck's waistband. He considered this an example of Calendar's peculiar genius, the ability to have others appear guilty in his place.

The agent knew the city well. He took a backstreet route west to Lammeck's house. The rain kept the *Habaneros* inside; this was the first time Lammeck had seen the city without its vendors, strollers, workers crowding the ways, cobbled squares, and cafés. Damp, quiet Havana seemed aged and dingy.

Lammeck's bandaged hand pulsed with the windshield wipers, the cut started to sting. Calendar drove the Czech car without speaking. This annoyed Lammeck, who'd taken beatings, gashes, and scares in Calendar's service, then witnessed him commit a brutal killing. Questions swam in Lammeck's head: Where was Alek? Why did Calendar murder Felix without questioning him first? What about Rina? Was the sniping plot canceled? Would Calendar give the signal for the poison pills now? He watched the agent's face, asking nothing. Again, Lammeck submitted himself to Calendar's authority and threat, silently chafing at it.

At the house in Miramar, Calendar pulled to the curb. The agent seemed uncomfortable out in the open like this, given his penchant for gloom and alleys. Perhaps he allowed himself this indulgence because of the drizzle; Lammeck didn't inquire but opened the car door without acknowledging the favor of the ride. Calendar shut down the Skoda and got out behind him.

"What are you doing?" Lammeck asked.

"Just making sure."

"Of what?"

"Gimme me your key, Professor."

Lammeck handed it over. Calendar walked in the lead. Opening the front door, he strode inside. Lammeck moved onto the porch, out of the rain, and stopped.

Calendar paced through the house quickly, room to room. He stepped over cushions thrown to the floor, the spilled contents of closets and cabinets. The back door hung wide open. A glass pane in it had been smashed, broken bits reflected the day's gray light.

Lammeck entered and hurried to the kitchen. He saw what he expected. All the cabinet doors were flung open.

"It's gone."

"I was afraid of that," Calendar said, standing beside him.

The agent left the kitchen, headed for the front door. Lammeck followed. He watched Calendar go to the car and return with the rolled-up plans for the assassination.

Inside, Calendar stooped to pick a cushion off the floor, replaced it on the sofa, and sat. He spread the plans on the coffee table. "Well, we know the kid got away clean. Come over here and look at this."

"What're you saying?" Lammeck refused to move.

When Calendar did not look up, Lammeck answered his own question.

"You mean Alek's still going through with this."

"Looks that way."

Lammeck couldn't believe his senses. The whole operation had collapsed. There'd been a betrayal, a raid, shooting, arrests. People had died, the rest were in prison. And Alek was still going to try and assassinate Fidel on his own! This was incredible.

"Come over here."

"No. Calendar, for God's sake, the mission's blown."

"The kid doesn't think it is. Now come look at the plans."

"Why?"

"Because we gotta stop him."

This was the last thing Lammeck expected him to say.

"I thought you wanted Castro dead."

The agent ran a meaty hand over his crew cut, displeased with having to explain himself.

"I do. But nothing is gonna be allowed to implicate the United States. Understand me, Professor. Hidell is gonna get himself caught. There's no doubt about that. He might be a good shot, you might've taught him some tricks, but he's a lousy little spy. He'll talk, he'll show off, he'll do something stupid, and he's fucked. Or one of Heitor's boys'll break early, and a search will go up all over the island for the kid. Any way you look at it, he's got no backup support, no vehicle, no escape route, no alibi. He's headed for a Cuban jail. And the worst that can happen? He'll actually manage somehow to pop Fidel before he gets grabbed. That's an international incident the CIA seriously wants to avoid. At any cost. And I mean *any* cost. So you've got to find him. Fast."

Lammeck crammed a finger into his own chest. "Me?"

"The book on you is nobody in the world knows assassins better. So figure out what he's gonna try and head him off. He likes you, he trusts you. You're the only one who can bring him in with no commotion." The agent tapped the sheet in front of him. "Alek has this plan in his head. He broke into your house for the rifle. So he's still going after Castro. He thinks he can do this all by himself. Before that happens, you find him, you stop him, and you bring him to me in Luyano."

"Then what?"

"Then I hustle him and his Russian off the island before the invasion hits."

Lammeck recalled what he'd seen of Calendar only one hour ago, the last time someone crossed him up. "Like Felix?"

"Felix was a double-dealing piece of shit. The kid's just doing the job I gave him. Big difference."

"A few things first." It rang false that Calendar cared a whit about Alek and Rina. The CIA would sacrifice all of them without hesitation, to preserve plausible deniability for America. At any cost.

Calendar leaned back on the sofa, crossing his arms. "You know me, Professor. I'm not much for negotiating."

"What about Rina?"

"Leave her in the dark. If you have to, you can ask her questions but under no circumstances are you to let her know what Alek's involved in. If she can help you find him, use her. If not, she's off limits. Next."

"Why isn't Alek walking away? What's the CIA got on him?"

"You don't need to know that."

"I've got to figure out what's driving him. How badly he wants to go through with it. So I need to know what you've got on him."

"I've already told you, Professor. But you weren't paying attention. Think back." Calendar tapped the finger against his temple. "You asked me what I'd do if Alek didn't go through with the job. What'd I say?"

Lammeck flashed back to yesterday, in the early morning darkness. To Calendar's voice at the foot of his bed, a skulking shadow in the room. *You want to argue with me about this, Professor?*

Yes.

We ship the kid back to Mother Russia. And we let him stay there.

Lammeck recalled, too, Alek's plea in the scorched field.

Promise you won't try to stop me.

"He wants to come home. That's it, isn't it? That's what you're holding over his head. The U.S."

"I guess the workers' paradise wasn't all it was cracked up to be. Look, the deal's simple. The kid kills Castro, he gets a ticket back to America. He refuses, he rots in Russia."

"Does Rina know he wants to leave?"

"No. And you don't tell her."

"How long have you been setting this up?"

"A year and a half, since the kid landed in Moscow. We had other defectors we were watching. Hidell wasn't my first choice. He's too young. But, a couple months ago he went crying to the U.S. embassy that he wanted go home. The timing was right, so somebody in the CIA went to see him. Who knew he missed apple pie and baseball that fucking much? The deal got made."

Lammeck shook his head.

"That's not a deal, Calendar. It's extortion."

"Correction. It's politics. I figured you knew something about that. I thought you taught history up at that college of yours, but I reckon you just teach pattycake. Now, is that all you got for me?"

"What about Orta?"

"Let me worry about Orta. You just do the kid a big favor and get him back."

"If I find him, what do I tell him? Will you let him go home?"

The agent shrugged. "Sure."

Lammeck was getting better at spotting Calendar's lies.

"And, Professor, you got only twenty-four hours."

"Why so quick?"

Calendar jabbed a finger into the center of the map. "Because that's when Fidel's gonna be standing right here."

★ ★ ★

Miramar

Lammeck showered. Finding a first aid kit under the sink, he changed his bandage with a gauze roll. He picked clean clothes from the litter on his bedroom floor. Out in the backyard, he lit a cigar with the assassination plans.

In his bandaged hand, he held the scroll like a torch, letting it burn from the top down. When the fire singed too close to his fingers he dropped the page to the grass. He stood by until the whole sheet was charred, then ground it into black dust under his heel.

The rain had moved on. Far to the west over the straits, the cold front that brought the damp weather ended in a sharp line of clouds. More tropical blue was headed for Havana.

He turned to face the rear of his house. With the cigar in his teeth, Lammeck puffed and re-created Alek's steps.

Three long hours ago, the boy had crashed through the hedge.

He'd quickly realized the chasing soldier had picked fatter, slower Lammeck for his pursuit. Alek took off, not knowing if Lammeck would get away. After he was in the clear, the boy stopped running, found a still place, and reviewed his dilemma.

What did he know? That Heitor, Susanna, and the conspirators had been caught, some killed. Lammeck might have been captured, but Alek couldn't be sure. He had to guess that Heitor, his men, maybe Lammeck, anyone who survived the raid, would be in prison and interrogated before the afternoon was over.

What was Alek unaware of? That the meeting had been betrayed. That the informant was dead, at Calendar's hand. That Calendar knew what had happened and put Lammeck on his trail to stop the assassination, to bring Alek in. That there was an alternate plan, Orta the poisoner.

The boy had to make a decision: go forward alone, or try to get his girl safely off the island before someone cracked under pressure and gave him up.

Lammeck had run beside Alek with the plans rolled in his hand. The kid was smart; if Lammeck had been captured, he'd know the plans would've been, as well.

So he came here first, to Lammeck's house. He broke in for the duffel bag, before Castro's people could beat him to the punch. Once he had the rifle, the scope, and ammo in his hands, he could keep his options open.

Standing in front of the door, trailing smoke off his lips, Lammeck envisioned Alek as he smashed in the glass pane. Reach inside for the lock. Open and enter. Lammeck followed.

The boy was in a hurry. In the bedroom the mattress had been yanked off the bed. The closet had been rummaged, dresser emptied. In the living room and dining room, every drawer hung open. In the kitchen, the last place Alek searched, pots and pans were scattered on the floor. But nothing in the entire house, save for the back door window, had been broken. Alek, frantic over who might find him here—Lammeck or the police?—tried even in his haste to be considerate.

Lammeck traced Alek's steps out the back door, around to the front yard. With the duffel over his shoulder, the boy walked in the rain to Avenida 5 for a taxi. Where would he go next?

What were his needs? To stay out of sight until one o'clock tomorrow. He'd keep alert, to see if he was being hunted. He'd watch for added security around the platform in Parque Central where Castro was scheduled to observe the parade down Prado Boulevard. Alek would need food and shelter. He'd require money for that.

And Rina. Could Alek disappear with no word to her?

Lammeck kept walking away from the house. He figured he'd clean the disarray inside later, or never.

He headed south, to Avenida 5, for a taxi to the Nacional.

He climbed the hotel steps. A doorman pulled aside the large portal. In Lammeck's imagination, Alek walked in beside him carrying the duffel.

He would have stashed the bag, Lammeck decided. Left it downstairs at the concierge desk. I'll be right back for it, he'd say. He had no way to know if he was only minutes ahead of the police or the army.

Lammeck went to a hotel phone. The operator connected him. Rina answered.

"It's Mikhal."

Immediately, she sounded tense, troubled. In Russian, she urged, "Where are you? Where is Alek?"

She knew, or feared, something was wrong. Something more than just Alek coming home late from a meeting.

"Come downstairs."

The phone went dead.

Lammeck pictured Rina flying from the room, excitable, a teenager. Inside a minute, she emerged into the lobby as he predicted, rounding the corner from the elevator bank.

She collided with him, opening her arms for an embrace Lammeck had not anticipated. She hugged him hard, trembling.

"He came. I was not in the room, I was at lunch outside in the garden. He left a note. I have it." Her Russian gushed almost too fast for Lammeck.

Lammeck patted the back of her head. Above her, he glanced about the grand lobby of the Nacional, his heart pounding.

"Walk with me," he told her.

He steered Rina through the rear door to the hotel courtyard. Neither spoke until they were well outside, moving across the grass with the ocean, Castro's newly dug defense works, and the Malecón in view.

"Why didn't you come upstairs?" she asked.

"I don't know if your room is bugged."

"Ahh." She nodded, as if this made perfect sense. "You have a knife under your shirt. I felt it."

"I'm sorry. I do."

"No. I'm glad of it. I knew you would guard my Alek. I believe you have tried to do that. And you are safe, too. If you have a weapon, then you were the best man to ask. I am the one who is sorry."

Lammeck stopped only when they reached the middle of the lawn. He faced the courtyard. "Give me the note."

From her handbag, Rina produced a sheet of hotel stationery. Three lines of Cyrillic had been scribbled on it. Lammeck translated:

*I'll be back tomorrow afternoon. I'm OK. If I don't come,
you'll know why. Then get out of Cuba as fast as you can.
Wait in Freeport. I'll make it to you. I love you. A.*

Turning his back to face the Malecón below and the ocean beyond, Lammeck reached past the poison pill in his pocket for a
lighter. Distracted, he flicked the Zippo with his right hand; the action made the wound in his palm nip. He switched to his left and
lit the note.

He waited for the fire to consume it before releasing the paper.
Beside him, Rina gazed at the curling page on the grass, unconcerned. When nothing was left, Lammeck asked: "Was that why
he came back to the room? To leave you that message?"

"He also took his passport. And money."

Lammeck took out his wallet. He handed the girl eighty pesos,
keeping ten for his own taxi fare.

"Here. If you have to get off the island, this is enough to get you
a ticket and a hotel room."

"Thank you." She stowed the bills in her purse. "Mikhal,
please. What is happening? Tell me."

He set his good hand on her shoulder. The ash of the letter blew
away at their feet.

"Rina, you shouldn't be here. This should not have involved
you. It was wrong, but there's nothing to be done about it now
except to keep you out of it. I'll only say that something went
bad at the meeting this morning. Alek has run off because of it.
He might be in trouble. I don't think he's injured. I'm trying to
find him to bring him back before anything can happen to him. If
I can do that, I'll get you both out of here safely. If there's something you can think of to help me, tell me now. I don't have much
time."

The girl enfolded herself in her arms as though suddenly cold. She turned her back. "You have to stop him."

This jolted Lammeck.

"I didn't say anything about stopping him. Stop him from what?"

He took the girl by the shoulders, spun her to look him in the eyes. Her mouth was grim and set. Lammeck lowered his hands.

"What do you know?" he asked.

"Very little more than you. It is of no consequence. Only this I will tell you, you must find Alek. It will be terrible if you do not. Bring him nowhere but to me."

Her tone had changed from the teenage girl scared because her fiancé was missing, worried to be left alone and in the dark. Suddenly, Rina was a part of the mystery, another sticky thread of the web Lammeck struggled in. What could he do? Shake her? Threaten her? Refuse to help unless she told him everything? Lammeck wanted Rina's information, but he didn't need it or her reasons for finding Alek. He had enough of his own. As for where he would take Alek if he found him, Lammeck would not decide that now.

The boy had money and a passport. He'd warned Rina he was in trouble. Told her to wait only until tomorrow. He planned for Castro to be dead at one o'clock, with all Cuba in an uproar. If Alek managed to dodge the frenzy and manhunt that would follow, he'd lay low and come to her in the evening. If not, she'd know with the rest of the world the reason why. She should go from Cuba without him. He told Rina he loved her.

In a few hours the sun would sink into the ocean. Lammeck believed that Alek had no interest in sunsets, so he looked north toward America, the thing Alek wanted most. The boy hadn't shared with Rina that he was risking everything to return to his homeland.

Would she be heartbroken when she found out? Would she go with him? Could she? Would either of them live long enough?

Lammeck stepped away from the girl, to follow Alek again.

A half-dozen carpenters put finishing touches on the reviewing stand in Parque Central. The statue of José Martí oversaw their work. Lammeck moved closer to their hammering, trying to see tomorrow the way Fidel would.

The parade down Prado Boulevard was going to be an agricultural display. A thousand young men and women in straw hats and denims would march in lockstep, rakes and hoes over their shoulders, tractors pulling floats. Songs would be raised to the glory of the fields.

At one o'clock, Fidel will stand elevated on his platform, ten strides from where Lammeck now watched the carpenters. With his amazing stamina, Castro will stay on his feet for hours until the last farmer moves past. Then he'll give an equally long speech to the throng that will swell in the wake of the parade. Waving to his people, will he think of the *petaca* that might have been under his boots, set to blow him to pieces, prevented only when Johan's security force captured Sorí Marín? Will Castro feel safe, unaware of Alek Hidell?

Lammeck turned away from the banging carpenters. Royal palms ringed the perimeter of the small, paved commons of the park. He walked to the edge of Prado to lean against the fat gray trunk of a tree. He envisioned the sounds: bands marching by, diesel engines spitting fumes, shuffling boots, the voices of farmers in a mile-long column.

No one would hear the shot. Only Fidel and those standing near him, too late.

Lammeck pivoted back to the platform. He envisioned Castro down, clutching his chest. Blood pumps through his fingers. The others on the dais dive to his side to shield him and help, or they cower for their own safety, depending on their makeup. The parade does not halt, it's twenty blocks long, with a convoy's momentum. A murmur rises first among the onlookers closest to the platform, then screams break over the crowd. From Castro's prone body a shock wave goes out, as if from a blast. Every vehicle, marcher, every person in the crowd, presses forward to see or recoils in fear, to run in case of more danger. In seconds, the bottleneck of cars and legs becomes enormous. Guns drawn, police can do nothing with the chaos; they might fire into the air, adding to the panic.

Heads jerk in every direction, searching for the source of the bullet that felled Castro.

Lammeck gazed south, three and half blocks down Prado to *El Capitolio*. He knew from Heitor's plans that the distance was four hundred fifty yards from the cupola. Five hundred from the roof of the building's south wing. The boy would be allowed his preference.

For a shot on the platform behind Lammeck, *El Capitolio* was ideally chosen. The distance, the unfettered view. The building was abandoned.

Lammeck continued his imagined vigil on the boy. With the bullet away, Alek takes one last look through the 10X scope to see that Fidel is hit hard. Then he uses a rag to wipe down the Winchester 70. This requires only a few seconds. He rises, leaving behind everything, the gun with a busted bleach bottle taped to the barrel, the lone .308 shell casing on the floor, the scope, the canvas rifle bag. The rifle and Weaver sight are both American but they're also common, anyone can get them, that's why they were an excellent selection.

Tomorrow at *El Capitolio,* there will be people everywhere on the lawn. A Sunday, the grounds will be jammed with Cubans picnicking, playing ball, watching the parade, plus vendors selling them everything from sodas to lottery tickets. Because of the clamor of the parade, no one will notice the Winchester's report, suppressed by the plastic bottle.

The only ones who will know a bullet has been fired will be those close to the projectile's path. They'll hear only a supersonic crack when the round passes overhead, with no way to tell the direction it came from. These few will likely be the people in the crowd closest to the reviewing stand, those officials standing on it, and Castro himself, a millisecond after the bullet strikes.

Then, in his mind's eye, Lammeck lost sight of Alek. He didn't know how the boy got into the abandoned building—a vulnerable window, an old door easily jimmied, a flimsy lock that could be forced—but he was certain that Alek would retrace his steps off the roof. The boy will stay calm, his training coming to the fore. Unseen, he tries to make it down some ladder or steps, back inside the capitol building, then out to the street to join the pandemonium. He'll hope to use the turmoil as cover.

Alek, descending from the roof, will have no one to act as lookout. No car waiting to whisk him off.

This will be when he gets caught.

Someone will see him emerge from an off-limits door, or slide under a broken window frame. They'll yell for the police. Alek will run: He will not get far.

As Lammeck watched Alek sprint in his imagination, he saw something he hadn't anticipated. The boy got away. He rounds a corner, ducks into an alley, flies over a fence, and dodges pursuit.

Lammeck closed his eyes and repeated the scenario in his head again, and again. Alek fires, Castro falls, the boy makes his way off the capitol's roof, into the heart of a citywide turmoil. Half the time someone catches him, the other half he slips into the crush and disappears. It was possible, yes.

What if the boy *doesn't* get caught? What if Calendar was wrong to say his capture was a lock-tight certainty? Some *mala suerte* was needed for Alek to be seen. Certainly the boy could be careless with his mouth, but he seemed that way only with Rina. With Lammeck he'd been tight-lipped and wary. Alek was a quick learner, adaptable, calm behind the trigger.

What if Alek kills Castro and gets away?

Calendar must know this. The odds were against it, but Alek could pull it off.

Lammeck looked up into the palm tree rising behind him. Not a wisp of wind waved in the fronds. He searched the blank blue sky, lowering his gaze to the tops of the several grand structures surrounding Parque Central. Traffic puttered past, the carpenters finished their work on the dais. Across Prado, Lammeck caught sight of his waiter Gustavo serving an early dinner on the Inglaterra's crowded patio. The hotel's five-piece band struck up a tune. The first strollers began their pre-dinner promenade beneath Prado's shade trees.

Where was Alek in all this? Was Lammeck really expected to find the boy?

Or...the other way around. Did Calendar expect the boy to find *him*?

Lammeck fixed his eyes on the roofline of the empty *El Capitolio* a third of a mile away. The building was eerily similar to the U.S. Capitol, just as Johan had described it.

This would catch Alek's eye, too.

America was what Calendar held over the boy's head. Alek wanted desperately to go home, so much so that he would risk his life, become a killer, and hide it all from his fiancée.

Alek needed to stay out of sight, until one o'clock tomorrow.

Lammeck leaned away from the trunk of the palm tree.

Facing *El Capitolio,* he waved his bandaged hand high over his head, certain the boy was watching.

Like the crack of a whip, the air around Lammeck split open. Before he could blink, instinct drove him to the ground; adrenaline exploded in his chest. Lammeck scrambled to cover behind the tree. He pressed himself against the trunk's width.

He checked himself, knowing how panic could repress pain for seconds, a fatal wound could be a surprise. He found no blood. No tears in his clothing. He drew a breath, put his back against the palm tree. The gash in his right hand drummed from the sudden surge in his pulse.

Lammeck looked around. The carpenters on the platform had all stopped to gape at him ducking behind the tree. On Prado, cars flowed past, but people on the sidewalk had halted in midstride to stare at him on the ground, patting his pants and *guayabera* for holes. Across the street at the Inglaterra, Gustavo and his patrons peered curiously. All of them would have heard the supersonic snap of the bullet, perhaps without recognizing what it was. None gazed anywhere but at Lammeck.

He stood, keeping behind the palm trunk for several more seconds to compose himself. Then he rounded the tree, ignoring those people on the street who probably believed he was just some hypersensitive fool who jumped at a car's backfiring. Lammeck turned to the tree. He put his left index finger into the .308 bullet hole punched only ten inches above the top of his head. He knew that Alek was good enough, fast enough, the Winchester zeroed to precision at this distance, that if the boy wanted Lammeck dead, he would be.

He turned back to *El Capitolio* in the distance. He held his hands away from his sides, to signal to the boy: *Why?*

Standing like this, Lammeck projected himself again beside Alek on the roof of the capitol. He saw his own rotund figure through the Weaver's crosshairs, watched himself stretch out his arms. His chest itched with the invisible reticle he knew was stitched right now across his torso. Alek watched him closely. His finger lay off the trigger; he'd need to replace the busted bleach bottle at the end of the barrel before he could safely fire again. But he won't shoot, not yet. He doesn't want to kill Lammeck. He's trying to warn him.

What's he saying?

Don't follow me.

Why?

Lammeck glanced around. The carpenters had bent back to their chores, the folks on the sidewalks resumed their strolls. Gustavo at the Inglaterra set down the plates of food he'd held in midair.

Lammeck took a stride toward *El Capitolio.*

Alek sees him coming. With swift hands, he strips the plastic bottle off the barrel and tapes on another. He finds Lammeck again through the Weaver. This time he fingers the trigger.

The boy likes Lammeck. Looking for the duffel bag, he rifled through Lammeck's house with as much restraint as he could muster.

That was why Alek cut off conversations when they were shooting in the cane field and in the car. He didn't want to get to know the old man too well. In case he had to kill him.

Promise you won't try to stop me.

Lammeck had been warned once. He wouldn't be again.

Lammeck stopped walking.

Bud Calendar. He felt the agent's hand on this like a chokehold.

Motionless, still sensing the crosshairs painted over his breast, Lammeck calculated. Calendar's voice played in his head: *The kid's just doing the job I gave him.* What did that mean? That

Calendar had sent Lammeck after Alek, knowing the boy had in-structions not to be stopped? Did Calendar actually set Lammeck up to be murdered?

Again the question; like a maypole, everything revolved around it: *Why?* Nothing made sense. What would Lammeck's death at Alek's hands accomplish for Calendar and the CIA?

Maybe Lammeck was overthinking this. Alek was just scared and reacted, yes? Lammeck shook this notion off. The boy's warn-ing shot had been dead center into the tree trunk. It was coolly done. Alek had followed Lammeck through the scope the whole time he was in the park. The boy knew Lammeck would come. The instant Lammeck waved, telling him *I know where you are,* he'd fired.

Lammeck nodded, certain the boy saw the gesture. Alek wasn't afraid, not a bit. He was determined, and he was deadly.

Lammeck took a step backward. This signaled to the boy: *Take your finger off the trigger. I'm not coming.*

What now? Lammeck couldn't advance. The boy might shoot and choose not to miss. If he didn't fire on Lammeck, he'd just dis-appear from *El Capitolio*'s roof before Lammeck could reach him. Lammeck would have no chance to find him, not before tomorrow at one o'clock. The boy could relocate in any of the other buildings around the park with a clear path to the reviewing stand. Calendar knew this. What was the agent's gambit?

What if Lammeck simply took a taxi back to Miramar and waited events out? Alek would gun down Castro. The CIA didn't want that. Or did they? Lammeck had no idea at this point. He was certain only of two things: that he'd been sent into harm's way with-out knowing the reason, and that Calendar would take a vengeful view of Lammeck's failure. The rest was confusion and guesses.

His thoughts jumped to Rina. What was she angling for? Why did she really send Lammeck to the meeting between Alek and

Heitor? What did she want Alek to do? Kill Castro? Or come back to her, as she claimed? Did she want Lammeck dead, too? Nothing added up. But now that a bullet from her fiancé had passed so close to his head, Lammeck was much keener to know Russian Rina's role in the mystery.

He gazed south down Prado, over the tops of traffic, trees, hundreds of unwitting Cubans, to the deserted capitol. At that moment, Alek was surely fixed on Lammeck's magnified image. Both men, old and young, gazed and wondered at the other's next move.

Lammeck focused in on Alek as tightly as the boy must be on him. What was the boy thinking right now?

Was he concerned that Lammeck would turn him in to the police? No. He had no reason to think that. Lammeck had Heitor's assassination plan; if he was going to betray the mission and come for Alek in force, he wouldn't be standing here alone and unprotected. Besides, how could Lammeck turn the boy in without incriminating *himself*?

Why was Lammeck here in the first place, instead of Calendar? Did Alek sense betrayal by the agent, the same way Lammeck had? That's why he fired high. Alek won't play along, not unless Lammeck pushes him to it.

Will the boy sleep on the capitol's roof tonight, since Lammeck knew where he was? No. Alek still had the Cuban's pistol. Lammeck recalled the flinty look on the boy's face this morning in Heitor's back room, again in the alley ready to square off against the pursuing soldier. Alek would use the sidearm to defend himself. So he would leave, spend the night in a hotel, and avoid a confrontation. He'd find another sniper's nest before sunup. He had the money he'd grabbed from the Nacional along with his passport.

In that instant, with the speed of the bullet that had slammed into the tree, Lammeck was struck by a new question. It staggered him into another backward step.

The answer was just a detail, harmless and small. But it might finally begin to unravel the web tightening around him.

He raised both palms, flattening them to Alek's eye. He pushed his open hands slowly downward, indicating: *Stay calm, son.*

He had to leave Alek for now. Lammeck stepped into Prado, and hailed a taxi.

She answered the phone on the first ring.

"Don't move," Lammeck told Rina, forgetting for the moment to speak to her in Russian. "I'll be right up. What room?"

"Six twelve."

He pushed inside the room even before the girl could swing the door fully open. She staggered backward slightly. Lammeck shoved the door shut behind him.

He switched to Russian. "Is this room bugged?"

"No."

"You checked?"

"Yes."

"You know what?" Lammeck said, striding to the center of the room. "I don't care if it is. If somebody's listening in, I want them here. Now."

"No one is listening, Mikhal."

The view from the room's picture window caught his eye. The long ribbon of the Malecón lay dry this afternoon. The Florida Straits shone blue as an opal. A mile and a half east from the hotel, old Havana rose craggy and sunny. Lammeck moved closer to the window. There, in the heart of the city, rose the dome of *El Capitolio.*

"You would know if they were, wouldn't you." It wasn't a question.

Rina sat on the edge of the bed.

"Yes."

Lammeck turned to her.

"You are upset," she said. "Tell me what happened."

"I found Alek."

The girl jerked on the mattress. She kept herself from rising off it in excitement. "Where is he?"

"He's exactly where he thinks he's supposed to be. But I'm not going to tell you."

Rina opened her mouth to object. Lammeck cut her off.

"He shot at me."

"Oh my God—"

"Why would he shoot me, Rina?"

She stared at Lammeck. "I don't know."

Lammeck glanced around the room, angry. The wound in his hand ached. He felt the impulse to snatch a lamp off a table and smash it. Or to unsheathe the blade at his back.

"Yes, you do know. You're CIA."

Again the girl shook her head. Her eyes had calmed. "No. I am not."

"When are you going to get tired of lying to me?"

"Mikhal, believe me. I am not CIA. What I am will make no difference in our situation."

"Fine. If it makes no difference, tell me."

The girl kept silent. Lammeck turned for the door.

"Screw this."

"Mikhal"—she stopped him with her voice—"I am KGB."

He spun at her, doubling at the waist as if the disclosure had punched him in the gut. He groped for a chair and fell into the seat.

"You're what? You can't be."

She drew herself up at his response, looking almost offended. "Why not?"

"Because...because the CIA's trying to *kill* Fidel. Christ, that's the only reason Alek is here. But you've been playing along the whole time. If you're KGB, wouldn't you be trying to stop him? Russia doesn't want Castro dead!"

"I must stop him, because he has gone on his own. But before, when he was part of a plan, no."

"Part of a plan?" Lammeck's hands came to his temples, as if to contain the eruption of revelations going on inside. "You're saying this is a joint operation? KGB and CIA *got together* to assassinate Castro?"

"CIA recruited Alek. KGB learned of the plot. As you have seen, Alek is quite the talker, quite in love with playing at espionage."

"In other words, he told you what the CIA was planning."

"I'd only known him a week. I informed my uncle, who is a colonel in the MVD. He reported this, of course, to KGB. Instead of interfering, KGB contacted CIA and gave the idea its approval. They insisted only that I be allowed to come. To support and encourage Alek. And to make a report. Alek came to me and suggested a sudden vacation to Cuba. I agreed, of course. Five days later, we are here."

"Does Alek know? That you're his KGB case officer?"

"He does not. There was no need for him to know. And I see no need for him to know in the future."

"Unbelievable."

"Not so much, Mikhal."

"But why? Why on earth would the Soviet Union want Castro dead? The man's leading a Marxist revolution south of the United States. This is the best thing that could happen for Khrushchev. For the whole Communist movement worldwide."

"Think for a moment." Rina mimicked Lammeck by touching a fingertip to her own temple. "Have you heard Fidel say one word that this is, in fact, a *Communist* revolution in Cuba? No. He has never made a single public proclamation to this effect. Yes, many of his programs are socialist. And yes, he has accepted much assistance from the Soviet Union. But Fidel continues to hedge his bets. He still believes he might somehow make a rapprochement with the West. Even now, on the eve of an invasion."

Lammeck listened, amazed. Rina did not sound like a nineteen-year-old girl. Why had he forgotten she must have been raised in the cant of Communism? She spoke like a seasoned ideologue.

He asked, "You know about the invasion?"

"The world knows about it. The only questions are when and where. Your CIA believes that if Fidel lies dead when the rebels land, the people of Cuba will rebel against the revolution. Or chaos will follow his killing and there will be little organized resistance. KGB believes otherwise. Once Fidel is gone, other, bolder leaders will step forward. They will beat back the exiles. They will fortify the revolution in Cuba. And they will do this as dedicated Communists."

Lammeck reeled back in the chair. He felt a flash of empathy for Fidel. How did the man stand a chance, when both his enemies *and* his benefactors wanted him murdered?

Rina continued. "Ask yourself. Who is next for power in Cuba after Castro?"

Lammeck considered. "Most likely his younger brother Raúl. And, of course, Che Guevara."

"Exactly. The brother has long been an open member of the Communist party. Che is a committed Marxist revolutionary. Both are more radical than Fidel. Both would make more willing partners for the Soviet Union. Fidel will serve Communism far better as a martyr than a leader. That was the decision in Moscow."

"So Castro must die."

The girl wagged a finger. "Do not scold me, Mikhal. For separate reasons, the same decision was made in Washington. There are no saints here."

Sitting on the bed, the girl crossed her arms. She was pretty and still so young. Now that she'd been candid, Lammeck's bitterness at being lied to subsided. He feared for Rina's future; being a conspirator in an assassination plot rarely led to happiness or even a long life, at least not so far as Lammeck's study of the subject could show him. He thought of the attempt on Lorenzo de Medici's life in Florence in the late fifteenth century. Lorenzo was marked for death by the archbishop of Pisa and two leading Italian bankers, all competitors for power. The Florentine crowd, when they heard of the unsuccessful assault on Lorenzo, reacted swiftly to protect him, torturing, hanging, and slaughtering almost a hundred men, many of whom had nothing to do with the plot. Adolf Hitler destroyed the lives of tens of thousands in an ever-reaching circle of vengeance for any attempt on his life or his minions'. In 1793, after young Charlotte Corday murdered Jean-Paul Marat in his Paris bathtub, the spasm of retribution that erupted out of the French Revolution cost thousands their lives, many more than a living Marat might have sent to the guillotine and gallows. Again, Lammeck grew aware that his inclination to protect both Rina and Alek might prove hopeless. It pitted him against the great tide of historical events. He thought of the boy at his post on the roof of the empty capitol.

But Lammeck had grown tired of being a pawn. He'd come here for answers.

"Why did you send me to that meeting with Alek?"

"Just as I have said, Mikhal. To keep an eye on him. Besides, I'm aware that the Cuban underground can be brave but sloppy. I know you to be wise and seasoned. You are smart and, most important, you are loyal." The girl paused. "As I have told you many times, I do love Alek. I intend to marry him when we return home. So I sent you to do exactly what you did."

Lammeck had no way of telling if this was the whole truth. She was KGB. He expected every word she uttered to be nothing more than the opening steps into a labyrinth of facts, lies, and veiled intent. On his own part, he chose not to tell her of Alek's desire to leave the U.S.S.R. That was a personal matter between the two of them, and he'd leave it there. Besides, it made him feel less of an imbalance, keeping another secret from her.

She asked, "You said Alek shot at you. Tell me."

Without relating any clues to the location, Lammeck described the incident. He'd guessed correctly where Alek was hiding, then waved his arm. The next second, Alek put a round into the center of a tree inches above his head.

"He was telling you to go away."

"Or he'd kill me."

"I think so, yes."

Lammeck was stymied. "It doesn't make sense, Rina. What's he gain by gunning me down in the street?"

"He wouldn't have done that on his own. He was following instructions."

Lammeck waited her out.

"Calendar," she said.

With that name, everything Rina claimed to be true was driven home. She wasn't just playing spy, the way Alek often did. Rina wasn't pretending to be KGB. She knew Agent Bud Calendar.

"He sent you to be shot by Alek, Mikhal. I do not know why. But the CIA is playing a separate game from what the rest of us are."

Lammeck glanced out the window. Dusk began to feather over

the straits, a deep indigo beautiful above the aqua waters. Silently, he thanked Alek for allowing him to sit here to see it.

"One more question, Rina. I need you to trust me right now, and not ask what I'm going to do. Just tell me what I want to know, don't ask me why, then do what I say from this point on. Alright?"

The girl studied him a moment. Lammeck stood out of the chair to step into her embrace. Against his *guayabera,* he felt her head bob in assent.

"You said Alek came back here. That he took money and his passport."

"Yes."

"What nationality is his passport? Soviet? Or American?"

"American."

Lammeck held her for a long minute. He looked down at the top of her head.

When he let her go, he turned for the door. "Stay where I can find you."

CHAPTER SEVENTEEN

★ ★ ★

Miramar

INSIDE OF AN HOUR, Lammeck restored order to his house. He showered, careful to keep his bandaged hand dry. He changed clothes, then foraged in the kitchen for a quick meal of chicken and beans.

On the back porch, he lit a candle, as if expecting a woman. He'd missed the sunset while cleaning and showering, catching only glimpses through his busted rear door. He sat in his wicker chair with a glass of *añejo* from a fresh bottle. On the table beside the vacant, matching wicker chair, a second empty glass waited.

He sipped, observing the candle flame. The fire stood straight, with barely a waver. What breeze there was came out of the southeast. Tomorrow it would whisper at Alek's back, causing him to make only a little adjustment.

One by one, stars attended the darkness over the straits. As he did whenever he looked north across the water, Lammeck thought of America, so close. Unseen, his country pulled at him. He tried to sense the tug Alek must feel after two years of self-imposed exile in the Soviet Union. So close, the boy must be thinking too, gazing north from his high roof. Just pull a trigger, a tug of the finger, a few millimeters.

Lammeck's mind wandered into the house, to his briefcase and research. He hadn't touched either in a week. He didn't know if his work had all been for naught, if his book on Cuba would ever be written. He couldn't even guess what the next several days would bring. A dead Castro and international chaos? A living Fidel and a rescued Alek? A dead boy? An invasion that returned America to power on the island, or a landing that would be ruthlessly swept off the beaches? Lammeck finished the last swallow of rum in his glass, and poured another.

He waited two hours on the porch, resisting the lure of the bottle beyond the initial tumblers. Enough time passed for Lammeck to fetch another candle. Of all the guesses he'd made, the one he had the most faith in was proven correct a minute after the new candle was lit and the old stub tossed into the backyard.

"Should I have brought flowers?" Johan asked, coming around the corner of the porch.

Lammeck responded by reaching for the rum bottle. He poured first into the clean glass set out for the police captain, then for himself. The two raised their rums with nods to each other and drank.

"I'm sorry," Johan observed, "that I have not been to visit in a while. But apparently you were expecting me this evening."

"I thought events might bring you around."

"Yes, well, it seems that your sources are beginning to rival my own." Johan looked at the busted back door. "I heard, for

instance, that your house was broken into. I did not know, however, that you had been hurt." He indicated Lammeck's hand.
"Did you cut yourself on glass?"

"Yes."

"Let us hope you will heal quickly. You'll find that the salty air
this close to the ocean will speed the knitting of your wound."

"I'll try that, when I get time."

"Have you been busy, Professor?"

"Johan."

"Yes, *amigo*."

"I'm very tired. I've had a day. Honestly."

"I understand. How can I help?"

"I want to ask you some questions."

Johan tipped his glass toward the candle flame, as if both were
evidence. "With respect, Professor, you are in possession of facts
or at least presumptions about me that led you to believe I would
come here tonight. As it turns out, you were correct. So, since you
are in my homeland and I am not in yours, and I am a policeman and you are not, I will for the first time in our friendship insist
on something. You will tell me what *you* know. But first, *por
favor*—" Johan waggled his emptied rum glass.

The flame between the two men jittered, casting nervous shadows across Johan's round face. It didn't matter to Lammeck which
of them asked and which gave answers. He figured the destination
would be the same tonight. He refilled their glasses, then said,
"The *Unidad* meeting this morning in Mendares."

Johan's eyebrows went up. The rest of his features remained
composed.

"Why would you admit to me that you know this? Have you
gone suicidal, Professor?"

Lammeck kept his tiredness and impatience out of his voice.
"Heitor Ferrer."

Johan touched fingertips to his chin, making no reply. He seemed reluctant to let Lammeck go farther.

"Captain, please," Lammeck said. "Heitor Ferrer. His wife, Susanna. Four others from the underground. Are they dead?"

Johan stared down into his rum glass. He swirled the brown liquor, considering.

"No. Heitor was wounded but he will live a while longer. We have them all in La Cabaña."

"Has anyone talked?"

"Not yet."

Lammeck made himself move past images of Heitor, his wife, and the others being interrogated. Nothing in the captain's tone hinted at what they were suffering inside the prison.

"I was at the meeting. When the army showed up, I jumped out a window and got away. That's when I cut my hand."

The policeman's face didn't flinch. "What were you doing there, Professor?"

"You don't know?"

"What I know is irrelevant at the moment. All that matters is what you choose to tell me, and what I choose to do about it."

Earlier, waiting for Johan to arrive, Lammeck had concocted a dozen lies for this moment. All of them were elaborate, all flawed. He raised his glass for a quick fortification of rum. He swallowed deeply, then set the tumbler on the table.

"I'm involved in a CIA plot to assassinate Castro."

Glumly, Johan smiled. "It seems everyone is, these days. Go on."

"I came here for research, just as I told you. Then the CIA approached and said they needed me because of my background in weapons and assassination theory. They just wanted me as a courier, nothing else."

Johan nodded. "Plausible deniability. The watchwords of your CIA. What did they promise you in return?"

Lammeck described the offer, authorship of the secret American history of Castro's assassination. He did not mention the exiles' coming invasion. He said nothing of Calendar's identity, or of the agent's threats of ruination and death if Lammeck failed to cooperate. He didn't produce the poison pill in his pocket.

"I did what I was told. Then they kept demanding more."

"Deals with the devil," Johan said, "often end up that way. Continue."

Lammeck felt the understated lash of Johan's disapproval. He figured he deserved it, and his situation was a testament to that.

"Before I knew it, I was told to train and evaluate a kid, a sniper the CIA brought in."

"The defector Hidell."

Lammeck swallowed his surprise; Johan's admission confused him for a moment. He hadn't expected candor from the policeman. But the two of them were playing a chess game of information; pieces were withheld and pieces sacrificed.

"I was at the meeting, with Alek. Your troops raided it."

"We received a tip this morning."

From dead Felix, Lammeck thought.

He said, "Heitor started shooting first. The soldiers opened up with automatic weapons. Alek and I barely got away."

"I should not be surprised, Professor. I have watched you dodge the sea along the Malecón. I know you to be nimble. You are a reluctant man of action, but a capable one. You received a cut hand. Was Hidell injured?"

"He wasn't when I last saw him."

"And where was that?"

"Running through the alley behind Heitor's house."

"I ask again. What were you doing at the *Unidad* meeting?"

"I was there to watch out for the boy."

"It seems that is, indeed, what you did. Were you there at the CIA's request?"

Lammeck chose a lie. So far, there was no need to move Rina onto the chessboard. "It was my own idea."

Johan rose from his wicker chair, carrying his glass with him. He stood before Lammeck's door, inspecting it.

"So when you returned home from your ordeal, your house had been broken into. What was missing?"

Lammeck eyed the candle, without a breath of air to stir it. "You know what was taken."

"Do I?"

Lammeck decided to test his authority now that he'd switched to the offensive.

"Have a seat, Captain."

Johan complied, sinking with a middle-aged sigh into the cushions of the chair. The candle flame quavered at the disturbance.

"You know Alek has the rifle. And you know he intends to kill Castro with it. What you don't know is where and when."

Johan's gaze fell on Lammeck without wrath.

Lammeck continued. "You've got a Marine-trained sniper armed and loose in Havana. But there's no manhunt out for him. That tells me one thing."

"What is that, Professor?"

Lammeck drew a long breath. He judged the move to the knife at his back using his left hand, should he need it.

"That you're in on it."

Johan's sole response to the accusation was to knit his fingers over his belly.

"I know who called in the tip this morning. He's been murdered, by the way, so don't look for any more out of him. He told you about Heitor's meeting and about Alek. What he left out was me. He didn't know I was coming. I was the wild card."

"You remain a wild card, Professor."

"When I jumped out the window, I took the assassination plans with me. I memorized them, and I burned them. A soldier chased me, but there's no way he got a good enough look to identify me. So, I figure until Heitor or one of his men breaks, no one knows I'm involved, unless they're part of the plot themselves. When you showed up here tonight, I knew for sure."

Johan shifted in the wicker chair, setting his chin on his balled fist, a patient posture. "And what do I want from you now that I am here, incriminating myself?"

"You've found out I'm trying to stop Alek."

"And I don't want you to do this?"

"No."

"You're saying I want Castro dead. That I am part of Heitor Ferrer's plot and I'm attempting to keep you from foiling it. Do I have this correct?" The policeman sounded skeptical.

"Yes."

"And why exactly are you trying to stop it? If, as you say, we are both part of a plot to kill Fidel, why not let the boy play it out?"

"Because I've been told to stop him. By CIA."

"Ah, yes. One would like America to stake out a position and stay there. It would make it so much easier for the rest of us. Tell me now, what do you want from me? You lit a candle, you poured me good *siete*. You are courting me for something, Professor. What is it?"

"I want you to help me bring Alek in. Quietly, with no bloodshed. I want him and his fiancée put on a boat and off this island."

Johan twirled a finger beside his head. "And poof, like magic, none of this ever happened."

"Right." Lammeck clamped his teeth against his growing annoyance and concern. Had he been wrong about Johan? Or was he dead on target? The policeman refused to give him a clear signal. "It never happened."

"But why should I do this, if I am so keen on the death of Fidel? Why not let Alek Hidell do what he came here for? Because you will expose me as a conspirator?"

"If I have to."

Johan laughed openly. "If that is true, do you assume I will allow you to continue living?"

Klaxons rang inside Lammeck now. His left hand slid off the arm of his chair, inching behind him.

"Do not reach for your dagger, Professor. At the moment, you are in no danger from me. Likewise, I wish to be in none from you."

"You've just threatened my life, Captain."

"I said that merely as a way to illustrate the many holes in your most improbable thesis."

"There's no other explanation for you coming here tonight."

"Really? Have you considered that perhaps the tipster this morning did in fact mention you by name, and I came to investigate, to see if you might know something to help me find this dangerous boy, so he can be brought in, as you say, without bloodshed? What if that is why there has been no manhunt so far? Or maybe I've been doing my job as Fidel's protector and already knew you had an involvement with Hidell and Heitor, and I've simply chosen to bide my time confronting you over it, until this evening? Worst of all, what if tonight was nothing more than a social call to a friend I have not seen in a week, and you have just blurted out that you are up to your neck in a plot to assassinate my country's leader?"

The candle shuddered on Johan's words. Lammeck considered snuffing it, but needed the thin light to help him gauge Johan.

"It seems," the policeman remarked, "that your conclusions are quite flimsy. I'm disappointed in you. I considered your deductive skills more keen."

"Alright," Lammeck said, having danced long enough on the end of Johan's flippancy. "Try this for keen. Hidell's passport."

The policeman untwined his fingers over his waist. He sat erect in the chair.

"Ah, you restore my faith. Proceed."

Lammeck knew that, despite Johan's claim to the contrary, his life depended on his being right.

"Something you told me when we first met. Ever since diplomatic relations between the U.S. and Cuba were broken off in January, your office has been in charge of approving all visas from Americans. You said you personally approved mine."

"An action I have not regretted until now, my friend."

Lammeck ignored this. He rose and strode past Johan, looking down, aligning his argument.

"Alek's a defector to the Soviet Union. That means he's given up his U.S. citizenship. He should *not* have an American passport. But he does. That tells me Alek Hidell isn't his real name. When the CIA recruited him, they ginned him up a passport for him to come to Cuba. And they did it in record time. Five days before leaving Minsk, he didn't even know he was coming."

"And I," Johan said mildy, "am implicated because I approved the visa for Alek Hidell, an American visiting Cuba?"

"And for his Russian fiancée. There couldn't possibly have been enough time for you to see any visa applications. CIA came to you. They told you to let those kids in. And you did it."

Lammeck stood in front of Johan. The policeman sat motionless, gazing up at Lammeck in the sallow glimmer of the candle.

Lammeck asked, "Do you even know his real name?"

"No. I don't want to. And I suggest you make no inquiries either. As a rule, the less we know, the better. Do you intend to expose me, Professor?"

"Like I said, only if I have to."

"And as I said, what makes you believe you will wake up to-morrow? If I am, as you claim, able to take part in the murder of my country's leader, what would save *you* from me? That we have shared a few rums together? You cannot be that naïve."

"What makes you think I won't cut your throat right here?"

"I am safe from you, so long as you need my help. You want to bring our young mystery marksman in without a fuss. I must as-sume you need my assistance because this is something you cannot do on your own."

"I tried this afternoon. He shot at me."

"Really? You found him?"

"Yes. From a distance."

"You are clever, Professor, as advertised. But the boy missed. Is Alek that poor a shot?"

"Believe me, it was on purpose."

Lammeck returned to the wicker chair. The woven fibers squealed under his weight. Lammeck poured fresh rum into both glasses.

"Thank you," Johan said. "This is all too intricate for me to consider with a sober head."

The two drank. They'd gone through half the bottle, but they were both large men, accustomed to liquor and crossing swords.

"Now tell me why I should do as you ask," Johan said, swirling the rum, contemplating it. "Tell me, please, why I should not have you disposed of, then do as I see fit with Alek Hidell."

"Because you're a CIA asset, just like me. And I've been told to bring Alek in, alive and under the radar. I expect that means you've been ordered to do the same."

The captain's hand stilled on his rum glass. The liquid settled in the bottom, dark and moody.

Johan set aside his rum. He stood. Lammeck tensed, but the policeman made no alarming move.

"Walk with me, Professor. I am beginning to feel cramped under this roof of your porch, in the light of this little candle. I want to see some stars and hear the ocean. Then I will tell you everything."

If Johan meant him harm, it could come anytime, anywhere, in the shadows along the coast road or here in his own house.

Lammeck stood with Johan.

"Alright. Thank you."

Johan smiled again, this time real and cheerless.

"Do not thank me."

Johan was unhurried. He strolled gazing at the constellations overhead. To their right, the flat water mirrored the silver light of the moon not yet above the horizon. No waves, no wind came off the straits. Tomorrow would dawn placid and warm, a perfect shooting day.

Johan drew a deep, appreciative breath. "I smoke too many cigars," he said. "I sometimes forget how to breathe such marvelous air as we have in Cuba. Is this your first time in Cuba, Professor?"

"Yes."

"Ah," the policeman said expansively, lifting his arms into the night to encompass the sea and constellations, "then you missed it. What a wonderland Cuba was. I am fifty-six years old, I suspect very close to your own age. I was born only seven years after the Americans threw the Spanish off the island. I grew up under your flag. Under American prosperity. But under Spanish culture. What a mix that was. Beauty, leisure, wealth, indulgence. My parents were land owners. We had money, influence. And I, Professor, I had it all. You understand?"

Lammeck did not. He was raised in New England in an academic tradition. Everything around him, family, weather, was cold.

"We embraced everything American, you see, because it served us well to do this. We had these lovely houses here against the ocean, and the mansions on the Malecón, we had fields of sugar and pineapple. We gambled on horses and cards, baseball and regattas. We had no conscience. We did not let ourselves see the millions"—Johan aimed a stern finger at the ground to make his point—"*millions* beneath us." He patted his breast pockets, looking for something that was not there.

"See, Professor, how dissolute I am? I cannot take a walk without a cigar. I cannot remember my youth without shame."

Lammeck didn't know what to say. This was confusing; Johan spoke not like a man plotting to murder Castro, but like a revolutionary.

"Many in my class left. They went north. To you. They took their money and bought new houses in a new country. They complain that Fidel has stolen from them. And they are right. Fidel stole the blindfolds off our eyes. He paraded in front of all of us the poor and uncared for, three of them for every one of us in our luxury. He showed us the corruption of American business and the American Mafia. Yes, Fidel is a thief. He took my comfort. He returned me only disgrace. And rather than escape to America, I chose to stay and wallow in it."

Johan said no more. Lammeck let long moments pass measured only by their heels on the gravel shoulder of the road.

After almost a block walked in silence, Lammeck prodded.

"But he's become a dictator, Johan. You know this. The revolution's more about Castro's personal power and vision than the needs of your people. The abuses are mounting up. Freedoms are fading. I can tell you from thirty years of study, that's when the people strike back. That's when leaders get assassinated."

The policeman tilted back his head, again to the stars.

"Just as you say, Professor. And it is heartbreaking for many of us who believed in Fidel. Even sadder, in the last year he has begun leaning too far toward the Soviet Union. That cannot be good for Cuba. Not with America, so strong and jealous, only ninety miles to the north. It has to be stopped."

Lammeck said, "Calendar."

Johan tucked his hands in his pockets. He kicked at a stone, sent it skittering up the road. To their right, the moon took its first white peek above the horizon.

"Yes. Calendar. An excellent example of American can-do attitude, that man. He believes there is no one he cannot kill."

"Johan."

"Yes, Professor?"

"Please. There's not a lot of time left for any of us. You, me, Alek, even Fidel. Tell me."

The policeman halted. He took a languorous look around at the deserted houses along the ocean lane, perhaps recalling more oblivious days when he was not so burdened. He pivoted, to return along the direction they had come. Lammeck fell in beside Johan.

The policeman said, "I was told very little about the plot. I did not know about Heitor or his plans. Nor was I informed of your participation, Professor. I accepted your visa in December for the reasons I stated. I appreciate your book. I wanted to meet you. I befriended you for those same reasons. Your involvement was purely happenstance, some opportunism on the part of our clever Agent Calendar once he learned you were coming to Havana."

"Lucky me."

Johan continued. "Two weeks ago, the CIA notified me that I was to order entry visas for the American Alek Hidell and his Russian girl. I did as I was asked."

"When did Calendar tell you Alek was a sniper brought in to kill Fidel?"

"He didn't. I already knew."

Lammeck stopped walking. He reached his good left hand in front of Johan's midriff to halt him, too.

"How? How did you know?"

"Because that was the plan all along. This is what you do not know, my friend. *La clave*." The key.

"Tell me."

"I would never have agreed with the CIA or anyone to take part in a plan to assassinate Fidel Castro. Never."

"But Alek . . ."

"The scheme did not call for Alek Hidell to shoot Fidel. I would not have consented to that. Your young American sniper was supposed to be captured before he could have the chance to shoot Fidel. As I said, that was the plan. It remains so."

Lammeck reeled under this revelation. He caught himself bending forward at the waist, jaw slackened. He straightened, but could not contain an involuntary gasp. Johan nodded, plainly pleased that Lammeck had been so fooled.

"The tip I received this morning," Johan said, miming a telephone receiver in his hand, "came at Calendar's direction from his informant. Immediately I ordered the raid. I fully expected to arrest Heitor, his conspirators, and Alek Hidell."

"Then I . . ."

Lammeck faltered. Johan finished the sentence.

"Yes, you, Professor. You were the 'wild card.' You were where you were not supposed to be. You somehow managed Hidell's escape, along with your own."

Beneath the gauze of his hand, Lammeck closed his eyes. Johan was snapping all the threads of the web Lammeck had believed were enclosing him. Now he was tumbling on those loose strands, falling onto another, larger, and totally unexpected web.

It was *Calendar* who told Felix to inform on Heitor's meeting.

That's why he'd knifed Felix so fast, to prevent the man from saying anything.

Rina. She sent him to the meeting. Lammeck had trouble believing her reasons. For love of Alek? To protect him? Had she known Heitor's house was going to be raided? Lammeck started to say her name aloud to Johan, to have her brought into the open. He checked himself. He had no reason for withholding the girl other than a need to cling to some piece of the puzzle that was his own.

He lost track of how long he'd stood in front of Johan with his wrapped hand to his forehead, staring up. He lowered his arm and his eyes. "Why arrest Alek? I can't figure, it doesn't make sense."

The policeman resumed the walk back toward Lammeck's beach house. Lammeck lagged a step, slowed as if tethered to his confusion. Johan waited for him to catch up.

"I have learned in my life as an investigator, that if something does not add up, there is always something I do not know. Perhaps your experience as an historian has been similar?"

Lammeck bit back his impatience for answers. Without facts, he perceived only danger, a growing sense of suffocation, and the time ticking away toward one o'clock tomorrow.

"You say the boy fired at you this morning," Johan said. "Why would he do that?"

"It was a warning."

"Certainly. But think. What else does it tell you?"

"He doesn't know he's not supposed to kill Fidel. He thinks the assassination plot was real."

"And he believes the plot remains intact, even after the raid on the meeting."

"That's right."

"It should also tell you that Hidell was instructed by the CIA to kill anyone who came after him, anyone who might stop him from his appointed task. That person was you, Professor. But, because of the boy's affection, he chose not to put a bullet into you. Now he is out there with a high-powered rifle, on his own, ignorant, and very dangerous."

"What are you saying? That I was supposed to die? That the plan called for me to be *dead*?"

"Yes. Of course. Consider. The object of this entire exercise is for the defector Hidell to be arrested. But what has he done to be put in jail? Hmm? Nothing, except attend a *Unidad* meeting that he cannot be placed at. Why not? Because you got him out of the house before the raid. The underground members we did arrest are understandably reluctant to inform on him. Heitor and his men, even his wife, are quite stubborn. This resistance was expected. *Unidad*'s opposition to Fidel is quite fierce. So Hidell had to do something quickly to draw the attention of the police."

"That's why Calendar sent me to find him. So I'd get shot."

"Once CIA learned you would be on the island, they developed this role for you. Calendar realized, and I agreed when he shared the idea with me, that Hidell might somehow evade arrest when the time came. We did not, unfortunately, envision your hand in that. But we did forecast this contingency, as unlikely as it seemed. The plan required a sacrificial lamb. Someone we could send to find Hidell. And, may I say, you were perfect. An expert in assassinations and weaponry. In human nature and the game of betrayal. Once Alek arrived, Calendar instructed Heitor to put you and the boy together, first at the Tropicana, then for a day of shooting, under the pretext that you would train and evaluate him. The real purpose, of course, was for the two of you to bond. You also formed a closeness with the Russian girl on your own. By attending the meeting and saving Hidell, you triggered your part. Calendar sent you forth with the story that you were to bring the boy in for his own safety. You reasoned out where he was hiding, you tracked him, and you drew his fire. Just as we knew you would. Alek's orders were to dispatch you. When he did, he would give me the basis to initiate a massive manhunt for him. To do so without reason, without Alek taking some overt illegal action, would draw attention to my own connection to the CIA's plot. You see the logic? The chain of events?"

Lammeck's mouth had gone bone dry.

"I was a sacrifice. The whole time."

"Yes. You and Alek both. But the two of you simply will not comply. It is frustrating."

Lammeck couldn't stop his left hand now from unsheathing the knife at his back. He stood with it pointed at Johan. Did Johan have confederates, were they closing in?

"Put that away, please." Johan showed Lammeck his back, making himself vulnerable. "We are alone, Professor. Only you, me, and Calendar know anything about this arrangement. It falls to you and me to fix it. At this point, we need each other quite a bit."

Lammeck held his ground, trusting little about Johan. The policeman strode away, pausing only to call over his shoulder, "Do come on!"

Without sheathing the blade, Lammeck stepped alongside Johan.

The captain continued: "You know where he is, Professor. And you know what he intends. I control the police. We cannot do this without each other." Johan indicated the dagger in Lammeck's left hand. "I see you still do not believe we must work together. Have I lost your friendship because I said you were to be killed?"

"Amazing how that gets in the way."

Johan shrugged. "It was not personal."

"It wasn't you in Alek's crosshairs."

"Fine. This is becoming tiresome. Where is Alek Hidell?"

"Not until you tell me the rest. Everything."

"I have told you enough for you to follow Calendar's orders. He said for you to bring the boy in. We will do that just as you desire. Quietly. Now where is he?"

Lammeck put the knife away under his *guayabera*. He stopped walking. He watched the policeman take several more steps before stopping. Johan turned his big girth slowly.

"What'll happen to Alek after he's arrested?"

Johan drew close, bringing his face near to Lammeck's.

"He will not survive the arrest, Professor. He cannot be allowed to say he is working for the CIA."

Lammeck leaned in more, until his nose almost glanced Johan's.

"Then fuck you. I'll let him kill Castro."

Lammeck watched Johan's features curdle. It pleased him to see the policeman lose his composure, for the captain to hoist his arms over his head and shout: "For the love of God, man! Why do you *care*!"

With both hands, Lammeck shoved Johan. The policeman stumbled backward, awkward and shocked. Lammeck's bandaged palm smarted. He ignored it.

"Because I promised I'd bring him back. That I'd get him out of Cuba."

Johan gathered himself. He tugged down his ruffled shirt to smooth it. His voice and demeanor showed no anger with Lammeck.

"Who did you promise? The girl?"

"Yeah. The girl."

Johan's big chest heaved once in a long sigh. He stepped forward, to come next to Lammeck again.

The moon had risen enough to cast a milky pallor on the coast road. Lammeck looked at the side of Johan's face, pasty and Spanish in the pale glow. Johan spoke.

"You, Heitor, and *Unidad*, even Alek himself, you all think he is the prize. The boy is not. He never was. It's the girl."

"Rina? Why?"

Instantly, Lammeck knew.

He said, "She's KGB."

"Yes."

"You're not trying to kill Fidel. You're trying to turn him."

"Against the Soviets, yes."

In a flash, all the strands of the plot wove together. Lammeck could not break free, but for the first time, he saw how they connected.

"You set Alek up to be involved in Heitor's assassination plot. Calendar alerts you to the meeting. You raid it. You make sure Alek dies during the arrest, or soon after in prison to shut him up. Then you grab Rina. You make her admit she's KGB."

Johan added, "She, of course, attempts to blame the CIA. But Alek, a defector to the Soviet Union, is dead. Her accusations would ring a bit hollow."

"Then you tell Fidel the Russians are out to kill him. They're not his friends anymore."

"As you say, Professor, such a thing does get in the way."

Lammeck let the plan sink in.

Johan pressed on: "Fidel will surely reconsider his attachment to Moscow after this news. He might even rekindle relations with America. Such a turn in events might even forestall the coming invasion." Johan poked a finger into Lammeck's shoulder. "Weeks ago, you said to me that Fidel was a classic candidate for assassination. Fidel knows this, as well. But, certainly, he does not suspect the range of his enemies includes Russia. That knowledge would sober him."

Lammeck strode sluggishly beside Johan.

"So you understand?" Johan asked. "It was an excellent plan."

A plan that the girl sniffed out, Lammeck thought. That's why she sent him along, to foil it.

Lammeck shook his head. "I'm not going to tell you where Alek is."

"Professor, there is no one left for you to salvage." The police-man's voice remained level. "Heitor and his people will be executed soon. They were conspirators, all of them. We will find Alek and he will be silenced. Then Rina will be swept up, to be taken to the *paredón* when we are through with her. The only one you can save is Fidel. And if you do not, I assure you there is nothing I can do to preserve your life. That is, if Calendar does not take it before I do. I'm sorry, but you make it necessary."

They'd reached the edge of Lammeck's yard. He stopped and faced Johan, indicating to the policeman that their negotiations had reached an end.

"I'm offering a trade, Johan. I'll tell you where the boy is. What he's going to do and when. In return, you let me bring him in alive. I want him and the girl safe off the island."

"No."

"You'd rather see Castro dead?"

"No. I'd rather jeopardize my own security by calling out every policeman and militia on the island to find Alek Hidell before sunup. I'd rather break every bone in Heitor Ferrer's body until he signs a document implicating the boy. I will do the same to the Russian girl until she admits she is a pawn in a KGB assassination plot. Then I would rather see my nation chart a path back to free-dom alongside the United States, instead of in thrall to the Soviet Union. I would rather see you dead before Fidel."

Lammeck stood stock-still.

"I see. Johan?"

"Yes."

"If you get your wish, if you get the freedom you're so willing to torture and kill for, you'll find your society has no more use for men like you."

"I pray for that day, Professor."

"There's something else."

"What would that be?"

"Does it make sense to you that I would stand here and refuse to tell you where Alek is? Even though, as you've put it so plainly, I risk my own life?"

"No. It does not."

"Then you've got to figure," Lammeck said, "there's something you don't know."

CHAPTER EIGHTEEN

★ ★ ★

April 9
Old Havana

A BASEBALL ROLLED NEAR Lammeck's feet, thrown by one child, missed by another. He stopped to pick the ball up and toss it back to one of the brown boys playing on the lawn. He tugged the panama hat farther down over his eyes and followed Jorge, the old janitor.

The man looked to be at least seventy, dried and cured as tobacco. He wore denim overalls and work boots without laces. He spoke in a nonstop fusillade of Spanish, mumbling about his sore feet, his vast family, and the rundown condition of his abandoned building.

The front of *El Capitolio,* the grand steps, grass, and sidewalk, were filling with picnickers and tourists angling for position to view the parade, scheduled to start in thirty minutes. Every bistro table of the Inglaterra and the other hotels and restaurants along Prado was jammed. Lottery salesmen in their tricornered hats wove through the crowd hawking numbers, buskers played flamenco for coins dropped in open music cases. The weather turned out as Lammeck had predicted, balmy with a trace of breeze from the south, blowing straight up Prado toward Parque Central. Lammeck did not tell Jorge he was hiding inside the crowd and beneath the panama. The old janitor did not know why he'd been instructed to guide this fat American to the capitol's roof.

The man led Lammeck to the rear of the building, the side facing Avenida Industria and the Partagas factory. Lammeck had not smoked one cigar all day yesterday, a horrible day. He promised himself a fat *robusto* as a reward if he was alive at dinner tonight.

Jorge led him out of the swarm of *Habaneros* carrying coolers and lawn chairs for the parade. The old man continued his gripes about bunions while traipsing down a set of forgotten steps to a basement door. A rusty lock and chain held the door shut. Jorge produced a key ring so large it would have been humorous on another afternoon. Uncannily, the old man selected the correct key out of the jangling mass, slid it into the lock, and pulled the chain away from the door handle. Without looking back at Lammeck, he pushed on the door and stepped inside.

Lammeck followed, shutting the door behind him. He stood on a raw concrete floor, beneath a low ceiling teeming with what seemed like miles of ductwork, asbestos-wrapped pipes, and bare electric wires. Jorge quieted. A reverent look eclipsed his face. Lammeck pulled off his panama to better see the metal jumble inches above his head, to keep from bumping it. He hung the hat on a protruding gauge that read no pressure. Jorge lapped a hand around one iron pipe he seemed to recognize. He shook his head, gazing at the pipe as if at a cold, dead friend.

"Jorge," Lammeck said, "with respect. There's not much time."

The old janitor took down his hand. He wiped dust on his overalls.

"There's not much anything," he said. "Come."

Again Lammeck followed, past boilers the size of cars, banks of fuse boxes, through doors marked *No Entre. Peligroso.* Jorge turned on lights, pulling the chains on bare bulbs along their path. The old man continued to grumble through the cavern.

When they reached a set of stairs, Jorge tramped up the first steps with his unlaced boots. The sound of his shoes on the concrete echoed through the stairwell. Lammeck put a hand on the man's bony shoulder.

"Jorge, please. We must make very little noise from this point on."

The janitor showed a peeved face. "Why? Is someone else in here? There's not supposed to be anyone here. Only me."

"I know. I'm going to bring him out. But we can't let him know we're coming. So, quit talking while you walk. And stop walking like a horse, alright, *viejo*?"

Jorge narrowed his eyes, deepening the creases around them. "How did he get in?"

"A broken window, a rusted lock. I don't know, perhaps someone gave him a key."

"Is there danger?"

"There might be."

"Good," the old man said, turning to continue up the steps. "My fucking life is so boring. Let's go."

With lips clamped and a lighter tread, Jorge rose up the stairs, emerging with Lammeck into a long hallway of vacant offices.

"We'll stay out of the concourse and the atrium," the janitor said. "I know ways to the roof the rats don't know."

"Don't take too long," Lammeck said, tapping his watch. Twenty minutes remained before the parade began.

"I said rats, *Americano*," the janitor snapped, "not pigeons with wings. Come on then, no dawdling."

Jorge ducked into one of the many doors in the hall, uncovering another narrow staircase. Lammeck followed, rising and huffing with the effort, amazed at the spryness of the weathered janitor. The stairs ran for three flights, then dead-ended. Jorge referred again to his extensive key ring to exit, once more knowing the exact key. He looked back to see Lammeck propped against the wall, wheezing. The old man made no comment beyond a shake of his head.

The door opened to a balcony looking down from four stories above the vast lobby of *El Capitolio*. Sunlight from a circle of windows in the dome overhead lit the expanse. White pillars, marble floors, balconies, statues standing in alcoves; the building exuded power, emasculated by Castro when he enthroned himself elsewhere. It seemed excessive to abandon such a structure, to leave it for Jorge because it reminded Castro of America. Lammeck was stunned gazing into such colossal silence. Nothing he'd seen on the island brought home to him like this empty palace the chasm between America and Cuba.

Jorge referred to his key ring, unlocking the door at the end of the balcony. He said, "This will take you to the roof."

"How many other doors lead up here?"

"Seven."

"Are they locked, as well?"

"If they are not, someone else is responsible."

"Pardon. Go down now, Jorge. Leave the building. Come back in an hour and lock everything behind me. Please walk quietly. If you see anyone inside, run from him."

"You do not need my help, *Americano*? I was a soldier. I can handle myself. You can barely catch your breath."

"I'll be fine. I have to go."

"Do so with God, then."

The janitor left the balcony and sank out of sight down the stairwell. Lammeck faced the door leading outside, hand on the doorknob.

Tasting fear in his throat, he faltered.

Beyond this door, Alek was armed. He not only had the Winchester but the pistol the *Unidad* man had put in his hand yesterday with the soldiers bearing down on them. The boy would not quit this roof or his mission willingly; he'd made that clear. Was he watching, did he know Lammeck was coming his way?

Fear was not the main reason Lammeck didn't open the door and stride into the open. He hesitated under a new wave of uncertainty—that saving the boy, in fact, was the right thing to do.

Should he reconsider? Or should he let Calendar's plan play itself out? What if the CIA was right? What if exposing the KGB's assassination plot would actually turn Castro away from Russia, back to relations with the U.S.? What if the invasion could actually be called off? Why shouldn't Lammeck throw Alek and Rina into the chasm, to help bridge it? Wasn't that an important enough goal in history to warrant sacrifice? Heitor, Susanna, and countless others had already been tossed in; could Lammeck, one man—an academic out of his element, playing spy—really block the plots of the CIA, defy Johan's police?

Or should Lammeck continue with his own scheme? Rescue Alek and Rina. Save himself. Save Castro.

Could he actually stand in the path of history with his hand jutted out, telling it to stop?

Let's see, he decided.

Lammeck pushed the door open. He stepped onto a gravel and tar surface. Above him, against an unbroken canopy of blue, the great dome of *El Capitolio* rose another six stories. Alek would not be up there. The boy didn't need the extra height for an excellent view of the park and the reviewing stand on Prado. Also, he'd be very exposed up there; the dome was visible across the entire old city. Days ago, Lammeck had told him not to climb too high, it would slow his escape.

Jorge had brought Lammeck to a parapet above the north wing. The roof stretched almost a hundred yards to its tip. The expanse was broken by a small, concrete blockhouse and several mechanical apparatuses for heating and cooling the building below. Lammeck didn't expect to find Alek here. The boy was more likely to have set up on the capitol's south wing, for the added cloak of distance from the park. Lammeck checked his watch. Eleven minutes to the start of the parade. He made his way around the great base of the dome, careful to ease his footfalls on the gravel.

Moving, Lammeck peered over the rampart to the milling crowd below. A thousand Cubans brightly dressed sat in lawn chairs sharing baskets of food and bottles, anticipating the parade after church. Even from this height Lammeck could hear children and music. *Unidad* had chosen an ideal perch for Alek's shot. In ten minutes, the people's festive din would be added to the parade's marchers and bands. The pop of a suppressed rifle report might go completely unnoticed.

Lammeck trod to where he could see out over the south wing's roof. It was identical to the north. He paused to scan for any sign of Alek: the Winchester on its tripod, the spotter's scope, trash from a meal, a blanket. Lammeck saw what he expected, nothing. The boy was no fool. Few Marines were.

Lammeck swept the area one more time with his eyes, his skin prickling. What if he'd guessed wrong, and Alek was not here?

His watch read seven minutes to one.

Lammeck turned his back and descended the ladder. At the bottom, his concerns about Alek's whereabouts were put to rest. The boy came from behind the blockhouse, jogging, pistol raised in a two-handed grip.

On reflex, Lammeck held his hands in plain sight. He said, "I'm not armed."

Alek said nothing. Arriving, he took one hand from the revolver to turn Lammeck roughly by the shoulder, spinning him to face the ladder. He searched under Lammeck's *guayabera* to check for the knife. Lammeck had left it behind. Quickly, the boy patted Lammeck, armpits down to his ankles.

He set the barrel of the gun against Lammeck's temple.

"Goddammit, I told you not to follow me. You alone?"

"Yes."

"You didn't think I'd be watching? You sounded like a herd of sheep coming up them stairs."

"We were supposed to be rats."

"What?"

"Never mind. It was just an old janitor. He's gone, and I'm by myself. Can I drop my hands?"

"Yeah. Turn around."

Lammeck pivoted. Alek backed off with the revolver.

"Why did you shoot at me yesterday?"

Agitated, the boy yanked the gun back up. "For the same damn reason I gotta shoot you today."

Facing the pistol, Lammeck did not raise his hands this time. "Because Calendar told you to do it."

"That's right. Anybody who came after me, except him. What the hell am I supposed to do? Calendar's got me by the shorts. Why didn't you just stay out of it? Damn it, I made you promise, 'cause I knew this would happen."

"But you didn't hit me. Why not?"

" 'Cause you're a nice fella. I figured you were smart enough to take a hint. The point was for you to leave me alone and let me do what I gotta do. I hoped I didn't have to kill you for you to get the message."

"Oh, believe me, I got it."

"But I reckon I was wrong, 'cause here you are."

"I had to come back, Alek."

"Why? Why in the hell did you come up here, *knowing* I had to do this?"

"Because I made another promise."

"To who?"

"Rina. She made me swear I'd bring you back to her in one piece. I'm pretty sure that includes me coming back in one piece, too, son. Put the gun down."

Alek eased the revolver to his side. "What'd you tell her?"

"That you're working with the CIA. That you're a spy. Nothing else. You tell her what you want. But you'll have to get back to her to do it. I'm here to take you."

Alek shook his head. "I can't do it. What about Castro? What about... what about me going home?"

"Calendar sent me to come get you. He said the deal stands, you can come back to the States."

"He sent you, and he knew I was supposed to shoot you?"

"Yes."

"That's fucked up."

"That's CIA. Don't ask me to explain it. But I am sure of one thing. Calendar doesn't want you to shoot Fidel."

"Why not?"

"Because if you do, you'll get caught."

At this, Alek turned to stalk away. The boy led Lammeck to the concrete blockhouse. Tucked behind the structure, where Lammeck could not have seen it from the parapet, was the Winchester 70. The rifle rested on a stack of crates topped by a rolled blanket. A plastic bottle had been taped to the end of the barrel, just like Lammeck had taught the boy. Next to the gun, the spotter's scope stood on its tripod. On the ground, the duffel bag lay open.

Alek let Lammeck come within a few strides of the rifle, then stopped him. Lammeck looked down the black length of the barrel. There, five hundred yards away in an unhindered view, on the rim of Parque Central, was the wooden riser decorated with bunting and the lone star Cuban flag. Lammeck glanced at his watch. Two minutes to one. He saw people standing on the viewing platform. Prado Boulevard was lined five deep with spectators. Barricades halted traffic on all the side streets.

Alek said, "I don't need Heitor or any of his guys. No one'll hear the shot. I found me an open duct to throw all this stuff down into. After Castro's hit, I head down the stairs, sneak out a side door I busted into, and start running with everybody else. I run all the way back to the Nacional and get on a boat with Rina off this damn island. The rest of y'all can sort it out from there. I'm done."

Lammeck wanted to touch the boy's thin shoulder, to make a firmer connection than words. But Alek was out of easy reach, he'd already put himself on the verge of murder.

Lammeck said, "I told you. Calendar's called it off."

The boy pursed his lips. "Calendar wouldn't have sent you with that message. He'd know I'd shoot you."

"You're being set up, Alek. Calendar told me the Mafia was going to take the blame for you shooting Castro. But that was a lie. You're the fall guy. That's all I can tell you right now. If you kill me and shoot Castro, the police will arrest you. I guarantee it. And you'll be dead sixty seconds later."

"That isn't gonna happen. The police aren't gonna catch me."

"Yes, they will."

"How do you know?"

"Because I brought them with me."

Angrily, the boy stomped forward. He rammed the nose of the revolver into Lammeck's chest over his heart.

"You *what*?"

Lammeck started to explain. Alek cut him off with another jab of the gun into his breast.

"I can't trust none of you sons of bitches."

Lammeck stared into Alek's wide eyes, white with anger and hurt.

He kept his voice even. "I had to make a deal, for your life. If you come down with me peacefully, there'll be no trouble. You pull that trigger"—Lammeck looked down at the revolver pressed into his *guayabera*—"and you're a dead man. Rina will never leave Cuba either. You shoot me, you kill all three of us. I'm the only one who can get you both out of here alive."

"What about Calendar? Why didn't he come get me himself if he didn't want me to shoot Castro?"

"Don't ask me to explain it. You just have to trust me."

At that moment, beyond the ledge of the capitol's roof, the first clamor of the farmers' parade rebounded from Prado below. The crowd roared, diesel tractors cranked up to pull floats, and the first strains of a brass band arced around Alek and Lammeck, who stood with a gun between them. The boy could pull the trigger, muffled against Lammeck's chest, and no one but them would hear it.

Lammeck took a chance. He set his bandaged hand over Alek's wrist, shoving gently down. "Please, son."

The gun stayed firm. "No. You're a liar."

Lammeck licked his lips. "Will you give me one more minute?"

"What for?"

"Because I know who you will believe. Look through the scope. Down at the reviewing stand."

Skeptically, Alex waved the pistol. "Stand over there. If I hear one piece of rock on this roof move, I shoot."

Lammeck backed off to give the boy room. Extending the gun at Lammeck, Alek turned his face to lean over the spotter's scope. The boy did not focus or adjust the eyepiece; the magnification was already trained on the reviewing stand.

"What the hell's going on?"

Lammeck said nothing.

Alek raised his eyes to him. "I said what's going on?"

"Keep looking." Lammeck indicated the scope. Alek breathed hard out of his nostrils, losing patience, drowning in confusion. He returned his eye to the scope. Lammeck stared into the dark circle of the barrel pointed blindly at his belly.

In seconds, Alek's hand holding the pistol at Lammeck wavered.

"He's not there, Alek," Lammeck said. "He's not going to be there. Keep watching. I won't move."

Far below, the sounds of the parade began to slither right to left as the marching workers took their first steps along Prado toward the reviewing stand. Lammeck checked his watch.

One o'clock.

"Watch," he told the boy riveted to the scope. "Listen."

Lammeck envisioned what he was betting, with his life, Alek was looking at: a slender figure stepping onto the raised platform, escorted by Johan; she passed the lineup of Cuban dignitaries, absent Fidel; she approached the bank of microphones; Johan stepped back, perhaps he searched the roofs and high windows of the many buildings ringing the platform; perhaps he looked right at Alek.

Rina.

Only a moment after imagining it, the girl's voice broadcast out of the loudspeakers hung around Parque Central. Her words cut through the commotion of the parade, sharp and clear.

"Ya govoryu ot vsego serdtsa."

Rina paused. A second voice translated the Russian into Spanish for the crowd:

"I bring you this message, from my heart."

"Pozhaluista poverite, ato lyubov."

"Please. Believe that you are loved."

"Verite tomu, kto ryadom s vami."

"Trust the one beside you."

"Ii kogda deni zakontychen i khochu, tchto by pryidia domoi be chyvstvovali by sebia b besopasnosti."

"And when this day is done, come home where you are safe."

The crowd below the white face of *El Capitolio,* arrayed in thousands along Prado, cheered Rina's cryptic message, believing it brought to them from some pretty ambassador of the Soviet Union. Alek kept his eye glued to the scope, the pistol forgotten in his hand. Lammeck guessed he was watching her leave the stage, again with Johan at her side.

Alek raised his gaze from the scope. "Goddammit. I can't believe you got her involved in this."

"Okay," Lammeck said, lifting his bandaged hand, "that's enough. You involved her when you brought her to Cuba. You involved her when you bragged about being an assassin."

"Shut up, Mikhal."

"No, Alek, time for you to shut up. We're done now with you running the show just because you've got a gun in your hand. Guess what? That pistol doesn't make you smart, and it doesn't make you brave. You're a patsy. So am I. We're both putting a stop to that right now. You need to show me where that duct is. Let's dump everything down the shaft and get off this roof. You and Rina have to catch a boat to the Bahamas tonight."

Lammeck strode forward before Alek could reply. He grabbed the

Winchester off the stack of crates. With a swift flick, he snapped back the bolt to eject the chambered .308 round into the air. He snatched the bullet and stuck it in his pocket beside the poison pill. He took down the blanket and pointed at the range scope and tripod.

"Let's go, boy. You've got no one to shoot today but me. Fidel's not showing up. It's over. So pull that trigger and kill me and you can go to hell. Or grab that scope and the duffel, and let's all get out of Cuba."

Alek shifted his gaze from Lammeck to the *parque* in the near distance. The boy seemed to be trying to sense Rina through the air, her words lingering in his ears. Could he trust them? *Come home,* she'd said, *where you are safe.*

"Choose," Lammeck ordered, "right now."

The boy lifted the pistol. Lammeck's breath snagged. Alek laid out his palm flat, handing the revolver over. Lammeck took it.

Alek scooped up the tripod and the duffel. Without a word, Lammeck followed him to the far edge of the roofline. Alek ducked low to avoid being seen from below as he approached a corrugated tin sheet. He slid this aside to reveal a vent wide enough for a man's shoulders. The boy lifted his chin to Lammeck, to say, *You first.*

Lammeck bent at the waist and crept to the rim of the shaft. He opened his arms and let the Winchester with the bleach bottle taped to the end fall into the hole. The rifle bashed the sides of the duct on the way down, then made an echoing crash four stories below. Lammeck threw in the blanket. Alek hurried beside him and dropped in the duffel, then the scope and wooden tripod. The clatter of their plummet was tinny and loud, but that couldn't be helped. If Jorge had left the capitol like Lammeck told him, no one on the grounds watching the parade could likely hear. Out on Prado, a marching band's drums and cymbals had struck up.

Last, Lammeck tossed in the revolver.

* * *

He led Alek down along the same stairs and hallways Jorge had used. When they reached the basement, Lammeck followed the bare lightbulbs the old janitor had left on, like a trail of bread crumbs out of a cave. Passing all the great boilers and ductwork, Lammeck wondered which unit had the broken jumble of Alek's weapons and bags heaped at the bottom. He imagined Jorge finding them; the *viejo* would mumble for the next year about it.

Lammeck recognized the correct door by finding his straw panama hung nearby. Before taking the boy out of the building, he stopped to put on the hat.

"Don't leave my side," he said to Alek. "I've got something the police want. They'll get it when you and Rina are gone. But I don't trust them enough for us to be separated. Alright?"

The boy said his first words since leaving the roof. "What about you?"

"I've got some details to handle. I'll get out tomorrow or the next day."

Lammeck pushed the door open. Alek almost trod on his heels.

On the grass, Johan waited. The policeman held a military-style two-way radio. Lammeck looked behind Johan to see that he'd kept his word. As far as he could tell, Johan had: There was no evidence of other security.

Lammeck said, "Captain, this is Alek Hidell."

The policeman approached. "Mr. Hidell," he said in his fluid way, "I will spare you the lecture you would otherwise get for attempting to assassinate my country's leader. If I had my way, that lecture would be the highlight of your day. But I am not getting my way this afternoon, and you may thank the professor for that. We will put you on a boat and be rid of you soon enough. Professor, a word."

Lammeck stepped only a few strides away from Alek. The boy, without his pistol and rifle, or the invisibility of the roof, seemed stricken, afraid. He reached for Lammeck, childlike. Lammeck assured him he would stay close.

"He is not much to look at," Johan said low enough for only Lammeck to hear. The racket of the parade echoed off the capitol and surrounding facades.

"Maybe not," Lammeck replied, "but he would've done it. Don't doubt it."

"Is everything as you wish it, Professor?"

"So far, so good."

"Excellent. One moment."

Johan brought the walkie-talkie to his lips. He pressed a button and spoke into the mouthpiece.

"Este es Johan. Dejalo que páse."

He released the button; static answered him, then a voice. *"Sí."*

Johan lowered the radio.

On the roof of the Partagas factory across the street, a flash of movement snared Lammeck's eye. Three figures, maybe more, stepped back from the ledge and disappeared.

Police snipers.

Lammeck glanced back at the boy. Alek had his hands stuffed in his pockets, shoulders hunched. He looked cold.

Lammeck asked Johan, "How'd you manage to keep Castro off the viewing stand?"

"At this moment, Fidel is cursing his driver. Unlike other world leaders, he enjoys very few of the trappings of power. He does not move with motorcades and sirens. Fidel is stuck in traffic at a roadblock arranged by my office. He will fire his driver, whom I will quietly promote and relocate. Fidel will arrive before the end of the parade, in time for his very long speech. Now, Mr. Hidell."

The boy pulled his hands from his jeans. He stood straight, his nerves making him eager.

"Yes, sir?"

"A car is going to drive you and Professor Lammeck to the Nacional. Your fiancée is waiting there. By the way, she also saved your life today. I suggest you thank her. You will all three stay at the hotel under my protection, which is a more pleasant way of saying under guard. You will not leave the grounds until six o'clock this evening, when I will come to take you and the girl to your ship, bound for Freeport. Professor, I will then escort you back to your house, where we will continue our discussions."

"Once they're out to sea, Johan. Not before. That was the deal."

"And so it shall remain. If you will follow me."

Johan pivoted to face the road, raising a hand. In moments, a brown Skoda sedan pulled up on Avenida Industria. Two hard-faced policemen sat in the front. Johan opened the rear door. Alek climbed in first. Johan stopped Lammeck. He leaned close and whispered in Spanish, "If you are wrong, Professor. If you have miscalculated. If you've in any way taken some romantic notion of trading your life for those two, understand me. I will accept that trade, without hesitation."

Lammeck climbed in the backseat beside Alek. Johan closed the car door and banged a fist on the roof above Lammeck's head.

At the stone gates to the Nacional, Rina stood waiting. When the police car swerved into the oval drive, Alek saw her and pressed against the window. She waved and shouted. The driver did not stop for the reunion. Rina ran alongside the Skoda to the steps of the hotel. Lammeck noted two dark-clad men jogging in the background, tracking her.

Alek burst out of the car into Rina's embrace. One of the police-men climbed out, to stand aside. He was joined by the armed pair who were shadowing Rina. The driver sped away the moment Lammeck reached the pavement.

The trio of guards watched the couple, silently. Lammeck moved to usher Alek and Rina inside. Immediately, the girl re-leased Alek and encircled Lammeck, squeezing him hard enough to make him labor for a breath.

"*¡Spasivo, spasivo!*"

Gently, aware of his bandaged hand, Lammeck patted her on the back.

He spoke in Russian to both. "Let's go inside."

Alek answered in English. "I'm starving."

Only one of the guards followed. Rina hugged Alek, wrapping the boy's thin waist, as they crossed the lobby. Seconds of uncom-fortable silence followed into the elevator, packed tight with the stony policeman. The man, in black T-shirt and khakis and with an American S&W .32 holstered on his belt, glared malevolently at Alek. The boy kept his eyes on his shoes. Rina, perhaps because she was Soviet, or because she knew how close she had come to killing this Cuban policeman's leader, stared back at the cop.

The guard took up position outside their door. After Alek and Rina had gone inside, the guard hooked Lammeck's elbow.

"My name is Blanco," he said in English. "Please, Professor, none of you must try to leave this room. Understand?"

"Of course."

"And no one will get in."

"Thank you."

Inside, Alek had flopped spread-eagled on the bed. "I'm ex-hausted," he announced. Rina jumped on beside him, making the mattress bounce. She fit herself inside his outstretched arm.

Alek spoke in English. "Professor, call up room service. Get me a steak and get yourself anything you want. The Cubans are payin' for it, 'cause we're outta here tonight."

Rina laughed, not understanding everything Alek had said but enjoying the vivacity of his tone. Lammeck stood back, fascinated at the turn in the boy the moment the hotel room door closed behind them. No longer frightened, he put on this show of bravado for his fiancée, the manner of a man fresh from a success. And in a way, wasn't he exactly that? The success was that he was still alive. All of them were.

Lammeck didn't pick up the phone immediately to order the boy's food. He stood beside the bed gazing down at the pair of young people he'd rescued. The two clasped each other and gazed with affection up at him. But there were still so many secrets unrevealed in this room, standing between them as stolidly as that Cuban guard outside the door. Alek had no idea his fiancée was KGB. He didn't know that last night, when Lammeck gave her the plan he'd devised to bring Alek back, he'd told her everything of the CIA's and Johan's plot, how they were all three marked for death in order to sour Castro on the Soviet Union. Alek was oblivious to it all, still believing that he'd been the centerpiece of the betrayal, not Rina. She knew nothing of Alek's desire to return to America. Lammeck didn't even know the boy's real name. Secrets.

Neither of them knew, or would ever be told, what Lammeck had to promise Johan in return for their safety. Or the danger he would soon face from Calendar for that promise.

"Get us some food, Mikhal," Alek repeated in his high spirits, and was gone into the bathroom.

Lammeck made the call, ordering steaks for all of them, even one for Blanco outside the room.

When he turned from the phone, Rina said in Russian, "Yes. I know. I owe you. You have brought him back, as you said you would." She gazed at him not with the smile she'd mounted for Alek, but with the countenance she'd shown Lammeck last night, the impenetrable face of a KGB operative.

Behind the bathroom door, water ran as Alek busied himself inside the shower. He would not hear them.

"Tell me now," Lammeck said.

The girl nodded.

"I had no knowledge the meeting was to be betrayed. But, before coming here, I was briefed to suspect such a move from CIA. I sent you to the meeting in hope that your presence might thwart Calendar, should he have such intentions. Perhaps he might hold off, tip his hand, if you were endangered as well as Alek. I had no idea Calendar was so ruthless. I am sorry you have been used this way."

"You used me, too, Rina."

"Not to kill you, Mikhal. Only to be a distraction. I cannot repay you for what you have done for me and my country. I will not ask what other arrangements you have made for Alek's and my benefit, and at your own expense. I thought only to give you this one last truth, for my debt."

One less secret, Lammeck thought. Still, there were too many. He wanted Alek and Rina on the boat, out of Cuban waters. Then he could concentrate on getting himself out of the web of deceits, and off the island.

The meals arrived. Lammeck struggled with his bandaged hand to slice his steak. Rina told him to call the front desk for a first aid kit. Blanco knocked when it arrived. After eating, Rina inspected Lammeck's wound. The furrow in the meat of the palm was deep but clean and pink. Lammeck gritted his teeth while Rina spun fresh gauze around his hand. Alek, showered and fed now, kept his attention out the window, gazing at old Havana.

Conversation died soon after the meal. Alek, selfish and continuing in his drama as returning warrior, collapsed on the bed, soon snoring. Rina and Lammeck in their chairs gazed at each other above the boy's prone body, patient with him. The girl was wise beyond her years. She had a steely nerve and a wild streak. The American boy on the bed was going to be her adventure.

Lammeck checked his watch. Three-thirty. He closed his eyes, lulled by the silence and the late afternoon light behind Rina. He heard her climb onto the bed beside the sleeping boy.

They all awoke to a knock on the door. Lammeck checked his watch again. Two hours had passed.

Johan was early.

CHAPTER NINETEEN

CALENDAR BECKONED THE WAITER with an impatient signal, a street-fighting gesture, indicating, *Bring it on*.

The man arrived with a tray in his hands full of empty dishes. *"Señor?"*

Calendar asked in Spanish, "What's your name?"

"Gustavo, *señor*."

"Gustavo, I've been sitting here for an hour, waiting for a sandwich and a second beer."

"I am sorry, *señor*. As you see, the patio is very busy today. The parade, Fidel's speech. We are doing our best."

"Your best is going to starve me."

"I will do what I can."

"Yeah. Do that."

The waiter whirled away with the tray. Calendar heard his

muttered curse, *"Coño."* Calendar shook his head. He was eager to be done with Cuba. *Communism,* he thought. *It always ruins the service.*

His food and beer appeared minutes after the parade lurched forward and began to file past the reviewing stand across the boulevard. Calendar munched. He cut his eyes between the platform and the roof of *El Capitolio*'s south wing four blocks off.

He set the sandwich down, drained the beer instead, hoping it might quell the acid burn in his gut.

He fixed his eyes on the platform, ignoring the capitol for the moment. He couldn't see the boy anyway, not at this distance.

Questions, all unanswered, fed the furnace in his stomach. He wanted another beer, a glass of water, something to pour on top of it, but Gustavo was swamped and surly. Calendar clenched his teeth.

Lammeck. The fat man wasn't dead. Why not? Did Hidell miss him? Not likely, the kid could flat-out shoot. Did Hidell get softhearted at the last minute?

Where was Lammeck? Chances were he was up on the capitol roof right now, trying to talk the kid down. The professor knew his own life was forfeit if he didn't do to the letter what Calendar instructed. Lammeck was a teacher and aging, but when the chips were down he was no puss. Calendar had to keep him on a short, tight leash.

It'll all work out, Calendar decided. The kid will plug the professor up on the roof. Johan will arrest Hidell. The plan will stay intact.

But what if Lammeck wasn't up there with Hidell? What if Hidell wasn't even up there anymore?

Those weren't insurmountable problems. Why?

Because among the dozen suits and uniforms on the stage, Fidel was absent. Hidell had no one to shoot. Lammeck must've gone to

Johan for help. The cop had done something to keep Castro away. Risky but smart.

Calendar still had time to work with Johan to trump something up against the kid. Get him arrested. Get him dead. Then pick up the Russian girl. With a little luck, that could all be done before day's end.

Later, Calendar would deal with Lammeck. That posed no challenge.

A tractor hauled a float between the patio and the platform. For several seconds, Calendar couldn't see around a great papier-mâché cow. When the obstruction had rolled past, he saw Johan rising up the steps of the reviewing stand.

Rina was on his arm.

Calendar's gut roiled. He looked into his beer glass. Only drops remained in the bottom. He drank them. Reaching into his pocket, Calendar pulled out a ten-peso note. He raised the bill and the empty glass together in the air. In seconds, a passing waiter snatched them both.

Before the girl approached the microphones, a fresh drink was on Calendar's table. He swallowed a third of the glass, wondering, *Now what?*

Into the mikes, casting her voice over a square mile of the city, the girl spoke Russian. Who in the hell in this crowd spoke Russian?

Calendar shot his eyes to the roof of *El Capitolio*.

Hidell. He was up there, listening.

She was telling the boy she loved him. To trust the one beside him.

So, Lammeck was up there, too!

She told Hidell to come down.

The ten thousand Cubans along Prado applauded the translations of what she said. Then Johan took the girl by the elbow to escort her away from the bank of microphones past confused but clapping dignitaries on the stage. Calendar watched the policeman guide the slender figure back down the steps, feeling the acid rage in his stomach. Johan handed Rina off to a pair of Cubans in dark garb and pistols. She let the two take her in hand without a glance around. She'd done her part.

Was she under arrest? No. There was no reason to grab the Russian at this point. Not until Hidell was in custody. What was going on?

An assistant handed Johan a fat green walkie-talkie. With a hurried stride, the captain lit out south along Prado, avoiding the crowded sidewalks by skimming the parade's edge.

On his feet now, Calendar grabbed his glass. He tipped it like a sword swallower and gulped the rest of the beer. He tucked another ten-peso note under the sandwich plate. Elbowing past patrons, brushing against Gustavo on his way out, Calendar moved into Johan's wake up the boulevard, pressing against the current of marchers and floats.

Inside the parade like this, the bands were blaring. Calendar's heartburn snarled at him. He popped himself in the sternum with a fist to try and calm his gut, break some logjam inside him. Johan set a pace that made Calendar break into a slow jog. Calendar's mood, not good to begin with, began to plunge on the weight of the unknown. Lammeck, Johan, the KGB girl, they'd come up with some plan on their own, something that didn't include Calendar.

Not yet it didn't, he thought.

He stayed half a block behind Johan to the capitol building. The policeman hastened across the lawn to the rear of the great structure, the side facing Avenida Industria. Calendar slowed, keeping himself hidden inside the throng along Prado, then doubling back. The police captain had positioned himself near a door leading down to the basement. Above and behind him, Calendar caught sight of three police snipers arrayed on the roof of the cigar factory. Johan spoke into the walkie-talkie; the snipers knelt and brought their long-barreled rifles up to their cheeks, scopes to their eyes. All went still as gargoyles.

Two minutes passed. The parade skipped blithely by. The vast crowd cheered the floats and farmers, all ignorant of the real event unfolding at their backs, the one that could change their lives, not just their sunny Sunday. Calendar loved these moments of life and death and shifting world power, knowing he'd set it all in motion. Then Lammeck and Hidell came out of the basement door. Calendar crept closer.

Johan spoke to them both, then into his two-way radio. The snipers on top of the cigar factory withdrew. Calendar half-expected them to shoot the defector down where he stood, but Johan must have decided to silence him at La Cabaña instead. Just as well. Do it out of sight.

An unmarked police car pulled up on Avenida Industria. Johan put Alek and the professor into the rear seat. The car pulled away. Standing alone, the captain watched it go, walkie-talkie at his side. Like Rina, he acted like his role had been played out. Calendar kept an eye on him. Johan crossed the capitol lawn to stroll along Prado. This time he made his way behind the crowd, in no rush, back toward the viewing platform. At a distance, Calendar followed.

Why didn't the police captain get into the car? Why wasn't he on his way to the prison right now? He should be staying close to Hidell, poised to shut him up permanently, before the kid could open his yap to spill how he was CIA, not KGB. Rina needed to be arrested. What the fuck was all this about, putting the Russian in front of the mikes, sending Lammeck up on the roof, bringing Hidell down alive, arresting him, if not to keep the plot on course?

And Lammeck? Why'd he get into the car? His part in this was over.

If he could, if Johan weren't ambling around in public, Calendar would grab him by the lapels and fling him against a wall or two, get to the bottom of what was going on. Calendar peeled away from trailing Johan, quickening his step, south from the parade route, deeper into old Havana. He dodged around barricades until he found flowing traffic.

He stepped in front of an oncoming taxi. The driver braked to keep from mowing him down. Calendar looked in the back. He handed the Cuban riding there twenty pesos to get out. He gave the driver another twenty to drive him to Miramar.

Calendar knocked again. He went around back. He reached past the broken glass pane in the door to turn the knob from the inside.

"Lammeck!"

Calendar bolted through the rooms, looking for clues where the professor might be. Bed neatly made. Breakfast dishes in the sink, with two glasses that smelled of rum. Who'd he been drinking with? Johan?

If Lammeck hadn't come home after the parade, where else could he be? Did Johan clap him in La Cabaña along with Hidell? No, the captain wouldn't do that. He'd have to silence Lammeck, too; both the boy and the professor knew this had been a CIA operation. Johan was too slick to make that mistake. If Alek Hidell disappeared in a Cuban jail, no big deal. Who was going to complain? The kid wasn't American and he wasn't Russian. But if hotshot professor Mikhal Lammeck dropped out of sight, someone would notice. That act, if it became necessary, would require a more deft touch. Calendar's.

He stomped out of the house, back to the taxi idling at the curb.

Was Lammeck in a bar, calming his nerves? Back at his favorite spot, the patio at the Inglaterra? The man liked his beer and rum. Was Lammeck getting soused watching that fucking parade?

Was he ducking Calendar? No. Lammeck knew better.

Where did Johan's bullyboys take him?

Calendar shrugged. He'd have to find the professor later, after the crowds left downtown and the streets cleared.

He climbed back into the taxi.

"The Nacional. *Rápidamente.*"

The taxi sped along the Malecón. Sunday revelers strolled on the sidewalks. The sea lay flat and the road glistened only with a light traffic of shining American cars. The Nacional Hotel, the former crown gem of Meyer Lansky's empire in Havana, stood high on its escarpment above the boulevard. Calendar ignored the city's beauty, paying attention only to his grinding gut. He rapped himself again in the chest and tried to belch.

At the Nacional's front door, he let the taxi go. Calendar strode without slowing to the elevators. He punched the button for the sixth floor.

Arriving with a bell, the doors slid aside. He stepped into the hall. To the right, at the far end, was Alek and Rina's room. Calendar did not take a step that direction. Outside their door, the armed guard, all in black, would have seen him.

Calendar pretended he was on the wrong floor. He slinked back into the elevator before the doors shut behind him.

Going down, he stared at himself in the mirror inside the elevator cabin. He wanted to smash the image. The stress in his stomach moved to his hands. He squeezed them in and out of fists, watching himself fume until the doors parted. The bell sounded again, like the start of a boxing round. A tourist couple stood in the lobby, waiting beside a bellhop with their luggage stacked on a brass cart. Calendar pushed them aside and knocked the cart into a spin. The man cursed in French. Calendar jammed fingers into his pocket for the mouthpiece, kept moving.

He emerged outside, at the swimming pool. Guests lounged in the weekend warmth. Calendar stopped and surveyed them: flabby men, cigar stubs in their teeth, women lying on their stomachs with straps loosened to prevent tan lines, books, towels, and drinks beneath paper umbrellas. Calendar stood panting. He wanted to break something. He saw himself uproot a light pole and swing it like a berserk superman, swatting everyone and everything until he was alone and could scream: *What the fuck?*

People began to look back at him. A waiter came his way, mounting an inquisitive smile. The man's approach centered Calendar's instincts again, to be invisible, make no imprint. The waiter asked, "*Señor,* may I help you?" Calendar shook his head.

He left the pool through a gate in the surrounding wooden fence. He found himself by a dozen metal trashcans. One kick, one deep dent, would make him feel better but the noise would be too loud. Calendar remembered who he was supposed to be, a shadow unstaked from the ground. He was Bud. Everybody and nobody.

His heartburn eased.

"Alright," Bud Calendar decided, "alright. Enough of this. So long, Fidel."

CHAPTER TWENTY

★ ★ ★

Nacional Hotel

LAMMECK'S BACK ACHED FROM sleeping in the chair. On the bed, Rina and Alek stirred but did not rise.

Blanco opened the door.

"Professor?" the guard said. "Captain Johan has arrived. He would like to see you downstairs in the courtyard. Alone."

"Is something wrong?"

"I cannot say. He asked me to send only you down. If you please. Tell the boy and girl to pack."

"Just a minute."

Blanco closed the door. Lammeck stepped quietly into the bath to splash his face. When he came out, Rina eyed him from the bed.

"Is it time?"

"Not yet. Johan wants to see me downstairs. Just some last-minute details. I'll be back. Start packing."

Lammeck left the room. In the hall, Blanco stopped him.

"Captain Johan says you saved Fidel."

Lammeck nodded.

"Thank you," the Cuban said. "That boy . . . If the captain allows it, I will kill him myself."

Lammeck was stunned. Alek wasn't going to be killed. That wasn't the agreement. He was on his way to the docks, to Freeport—

"I'm sorry, Professor. I should not speak. The captain waits. Please."

The guard looked down the hall, for him to go. Lammeck stepped away toward the elevators, glancing over his shoulder at Blanco. The guard made his face stony, regretting his indiscretion.

Another of Johan's men, pistol at his hip, waited for Lammeck at the elevator bank. This one said nothing but pushed the button and stood aside for the car to arrive. They rode down together. Johan waited on a bench in the hotel's rear gardens under waning sunlight. The guard stopped several strides away but remained in range.

Johan stood.

"Professor."

"Captain. You're early."

"A trifle. I am eager to be going, I suppose."

Johan motioned for the guard to stand elsewhere, to stop hovering so conspicuously. The captain sat, motioning for Lammeck to join him.

Lammeck asked, "Did Fidel make it to the parade?"

"Yes, halfway through. When it was done, he spoke for two hours. Astonishing, the stamina that man has."

"It's the audience's stamina that's astonishing."

Johan chuckled. "Perhaps. Are the children awake?"

"They're packing."

"Have them ready in five minutes."

"That's not much time."

"I'm in a hurry. Also, you will be coming along."

Lammeck did not move. "What's changed?"

"The only thing in this world that is permanent is change, Professor. You're an historian, you know this. We shall play the game to its conclusion, the two of us. I will see you shortly." The captain stalked off without explanation.

Lammeck headed for the elevators. The guard swung in behind him. Lammeck wiped concern from his face before walking past Blanco, into the room on the sixth floor.

Alek and Rina packed at a leisurely pace. Clothes were spread everywhere.

"No time," Lammeck said in Russian. "Take what you need for the next few days. One bag each. Leave the rest. Johan's waiting."

Rina continued to fold a sundress on the bed. Lammeck laid a gentle hand across her wrists. "Leave it."

The girl read on his face what he did not say. She said to Alek, "Empty the bathroom. I will take clothes for us. We will get what else we need in Freeport. Quickly."

The boy seemed not to care either way and did what she told him. Blanco knocked and stuck in his head.

"Now."

The guard ushered them to the elevator. A second one joined them in the lobby. Two black Skodas waited at the bottom of the hotel steps. Another pair of Johan's armed men took the bags from Alek and Rina, tossed them into the trunk of the second car. The rear door was held open for them; the young couple looked questioningly at Lammeck.

"I'm coming in this car." He pointed to the lead vehicle. "I'll see you at the docks."

Alek got in. Rina kissed both of Lammeck's cheeks. Spinning

away, she climbed into the second Skoda. A thick wire mesh separated the couple from the policemen.

Johan rose from the passenger side of the lead car. "Professor. Join me."

Blanco held open the rear door. Lammeck stuffed himself in behind the same wire barrier. Johan did not turn to address him. Blanco got behind the wheel.

"Johan," Lammeck asked, *"¿Qué es diferente?"*

The captain glanced quickly through the wire back at Lammeck. His expression said: *Be quiet, Professor.*

The road ran alongside Havana Channel. Ahead were the gargantuan piers, with a dozen cargo ships moored alongside. Which one was headed for the Bahamas? Lammeck glanced back to the following car. He saw the outline of the couple's heads in the rear seat, behind the wire. Were they wondering the same, which boat was theirs?

The car slowed.

"What's going on?" Lammeck asked through the screen.

Blanco steered off the main road, past a high fence of black iron pickets. Both cars stopped on a stone drive, at the foot of a foreboding, rocky keep with many turrets and towers, a drawbridge gate. Uniformed, armed men moved to surround the second car.

Police headquarters.

"No." Lammeck gripped the wire with his left hand and shook. "No!"

Blanco shut down the engine. Johan signaled the guard to leave the car.

Lammeck tried to open his door but the lock was controlled from the front seat. He whirled to look out the back window. A half dozen policemen formed a phalanx at the rear door of the second Skoda. Blanco approached and bent to speak inside. The boy got out. Immediately, policemen engulfed him. Alek's shocked face found Lammeck gaping back at him. The boy was hustled under the dark arch leading inside. Blanco and the rest of Johan's men stayed behind, guarding the second car.

"Johan," Lammeck growled, "we had a deal."

Lammeck rattled the wire mesh in Johan's face. In the backseat of the other Skoda, Rina pounded on the window, howling, rocking the car like a caged wildcat.

Lammeck dropped his hand from the wire. "You son of a bitch."

The captain said, "You were correct, of course. Things are different. The boy's luck has failed to hold. Actually, it wasn't the boy's luck that collapsed. It was Heitor."

Lammeck looked across the channel, at La Cabaña prison. He imagined the old engineer inside the battlements, broken and bleeding secrets to Johan's inquisitors.

"When?"

"An hour ago. He identified Alek Hidell as the sniper. He named CIA as being behind the conspiracy, with *Unidad*. Once he'd blurted the raw facts, I did us both a favor."

Lammeck did not take his eyes from the prison.

Johan said, "I stopped him before he could mention you. It was merciful. And it was for the best. Trust me."

Lammeck wanted to smash his one good fist against the wire, like Rina in the car behind. "What good did breaking him do? You couldn't wait two more hours until they were on the boat and gone? Christ, Johan."

"It was not me, Professor. Fidel himself ordered the interrogation. Two days ago, he was told of Heitor's arrest. They were old comrades from the Escambray campaign, you know. He took Heitor's betrayal very seriously. Young Fidel hides behind the demeanor of a warrior, but in truth he is only a lawyer. Every day the people see him in fatigues. He does this to remind them of the struggle, to make them believe he was a true *guerrillero*. They say Castro learned in the mountains to survive. What the people do not yet realize is that he also learned to be unbending."

Lammeck asked, "What about the girl?"

"She'll be taken back to the Nacional. Kept there under guard until she's summoned back here."

"Why'd you have them pack? Why the ruse of going to the docks?"

"To avoid this unfortunate scene at the hotel. Look at her."

Rina had not stopped battering the car window.

"Is Alek dead?"

"No. My plans have been trumped. I cannot silence the boy. Fidel intends to speak with him personally. Then it merely becomes a game of connect-the-dots. Your defector will tell Fidel about you. You will be questioned. You will tell about me. I will be arrested and reveal everything I know about the girl, the CIA, and KGB. She will be next. Fidel will become incensed, and we will all hold hands at the firing wall."

"And Calendar?"

Johan loosed a sardonic laugh. "He will fade into the woodwork. He's not the sort to face consequences. His kind rarely do." The captain sighed. "Saddest is that after all is said and done, we'll have had little effect on Fidel's attachment to the Soviets. The boy will live long enough to name the CIA as the origin of yet another plan to assassinate Castro. The KGB's role will be seen as minimal. Moscow will, of course, officially disavow it. In a few days, or hours, CIA-trained exiles will invade my homeland. Fidel will have more reason than ever to loathe America. I will die, Professor, and I will have failed Cuba."

Lammeck didn't know if Johan was right about Fidel, but he was sure that neither Russia nor the U.S. was going to interfere;

that would be an admission of guilt. Alek, Rina, and Lammeck would be written off as rogues. Johan as a traitor. Plausibly denied.

He set a hand over his pants pocket. The botulinum pill. It could break him out of the chain, save Johan and Rina behind him. At least that would be something salvaged. But as always, the thought of suicide, even nobly done, sickened him.

"Put me and Rina on that boat."

Johan lofted an eyebrow. "Do I hear cowardice or mere pragmatism?"

"It's the only way to keep yourself alive, Johan."

The captain brought his face close to the wire. The mesh pressed against his nose.

"You are a pawn, Professor. But even a pawn can have awful choices. You can tell me what I do not know about the CIA's plans to murder Fidel. That will save his life. Then I will allow you and the girl onto your boat to Freeport. But Calendar will surely come to Providence to repay you for that betrayal. And I supsect a similar fate awaits the girl in the Soviet Union. Or you may continue to stay closemouthed with me. In that case, I will have Blanco drive you across the channel to La Cabaña. You will be questioned with whatever ferocity is required. You will tell me what I need to know, and my police will stop the CIA plotters. After that, you and the girl will face the *paredón*."

"Why?" Lammeck asked. "It's senseless. You'll die, too."

"Do you recall yesterday when I said I would rather see you dead than Fidel? I would also rather see myself dead than to allow his murder. He is my country's leader. He has gone wrong by taking Cuba down the path of Communism. Many of us oppose that. But to kill him? That would make us unworthy of the democracy we wish for. I believe Fidel is a rare man, that he has greatness left in him. I want him to realize his mistake, his betrayal of the revolution. I want him to lead Cuba as only a great man can."

"And what if you're wrong?"

"Then I will die as a man of sins, but not as a traitor."

Lammeck glanced at the fortress across the channel. He saw himself behind the prison walls, in poor Heitor's place.

One slim path opened in his head, a way out. He looked up to gauge Johan, how much tolerance was left in the man. Lammeck saw the last trace of patience drain from the policeman's face.

"Choose," Johan said.

"I want to talk to Castro."

"You jest."

"I'd have to be a lot braver to make a joke right now. I'm serious."

"What good will speaking with Fidel do?"

"I'll tell him about the plot myself. You said he was still a lawyer at heart. I'll negotiate."

"What for? Your life?"

"For the boy's life. If we can get Alek and Rina out of Cuba before he's interrogated, you and I are safe."

"And have you considered Calendar? Once you spoil the CIA's assassination, *you* become his target."

"I've been Calendar's target for a while now. I'm getting used to it."

Johan covered his mouth with his fingers, considering.

Lammeck said, "I've got nothing to lose. Like you said, I'm dead either way."

The policeman smiled bleakly. "That does play to our advantage."

"Where's Fidel right now?"

"He has a routine after a speech. He takes several of his *barbudos* to dinner. They relive the campaign days and compare their beards."

Lammeck's other hand shot to the wire screen. "Where?"

"Various places. He has a few favorite restaurants."

Calendar's voice from three days ago replayed in Lammeck's brain, talking of Juan Orta and the botulinum capsules: *He's going to hand them off to a connection of his in town, a cook in one of Castro's favorite restaurants. The cook's been told not to do anything until he gets the signal.*

Had Calendar given that signal? No way to tell.

"Do you know which restaurant Fidel's going to?"

"The Peking, in Vedado, on Twenty-third Street."

Lammeck pushed against the wire. "Get behind the wheel, Johan! Drive!"

The Skoda did not have a siren or lights. Johan dashed down the Malecón at a frightening rate, weaving into oncoming lanes to pass slower vehicles. Cars honked and flashed at them; Johan leaned on the horn and mashed the gas pedal.

Lammeck sat forward in the backseat, linking his fingers into the wire barrier to hold himself in place while the Skoda careened. Between moments blowing the horn, Johan shouted into the backseat.

"Botulinum! Calendar gave you botulinum! *Ai,* that *comé mierda.* How does it work exactly?"

In short bursts, not to divert the police captain's attention from the flying road, Lammeck explained the effects of the poison. Twenty-four to forty-eight hours of creeping paralysis, death by asphyxiation. How the capsules were only to be sprinkled on foods or in a cold liquid. Five pills. He made no mention of the one in his pocket.

"After Calendar gave the capsules to you," Johan called, "you took them to the Peking?"

"No."

Johan swerved to avoid a slow-going truck.

"There was a middleman then. Who did you give them to?"

"I won't tell you that, Johan. There's enough of a body count already."

"Fidel will ask, *amigo*. You will have to give him the name. You may as well tell me now."

Lammeck let go of the wire and sat back.

So complex, Lammeck thought, this assassination business. Not as simple as just pulling a trigger, thrusting a dagger, pouring a cup of nightshade. There were wheels within wheels, mysteries inside lies, shifting loyalties, losses to be cut. Good and bad men, good and poor plans, far too much bad luck.

Lammeck let go of responsibility for Orta's fortunes. When the man accepted the pills from Lammeck's hand, he surely knew events could turn against him. It would not be Lammeck betraying Juan Orta Córdova. It would be inevitable, heartless, history.

"If Fidel asks," Lammeck said.

With screeching tires, the Skoda turned left onto Twenty-third. The street was the main business avenue heading west from the old section of the city. Restaurants, banks, tightly packed shops lined the road. Pedestrians crossed without warning. Johan drove in fits and starts, cursing.

Johan asked no more questions and focused on his driving. He ran red lights and stop signs, blaring the horn almost without cease. Lammeck sat back against the rear seat, unable to hang on to the wire anymore with his bandaged hand. The constant jostling, and the fear of a collision, kept him from arranging his thoughts about meeting Fidel. He settled for steeling his nerve.

The road neared the reaches of a gigantic cemetery on the left.

Inside an iron fence, an uncountable number of headstones stood like marble dominos arranged in rows; there were so many, Lammeck thought, if one fell into another, they would topple for days. With his eyes on the cemetery, Lammeck wasn't watching when Johan swung the car off the main road into a sharp right turn onto Fourteenth Street. Lammeck smacked his head against the window. The thump was the opening gavel; Johan slung the Skoda to the curb. Lammeck had to wait for the captain to open his door from outside.

"Say nothing, Professor. Not one word until I tell you to speak. Inside this restaurant, there are suspicious and loyal men around Fidel. And there are many guns."

Lammeck nodded. He followed Johan into an alley off Fourteenth, to enter the Peking from the back. Johan walked as he had driven, urgently. Lammeck understood that the man did believe in Castro, did love him, and would truly try to save him at any cost.

An armed guard in fatigues, a submachine gun slung over his shoulder, put the weapon into his hands on sight of the two approaching. Johan raised a palm in greeting.

"Rafael, I'm late. How long has he been here?"

"Ten minutes maybe." The guard plucked a cigarette from his lips. He pointed it at Lammeck. "Who's this?"

"An American. Fidel wants to meet him."

"*El Commandante* said nothing to me about this."

"If you were one of Fidel's confidants, you would be inside eating and not out here on watch. Step aside."

The guard eyed them both. Lammeck put a look on his face of innocence, as if he did not speak Spanish. The guard shuffled backward a reluctant step. Johan walked past him. Lammeck followed.

In the restaurant's kitchen, two small Orientals in undershirts were busy at sinks washing dishes and pots. Another, a tall Cuban in a white paper hat and apron, turned to look at the intruders, a chopping knife in his grip. Johan glanced at this one, then back to Lammeck, to see if any recognition sprang between them. Lammeck had never seen the cook before, but the man glared back.

"One last thing, Professor. Fidel is twenty years younger than you and I. But do not, for an instant, think you are speaking to a pupil."

The policeman patted his shoulder. "Good luck. And thank you."

Johan turned on his heel. He left the kitchen, pushing open a swinging door. Lammeck stayed a stride behind.

The place was decorated in classic Chinese-restaurant style, with red leather seating and murals of pagodas and floating junks on every wall. The room was empty save for eight grizzly men seated around a long table. Each wore olive drab fatigues and high laced boots with pant legs tucked in. All kept their campaign hats or berets on. Over the backs of chairs, a collection of rifles were slung by their straps. A pistol rode on every hip. Only one of the bearded faces that looked up wore large, black-rimmed glasses.

Beside the table stood a heavyset Negro waitress. She busily set plates from a tray onto bamboo place mats before each *barbudo*. Castro had no food in front of him.

"Johan," Fidel called. "Come in." Fidel picked up his fork for the waitress to place a heaping dish on his mat.

Lammeck's gut squirmed.

Fidel asked, "Who is this?"

Before Johan could move or speak, Lammeck charged from behind. He yanked up his bandaged palm, held it at arm's length to Fidel, a white warning. He disobeyed Johan. He had no choice.

"No."

Lammeck took only a single step before halting. The soldiers scrambled for their weapons. In a second of racking metal, Lammeck stared down a collection of barrels long and short.

Fidel, the only one at the table who hadn't moved, laid his fork beside his plate. The waitress scurried out of the way.

Fidel studied Lammeck.

"No what, *señor*?"

Johan pushed Lammeck back a step, to stand beside him. He answered for Lammeck.

"No, *Commandante*. Do not eat that food."

Fidel did not flinch. The others at the table dropped their silverware to push their plates to the middle of the table. The dark face of the waitress was impassive.

"Why, Johan? Is it poisoned?"

"I do not know. It may be. This man, he must speak with you. And you must listen to him." Fidel nodded at one of the soldiers at the table with him. This *barbudo*, the only one with a blond beard, rose and moved behind Lammeck. He ran his hands up and down Lammeck's legs and raised arms, checking for weapons.

Watching the search, Fidel said, "I ask you again, Johan. Who is this? Is he a crazy man?"

The search was finished quickly. The blond soldier stepped away.

"This is Professor Mikhal Lammeck, *Commandante*. An American."

Fidel nodded, amused. "Of course he's an American. He thinks he's bulletproof." Fidel waggled two fingers in the air for Lammeck to come closer. A bead of sweat trickled down Lammeck's back where the ancient priests' knife would have been. Again, he was relieved he'd left the dagger behind.

Lammeck stared at the plate in front of Castro: mushrooms, pork, shredded greens, bamboo shoots, brown rice.

"Professor," Fidel asked, "do you speak Spanish?"

"Yes."

"Excellent."

Lammeck said, "I must talk with you. It's urgent."

Fidel looked to Johan. The captain nodded.

"Alright."

Castro stood. Lammeck was impressed with the man's height and physicality. He moved like an athlete, limber and long, away from the crowded table. He led them to a separate, scarlet booth. The three sat. Behind them, the waitress retreated into the kitchen. Fidel snapped fingers at his *compañeros*. Two men went with her. At the table, all the plates sat cooling, untouched.

Fidel cut his eyes to Lammeck's wrapped left hand. He pointed at Lammeck's forehead.

"What happened to you? You've got a lump and a bad hand." Castro grinned, charming and concentrated. "If you've been fighting, I hope at least it was in my behalf."

"No. Just clumsy."

"Well, be careful. Johan here is the most careful man I know."

Castro set an elbow on the table. He leaned forward, scratching a finger deep in his beard.

"Did you see the parade today, Professor?"

Lammeck answered, "I did."

"What did you think?"

"I was impressed."

"You realize, it was all farmers. Under Batista, and before him Prío, for my entire lifetime and longer, the people of Cuba did not get parades. The army did, and the Americans, but never the workers. The cane cutters, charcoal makers, fishermen, plowmen, tobacco pickers, all of them were ignored until the revolution. I was very proud today. Did you hear my speech?"

"No. I had to leave early. My apologies."

Fidel appeared to be laying out his credentials as a revolutionary.

He gave the sense he might launch into an hours-long lecture across the table, for just Lammeck's ears, to recruit the heart of one man at a time.

Odd, Lammeck thought. He and Johan had said the matter they'd come for was urgent. Johan even announced that Fidel's meal could be poisoned. But the man was not pressed, and he was not afraid. His manner seemed to Lammeck self-consciously bold, a performance, as if he had not climbed down off the afternoon's rostrum.

"You are a professor," Fidel observed. "Of what subject?"

"Political science."

Castro's eyebrows arched. Inside the rough curls of his beard, his lips puckered.

"The two of us are interested in much the same ideas. Politics. History. The worthiest of endeavors. How to save mankind from itself, eh?"

Despite Johan's warning not to consider Castro a student, Lammeck tamped down a burr of irritation. In his own long career, Lammeck had read most of the major historical treatises and documents from two thousand years of civilization, had written one himself. Fidel Castro was, essentially, a courageous young attorney versed in rebellion. The man was no scholar, despite his self-stylings. Lammeck would share little with him in a contest of ideas.

Lammeck said, "My specialty is assassinations."

"Ahh, have you come to save me, Professor?" Fidel's eyebrows bent a notch higher.

Castro asked this theatrically, loud enough for the *barbudos* to hear at their table. They, the men who would die for Fidel, who would save him and perhaps had already done so in the mountains, laughed at the American *viejo* come to rescue their *commandante.*

Even so, Lammeck noted none of them touched their plates.

He reached into his pocket, and set the poison capsule on the table.

"Yes."

Fidel picked the pill off the tablecloth. He jiggled it in his wide palm. "What is this?"

"Botulinum."

Castro put the pill down, as if it could infect him through his hand.

He asked Johan, "CIA?"

The captain stared at the pill on the table, surprised. Lammeck had not told him of the one he'd kept. Johan nodded to Castro.

Lammeck continued: "The CIA gave me six pills. I hung on to one. The other five were delivered to one of your favorite restaurants here in Havana. At a signal, you were to be poisoned."

"Who gave this signal? You?"

"No. I'm not even sure it has been given. But it'll come from the CIA."

"Yes," Fidel agreed, lifting a long, pale finger. "I know your CIA. I was supposed to die today. The American sniper on *El Capitolio*. But he is in prison, and I am not in the ground. Be assured, Professor, the CIA has given the signal."

Lammeck believed it, too, but did not say so.

Fidel put his tongue into his lower lip, considering.

"You say I was to be poisoned in one of my favorite restaurants?"

"I wasn't told which. Johan said the Peking is one."

Castro leaped to his feet. He stamped away, past the quizzical *barbudos*, who watched their leader shove open the kitchen door and disappear. They turned their eyes on Lammeck.

Fidel returned in seconds. With him were the two men he'd sent into the kitchen. They herded out the entire staff of the restaurant.

Castro had his guards put them in a line in front of the red booth, then returned to his seat opposite Johan and Lammeck.

"I wanted them to hear what you say, Professor. They should know how their fate is to be determined."

Castro asked the row of five workers, pointing at Lammeck, "Do any of you know this man? Have you ever spoken to him?"

The two cooks, the black waitress, and the pair of Asian dishwashers replied in unison, "No, *Commandante.*"

"He says you wish to poison me. Yes? Is this true?"

Heads shook violently. Again all said, "No, no, *Commandante.*"

Castro drubbed his finger into the table beside the botulinum capsule. The pill danced on the vibration.

"Did you bring the pills here, Professor?"

"No. I gave them to someone else. He had the connection. I don't know which restaurant he took them to."

"What is the man's name?"

Johan glared along with Castro at Lammeck. The restaurant staff, the *barbudos* at their table, all mounted angry stares.

"I'll tell you," Lammeck said. "But in return I want something."

Castro sat back against the leather booth. He pulled down his black-rimmed glasses, tossing them onto the table. He pinched the top of his nose, closing his eyes as if from strain.

"You wish to haggle with me, Professor?"

"Negotiate."

When Fidel fixed his gaze again on Lammeck, he smiled. "You see, Johan, this is capitalism. There are no Americans left who want nothing in return for their good deeds. Professor, I want to believe you. I would like nothing better than to think that one more plot to kill me has been prevented. Your CIA. They come at me."

He circled a finger in the air beside his head.

"I know they will land several thousand exiles somewhere on

the island soon. Your country would like me dead before that happens, in their mistaken faith that *I* am what holds the revolution together and not the people. But, it is in them where I place my own faith, you see."

Fidel indicated the black waitress. "It is María, yes?"

The woman started. "Yes, *Commandante*."

"Bring my plate of food here."

All eyes watched her fetch the dish of pork and vegetables. She set it in the center of the table.

"Bring my fork." The woman did so.

Castro held the utensil up, tines beside his temple.

"So, Professor, I am to be killed."

"Yes."

"You say you have made a study of assassinations. Do you have an opinion? Is it not a barbaric practice?"

"It's politics. There's never been a culture that didn't resort to it at some point."

"Perhaps. But it seems frantic. Lacking confidence. It's a sign of a decaying culture. If the United States is so certain it has the best way of life, then it should focus on spreading that, not violence. Do you know why I am a Communist?"

"No."

"I will quote my friend Nikita Khrushchev. He told me that he had worked in the mines for the Belgians, in the factories for the Germans, in the fields for the French. The capitalists made him a Communist."

"Why haven't you announced it?"

"I have been trying to avoid kicking the hornets' nest of the United States. You are a close and powerful neighbor, and not one I care to upset unduly. But, with that ugly pill on the table and the Marine sniper in jail, and a hundred other ways, I see that the hornets buzz at me regardless. Can you tell me this is not so?"

"I'm not a politician."

"No, you are decidedly not. You are a conspirator. An assassin. But you are also an American, a citizen of a desperate nation. I suppose I have been foolish to expect anything beyond the back of a hand from your country. But what I find most painful is that here, in Cuba, in the midst of the revolution, we still have wreckers. Those who cling to the old abuses and privileges of capitalism."

Castro leveled the fork at the restaurant staff, all five of them listening in their lineup. Eyes went wide with Fidel's interest on them now.

He addressed them. "Do you recall how we made the revolution? We were certain. Not a man or woman among us doubted or feared, never for a second. We fought and died with conviction. Now, my friends, if I am to believe that all of you are innocent, if I am to restrain myself from taking you out back and having you shot, you must show me your conviction, that you are not wreckers. That if the professor is correct that the CIA has turned one of my favorite restaurants against me, it is not this one."

Fidel reached the fork to the first in line, the tall cook.

"Your name?"

"Cruz, *Commandante.*"

"Take a bite, Cruz."

The cook scooped a large portion into his mouth, then put down the fork with vigor as if he'd used it to sign a declaration. With less enthusiasm, each of the staff ate from the plate. The waitress María came last. She accepted the fork and hesitated.

"Him," she said, pointing at Lammeck.

Fidel asked, "What about him?"

"He came in shouting no, you should not eat, *Commandante*. I am afraid he has done something to the food that we do not know about. He is CIA. They are devils."

All in line nodded, Castro, too. He said, "A valid concern, my dear. May I?"

He took the fork from her, extending it to Lammeck.

For a moment, Lammeck let the fork hang in Castro's hand. He looked across the faces of the staff, seeing nothing to ease his apprehension. Their options were the risk of poison or the certainty of a submachine gun. Lammeck shared their predicament. How could he rely on them?

Spearing a strip of pork, he closed his lips around it and shut his eyes, to fix on the meat, desperate to taste anything untoward, to separate spices from the shadow of toxin on his tongue. He chewed. When he swallowed, he felt an hourglass turn over in his stomach.

Then María ate. When she was done, Fidel ordered the staff to sit together at a table across the room. Quietly, the *barbudos* dug once again into their own plates. Fidel pushed his meal away.

He spoke to Lammeck. "You were not afraid?"

"There's nothing to fear where there's no choice. Like you said, conviction."

Fidel glanced at Johan, intrigued.

"This continues to get more interesting. Captain, do you trust him?"

"Yes, *Commandante*. It was Lammeck who went on the roof of the capitol today and brought down the sniper. He will do what he says. And he is not CIA. He is a teacher who has been threatened by the CIA."

Fidel lifted his black frames from the table to slide them over his eyes. He blinked behind the lenses, keen.

"Proceed, Professor. Make your deal."

Lammeck forced aside his distraction with the poison that might be ticking in his gut now. Dying or not, he had to press forward.

"The boy arrested today, his name is Alek Hidell."

Fidel stopped him. "You call him a boy? Johan tells me he is a U.S.-trained sharpshooter brought to Havana to murder me in front of ten thousand people, on the eve of an invasion. Do not call him a boy and expect this will get sympathy from me."

"He's young, and he's confused. The CIA took advantage of him."

"As they did you, Professor?"

Lammeck began to answer, but Castro waved him off. "Continue with Hidell. We will return to you before we finish."

"Hidell was made part of Heitor Ferrer's assassination plot. But the CIA never intended the assassination to happen. The meeting with Ferrer and Hidell was betrayed."

"Yes," Castro said, indicating Johan, "through the excellent intelligence work of the captain here. Heitor." Fidel said his old friend's name as if it had a sour taste. "Traitor."

"*Commandante,*" Johan spoke up, "Ferrer was not uncovered by my department. He was purposely exposed by CIA."

Fidel shook his head. "Impossible."

Lammeck said, "Hidell was meant to be captured. He and Ferrer's cell were set up by the CIA."

"Why would the CIA bring a sniper to Havana just to have him arrested? It's absurd."

Lammeck opened his mouth, but Johan gripped his wrist, silencing him.

"Hidell is an American defector, *Commandante*. To the Soviet Union. He was accompanied to Havana by his Russian fiancée. She is KGB."

Castro winced behind his glasses. "What are you saying?"

"Hidell was never intended to kill you. He was an unwitting decoy, to lead us to the girl. The assassination plot was an elaborate hoax."

"So I would learn that the KGB and CIA have joined forces to assassinate me? This is . . . this is unimaginable."

"That is why the CIA sabotaged Ferrer's meeting. The CIA hoped the shock of realizing the Soviet Union also opposed you would sway you away from them."

Castro took long moments before bringing his gaze to Lammeck.

"It would seem, Professor, I should have kicked the hornets' nest sooner."

Genuine dismay stained Fidel's features. Lammeck said only, "Perhaps."

"Raúl and Guevara will be flattered when I tell them." Castro eyed Lammeck before asking, "Very impressive. Like chess masters, your CIA. They play several moves ahead. Now tell me, what is your role in all this?"

"I met Alek and his fiancée, Rina. After he escaped the Ferrer meeting, Alek went ahead with the plot on his own, thinking it was the only way the CIA would keep its end of the bargain to let him go home. Rina asked me to stop him. The CIA did, too."

Fidel tapped the table beside the botulinum pill. "Why did the KGB girl want to stop him from killing me? That was her goal from the beginning, yes?"

Lammeck said, "As it turns out, she actually loves Alek. More, I think, than she loves Russia."

"Russians. An unpredictable people. Where is the girl?"

Johan answered: "Under guard at the Nacional. There has been no reason to arrest her yet. She is Soviet, and I assumed you would want me to use discretion before acting."

"Exactly. Well done. Professor?"

"Yes."

"Hidell is in jail. The Russian girl is in custody. It seems the

CIA's plan has been carried out. Why do you believe they still want me dead?"

"Because the plan called for Hidell to be killed before he could be questioned. You were never supposed to know CIA was involved. Only KGB."

Castro leaned to an elbow.

"So it seems, Professor, with the plot in shambles and the invasion coming, the CIA has decided to give up turning me away from the Soviet Union. The backup plan is to assassinate me before the *gusanos* land on the island. I am to be poisoned."

"Yes."

"But you decided to come warn me. In return, I am to make a bargain with you. Let me guess. You want me to spare Hidell and the Russian girl, in return for the favor of my life."

"I want them freed and allowed to leave Cuba."

Castro nodded, appreciating Lammeck's brevity.

"They will both go back to Russia?"

"Yes."

"Johan says you were the one who brought Hidell down off *El Capitolio*. You could have stayed quiet. You could have let him shoot me. Your government would have been appreciative of that."

"Yes."

"But conscience intervened, eh?"

Lammeck said nothing. Castro snickered at himself.

He snapped his fingers at the table where the staff sat. "María."

The woman jumped to her feet. Castro swept a hand over the cold plate.

"Take this away."

Next Castro pointed at the botulinum pill. "Put that back in your pocket, Professor. It makes my stomach sink to look at it."

Castro said to him and Johan, "I despise this part of politics. The machinations, the wheedling. Every decision strained through the greater needs of a nation. I wanted it to be simpler. But with Cuba such a poor country, there are too many eggshells for a man to put his foot down firmly. Compromise is the rule. It is unfortunate."

Castro removed his olive drab hat.

"Hidell is lucky he is a defector. If he were just an American, I'd wave him in front of the world. Let them see what the Yankees are doing. Then I'd either have him shot or I'd trade him back to Kennedy for something humiliating. But this pleasure is denied me, because Hidell is a guest of the Soviet Union. And considering Russia's low opinion of me at the moment, I cannot shoot the KGB girl either. Johan?"

"Yes, *Commandante*?"

"Although I am certain there are other sinister little bits of this tale, it seems the professor has told us enough. I see no point to interrogating the young couple. That would bear little profit for the political cost. Do you agree?"

"Yes."

Castro brought his attention back to Lammeck. "So, actually, Professor, letting the two of them go plays somewhat to my advantage. I now know their plot, and the roles of both governments. But only you, me, and Johan are aware of this. So, I accept your proposal."

Lammeck was stunned at the suddenness of Fidel's agreement. "Alek and Rina can go?"

"Johan will release the boy—I will call him that now—and put them both on a plane leaving the island. Tonight."

"Thank you."

"Johan's police will make inquiries and we will locate where your poison pills have gotten to. I will watch my Russian allies with a jaundiced eye. And I will find some new favorite restaurants."

Fidel tugged his campaign hat down over his locks.

"I will become a far more public Marxist. If that is what is demanded of me, I intend to perform like a Russian bear. Kennedy will not be pleased, but he will have his chance soon enough to display that, I believe."

Castro patted the pockets of his tunic, looking for something. Coming up empty, he called to the table of *barbudos*.

"Eduardo, a cigar."

One of the bearded ones rose swiftly and shuttled a cigar to Fidel. While the burly man dug in his pocket for a lighter, Castro bit off the tip and rolled the stogie in his mouth. The *barbudo* brought a flame to it and Fidel puffed the tobacco to life.

"Do you like Cuban cigars, Professor?"

"Yes. The best in the world."

"They are indeed. When we have concluded our business, I will offer you one." Fidel breathed in a full load of smoke, emitted it above the table. "Perhaps."

A chill struck across Lammeck's shoulders.

Castro spoke to the table of waiting restaurant staff. "Cruz?"

"Yes, *Commandante*?"

"Back to your kitchen. We'll be leaving in five minutes. You can open for business then."

"Thank you, *Commandante*."

Castro puffed again, blowing the haze directly at Lammeck. He addressed the soldier waiting beside him.

"Eduardo, you and Calderón take the professor outside to the alley. Bring your weapons. The rest wait inside."

Johan said, "*Commandante,* with respect, Professor Lammeck has saved your life."

Fidel stared at Lammeck when he spoke. "Yes, Captain. Now he will be given the chance to save his own."

Lammeck stood. Johan jumped to his feet. Fidel rose gradually, his long frame unfurling from the booth, the cigar fuming above their heads.

Lammeck looked to Johan. The policeman's face was frantic and pleading. He knew that, with one sentence, Lammeck could have Johan condemned and standing next to him in the alley facing the guns of the *barbudos*.

The pair of soldiers bracketed Lammeck front and back, headed for the kitchen door. Passing their table, they snatched submachine guns off the backs of chairs. The other *barbudos* stayed silent.

Lammeck walked, stunned. The poison that might be in his stomach began to churn up into his throat. He kept his own bearded chin high, trying to maintain enough composure to lobby for his life in the coming minutes. But he was frightened, almost past his ability to bear it.

They entered the kitchen in a column, Eduardo in the lead, then Lammeck, followed by the blond *barbudo,* Fidel, and Johan. The two Oriental dishwashers were already at work in clouds of steam and spraying water. One cook diced vegetables on a chopping block. The tall cook Cruz closed a door on an old refrigerator. He carried a cold and fragrant plate of flan to a large sink and dumped it under a stream of water.

Cruz looked over his shoulder at Lammeck. The man scowled.

Some of the turmoil in Lammeck's gut disappeared. He had one less menace to kill him now, he was not poisoned. The botulinum had been in the chilled dessert.

This failed to lift his confidence.

Eduardo pushed open the back door. Without being told,

Lammeck walked to put his back against a high brick wall. The rest took natural positions for an execution; Eduardo and the blond stood opposite Lammeck ten strides away, submachine guns in their hands. Johan moved beside Fidel, off to the side.

Fidel inhaled a great breath through the cigar. The red ember tip glowed in the thin light, illuminating Castro's face. The moment was calm and devilish.

Fidel released the smoke, then said, "Professor Lammeck. I have agreed to free the sniper and the Russian girl in return for my own life. But we have some unresolved issues, you and I."

Lammeck said nothing. He cut his eyes to Johan. The policeman stood with his hands behind his back, eyes cast down to the stones of the alley, as if he were already accused.

Castro put the cigar between two fingers. He shifted it around as he spoke.

"You understand, nothing you told me this evening excuses the fact that you were involved in a secret CIA plot to murder me. Though you may have spared me from it, you have not yet spared yourself. You have had dealings with the turncoat Ferrer, the sniper Hidell, the KGB's treachery, and I cannot imagine what further collaborations with the CIA. So, Professor?"

Lammeck licked his lips to be sure he had enough moisture in his mouth to speak.

"Yes."

"What do you have to offer me in trade for your own life?"

Lammeck took his own deep breath to force down nausea. The alley was dark, but enough light spilled from streetlights elsewhere for him to see Eduardo's finger slide to the trigger of his submachine gun. Johan audibly held his breath.

Lammeck made a silent apology. This was the game everyone else had played, on every side of him since arriving in Havana: Calendar, Johan, Rina, Heitor, they all turned on someone else.

Like spiders, they spun webs and ate their own. Lammeck had tried to keep the secrets and names entrusted to him. But clearly, that way lay his death. This world of assassins, Lammeck thought, was far more savage than he'd ever dreamed.

"Juan Orta Córdova."

Fidel's cigar stopped waving in the air.

"Orta? My old secretary? What about him?" Before Lammeck could say more, Castro's cigar went on the move again, rising with the two fingers to tap himself on the noggin over the campaign hat. "You gave *him* the pills! Of course."

"That's right."

Fidel laughed.

"I fired Orta three months ago. He's a corrupt worm, a dissolute gambler, in the pocket of the Mafia. Oh, this makes perfect sense, Professor. He sold himself to the Mob, then they sold him to the CIA. Yes, yes, I see. After I am dead and the Americans are in charge again, Orta will be rich in influence. Thank you, Professor. Johan?"

The policeman lifted his face to respond. *"Commandante?"*

"Tomorrow, find Orta for me."

Johan nodded and said no more.

"Professor Lammeck?"

"Yes."

"Thank you again for another valuable bit of information. I continue to be amazed and a little saddened at how many people I have trusted wrongly. But Orta is nothing. He is not a counterbalance to you and your involvement. I need more. What else have you got? Who weighs the same as you?"

Johan's features caved. He looked as distraught as Lammeck felt, as if he were a second away from blurting out his own role in the plot. The policeman was clearly convinced Lammeck was ready to sell him out to save his own skin.

Lammeck brought up both his bandaged and good hand in front of him. He raised his two index fingers, a gesture he'd used in untold numbers of classrooms to make summations and his most important points.

"What would you say, *Commandante,* if I told you there was one last CIA agent left in Cuba?"

"I would say that is one too many."

"What if I eliminated him?"

Castro yanked the cigar quickly from his lips. He coughed on smoke that caught him by surprise.

"You mean kill him?"

"Yes."

"*You* will do this?"

Lammeck nodded.

Fidel motioned for the pair of *barbudos* to lower their weapons. He held out a hand to Eduardo. "Another cigar. And your lighter."

Castro approached. He handed Lammeck the stogie, then waited for him to bite the tip and spit it away. Lammeck accepted the flame from inside Castro's cupped palm. The smoke stung his tongue, already tender from the taste of bile.

Castro leaned in more, coming within range to whisper. Lammeck smelled the starch in his olive uniform.

"Tell me the name. How to find him. I will have it done."

"No," Lammeck said, matching Castro's clandestine tone. "I'll do it."

"Why?"

"Plausible deniability."

CHAPTER TWENTY-ONE

★ ★ ★

Colon Cemetery
Twenty-third Street
Vedado

CALENDAR RAISED A BOUQUET of white daisies to his
nose. He breathed in a pleasant, earthy scent.

He watched above the stone cemetery wall, across the street to
the Peking. Castro emerged with five of his *barbudos*. Odd.
Twenty minutes ago, the man had entered the restaurant with an
entourage of seven. Where were the other two?

Fidel hadn't stayed long enough for a full meal, coffee, and
dessert. He and his men got into their pair of jeeps and pulled
away. As soon as they roared off, the black waitress flipped the
CLOSED sign on the door to OPEN. Calendar dropped the flowers
on a grave. The flowers didn't help. Something stunk.

After Castro rode off with his cadre, Calendar hopped the low
wall surrounding the massive graveyard. It had been a spooky

place to wait after the sun went down. The weathered old marble
and quarried stone markers dated back two hundred years. Now,
in the dark, they were sooty and murmuring. Calendar crossed
busy Twenty-third and entered the restaurant, expecting to find
Fidel's two bearded *compañeros* lingering at a table. Instead, the
place was empty. The waitress greeted Calendar with a hand out,
gesturing he could sit where he liked.

"I want to see Cruz."

"He is in the kitchen, *señor.*"

"Get him."

"He is preparing meals—"

Calendar strode away from the short woman. She called after
him, "You cannot go back there!" Calendar snorted at the feeble-
ness of people who tried to stop him.

He pushed on the swinging door to the kitchen. He didn't know
which of the staff was Cruz and called out the name. One man, a
tall Cuban in an apron with a bitter look to him, turned. The others, two Asians and another Cuban, glanced up from their labors,
then ignored him. The tall one came forward.

"Outside," Calendar said.

Cruz followed into the alley. Calendar closed the door behind
them. He scanned in all directions before speaking.

"You know who I am?"

"No, *señor.*"

"Orta works for me. You know me now?"

"Of course."

"What happened?"

The man said nothing. Calendar could not hold his eyes. Cruz
dropped his chin. The cook's mouth worked like a landed fish, he
seemed close to weeping.

Calendar pushed one finger into the apron over the man's lean chest. He walked Cruz backward, as if his finger were the tip of a dagger. Cruz stopped retreating when his back hit the bricks of a wall. He did not lift his head. He sniveled.

"What happened, Cruz?"

"*Señor,* please. It was not my fault."

Calendar wanted to spit, the words rose so foul in his mouth.

"You didn't poison him."

The cook shook his head fast, in a tremor. "Orta said only to serve the poison in food or a cold liquid. Fidel always eats flan for his dessert. I had it ready, hidden in the back of the refrigerator. But a policeman came. And a professor. I threw the flan away and flushed the rest of the pills. What else could I do, *señor?*"

Calendar couldn't stop his hand. It flew around the cook's neck, plugging any answer. The man gagged. Calendar let him choke red before letting him go. Cruz collected his breath, afraid to lift his own hands to his throat.

Calendar asked, "A professor?"

Cruz nodded, again in quick, small motions. "A fat American, older. A gray beard . . ."

"I know him," Calendar said. "What did he do?"

Cruz explained how the American had come to warn Fidel that his food might be poisoned. Fidel made the staff eat from his plate, the American, too. After that, Castro, the professor, and a policeman spoke of a sniper. They talked of a girl, CIA, and KGB. The professor wanted to bargain with Fidel for something.

"For what?"

The cook's voice quaked. "I . . . I could not hear, *señor*. For his life, I suppose."

"No," Calendar said, lowering his hand, "not for his life. He'll have to come to me for that."

He backed away from the cook. "Castro entered with seven *barbudos*. He left with five. Where are the other two?"

"They went out through the back door with the policeman and the American. They did not return."

They're with Lammeck, Calendar thought. Castro's put watchdogs on him. Why? Until he does something. What?

Calendar was weary from the rage he'd expended already today. He had none left for Cruz and this latest debacle wrought by Lammeck. The professor was a pariah, an obstruction to everything Calendar had hoped to accomplish in Cuba. Bringing him into the mission was the worst decision of Calendar's long covert life.

"Go inside," he said. He turned away from Cruz. He needed to find and attend to the professor. He didn't know what was happening with Hidell and the girl, or Johan. Calendar had no notion how he was going to get to Lammeck past Castro's boys. But he would, either here in Havana or soon, back in the States. Before he was done, the professor would provide answers. On top of all that, he still had to find a way to kill Castro.

"*Señor?*"

"What."

"I...owe a great deal of money. Tonight was supposed to take my debt away. I am not to blame. Orta will call. What will I say?"

Calendar blew out an aggravated breath.

"Tell him exactly what happened. Tell him the American probably gave his name to Castro and he needs to drop out of sight. And if he isn't out of the country in forty-eight hours, I'll have to kill him."

The cook jerked at this. Calendar had little subtlety left in him for repairing the damage.

"And what of me, *señor?*"

"The money you owe. Is it to the American Mob?"

"Yes."

This is one, Calendar thought, *I won't have to shut up.*

"You're on your own."

He left the cook standing against the wall.

★ ★ ★

Nacional Hotel

Lammeck flung his bad hand up to protect his face. He flinched and braced, unsure of what was flying toward him. He fell backward against the still-open door. The impact against his arm was slight. She had thrown only a lampshade.

The paper shade landed at his feet. The soldiers taking up station in the hall laughed as Lammeck closed the door fully. She stood on the far side of the bed, the still-glowing lamp cocked and ready to sail in her hands.

"Put it down," he said in Russian.

Rina dropped the lamp to the mattress. She bounded over the bed, jumping across the springs with arms spread wide. In the second before she reached him, he saw how crimson and tearstained she was.

"What's happening?" she implored.

He looked above her head. The room was in shambles; the bed coverings were strewn, a chair had been smashed, the mirror above the dresser cracked. Rina had continued her tantrum after Johan's guards returned her here.

Lammeck tried to peel the girl from him, to look into her face. She clung, resisting his pulling away, crying "No, no, no," as if his purpose was to give her more bad news. He took her by the shoulders, making hushing sounds, and sat her on the wreckage of the bed. He noted bruises on her knuckles, marks from beating at the windows of the police car.

"It's alright," he said. "Rina, listen to me. It's alright. Alek is coming back. You're going home."

The girl blinked. She shook her head in disbelief. Lammeck repeated himself. Slowly, she lowered her fingers from her lips and gawped, still not fully comprehending. She'd had a bad scare, but Lammeck's day had been considerably worse. Alek had jammed a pistol over his heart, he'd thought he was poisoned, he had stared down the barrels of twin machine guns, and now he had to face what was certain to be a lethally angry CIA agent. But Lammeck found himself consoling young Rina, who'd torn up her hotel room.

"Be quiet," he said.

Lammeck collected the shade off the carpet, the lamp from the mattress, and put the two back together to ease the garish light from the bare bulb. He set the lamp upright on its table, moved across the room to the remaining unbroken chair, and sat. Some pink restored itself to the girl's face, replacing the swollen, shiny red.

She sniffled once and focused on Lammeck.

"We are not going to die?"

Irritation flared in Lammeck's chest. He wanted to shake her by the shoulders, shout at her so that the broken mirror would rattle: *What did you think would happen when you came to another land to kill its leader? That there'd be no danger? No fear? This is* killing, *girl!* Lammeck bit his lip and stared at Rina. Lammeck had trained boys this age to go kill. He could instruct their hands and eyes to do the job but their spirits always suffered when the first bullets flew, when the enemy turned on them. Dying, he thought, seems remote at nineteen, without enough life lived to consider what a life really is. But, conversely, when fear grabs hold and sinks in its teeth, an old man stands it best.

"No. Johan's going to bring Alek here in a little while. The two of you are getting on an airplane tonight. You're leaving Cuba."

She dragged a forearm beneath her nose. "How ... how did this happen? Why was Alek arrested?"

"I spoke with Castro myself. He agreed to let you go. More than that you don't need to know."

She glanced around the waste she'd made of the room, as if somehow she might have been responsible for the reprieve. She took only moments to rein herself in. Lammeck admired how fast she did it.

"Mikhal, I said before I would not ask what things you have given up of yourself for Alek and me. But that is not proper. I must know. What have you promised? What have you done?"

"You're a Russian. Alek is a defector. With the invasion coming, Castro can't risk harming either of you. He's going to need Soviet support. I helped convince Fidel it was best for everybody if he just let Alek and you leave."

The girl squeezed Lammeck's knee.

"And what of Calendar? Is he convinced?"

Lammeck waited, thinking of no lie to tell.

He shook his head.

Rina's face grew doleful. "Mikhal, no. Please. Do not confront that *ublyudok*." She called Calendar a bastard.

At least here in Havana, Lammeck thought, he and Calendar would square off face-to-face. Because of this, he had a chance. He meant to say this to Rina, but footsteps sounded through the door. Voices were exchanged between Johan's guard and Lammeck's *barbudos*. The door flew open.

Alek leaped in. Behind him came Johan. Rina squealed. The boy and girl collided and ran hands over each other as if to confirm the reality of Alek's return.

Alek caught Lammeck's eye above her shoulder pressed tight under his chin. The boy smiled. Lammeck noted the boy's left socket was swollen and bluing.

Johan came to stand beside Lammeck, ignoring the young couple. Lammeck spoke in Spanish, for privacy from Alek and Rina,
who likely were not listening.

"Was he questioned?"

The policeman shook his head. "No. One of my men got a bit
zealous. Actually, Hidell swung first, I was told."

"Do you believe that?"

Johan now looked at the embracing boy and girl.

"Oh, yes. I do. There's something about you Americans. Even
the defectors. All cowboys and spies. Perhaps it is your movies that
make you this way."

Lammeck grinned.

Johan announced, "Time to go."

Rina released Alek first. She turned from him and approached
Johan. Her blue eyes were dry and restrained.

In English, she said, "Thank you, sir."

Johan accepted her hand and nodded. For that moment, he and
the girl seemed to Lammeck as equals. Johan had laid a trap for
her, she'd eluded it, they'd both survived. The handshake was that
of respected adversaries and, in keeping with the code of their
trades, left volumes unspoken.

Rina took her hand from Johan. She stepped in front of
Lammeck but said nothing, only laid her open palm over his heart.
She looked there, not into his face, as if what lay inside him were
what she committed to memory. She turned for the door.

Alek glanced around the room, at the mess. The boy looked at
Rina, then shrugged. He came to Lammeck, hand extended. He
did not look at Johan.

"Hey, look, I'm sorry and all. I'm glad I didn't shoot you."

Lammeck took the boy's thin hand gently with his bandaged
mitt. Up close, he saw Alek was going to sport a fine black
eye.

Beside Lammeck, Johan cleared his throat. The boy looked at him now, sheepish.

"I reckon I'm glad I didn't shoot Castro either."

Johan inclined his head. "Gracious of you. Shall we go, Mr. Hidell? The sooner you are away, the better."

Alek tugged his hand away, but Lammeck held on. The cut in his palm stung.

In a low voice, he said, "Tell her, son."

"Tell her what?"

"That you're trying to get back to America. She loves you. She thinks you're going to stay with her in Russia."

"I *am* gonna stay with her. I'm gonna bring her back with me."

Calendar would never allow that. But Calendar had yet to be dealt with.

"Then at least tell her you were under a threat from the CIA."

"Why would I do that?"

"Because she doesn't know you were forced to do this. Right now, she thinks you're just an assassin."

Alek crossed the room to Rina. He put his arm around her waist and ushered her out the door. When she was in the hall, out of hearing range, he leaned back through the doorway, grinning.

"An assassin. Maybe that's what I am, Professor."

The boy raised his thumb and stuck out his index finger at Lammeck's midriff, making the hand a little gun. He crooked the thumb as if the gun had gone off, and smirked. "See you."

Behind Alek, the door eased itself shut. Johan, with Lammeck, stared after him. The policeman sighed. "I'm sure it's in your movies."

The policeman walked around the ruined bed to a window. He gazed out at old Havana. Lammeck moved to another window. The wind, absent all this drawn-out day, had kicked up.

Whitecapped waves whipped the island, drenching the Malecón. Puddles shimmered on the road beneath the traffic, evening strollers on the sidewalk scuttled and laughed.

"I'll put you in a different room, Professor."

"Thank you."

"Fidel's *barbudos* will stay on guard. Blanco will bring dinner from outside the hotel. I will join you after I have seen those two off the island."

"I'll have a steak. And beer. Ask Blanco to join us."

"Certainly."

Lammeck left the window. He found an ink pen on the floor and a piece of hotel stationery. He ripped away the Nacional Hotel's logo and scribbled a note. He folded the page, then handed it to Johan.

"Take this to my house. Leave it out where Calendar can find it."

"May I look?"

"Go ahead."

Johan opened the crease. He smiled at the words.

Tomorrow. Inglaterra. High noon.

"High noon, Professor?"

Lammeck returned to the window. He watched a wave batter the seawall. Johan left the room, muttering, "Just as I said. Cowboys and spies."

CHAPTER TWENTY-TWO

★ ★ ★

April 10
Nacional Hotel

LAMMECK STARED AT THE blank, white ceiling of his hotel room. The sun would not rise for another hour; the plaster was lit only by streetlights far below on the Malecón. He rose from bed, went to the windows to check the morning winds. A front had passed in the night while he tossed. The coming day promised to be calm.

Lammeck dressed. He opened the door slowly, letting it click to alert the guards outside. One *barbudo* stood facing him, the blond from the restaurant. The other was on the hall floor, slumped against the wall, sound asleep.

"Wake him," Lammeck said. "Do you have a car?"

"Yes."

The ride to Miramar in the open jeep was bracing. Lammeck

enjoyed the antique feel of it, recalling younger days when he trained fighters for the OSS in Scotland during the war. This set off other memories in his heart, of friends and classrooms, a snowy childhood, women, on this day when he would commit murder, or die.

He guided the *barbudos* to his house. One stayed in the idling vehicle, the blond put a pistol in his hand and went inside first, clearing the rooms before beckoning Lammeck to come. Lammeck grabbed what he needed. He found the priests' knife and the sheath. He picked up the dagger, admiring again the heft and balance. The blade, like the ride in the jeep, launched him into another reverie, of his studies and work. He wondered about the book he'd come to Havana to research, feeling it could be great and wanting to live to write it. Lammeck put down the knife. Before leaving, he looked for the note Johan was to have set out. He could not find it.

He stood in his backyard, looking toward the old city in the east, until the orange cap of the sun peered above the horizon. The two *barbudos* guarded Lammeck from a distance, leaving him alone in the dawn, as if he were a condemned man.

He turned from the flat sea and the waning stars.

"Let's go," he called to the soldier eyeing him from the porch of the house.

Monday morning traffic joined them on the roads, office workers trudged the sidewalks, a horse-drawn cart of construction workers slowed a lane on the Malecón. Pulling into the grounds of the Nacional, the jeep cruised past gardeners spraying hoses over the lawn. Taxis pulled up to the front door with the day's first arrivals from the airport and harbor. The silent *barbudos* accompanied Lammeck inside. Again, the blond led the way, his hand on the butt of his pistol. He did the same when they arrived at

Lammeck's room, then planted himself beside the door. The other soldier, darkly bearded and portly, asked Lammeck what he would like for breakfast. He would go out of the hotel for the food.

"Nothing," Lammeck said. "I'll wait for lunch. Get yourselves something."

Closing the door, he heard the blond guard order *huevos y jamón* and *café con leche.*

"Get some for the professor," the blond said. "In case he changes his mind."

Lammeck took off his khakis and *guayabera,* lapping them over the back of a chair. He lay on the ruffled bed, his head to the pillow. The ceiling remained bare but this time glowed with a golden morning light. Lammeck closed his eyes and found to his relief that he'd finished thinking. Finding no reason or way to turn back, he did what he could not in the darkness. He slept.

Lammeck awoke to the aroma of eggs. He lifted his head to see a foil-covered paper plate on the dresser. Napkins and a fork were set beside it. He peeled back the foil to find cooled scrambled eggs, chorizo sausage, and two limp slices of white bread. He opened the door to thank the dark-haired guard there, and to make sure it had been he who'd brought the food.

After eating, Lammeck showered and dressed. At ten o'clock, he opened the door to his room.

"We'll walk," he said to the guard.

The blond *barbudo* had talked a maid into letting him sleep in an empty room. He was found and awakened. The soldiers moved to Lammeck's sides and stayed there out of the hotel. Lammeck strode between the two olive uniforms, not certain if he looked like a dignitary or a convict.

He took pleasure in the sunny Malecón. He would miss Havana

when he left, if he managed not to be buried here in the next few days. Soon, if the exiles succeeded and retook the island, Lammeck would come back. He'd observe and record the next cycle of Cuba's history. He'd try to buy that house in Miramar. Maybe he would be buried here, after all.

At eleven o'clock, Lammeck and his escorts arrived at the Partagas factory behind *El Capitolio*. He purchased a half dozen Diplomaticos, gave two each to his *barbudos,* lit one, and pocketed the other. Out of curiosity, and to kill the last bits of time, he marked off the steps between the south wing of the capitol where Alek had been and the spot where the viewing platform had stood on Prado. He counted five hundred and ten strides.

At eleven forty-five, Lammeck crossed the boulevard to the Inglaterra. His guardians melted away. For the first moments, he felt vulnerable, searching the sky, buildings, and crowd around him, magnifying Calendar's power to reach him. Then Lammeck dropped the last of his cigar, patted his pants pocket, and stepped through the iron gate of the hotel patio.

The waiter Gustavo greeted him. A table had been reserved for Lammeck in the center of the bistro. Already, lunching Cubans were seated with beers and sandwiches. Lammeck took a chair, knitting fingers in his lap to keep his hands from showing his nerves.

"Beer, Gustavo."

The waiter brought the drink quickly. Lammeck was relieved, the glass gave his hand and eyes a focus. He resisted the need to swivel his head in all directions, looking for the *barbudos,* for Johan and his men embedded somewhere around the patio, and for Calendar.

To distract himself, Lammeck kept an eye on the hands of his watch sweeping toward noon. He keened his ears to the ticking, surprised at how slowly time moved when measured in the shivering of a second hand. The hand stuttered past the twelve. All of Lammeck's fear subsided. He felt only resignation and an unbidden sadness.

A hand grazed his shoulder from behind. Before he could turn, Calendar was beside him, moving into the open chair. The large agent collapsed with a gassy grunt, sounding tired. He spun a folded note on the table between them.

"Who're you all of a sudden, Gary Cooper?"

Lammeck took the sheet of stationery and read his own handwriting.

Gustavo appeared beside the table.

"Will you be joining the professor for a beer, *señor*?"

Calendar flicked a hand. "Cristal."

The waiter hustled off.

Calendar sat back, folding his arms on top of his big middle. Both eyes were reddened.

"Long night?" Lammeck asked.

"Yeah."

"Trying to find me?"

"You're just one of my worries, Professor."

"I'm glad to know that."

"Don't get too happy. You've got my full attention at the moment."

Calendar leaned forward over his crossed arms, setting them on the tabletop. He lowered his voice.

"Let me get right to the point. You fucked everything up. You know there's an invasion coming soon, right? There's gonna be fifteen hundred armed Cubans on a beach, all of 'em landing with one idea in their heads. Take Cuba back. The whole free world is counting on them."

"If you say so."

"Goddam right—" Calendar caught his volume rising. He leaned closer and eased his tone. "Goddam right I say so. And you know what? The odds are, the only chance they got is if Castro's dead when they show up. The people on the island have got to revolt, and they're not gonna do that if Fidel's alive and screaming into a microphone keeping everybody in line. You understand? We're talking about making history here. Who the hell should know that better than *you*? You got that last capsule with you?"

"Yes."

"Let me see it."

Lammeck dug into his pocket, set the pill on the table. "Is that what this is about for you, Calendar? Making history?"

"American history, Professor. I could give a crap about Cuba. This is for our security. Period."

"So you throw lives away left and right. Heitor, Susanna, Felix. You put others' at risk, mine included. You use torture, murder, and assassination, not to mention extortion. Is that the American history you think we should be writing?"

Calendar snorted. "Don't moralize to me, Professor. You don't have hands clean enough for the job. You were hot to play along with Castro's murder, so long as it got you into a plum position to write about it. You trained Alek knowing exactly what he was assigned to do. You handed Orta the pills knowing what they were for. So get off my back. Hypocrisy doesn't look good on you. Or wait a minute. Maybe you just got cold feet."

"What I got was a slap in the face when you sent me out to get killed. I found out real fast I was just an historian. Making history's for somebody else."

"Me." Calendar crammed a finger into his own girth. "It's for *me*, Professor."

Lammeck shook his head. "No. You're not a force of history. You know how I can tell?"

The agent looked to the sky to demonstrate his disdain. But when he brought his eyes down, he asked, "How?"

"Because you failed. Castro's alive. Alek and Rina are long gone. Johan wants nothing to do with you. From the standpoint of history, you never existed. Life goes on. Now it's down to just you and me. Bud and Mikhal. We're everybody. And we're nobody. Just like you said."

"Okay, enough," Calendar snapped. "This isn't one of your classrooms. I've got real-world shit to take care of. What'd you tell Castro?"

"Everything. Alek, Rina, CIA, KGB. Orta."

"What about Johan?"

"I left him out of it. Didn't see the point."

"Look at you. The same as me, deciding who lives, who dies. That's not a nobody, Professor. That's power."

"Indeed."

"So Castro knows Alek was a CIA sniper. And Rina was KGB. I guess he knows both agencies were in it together."

"Yes. And he blames the CIA. Correctly."

"Too bad. It was a hell of a plan."

"Castro was impressed."

"Still, I don't get it. Why'd he let Alek and the girl go?"

Out of the corner of his eye, Lammeck caught a glimpse of one of the *barbudos* moving on the sidewalk along Prado. He fixed his focus back on Calendar, to keep from drawing the agent's attention to the soldier. Chances were, Calendar knew about Lammeck's bodyguards, and was not concerned. He was that slippery.

"I made a trade," Lammeck said. "I offered myself instead. Fidel took it."

Calendar laid both palms flat on the table. "Why did you do that?"

"Be realistic, Calendar. Alek was going to give me up in the first five minutes he was interrogated. I was a dead man. So I figured at least I'd try to save somebody. I picked Alek and Rina. And Johan."

"And Castro."

"Yes. Him, too."

"But not yourself?"

"No. And Calendar?"

"What."

"Not you."

Lammeck lifted his beer and swigged the rest. Calendar waited. Lammeck watched the empty glass drizzle foam.

"Forget about it. You can't touch me, Professor. And Johan won't lay a glove on me, I know way too much about him. The moment I stand up and walk away from this table, I disappear. Guys like you, and that punk Alek, the Russian girl, you play at being spies. But this is what I *do*. You understand?"

"Vividly."

"Good. You also understand I can't let Castro put you in La Cabaña. Not on my watch. You're an American citizen. That'd be bad for my reputation if you got yourself interrogated, or even got executed. But I can't let you off the island either." The agent tapped on the table. "What to do?"

Lammeck nodded. Calendar's threat had been oblique, but clear enough. And inevitable.

"You can have one last beer with me."

The agent pursed his lips. "Why not."

Lammeck raised a hand to snare the waiter's attention.

The pause for the waiter to come created an intermission between them. Both sat back quietly in their seats. Another man, not Gustavo, wove through the tables to come take the order for two more Cristals.

When he was gone, Lammeck and Calendar stared at each other

for prolonged moments. Lammeck took pains to keep his face vacant. Calendar spoke first.

"You know the game. Where this is going."

"I do."

"Then why're you here? Why'd you want to sit down and talk? It's not going to change anything."

"I hoped it might."

"Go ahead. I got time."

"I wanted you to know that I'm done being scared of you."

"Good for you."

"I'm through wondering all day if you got to my food somehow, not sleeping at night, bodyguards, checking every shadow. That's going to drive me crazy if it goes on much longer."

"Don't worry. It won't."

"I know. So I wanted to sit down with you one last time. To tell you, face-to-face, what I told Castro."

"And that is?"

"I'm going to kill you."

Calendar didn't move, except to mount a predator's grin.

"I am," Lammeck said, unprepared for Calendar's stillness.

"Good luck with that."

"I know you can get to me a thousand ways. You'll bribe a guard at the prison. You'll get a cabbie to run me down, a thief to knife me, a cook to poison me."

Calendar nodded, enjoying Lammeck's assessment. "I figure it'll cost me a hundred pesos. More or less."

"Is that the going rate?"

"That's what Felix charged me."

"Maybe you'll threaten Johan into doing it for you."

"Better idea. I can get him for free."

"Then you'll go after Castro again. And when you're done with him, some other poor sucker on the planet who pisses off the CIA. You won't stop."

"No, I won't. It's my job. It's my nature. And here's a news flash for you, Professor: I like it."

"I know. So I'm going to stop you."

"Don't kid yourself. No one ever has. And I've played rough with some of the big boys. Guys that pansy historians like you only write about."

"You don't have history on your side, Calendar. Not this time. I can tell. Like you said, who would know better than me?"

The beers arrived. Setting them on the table, the waiter inclined his head to Lammeck. "They are very cold, *señor.*"

Lammeck reached for his glass. Calendar held out a palm to stop him from drinking.

"You remember what I told you, early on? That when the time came, if it looked like you were gonna get caught"—Calendar aimed a finger at the capsule on the table—"you would take that?"

"I remember."

"The time has come."

"No."

"Okay," the agent said. His voice was straightforward, like the knife thrust that killed Felix. "Here's the deal. Don't make me come after you, Lammeck. Don't make me hunt you down, crawl around in your shadows anymore. Pop that pill in your mouth and chase it with that beer. Then our business is done."

"And what if you have to come after me?"

"I'll make it as miserable a death as I can manage. And not only will I kill you. I'll ruin your name. I'll do everything I promised you I would and more. Your legacy at Brown, in academic circles, in publishing, I'll steal it and wipe so much shit on it that people will spit on the floor when you come up in conversation."

Calendar sat back, folding his arms again. His voice remained a low, even rumble.

"You're not gonna kill me. That was nice brave talk. But you don't stand a chance. Like I told you, this is what I do. You're a teacher. School's out. Take the pill."

"And if I do?"

"Then I leave you alone to die. I'll forget about you the minute we get up from these beers. You got my word on that. And don't give me any malarkey that my word's no good. I don't double-cross a dying man."

Lammeck's eyes fell to the capsule.

"Is that the only kind you don't double-cross?"

"Just take the pill. Make it easy on us both."

Lammeck stared at the capsule. He did not lift his eyes when Calendar said, "You know this is where we been headed since day one."

With a quick motion of his bandaged hand, Lammeck swept up the capsule, flipped it into his mouth, and swallowed a deep draught of beer.

"Okay," Calendar said, easing his expression and voice. "Okay."

Lammeck placed the glass on the table. He gazed into it like a fortune-teller's ball, watching bubbles flee up into the foam. He did not look directly at Calendar when the agent lifted his own beer for a swallow. He let Calendar take a swig, then, keeping his head down, raised his glass and drank again.

"How's the hand?" Calendar asked.

"It hurts."

The agent snickered, cruel.

"It'll get better soon."

Lammeck stood from the table. He pulled from his wallet a pair of hundred-peso notes. He tucked them under the bottom of his beer glass.

He looked at Calendar now. "Make sure the two waiters get these."

"That's a big tip. Giving away all your wealth?"

"The first one's name is Gustavo."

"Him I know. How about the second guy?"

"Blanco. And, Calendar?"

"Yeah."

"Just so you know how I figured it out. Alek Hidell can't be the kid's actual name. He couldn't have gotten a U.S. passport under his real identity. He's a defector. That means he's given up his American citizenship. Johan had to issue the entry visa to a fake passport. That's when I guessed he was in on it. The rest was easy."

"You're a smart man, Professor."

"And you're a *pendejo*."

Lammeck watched the agent take one more drink. Calendar licked his lips when he put down the glass.

"Hey, Lammeck."

"What."

"You still gonna kill me?"

"Yes."

"Well, pal, the clock's running."

Lammeck took a step away from the table, then halted.

"One last thing, Calendar."

"That's well put. One last thing. Tick tick tick."

"Just out of curiosity. What's Alek's real name?"

Calendar hesitated.

Lammeck held up his hands, yielding. "I won't tell anybody."

The agent shrugged. "I guess you won't. It's Oswald. Lee Oswald."

Lammeck made no parting gesture, just left the patio. He crossed Prado to stroll back to the Nacional. The two *barbudos* picked him up quickly. They fell in around him.

He reached in the pocket of his *guayabera* for the second cigar. He bit off the tip and accepted a light from the blond soldier.

After a long, savored puff, Lammeck dug into his pants pocket for another sugar pill. He tossed it onto his tongue and sucked on it. The thing tasted sweet.

CHAPTER TWENTY-THREE

★ ★ ★

April 12
Nacional Hotel

LAMMECK YANKED OPEN THE door. The guard, one he had not seen yet in his imprisonment, started.

"That's enough," Lammeck said in English, forgetting himself. The soldier did not register. Lammeck switched to Spanish. *"Bastante."*

"Enough of what, *señor*? Are you finished with lunch?"

"Do you know Captain Johan?"

"Yes."

"Tell him to get over here. As soon as he can."

The *barbudo* was young, with a black beard hardly grown in. Lammeck handed him an empty bottle of *siete* rum.

"More," he said, and closed the door.

★ ★ ★

Lammeck lay on the bed, arms and legs spread over the rumpled sheets, a disheveled starburst. He gazed at the bare ceiling, watching the changing light of his third sunset in this hotel room, first copper, then deepening to red, finally indigo to black. He did not rise or turn on the bedside lamp, but let the room darken until the white plaster was washed in the electric yellow of streetlights from the Malecón.

He closed his eyes, not seeking sleep. He simply wanted release, from the coop of this room, from Cuba, the killing of Calendar, from the labyrinths of assassination and betrayal. He needed to trim his beard and switch out of his khakis and undershirt. He had no razor, scissors, or fresh clothes, no toiletries. The only other items in the room with him were an uneaten dinner on the dresser and another well-used bottle.

When Johan arrived an hour after sundown, Lammeck knew the man was coming down the hall before he knocked. Lammeck's senses for what went on outside his door had grown acute. He stood from the bed, turned on the light, and checked himself in the mirror, in case there might be some instant improvement he could make in his appearance. There was none. Johan knocked.

"Come in, Captain."

The policeman poked his head around the door, careful, as though unsure what he would find inside. Lammeck waved him through the door. "Where have you been?"

Johan stepped in, closing the door behind him. He sniffed the air.

"Clearly away too long. It smells like monkeys in here. You need a shave, Professor. Have you showered?" The captain walked to the dresser. He poked a fingertip into the cold plate of food. Beside the stale dish stood the uncapped bottle of *siete*.

"It's been over forty-eight hours," Lammeck said. "He's dead. I want to go home."

Johan shook his head.

"I am sorry, *amigo*. That cannot happen just yet. We have no proof. Fidel was quite specific about the terms of your agreement."

"Goddammit." Lammeck sat on a corner of the bed. "Didn't your men follow him from the Inglaterra?"

Johan settled in a chair. "Yes."

"And they lost him?"

"Remember, Professor. We are talking about a career CIA field agent. This is a man who's worked in a hundred places around the world as a ghost. Calendar did not intend to be followed. So he was not."

Lammeck fell back on the mattress, his hands pressed against his temples.

"Do you think something went wrong? With the poison?"

"I have no way of knowing that."

"Blanco put it in his beer, you're sure?"

"Everything went the way it was supposed to."

"So until you find his body, I'm stuck here."

"Or until Fidel loses patience and revokes his arrangement with you."

Lammeck closed his eyes again, barely able to look more at the ceiling.

"That wouldn't be good for you either, Johan."

"I am aware of that. Trust me, I am using every man I can spare to find Calendar."

Without looking, Lammeck heard Johan reach to the dresser for the rum bottle.

"You know the way," Johan said, "when a dog has been hit by a car on the highway, it often dies where it has been struck in the middle of the road. But a cat. A cat will somehow drag itself off the pavement. It will die on the shoulder or in the ditch, out of traffic. I believe this is what our Agent Calendar has done. He has always been a tiger. He has crawled somewhere else to die, not in the middle of the road."

Johan set down the bottle. He rose from the chair and went into the bathroom. Lammeck heard the squeak of handles, then the spray of water. The captain came beside the bed to stand over him.

"Clean yourself, Professor. I am going out for an hour. I'll be back."

Lammeck sat up. He glanced into the open bathroom door. Steam began to spill across the floor tiles.

"Where're you going?"

"To find Blanco. He will arrange a security detail."

"For what?"

"I am going to transfer you out of this hotel before the other guests complain about your odor. You can wait for Calendar at your own house."

Johan took up the ignored plate of food and the drained bottle. Without another word, he carried them out the door. Lammeck was left alone with the running shower.

★ ★ ★

April 13
Miramar

"Professor, please." Blanco shrugged. "Move."

Lammeck's right hand, finally without the gauze wrapping, hovered above his remaining rook. He saw an opening that might develop in three or four turns.

"Quiet," he said, wiggling his fingers, enjoying the absence of the bandage. The gash in his palm was knitting well. He believed the salt air of the nearby ocean had helped his healing, as Johan had prescribed.

Blanco sighed, doing his best to restrain his impatience. Lammeck's wait here at his house, among his books and notes, with a television and human company and the sea, was better than the miserable two and a half days at the Nacional. Still, he was not a free man, and he drank more than he knew was good for him. His status was paradoxical; he needed to be proven a murderer to regain his liberty.

He tapped on the rampart of the little wooden chess castle. Dinner dishes sat unwashed on the table behind them. Lammeck had cooked chicken for the two of them, then delivered sandwiches to the four others out in the dark guarding the house, the men keeping Lammeck prisoner. Two glasses of rum waited beside the chessboard.

Lammeck pulled his finger away, exploring instead into his beard to consider a different ploy.

"*This,*" said Blanco, rising from the sofa, "is the difference between us. You deliberate, you analyze, endlessly. Just move!"

Lammeck watched the young policeman turn a frustrated circle in the living room before he plopped again onto the sofa.

Amused, Lammeck said, "Another difference is that I've won six out of seven."

"Yes." Blanco reclined farther into the sofa, leaning his head back to gaze upward. "And when the games are over, you are not exhausted."

"You're younger. I have to conserve my energy."

"No," Blanco said, sitting straight, then leaning over the table. "I know you. You have always been this way."

True, Lammeck thought, then said it aloud. "True." He returned to the rook and shoved it forward four squares. Instantly he regretted the move he'd been goaded into, seeing ahead the trouble he might have gotten into.

Outside, footsteps approached on the sidewalk. Blanco stared glumly at the chessboard. Before the young policeman could take his turn, Johan came through the front door. He carried with him a newspaper and a flashlight.

Blanco started to rise, Lammeck kept his seat. Johan waved the young policeman down. He dropped a folded *New York Times* into Lammeck's lap, then headed for the kitchen. While fetching himself a tumbler to share in the rum, he called to Lammeck.

"That is yesterday's paper."

"Anything of interest?"

Johan arrived beside the chessboard as Blanco made his move with a knight. Blanco did not counter Lammeck's blunder. The captain set the flashlight down to pour himself a shot while scrutinizing the board. Clucking his tongue, he reached down to take back Blanco's move. Instead, he pushed forward a bishop which, in two more moves, if the queen were involved, could capture Lammeck's rook.

The captain patted Blanco on the shoulder. "You need to slow down. You missed an opportunity."

Blanco slid sideways on the sofa to make room for Johan. "Please, sir, finish the game."

"No." Johan smiled. "I will enjoy watching the *viejo* teach you a few things. He's outmaneuvered me quite a bit lately."

The captain pointed at the newspaper.

"Your Kennedy said at a press conference that under no circumstances will the United States intervene militarily in Cuba. He claims the conflict is not between America and Cuba but between Cubans themselves. He is, of course, lying."

Lammeck looked at the chessmen, imagining the moves Kennedy was needing to make in advance of the invasion, now that one big strategy—the assassination of Castro—had failed.

Johan asked, "Have you been playing chess all night? Did you not turn on the television?"

Blanco answered, "What happened?"

"The El Encanto has burned to the ground."

"The shopping center?" The place was in the center of Havana.

Johan sipped his rum, turning to look through the open back door, to the stars and the sound of waves. "It seems that while the store was owned by rich men, there was no need to destroy it. Once it belonged to the people, it was marked for flames. The El Encanto is gone, completely. There were deaths."

The captain brought his head around. He circled a hand above the chessboard.

"The forces are gathering, Professor. I can feel it. A few more moves to go."

Blanco rose. "I will tell the men about the fire."

They waited for the young man to exit.

Johan said, "I have good news, and I have bad news. Myself, I always prefer the bad first. It leaves me something to look forward to."

Lammeck lifted his rum glass. He tilted it Johan's way.

Johan said, "You will not be leaving Cuba for a while longer. I am sorry. This is out of my control."

Lammeck brought the rum beneath his nose to inhale the fragrance before taking a swallow. The slow gesture, like his measured chess playing, helped keep his emotions in check, his reaction measured.

"Why not?"

"After the El Encanto fire, Fidel has decided to lock the island down. In Havana alone, over thirty-five thousand people suspected of anti-regime sentiment are being detained as we speak. Jails and prisons in every part of Cuba are overflowing. Fidel has suspended all commercial flights. Shipping has been advised to stay offshore. Castro suspects, as do we all, that the rebels are on their way. The invasion is only days, maybe hours, away. The only remaining questions are exactly when and precisely where."

Lammeck poured some rum across his lips. He let the liquid rest on his tongue, a pleasure in a world fast running short of them.

Johan continued. "I am sorry, my friend, I have not been able to visit with you during your own incarceration. I have been, to put it mildly, busy."

"Why do you call me your friend, Johan? You were willing to let me be killed by Alek. You would've put me in La Cabaña."

The captain picked a knight off the chessboard. "This is my favorite piece. But I do not hesitate to send him into harm's way to defend my king." He set the horse on the square where it resided. "Now, ask me about the good news."

"It'll have to be pretty good to balance out the bad."

"We will see. Come."

Grabbing the flashlight, the captain led Lammeck out the front door. The evening was balmy, the street deserted except for a few parked police vehicles. The only light for blocks in both directions came from his house.

Johan approached Blanco, who was speaking with one of Lammeck's guards.

"We will be gone a few minutes."

The young policeman asked, "Do you want me to come?"

"No. Professor Lammeck and I both lack the ability to escape each other."

Without cutting on the light, Johan walked into the empty street. He strolled with Lammeck down the center of the starlit road.

"Professor, you are renowned for your ability to think like an assassin. Since coming to Cuba, you have been personally involved with an assassination plot. You have poisoned a man. I must wonder whether becoming a murderer yourself has decayed your powers as an intellectual of murder. I fear Cuba has cost the world a scholar."

Lammeck stopped walking. "You found Calendar."

"I merely stumbled upon him. After all, I am not the genius between the two of us, just a poor administrator. You should have figured it out. Even I am embarrassed for you."

"Why?"

"Because his whereabouts, when I show you, are sadly obvious."

Johan walked more along the dark coast road, headed in the same direction they had a week ago, past deserted houses.

"Since you came to the island, I have enjoyed the few times I visited you here in Miramar. Our talks on your porch with a candle, the smell of salt, the breeze fresh on your face before it strikes the city. Just this evening I decided I would seek permission to take over one of these dilapidated houses for myself. This is appropriate, you know, as the number two man in my department. Besides, recently I have had a string of notable successes. Thanks to you. And, of course, Agent Calendar."

"Heitor."

"Spilt milk, Professor. Let it go. My point is, this evening, on my way to come tell you about Castro's restrictions on travel, I walked this road, looking over some of the homes. Though abandoned, you may have noticed they have not been vandalized."

Johan clicked on the flashlight. He stopped walking and shined the light on a one-story stucco house, three doors down from Lammeck's.

"This was the only one with a broken window in the rear."

Lammeck's throat tightened. "He's in there."

"Shall we?"

The back of the house featured a porch bigger than Lammeck's. A pane had been smashed in. The window frame, like all the others, remained shut. Lammeck said nothing, working to control his revulsion at the thought of what lay inside. But he had to see for himself the completion of what he'd set in motion.

Johan turned the knob to the unlocked back door. He pushed it open, moved inside. Lammeck hung back.

"Professor," Johan said without turning the flashlight on him. "Come see your handiwork."

Before entering, a wretched stench unfurled out of the doorway, draping itself over Lammeck. Feces. Putrefaction. He cupped a hand across his nose and forced himself forward.

The interior was bare. Johan's flashlight found Calendar upturned on a tile floor. He lay beneath a window facing the direction of Lammeck's house. The sallow flashlight beam gave his flesh the color of a pustule.

The house had been shut up, the only ventilation was the broken glass pane. The past two days had been warm. Lammeck lowered his fingers from his nostrils to test the odor. Instantly he fought down a gag and returned his hand over his nose.

The policeman kept his distance, focusing the flashlight on the corpse. Two days of death had changed Bud Calendar. Lammeck neared the corpse and kneeled. The agent's belly was swollen with unreleased gases. The violet of pooling blood splotched the backs of his arms and neck. The skin felt firm like wax. Lammeck pressed and pulled back, his touch left no impression.

The flashlight revealed no signs of struggle. Calendar's eyelids were lowered. No blood stained his mouth or hands. The cheeks displayed some broken capillaries from his last labored gasps, the final stages of the poison's paralysis. The toxin had simply lain Calendar down when it got the upper hand and choked him.

Lammeck leaned over the mound of the bloated torso. A .32 revolver had been tucked into the belt at the dead man's hip. On the other side of the body, on the floor close to Calendar's right hand, lay a long-bladed skinning knife.

Calendar had come to Miramar. Lammeck's mind raced

backward from this final destination. Hours after their encounter at the Inglaterra, perhaps as soon as dusk, Calendar must have felt the first awful symptoms of the botulinum. He knew. He must have gone into a fury.

He'd promised Lammeck a terrible death. Instead, that death was coming for him. With the numbness rising in his feet and legs, Calendar must have seethed an oath. He swore that a wicked end would not be his alone.

Angry, he struggled to the only place he was sure Lammeck would return to. He brought weapons to keep his vow. He kept watch, knowing the poison's clock. Twenty-four to forty-eight hours. He waited. He held out.

He died waiting.

Lammeck stood away from Calendar. He expected that he would want to retch but his stomach had calmed. He lowered his hand from his nose.

"Let's go," he said.

Lammeck walked away to the kitchen and out the back door. He walked off the porch to the weedy lawn. He spit. A deep breath of the ocean cleared his lungs. Behind him, he heard Johan open a window from inside.

The captain shut off the flashlight and came to Lammeck's side. Together they gazed north. Silver tinged the eastern horizon where the moon prepared to rise.

"I should like this house," Johan said.

"You're not bothered that Calendar died in there?"

"No. Quite the opposite."

Lammeck and Johan let a hushed minute pass, both gazing into the night. Lammeck wondered if the captain, a man accustomed to such violence as what lay behind them, was standing here like him, appreciating life more, the small miracle of standing here. Or was

Johan simply imagining what he might plant in this yard, how he would furnish the porch?

Johan said, "I will inform Fidel. You are a free man, Professor."

"Sort of."

"When events slow down, I will return Agent Calendar's body to the CIA. Perhaps even a man like him had a family."

"How're you going to explain what happened?"

"Simple. I will tell them what they already know. His plot to assassinate Castro collapsed. He did the brave thing for a covert agent in a foreign country and took his own botulinum pill. He will be a hero."

"Very tidy. You've got a gift for that sort of thing. Half-truths."

"We all have our abilities, Professor. Come."

In the dark, the two walked out of the yard, back to the road.

"I will have the body taken away in the morning," Johan said.

"Can't you do it tonight?"

"No. There are procedures. And please, do not come back over here."

"Not in a million years."

Johan eyed him. "You are a fascinating man. You are hesitant and squeamish, but when pushed can be formidable and dangerous. You are brilliant, but will disregard what is right in front of you. I have never met another man with such a spectrum inside him. I should enjoy playing chess with you. Let me see your palm."

Lammeck turned his hand up and set it in Johan's. The policeman shined the light into it. With his thumb, he prodded the red streak of Lammeck's wound.

"This will not leave a scar."

"No."

"When this is healed, there will be nothing left of what happened between you and me. Alek and Rina do not know. Only us. Please, Professor, keep our secrets. Do not write the book you came to research. It would not serve either of our interests. Let Calendar rest. And let him rest alone."

Lammeck took back his hand. "Is that your opening move of our chess game, Captain?"

"Very clever, my friend. Yes."

Lammeck patted Johan's arm. "Good. I'll enjoy playing you, too. *Buena suerte.*"

"*Y tu también.*"

"By the way. I asked Calendar what Alek's real name is."

"It is an average name, nothing noteworthy. Why did you care to find out?"

Lammeck flicked a hand in the air. "Just curious. In case I hear from him again. I don't think I will."

CHAPTER TWENTY-FOUR

★ ★ ★

April 15
Miramar

LAMMECK AWOKE TO KNOCKING. He answered the front door to find Blanco holding a mesh bag of fruits and vegetables, a loaf of bread, and meats wrapped in butcher paper.

"Turn on your television."

Lammeck set the groceries on a kitchen counter, then joined Blanco in front of the RCA. The screen took moments to warm, green sizzles swarmed its face. A reporter appeared at a desk in a bare studio, sheets of paper in his hands. Reading from the pages, he seemed hasty, chased by the news he was reporting. He pronounced the names of several Cuban air bases, and the word, over and over, *ataque*. Attack.

The image shifted to a scene of smoke and wreckage, an airfield. A dozen aircraft coughed flames and smoke, their wings askew, wheels melted.

Blanco spoke over the commentator's voice, impatient for Lammeck to know what had happened.

"At dawn this morning, B-26's hit three air bases in Havana and Oriente. It's the invasion, Professor. It's starting. I went to get you some groceries first thing before there was a run on the stores."

"Thank you. How much damage?"

"The first reports say five planes were destroyed on the ground. That's almost half our air force."

"Half?"

"They will not get the rest. Fidel has ordered all pilots to sleep under their wings. And we still have a few jets left."

"Who flew the raids? Americans or Cubans?"

Blanco laughed without mirth at this. "Watch, it will come up in another minute. You will not believe your eyes."

Lammeck settled into the sofa. Blanco, youthful and eager, rose to turn up the volume.

The news program continued describing the carnage. So far, seven deaths were reported, fifty-two wounded from the bombs. Castro had put all militia and army units on alert. The Cuban U.N. delegation was instructed to directly accuse the government of the United States for the aggression.

"Here," the policeman said, pointing at the tube, "here, Professor. Watch this."

The picture had switched to footage of a B-26, one of the American-built bombers that made up most of the Cuban air force, given to the island in the days of Batista. The plane sat on a runway, wings and fuselage punctured by small-arms fire. The camera zoomed in for close-ups of the bullet holes.

The narrator went on to say that at 7:00 A.M. that morning, a B-26 bearing the markings of the Cuban FAR air force had landed at Miami Airport. The pilot, named Mario Zúñiga, claimed that he and three of his comrades had defected from the Cuban air force. On their own initiative, they'd strafed Castro's airfields. Damaged by antiaircraft fire, low on fuel, they flew across the Florida Straits to seek asylum in America.

"Look!" Blanco almost whooped, jumping off the sofa when the damaged B-26 was shown in full. Zúñiga stood next to it, surrounded by American reporters. "See the cowling?" With his finger on the television screen, Blanco circled the plane's nose. "Solid metal. See? The FAR's B-26's all have clear Plexiglas there."

Lammeck was stunned. "That's not a Cuban B-26."

"It is an *American* plane!" Blanco fell back onto the cushions, rocking the sofa under Lammeck. "Ridiculous."

Blanco was right. This was a preposterous, transparent mistake to make, Keystone Kops. Was this the best the CIA could do? Once Castro's delegation at the U.N. made this known, the whole world would see America's fingerprints all over the invasion of Cuba. Kennedy was going to have a fit. Castro was probably having one right now.

Lammeck shook his head, amused at the ingredients of history. He imagined history seated with him, an old admirer, watching herself happen. You are everything possible, Lammeck would tell her, everything human. Somewhere, some low-level bureaucrat forgot to check one small fact. History, you are folly.

The television coverage switched to Castro, shouting into a bank of microphones at a press conference. The man launched into a peroration against the United States, labeling the attack on the Cuban airfields worse than Pearl Harbor. He called America liars, cowards, and aggressors.

Lammeck listened half-heartedly beside Blanco's rapt attention. He hearkened back over his last month spent trying to murder, then save, this man shouting into the microphones. In his mind, Lammeck silenced Castro, shot him or poisoned him, it made no difference. His gaze wandered away from the champing beard on the television set, his ears blocked out the stream of eloquent spleen. In his mind, Lammeck dug one good hole with straight walls and put dead Fidel Castro in it. He covered the grave, tamped it down. Then he asked history, standing there in his imagination with him, the question he'd put to her countless times. Just one more grave. What will be different?

Finally, after a lifetime, she spoke. Lammeck had his answer.

Todos, she said.

Everything.

I. ANNOTATIONS

Page 11—Cuban assassination team trained by CIA
Dozens of assassination and sabotage squads, called Grey Teams, consisting of CIA-trained Cuban exiles, were landed secretly by air or sea onto the island throughout the 1960s and '70s. Often these units were discovered and arrested soon after arrival due to massive infiltration by Castro's G-2 into the Cuban underground. Upon discovery, these men and women faced imprisonment or execution. However, successes were also frequent; much sabotage was accomplished on the island by returning covert exiles, and communications were kept open with the exile leadership based in Miami.

Page 31—alliance between CIA and Mafia to kill Castro
The partnership between the Mob and CIA to assassinate Fidel Castro has been well documented by a number of excellent historians. The question of whether President Kennedy knew of the alliance, code-named ZR/Rifle, remains unanswered. What is clear in the record, however, is that others in the administration, as high up as Attorney General Robert Kennedy, were briefed.

The original contact between the Mob and the CIA was facilitated by Robert Maheu, a former FBI agent and private security expert employed by Howard Hughes. Maheu acted as liaison between CIA agent James O'Connell and Mafiosi John Roselli (born Francesco Sacco), Sam Giancana, and Santo Trafficante.

According to the *1967 CIA Inspector General's Report on Plots to Assassinate Fidel Castro* (Ocean Press, 1996), neither Maheu nor O'Connell knew the true identities of the two men Roselli brought to Miami in early 1961 for the purpose of discussing the assassination of Castro. After the initial meeting, Maheu brought O'Connell's attention to a Sunday *Parade* supplement in a Miami newspaper that showed photos of the pair: "Joe the Courier" was, in fact, Santo Trafficante, and "Sam Gold" was Sam Giancana, two of the most powerful warlords in the American *La Cosa Nostra*.

Page 41—CIA *preference for gunning down Castro; Mafia insists on pills*

According to a comment in the *CIA Inspector's Report* (ibid.), the mobsters voiced a serious objection to a gangland-style gunning down of Castro:

> Giancana was flatly opposed to the use of firearms. He said that no one could be recruited to do the job, because the chance of survival and escape would be negligible. Giancana stated a preference for a lethal pill that could be put into Castro's food or drink. Trafficante ("Joe, the courier") was in touch with a disaffected Cuban official with access to Castro and presumably of a sort that would enable him to surreptitiously poison Castro.

Page 68—New York Times *articles detailing impending invasion of Cuba*

Preparations for the Cuban exiles' invasion of their homeland was a poorly kept secret. In addition to an immense and indiscreet rumor mill in Miami where the exile resistance was based, newsmen had little problem ferreting out reports of the rebel brigade's training regimens in Florida, Louisiana, and Guatemala.

On January 10, 1961, the *New York Times* ran a front-page story titled: "U.S. Helps Train an Anti-Castro Force at Secret Guatemalan Air-Ground Base." The article stated that "Commando-like forces are being drilled in guerrilla warfare tactics by foreign personnel, mostly from the United States."

On March 17, the *Times* ran a story claiming that, in the coming weeks, coordinated exile invasions would take place at various sites in Cuba.

The *Times* ran a related story on April 7 written by Tad Szulc, titled "Anti-Castro Units Trained to Fight at Florida Bases." The article reported the invading Cuban brigade's strength at 5,000 to 6,000 men (in fact, it was no more than 1,500), and claimed that training had been halted because the brigade had reached a point of sufficient readiness. Szulc sited sources at CBS as uncovering irrefutable signs that preparations for the invasion were in their last stages. Kennedy, alerted in advance of the article by *Times* publisher Orvil E. Dryfoos, managed to have the story reduced from a front-page, four-column lead to a single column in the center of page one. After reading the report in the *Times*, Kennedy commented that Fidel had little need of spies in the U.S.; all he had to do was read our newspapers.

Page 108—the Sorí Marín plot of March 18
On this date, leading officers of the Cuban underground, including Humberto Sorí Marín, Manuel Puig, and Rogelio Gonzalez Corso, were captured in Miramar. The meeting was held to complete the plans for an assassination attempt on Castro by placing a *petaca* (plastic bomb) beneath a viewing stand alongside a parade route where Fidel was scheduled to appear on March 27.

While Cuban historians maintain the clandestine meeting was broken up as a result of keen intelligence work, the truth is probably closer to serendipity and bad luck, seeming constants in the history of the anti-revolutionary movement on the island. A routine foot patrol in the Miramar neighborhood caught sight of a woman and child running through an alley from a home they were approaching. Curious members of the patrol followed the woman and child to a yellow home down the street. The woman had no idea a meeting of the military wing of the opposition was taking place in the back room.

Entering the yellow house, the patrol happened upon the meeting. Sorí Marín and his cadre exchanged gunfire with the soldiers before surrendering. Sorí Marín was wounded. He and eight others in *Unidad* were all captured. On April 19, on the day the rebel invasion surrendered to Castro's defending forces around the Bay of Pigs, Sorí Marín, Puig, and Gonzalez Corso were executed for treason.

Page 161—Dr. Manuel Antonio de Varona y Laredo

Tony Varona was part of the last democratically elected government in Cuba. He had served as president of the Cuban Senate, and took part in the effort to overthrow Fulgencio Batista. Though he worked with Castro early on, Varona was forced to flee to Miami because of his dedicated anti-Communist stance. In Miami, Varona remained a political force in the *Frente*. He developed relationships inside the Mafia for their shared wish to remove Castro from power. Varona also made a favorable impression with the Kennedys; he was selected to be part of the new government to be installed on the island after the invasion of the exiles in April 1961.

Regarding the many attempts to assassinate Castro, Tony Varona's story is another in the long tradition of myth blended with fact. In early 1961, Varona was approached by Trafficante with an offer of a large payoff in return for the death of Castro. In return for expense money of $10,000 provided by the CIA, delivered to him in cash by Johnny Roselli, Varona accepted botulinum pills. He caused them to be delivered to a Havana restaurant for the purpose of poisoning Fidel. If successful, Varona stood to reap a million-dollar bounty offered by Meyer Lansky in addition to a triumphant political return to Cuba.

Legend has it that Varona instructed the Havana restaurant worker not to execute the poison plot until a signal was received by telephone from Varona. However, on the eve of the invasion, he, along with other Cuban Revolutionary Council leaders, was sequestered by the CIA at Opa-Locka Air Base near Miami. This precaution was in anticipation of the *Frente* leaders being flown to the island to set up a provisional government after the rebel brigade had secured a beachhead. Because Varona was incommunicado at the American base, the story goes, the word was never sent out to the restaurant, allowing Castro to survive the plot.

(Author's Note—This is a popular, but likely apocryphal, explanation. The CIA agent responsible for the poisoning plot, Sheff Edwards, stated on the record that he believed the scheme failed simply because Castro stopped frequenting that particular eatery. It strains credulity to assume that, had Varona merely mentioned his role in initiating the poison plot, he would not have been handed a telephone by his CIA guardians to call Havana.)

In 1964, Varona left Miami for New York City, where he sold cars and became a language teacher for Berlitz. He died in 1994.

Page 180—*Juan Orta Córdova receives botulinum pills in Havana*

Juan Orta was the asset of Santo Trafficante. When the gangster gave this name to the CIA, Orta was touted as a high-level connection: the Office Chief and Director General of the Office of the Prime Minister (Castro), a man with access to Fidel. Trafficante explained that, prerevolution, Orta had been raking off a fortune from gambling operations, but became disgruntled when Fidel evicted the Mob from Cuba, shutting down his windfall. Trafficante had assured Orta that the return of the Mafia to Havana would be to his benefit.

In fact, Orta had lost his position as Castro's secretary on January 26, 1961. This was not reported to the CIA. A couple weeks after receiving the pills in Havana, Orta asked out of his assignment and returned the pills. He recommended a replacement for the operation who, the gangsters reported to the CIA, made several more unsuccessful attempts to poison Castro. (Author's Note—For the requirements of simplicity, I have stuck with Orta as the sole conduit for the pills.)

Page 190—raid on Heitor Ferrer's house

The fictionalized facts of this scene are based on the same set of circumstances of the actual raid on the Sorí Marín meeting of March 18, 1961.

Some confusion exists in the record as to the location of the house. Some say the meeting was held in a home on Calle 11 in the Mendares neighborhood of Havana; others mention an address in the far western Siboney neighborhood. (Author's Note—For the purposes of this novel, the Mendares address was used.)

Also, several Cuban authors, particularly former security officers, insist that Castro's G-2 knew in advance of Sorí Marín's *Unidad* meeting and broke it up as a result of their good intelligence work. That, too, is disputed by American historians, who claim the meeting was happened upon by chance (see the annotation above: *The Sorí Marín plot of March 18*). (Author's Note—

Due to Castro's infiltration of almost the entire underground network, I have chosen to believe the Cubans.)

Page 230—Castro's reluctance to state publicly that the Cuban revolution was socialist

According to one of Castro's principal biographers, Tad Szulc, Fidel had long dreamed of creating a socialist culture in Cuba. But in the early stages of the revolt, he did not believe that socialism should have been the immediate objective, not when his movement was fighting to remove Batista and supplant American dominion on the island. In Castro's words, he held back announcing his real intentions for the revolution, considering "the realities of our country, the level of political culture in our country, the level of preparation of our people, and the enormous objective difficulties if we tried to push ahead with this type of revolution."

Szulc also supposes that Castro, wisely, kept his Communist intentions under wraps to avoid undue and premature confrontation with his massive neighbor to the north, the United States. Nonetheless, Castro had spent a great deal of 1960 and 1961 quietly fusing his revolutionary movement with Soviet Communism. The impending exiles' invasion, plus sharpened American political rhetoric, increased pressure on Fidel to declare the true nature of his revolution. Still, he held back, waiting for what he considered a well-chosen moment.

In *Fidel, A Critical Portrait* (William Morrow, 1986), Szulc observes that this would imply that socialism was being created, in effect, behind the backs of most of the population—which was true. It would be an admission that Castro had been misleading the Cuban people, especially when he fulminated against the "lies about communism."

Page 255—the abandonment of El Capitolio

The Cuban capitol building was left vacant for the first four years of Castro's government. In 1962, the Cuban Academy of Science located its headquarters at *El Capitolio*. Today, the capitol remains well restored and utilized in the heart of old Havana. *Habaneros* of all ages can be seen playing sports and picnicking on the wide lawns.

Page 291—the Peking restaurant and the plot to poison Castro

Fabián Escalante, a former high-ranking Cuban security official and noted historian, notes in *The Cuba Project* (Ocean Press, 2004), that botulinum pills were delivered to a restaurant frequented by Castro, the Peking, at the corner of Twenty-third and Fourteenth in the Vedado neighborhood of Havana. According to Escalante, the contacts provided to the CIA by Tony Varona were Cruz Caso and María Leopoldina Grau Alsina.

According to Escalante, the Peking plot was known in advance to Cuban G-2. Because of this, he claims, the attempt on Fidel's life would never have been put into action. Other observers dispute this, noting either that Fidel simply stopped eating at the Peking, or that the pills were put inside a freezer in the restaurant and became stuck to the coils and ruined, or other, equally protean, explanations. Another frequently cited account is noted above in the Tony Varona annotation, that Varona, sequestered in Florida by the CIA, was unable to give the signal to initiate Castro's poisoning at the Peking. (Author's Note—The truth of how Fidel escaped this assassination plot remains unknown and is likely to be far less intriguing than the fictionalized account in this novel.)

Page 310—the disappearance of Juan Orta Córdova

The *1967 CIA Inspector General's Report on Plots to Assassinate Fidel Castro* reports that Orta "took refuge in the Venezuelan

Embassy on 11 April 1961 and became the responsibility of the Mexican Embassy when Venezuela broke relations with Cuba in November 1961. Castro refused to give him a safe conduct pass until October 1964 when he was allowed to leave for Mexico City. He arrived in Miami in early February 1965."

Page 350—Cuban B-26 pilots land in Miami, claiming to be defectors

While on the ground at Happy Valley in Guatemala (the CIA's secret base that served as a staging ground for the air support of the Bay of Pigs invasion), the pair of B-26's that landed in Miami on the morning of April 15, 1961, were machine-gunned by CIA agents to make them appear to have been in combat. Soon after the Cuban crews landed in Miami, claiming to have been defectors from the Cuban air force (FAR), local Miami reporters observed a cascade of discrepancies in that story. In addition to having solid metal noses where the FAR B-26's had Plexiglas, the pair of bullet-riddled planes had eight nose-mounted .50 caliber guns, instead of the six .50 caliber guns set in the wings of the FAR's B-26's. Also, none of the guns had been fired; tape covered the muzzles. The bomb racks were corroded and had clearly been long out of use.

The American ambassador to the U.N., Adlai Stevenson, had been assured by the Kennedys that all combat taking place on the island was between Cuban forces, with no support or intervention from the United States. The afternoon of April 15, following the appearance of the defecting B-26's, Ambassador Stevenson held aloft at the U.N. a wirephoto of one of the B-26's. He pointed to the FAR insignia on the plane and pronounced, "These two planes, to the best of our knowledge, were Castro's own air force planes, and according to the pilots, they took off from Castro's own air force fields."

After learning that he'd been sent unwittingly to the U.N. by the

Kennedys to spread this disinformation, Stevenson became incensed. He later was informed that Kennedy had referred to him as "my official liar." In retrospect, Stevenson referred to the episode as the most humiliating moment of his public career.

Page 304—Fidel's first public statement of a socialist revolution in Cuba

On April 16, 1961, the day after the initial bombing raids on the Cuban airfields, Fidel Castro attended the funerals of seven military personnel killed during the attacks. At this service, he announced for the first time publicly that the Cuban revolution was socialist.

Again according to Tad Szulc (ibid.), Castro has commented that he had no choice but to unveil the true socialist nature of the revolution on what he believed was the eve of the exiles' invasion. Castro explained that his people, specifically the tens of thousands of soldiers who would face the invading rebel force, had a right to know what they might be dying for. For this reason, Castro said, "I proclaimed the socialist character of the Revolution before the battles of Girón."

Early the following morning, the exiles landed, and the Bay of Pigs invasion began. Castro's relationship with the Soviet Union became open and strong, and remained that way until the fall of Communism.

(Please do not read until you've completed *The Betrayal Game*)

II. ANNOTATIONS

Page 113—the name Alek Hidell

During his two-year-plus stay in the Soviet Union as a defector, Lee Harvey Oswald went by the Russified version of his name, Alek. In 1963, Lee used the identity *Alek Hidell* to purchase the Italian-made 6.5 mm Mannlicher-Carcano bolt-action rifle soon linked to the assassination of John F. Kennedy. Some historians have supposed that the false last name, *Hidell,* was a rhyming homage to one of Lee's heroes, Fidel.

Page 113—the arrival of Alek Hidell and Rina in Havana

In Minsk, on March 30, 1961, Lee checked into an ear, nose, and throat hospital, complaining of a sinus headache. He stayed in the hospital until April 11. During this time, Lee was essentially out of public sight, visited frequently by his fiancée, Marina Prusakova. (Author's Note—It is this time frame, where no record of Lee's whereabouts exists other than as a patient in a Soviet hospital for treatment of what some commentors have called "the mother of all sinus headaches," that I have utilized for his presence, with Marina, in Havana.)

Page 115—Alek Hidell as a CIA asset

There continues to be intense speculation that Lee Oswald was, in fact, a recruit of the CIA, even before he defected to the Soviet Union. There is not room here to enumerate all the inconsistencies in Lee's military and personal records that point in this direction, or his many contacts with the intelligence community.

One of the most compelling summations of this theory came from Senator Richard Schweicker, a member of the Church Committee in 1975, which specifically delved into the connections between Lee Oswald and JFK's assassination. Schweicker had access to many classified files and concluded, according to one historian, that he considered it a serious possibility that "we trained and sent Oswald to Russia."

(Author's Note—For an excellent analysis of this issue, I recommend *Ultimate Sacrifice, John and Robert Kennedy, the Plan for a Coup in Cuba, and the Murder of JFK,* Waldron and Hartmann, Carrol & Graf, 2005.)

Page 228—Rina Prusakova as KGB agent

As there is with Lee Oswald, a school of conjecture has cropped up around the question of whether Marina Prusakova was, herself, an asset of Soviet intelligence. Several facts lead to this conclusion, among them:

1. Marina, part of the Soviet upper-middle class, reasonably educated, and an attractive young woman, met Lee Harvey Oswald and was so smitten by him that she agreed to marry him after knowing him a little over a month—two weeks of which he spent courting her from a hospital bed.

2. The Soviet government granted Marina permission to marry Lee in the span of ten days, despite the fact that she was an MVD colonel's niece marrying a U.S. defector.

3. One month after marrying Marina, Lee informed her he'd decided to return to the United States. In spite of any security objections her uncle had reason to make—and Colonel Prusakov, a ranking figure in the Soviet equivalent of the American FBI, could have easily stopped this, if he wanted—Marina was granted permission to leave the Soviet Union in the company of an American defector. The time between her formal request and receiving permission was a matter of weeks, an unheard-of time frame in a Soviet republic.

If the Warren Commission had the facts right, then it is clear that the Soviet government wanted Marina and Oswald to marry, and they wanted them to go together to the United States. Now, a leap is necessary, but a reasonable one: The only agency in the Soviet Union with the ability and interest to get this done in the fashion it was accomplished was the KGB.

(Author's Note—The above was adapted significantly from "The Mystery of Marina Oswald" by Dr. George Friedman, published in *The Stratfor Weekly,* 24 November 2003.

ABOUT THE AUTHOR

DAVID L. ROBBINS is the bestselling author of *The Assassins Gallery, War of the Rats, Liberation Road, Last Citadel, Scorched Earth, The End of War,* and *Souls to Keep*. He divides his time between Richmond and his sailboat on Chesapeake Bay. He is currently writer-in-residence at his alma mater, the College of William and Mary.